SOLDIER'S DUTY

RETURN OF THE AGHYRIANS BOOK 3

PATTY JANSEN

CAPRICORNICA PUBLICATIONS

GET FREE EBOOKS

DID YOU KNOW?

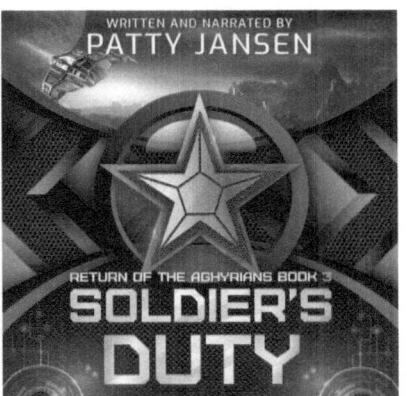

Soldier's Duty is also available in audio. Click the image or visit
https://pattyjansen.com to find out more.

1

———

IZRAMITH OPENED her eyes, flicked back the blankets, and rolled off her mattress onto her hands and knees. For a few dazed moments she remained that way, staring into the utter darkness where her hands would be if she could see them.

Something was very, very wrong.

Through the roaring of blood in her ears, she couldn't hear the sound of weapons fire or explosions. There was no shouting, no one was swearing and rummaging for clothes and gear in the tent. She wasn't, in fact, in a tent, and no supervisor was yelling orders. No group of fighters scrambling to get ready and armed for battle.

The soft stuff under her hands and knees was not sand, but the carpet in her bedroom. This was not a military base. She was at home, not in the war zone, and the noise that had woken her up was not the general base alarm.

That damn child was crying again.

She leaned back, rubbing her face with her hands. The roots of her hair were damp with sweat.

A cold draft tracked over the floor, making her shiver in her nightclothes. The hub at the door glared some impossible time in the middle of the night shift.

She jumped to her feet and was at the door in two steps, where she found her home clothes hanging on hooks on the wall. Her fingers brushed the tough fabric of her basic service uniform. She pulled her home pants and shirt from underneath, almost dislodging her gun from its hanger. It scraped against the wall, dangling to and fro.

The piercing cry of a baby grew louder when she opened the door.

"Thimayu!" Mother yelled from elsewhere in the apartment. "Go and feed that child or you pay off the neighbours' goodwill from your own account."

For two days in a row, that nasty Merani had filed a complaint about noise with the corridor caretaker, and twice Izramith had gone into the man's cramped office to deal with it. Pay up or we'll put in a challenge to the Good Neighbours regulation. Some neighbours were just insufferable, even when they knew what had happened, or maybe even *because* they knew what had happened, as Thimayu insisted.

Lights flicked on automatically when Izramith walked into the hall, their intensity low at first, so as not to be hard on her eyes. Before the light grew too bright, she crossed to the small room where the cot stood jammed in between the spare bed and the cupboard. The light above the cot gave an eerie blue glow that seemed impossibly bright.

The baby had kicked off his blankets and wriggled until he lay exposed and upside down in his cot with his feet where his head was supposed to be. In the time that Izramith had been awake, his cries had gone from loud to hysterical with great gulps of breath in between. With each cry, his mouth opened wide and his lips drew back over toothless gums. His little hands trembled. Poor thing.

Izramith prised her fingers between the mattress and the soft and sweaty body and lifted him, being careful to support the head. He was so helpless and fragile, a mere bag of loosely connected bones that felt like they would fall apart if handled too roughly. She held him awkwardly against her body, where he buried his face in her shirt, seeking something that he wasn't going to find. At least he stopped screaming.

The door to her sister's bedroom remained closed. Mother was nowhere to be seen, though obviously awake. Izramith hadn't seen either of them when coming off her shift last night, when the apartment had been quiet enough to look abandoned.

She went into the kitchen, cradling the baby in her arm as she had learned from watching the nurse teach her sister. He was still digging around in her shirt and getting frustrated, making protesting noises. For someone so young and so soft, his little hands were strong enough to pinch the skin.

Using only one hand, she found a bottle in the pantry, grabbed it between her knees and twisted the top to break the seal. A couple of drops of formula splattered on the floor. The baby started screaming again.

She flung the bottle in the heater, waited until it beeped, took it out and sat down with the bundle of screaming, shivering baby. The teat went into the mouth.

Silence.

The boy drank with great gulps, holding the bottle in both his hands. The milk behind the glass went down visibly.

While he drank, Izramith studied his fine-featured face. The skin below his eyes was wet from tears. How long had he been crying? She wiped the wetness away with the tips of her fingers, which felt coarse enough to damage his newborn skin. Poor, poor thing. If only she'd heard him earlier.

She folded her free arm around him and stroked his little head, ruffling the unruly mop of black hair that stood straight up from his head. It was so soft. He was so perfect against her rough, muscle-corded and scarred skin. New unblemished life in contrast with someone who made a living killing people.

He was her little nephew, the first of the next generation.

His birth two nights ago, in her sister's bedroom, had changed everything. Izramith couldn't get that horrible moment out of her mind. Thimayu sat, naked, on the birthing chair. Mother stood behind her, holding her shoulders, backlit by the light on the wall. The nurse crouched on the floor. The final moments of what had been—the nurse said—a pretty normal birth. But the emergence of the child and her sister's cries of relief were followed by a moment of silence. Stunned, horrible silence that said *there is something wrong*.

And into that silence, the nurse said, "He's *zhadya*-born."

Thimayu opened her eyes wide. "No," she shouted. "No, that can't be."

"Unfortunately, he is. Look at him." She held up the baby, thin, the skin pale, with his umbilical cord still attached.

"No. I don't want that. I don't want him. He's not mine."

Mother said, in a calming voice, "Thimayu, it's all right."

She whirled around. "No, it's not all right. I negotiated that this child would be mine, not Endar's. I don't want to look after some freak. I can't. I can't, do you hear me?"

Her sister's hysterical screams still rang in Izramith's ears. She had not wanted to hold the child, not then and not the next day when she calmed down. Since his birth, she had fed him only a couple of times, and then complained that he creeped her out.

But this little boy in Izramith's arms was helpless. He was now getting to the last dregs of his milk while his eyelids drooped and his hand kept falling off the bottle only to jerk back up when his eyes opened wide. He looked at her when he did this, as if he felt embarrassed by being caught asleep. It was so unbelievably cute.

Zhadya-born.

He looked healthy, if unusually thin. He would walk and talk long before any of his peers did, and grow into an extremely smart, precocious boy who outsmarted all the kids of his age. He would read and write at an unusually young age. He would know all his lessons backwards. Then, having grown bored with reading and writing, he would start playing mind games, manipulating teachers and elders with cold calculation.

He would become less coherent and withdrawn. Sometimes angry, usually brooding. Often scary, manipulative or downright malicious. He would lie to see what he could get away with, and he would set people up against each other. He would be nice or mean, often in the same sentence, continuously testing the boundaries of acceptance of the people around him. He would say one thing and do the opposite, and would never hold to his promise.

Everything in the house was fuel for fires, and fires would be his obsession. He would overheat his food until it burned, set his clothes on fire and watch the flames creep up his arms. Whenever they lost him, he would be found staring at the underground lava rivers. He would pluck mycelioids from the rocks and throw them in to see how they burned. Or undress himself and burn his clothes. Or he would climb down the rocks until the soles of his feet blistered with the heat. He might even push people into the lava and do nothing as they screamed and died. He would stick in his hands and peel the burnt skin off his victims.

Then he would be arrested by the guards and spend the rest of his life locked up, together with his twisted and crazy peers.

All that would be the future of this helpless creature in her arms. His eyelids drooped and his hands were slipping again. She took the bottle from him and set it on the bench.

His eyes jerked open and focused on Izramith's. His lips pursed and his face screwed up with a furrowed brow as if the very action was an effort.

People said newborn babies didn't see and didn't think, but she knew that wasn't true. Not for this boy. Two days old, and he knew everything. He watched her. He knew his mother didn't want him. He knew his grandmother wanted him out of the house. His mother and grandmother were afraid of him. He knew he only had his aunt to keep him out of the Respite Illness Centre, where people who were too ill to be in the community lived their lives in misery.

Izramith stared at his little face. As guard, she had seen the ugly side of the *zhadya*-born, she had seen the murders they had committed, the family members they had terrorised, locked in cupboards and fed rubbish. She had seen the scars one boy had cut into his sister's skin *because she annoys me*. She had spoken to bosses whose employees had played games of betrayal. She knew all that, but still couldn't believe that this helpless creature would do any of those things.

"Come, let's put you back in bed." She was on the early shift tomorrow, had been for the last few days, and these nightly escapades didn't help her level of alertness on the job. Nor would they increase her supervisor's satisfaction with her, and to be honest, after the war zone of Indrahui, coming back to a dull guard job had been hard enough.

The door to Thimayu's room opened when she walked back to the nursery.

Izramith didn't stop and didn't look at her sister, who stood in the doorway like a ghostly wraith in her nightclothes. She ignored the urge to start yelling and ignored the flick of her sister's head and the crossed arms over her chest and everything that screamed *Dare to criticise me*.

Izramith went into the nursery and put the sleeping baby in the cot. Her hands trembled and the skin on the back of her neck pricked with her sister's gaze.

The baby stirred only a bit when the warm arm at his back became a cold bed. His little hand flopped relaxed on the mattress with a soft thud.

Izramith pulled the messed-up blanket off the bed, draped it over him and tucked the ends in. She left the room after having planted a kiss on his head. The hair was so soft.

Thimayu still stood in the doorway, glaring.

Their eyes met. Izramith's anger flared. "Don't look at me like that, sister. I just fed *your* baby."

Thimayu said nothing. She looked pale, with hollow eyes and her belly still too big and floppy from carrying the child. Had she even slept since he was born?

Izramith reached her bedroom door. With her hand on the handle, she said, "You are allowed to say, *Thank you, sister*. That would be the least I expect."

No reply.

Another flash of anger welled in her.

Fuck it, fuck her stupid dysfunctional family who couldn't

even agree on being civil to each other. Was this why she'd made the effort to come back?

She slid the door aside, went into the room and slid the door shut again with more force than necessary. It crashed into the frame with a thunk. The walls rattled and the door bounced straight back open.

Izramith whirled around. Stupid piece of furniture.

Thimayu was still glaring.

"I didn't ask you to feed him and look after him." Her voice was prim.

"Then what were you going to do? Let him cry, like you did last time? Get complaints from the neighbours? That bitch Merani has probably told everyone in the corridor how you've gone to pieces and aren't fit to be a mother."

"I'm not a mother." Thimayu turned on her heel and slammed the door behind her. Not as hard as Izramith had slammed it. The door stayed shut.

Izramith glared at the door. Her sister would probably stay there for most of the day, and ignore everything to do with the child. Mother might take pity on him, but she wasn't much better.

Izramith was on duty and couldn't look after him.

And the fuck, her sister was going to take some responsibility.

In a few steps, she had crossed the hallway. She grabbed the door handle to her sister's room and pushed. The door moved a fraction but wouldn't open. Thimayu was trying to keep it closed from the inside.

"Open the fucking door so I can look you in the face."

"Mind your own business!" Thimayu's voice came through the door.

Izramith gave the door a huge heave. Something broke and slipped. The door opened. Thimayu screamed and retreated, holding up her hands. The nail on her left index finger had ripped off and blood streamed down her hand, dripping onto the floor.

"Now look what you've done."

"I don't fucking care. I don't know what's wrong with you.

Since when are your nails more important than your son? I've had enough of your stupid obsession with clothes and other selfish things. You are going to promise me to take responsibility. You are not going to cause any more complaints from the neighbours, because I'm not going back to that office and pay another fee. And if that means Merani will turn up at the door to beat the shit out of you, that will be your problem." Merani *would* do that, too, being an ex-guard. And Thimayu with all her style and pretty clothes would be no match.

"Mind your own business. You can't tell me what to do."

"Yes, I can, because you're pathetic, hopeless and weak. I have spent a year in war, crawling in sand and mud, in the cold, to keep people safe. People who are poor but grateful. You have everything you'd want and you can't see it for self-pity. You'd let a baby suffer. You'd embarrass Mother. You can hardly look after yourself—"

"Shut up, shut up, shut up!" Thimayu covered her face with her hands, smearing blood on the front of her nightgown. "Go back to the war if you're going to be such a prick about it. Go and be a hero. I didn't ask you to come back to mother over me."

"You need to stop this. There is a child who needs a mother—"

"I don't want him! Leave me alone. Get out of my room." Thimayu crossed the space between them, and shoved Izramith in the chest.

Izramith grabbed her sister's upper arms and pushed her back until she hit the wall with a thud that made the walls rattle. Mother shouted something in the next room, probably about annoying the neighbours.

Panting, Izramith glared into her sister's eyes. They were not as richly gold-flecked as those of most Coldi, and their defiant gaze evoked a deep emotion in her. It wasn't hatred or jealousy, but a feeling that she had tried to suppress most of her life: the urge to fight.

From as young as she could remember, Thimayu had been Mother's favourite, because she was older, and smarter, and always did what Mother wanted her to do. And now it all fell apart and what did she do? Complain and hide in her room and shirk her responsibilities like an entitled brat.

Thimayu tried to push Izramith away, but only succeeded in smearing both of them with blood. Izramith held her sister's arms in a strong grip. She said in Thimayu's face, "You thought you could beat me, big sister? Don't you know that no one beats a Hedron guard in a fight?"

"Has it come to fighting now? Didn't we finish with that when we were little?" She spat out the words. "I'm not afraid of you."

"What's this childish behaviour?" A voice sounded behind Izramith's back.

Mother. She stood in the doorway to her bedroom, her arms crossed over her chest. Her hair, now mostly grey than black, stood from her head like a fuzzy halo.

"She's bullying me," Thimayu said.

"Izramith, can you be more considerate with your sister? She's supposed to be resting, not being pushed against a wall."

Izramith let go of her sister's arms. She said in a low voice, "Of course you're not afraid of me while Mother is watching, coward."

Thimayu smirked and Izramith made a threatening gesture to her.

She knew what Mother would say. Fighting was not done. It was ugly and primitive. Fighting was how the Coldi people on Asto settled who belonged in which position in their *associations*. But they didn't do associations at Hedron. They were much more civilised than that.

Stuff like that. She had heard it so many times before.

Izramith met her mother's eyes, barely containing the anger. "Whether we fight or not, Thimayu is going to take responsibility for *her* child."

Thimayu said, "I've sorted it. I told you I want him to be looked after at the Respite Illness Centre. That's where he's going."

"What? He's only two days old. He hasn't even *done* anything."

Thimayu snorted. "For now. Don't be stupid. You know what

it means to be *zhadya*-born. You know all the trouble he'll get into. You'll know he'll never have a normal life. You know that if he's allowed to bond with us he's likely to try to kill us. I can't look after him. You can't look after him. You're hardly ever here anyway. We can't expect Mother to look after him, either. I don't want any of us to become attached to him and then for him to betray us in some horrible way, or worse."

Izramith protested weakly. "He's a baby." But he would do all those things. Her argument was slipping and she knew it.

She turned around and went to the room's door. The anger still burned inside her, but she had become used to that feeling. Thimayu did everything to *avoid* a fight, and fighting might resolve the issue of who had the right to speak, but it would not help the boy. In fact, she wasn't sure anything could help him.

She wanted to pick him up and run out with him. She wanted to take him somewhere safe. But that wasn't going to solve the problem. A young boy had faulty genes. And he was going to grow up in a terrible place, and, with time, become a terrible, manipulative person. And there was not a thing she could do to stop it.

"When?" she asked, feeling weak.

"He'll be gone by morning."

2

DRAINED AND defeated, Izramith went back into her room.

She lay on her bed, staring into the darkness, letting the awful truth seep over her.

Far too many families were destroyed by the malicious minds of their *zhadya*-born sons—people who thought they could look after them and contain the evil streak by giving the boys love, only to have that love used against them, like that awful case of a mother, her sister and a young girl being hacked to death in their sleep. A couple of Izramith's colleagues had caught the boy in a river cavern a few days later, still with the blood on his hands and clothes, rambling and incoherent. He had not changed, or eaten or slept.

There was no cure. The medicos' most recent advice was not to become too attached to the boys. They were best cared for by strangers with training to spot the precursors of violent behaviour.

These days, most babies went to the Centre.

Zhadya-born who managed to escape being taken to the Respite Illness Centre lived in the abandoned second level corridor of the old settlement. Most of those were older, but few lived past middle age. *Zhadya*-born had a habit of getting killed in violent ways.

When she was on internal patrol, Izramith had attended suicides and murders that happened with disturbing regularity in that horrible place that had long since been abandoned by the Mines Settlement Authority, its health and maintenance services. No outsider except guards went into that place.

Every now and then, a man would escape the area by way of a poorly-guarded or disused passage, and then the guards would have hunts all over the settlement, on the inter-settlement trains and sometimes even on the surface, trying to scout him out in the dark, because he was likely to murder someone or, worse, tamper with mining equipment or the bio-engineering plants.

That behaviour endangered the lives of the entire settlement, and they couldn't risk it. For all its strengths, the industrial settlements at Hedron were vulnerable. Without technology, most of its population would not survive for long in the perpetual darkness of the planet's surface. The threat of sabotage was huge.

At the bottom line, *zhadya*-born could not be trusted.

Many people made no secret of the fact that they wanted those children killed at birth. No doubt some even were, but the talk went that not even the Asto Coldi were low enough to kill their *zhadya*-born babies, so no one at Hedron did so either. They just locked them away instead. The difference of course was that Asto's climate meant that most *zhadya*-born never made it into adulthood and full-blown madness. At Hedron, they did.

By the time the alarm went off in the morning, Izramith's head resembled a big hollow space filled with packaging foam. She scrambled from the bed—she had no sense of the alarm being an exercise now—and pulled on her clothes, feeling like her arms and legs were held down by heavy weights. The hub next to the door glared the time at her. Shit, she was late.

By the sounds drifting through the door, someone was already up in the apartment, and when she stepped into the hall, the light in the hall already burned at full strength. It was harsh on her eyes.

Thimayu stood in the kitchen, with her back to the door, waiting for her porridge to cook.

Izramith walked around the table, while the heater pinged and Thimayu took her porridge out. Izramith did not meet her sister's eyes, afraid to trigger another urge to fight. There was no time for that sort of thing right now and no point.

She collected her own porridge from the pantry, pulled the lid off and shoved it into the heater. The apparatus hummed briefly and pinged when it was done. Meanwhile, Thimayu had sat down with her bowl and tongs and started eating.

Izramith took her porridge out and used the end of the tongs to stir it. She didn't want to sit at the table, because Thimayu would look at her, so she ate while standing up, facing her sister's back.

The silence was thick.

Izramith's throat felt tight. She knew that every day she put off a confrontation was a day she allowed this situation to fester, and she knew that her sister didn't understand it and possibly didn't even see it that way. She would rather hide, and keep doing things the way they had always been done before.

But that way wasn't working. You didn't solve anything with long, protracted silences or shutting yourself in a room and not talking to anyone. What was the point of a family if you were going to live like that?

Thimayu finished, rose and put her bowl in the cleaning cabinet, where the next water cycle would spray boiling water over it as soon as the breakfast timeslot was over.

"So. When I come back he'll be gone, right?" Izramith said when her sister was at the door.

Thimayu turned sharply. "What worry is it of yours? You're not going to look after him either."

It was a plain challenge, and Izramith had to do all she could to remain outwardly calm while her sister turned, crossed the hall and went back to her room. The door shut.

Izramith glared at it, clenching her fists.

Selfish brat.

Stupid family.

Izramith finished her porridge, put her bowl away and went into her room to change into the grey pants and tunic that was the general utilitarian uniform of the Hedron residents.

She eyed herself in the mirror. Her eyelids were puffy. If she kept feeling as tired as she looked, today was going to be a long day standing still and looking scary at the airport.

Izramith left the apartment.

She strode through the maze of the underground settlement as fast as she could without running. Winding passages flowed into community courtyards with planter boxes in which grew multi-hued mycelioids of all shapes, sizes and colours. Spotlights on the ceiling accentuated their grotesque shapes and sometimes fluorescent colours.

Often, Izramith would stop to admire the many weird structures—you could goad them into producing almost any shape out of the fibre that they grew for their fruiting bodies—but today, the winding corridors and playing children only provided an impediment to getting to work on time. This was not hurrying-up territory.

She came out into the large central hall of the settlement and joined the group of people waiting for the lift.

They were mostly people who lived on the higher levels in the settlement. Parents with children going to school, people with parcels of food from the lower floor cafes.

The atmosphere in the hall was one of relaxation.

A pond occupied the middle of the hall and water trickled from another set of living rocks covered in red moss. A colony of mycelioids grew on an artificial wall that was at least two floors high. The fruiting bodies were orange and flask-shaped and they mingled with blue ones that looked like hands with lots of fingers. They were about the same size as hands, too. Blue lighting made the edges glow fluorescent pink.

People sat at tables around the pond. The netted mycelioid that was owned by one of the cafes was flowering again. It was a huge thing, with a pink, fleshy-looking stem and tendrils hanging over several tables. There were shops around the outside of the hall, underneath the overhang of the balcony on the floor above.

Someone yelled behind her, "Hey." And a bit later, "Hey, Izramith!"

She turned.

The man walking towards her wore an administrative uniform with the lilac shirt and the mines emblem on his chest, two triangles, one grey, one purple. He wore his hair in the standard tight ponytail, but a curly strand had escaped it and hung over his forehead.

Several of the other people waiting for the lift—workers in all grey—raised their eyebrows.

"Hello Indor."

Damn, was there a more inconvenient time and place to meet him?

He smiled. "I didn't know you were back. I would have come earlier to say hello."

"It's been really busy. With debriefing and . . ." Izramith shrugged. What the hell would she say about her sister's baby?

"How was Indrahui? I heard it's pretty nasty out there. We've been getting so much news from there recently and I've been following it, because of you. That warlord at Pataniti was quite a nasty piece of work. So glad that you got him. That was really good work."

"Yeah." Seriously? Why would anyone at Hedron care about the tribal wars of Indrahui? A warlord died and another rose immediately. For the little people nothing changed. The news services wrote their beat-up, semi-heroic shit to justify the continued spending of money on a conflict that was a long-running vendetta that would never be solved.

He continued, "I heard they might be giving distinctions to all of those who served. That would be awesome and is the right thing to do to honour all those who fought. The people don't appreciate the work you do."

One thing Izramith hated more than a disregard for her

service: unbridled adulation from people who didn't know what the fuck they were talking about.

"There is nothing heroic about war."

"Oh, but because of you, a lot of people will be safe at night."

Because of me, a lot of people are dead. She glanced sideways at the closing lift doors, wondering if she could say *Look, I have to run,* but the lift was only up to the floor immediately above so even if she ran, she wouldn't be going anywhere.

"You're not working today?" Time to change the subject.

"I am, but I was on my way to get some food—look, why don't we meet in the next couple of days? We can continue our contract discussion where we left off."

"Sure."

"I'm really looking forward to it. I think it will be a very good thing for both of us."

"Sure," Izramith said again. Why was that lift taking so long? It was on the second floor now. Between the cage and the balcony railing she could see the silhouettes of people walking off.

"You're sure you're all right?"

"Yes, why?"

"You seem distracted."

"Just tired." She dragged a hand over her face to illustrate it. "I'm on my way to work." She glanced at the lift as if to make her point. Next time that lift came, she had better be on it. She was probably already too late.

A look of understanding came over his face. "Ah. I see. Protecting our settlement, eh? Doing all the good work." He laughed. "Oh, well, I better leave you to the important job to protect all us rule-pushers. I'll be in contact. Let's go out for dinner."

"Sure." She attempted to smile back at him, but every fibre of her being screamed with the agony of what she knew and he didn't.

And he was gone, leaving her to look at his retreating back.

Oh, damn.

Indor was a good man. Really, she meant that, because she

wouldn't have selected him from the matchmaker database if he weren't. She didn't want just anyone as father for her children, and he was intelligent and not unattractive.

But meeting her in a few days' time? To do what?

The only thing she could do was tear up the agreement between them. There would be no children, no matter how much she wanted them, no matter how jealous she was of the ex-guards who came into the guards' change room to show their initiation scars and brought their cute toddlers. They complained how hard life was outside the guards and how uncomfortable it was to be pregnant. Izramith saw through them: those women were happy.

But there would be no happiness for her. Once Indor found out that she carried the *zhadya* gene, he wouldn't want her anymore. No one would want her anymore.

No one wanted to add to the population of crazy and deranged men.

3

THE LIFT arrived and, via a couple of stops to let off passengers, it took Izramith up to the surface level.

The featureless arrival hall gave away nothing of the splendour of the settlement below. For many foreign visitors, especially commercial ones, their access to Hedron stopped here. Visitors needed a personal invitation from a resident to enter the rest of the settlement.

It was busy here, with departing travellers waiting for a shuttle. Most of them were Coldi from the Ezmi clan, most of them sales and administration officers.

A few foreign visitors lined up for the accommodation counter, where they would be allocated rooms in this lifeless and dull part of the settlement.

Izramith walked past all those people and pushed open the unmarked door on the other side of the hall. The light on the door blinked in response to the signal from her earring. She stepped into the pitch-dark entry dock. The door shut, plunging her into darkness. A second door ahead provided entry to the guards' change room, but right now it was too dark to see it. A beam of light intersected the darkness and tracked her body. The scanner hummed. A light on the scanner blinked blue: she could pass. The light came on in the dock and Izramith let herself into the change room.

Inside the base, the mantra was white efficiency. On the white and bare floor stood several rows of metal benches separated by metal racks on which hung the same grey garments as Izramith was wearing. Around the walls stood banks of lockers. The back wall was taken up by a row of change cubicles.

The locker area was busy, with women of the green shift hanging up their guard uniforms.

As per regulation, Izramith passed them without speaking to any of them. Anonymity was the power of the guards. When on duty, no one was supposed to recognise you, and you weren't supposed to know the names of your colleagues. Nevertheless, after having worked for the guards for so long, Izramith knew most of their names and could match those with their code names. After having come back from Indrahui, it had surprised her how many of the same women still served in exactly the same positions as before.

The only sound in the room was the scuffing of feet.

The side wall of the room was taken up by sets of shelfves on which lay a sea of dark purple clothing. Overalls, jackets, belts, shirts, armour, all stowed in meticulous precision. Izramith took one of each item and went into a change cubicle, and, as she had done since joining the guards barely out of adolescence, left her identity behind and became a nameless, faceless soldier.

First, she put on a grey shirt and tight-fitting leggings. Then the overalls—dark purple. Over that went the body armour, front and back, which clipped together at the sides. Then the jacket, the belt, and from the safe, her weapons—one at the right arm, one on the belt, comms devices, and finally her hood with face veil—which covered everything except her eyes—and helmet. As she left the cubicle through the door on the other side, she switched on the helmet comm. A tiny display sprang into life in the corner of her vision.

She flicked her eyes, and this made the tiny microphone pop

out of its recess inside the helmet. "Blue Forty-four reporting to Commander Blue for duty."

In the small silence that followed, her headphones crackled.

Then a voice belonging to Commander Blue said, "You're late, Blue Forty-Four."

"My apologies."

"That is the second time in three days."

"Apologies. It won't happen again."

"It had better not." The tone of Commander Blue's voice masked ill-disguised anger. "You assured me you were ready to assume duty after your debriefing from Indrahui. I'm beginning to think you might need to be referred to the clinic."

"I'm fine. There are reasons for my lateness. Nothing to do with me." She was *not* going to the clinic. That would go on her record and the label *stress-affected* was only one step away from dishonourable discharge. After leaving the guards, she was planning to work in security or safety patrol and a dishonourable discharge would prevent that.

Worse, she had the feeling that the higher command had been looking to find a label to stick on her ever since she returned.

"We will see, Blue Forty-four. You're on entry duty, post seven."

"Copied and out."

Izramith ran out the change room into the long and bare sloping corridor that linked the arrival hall to the settlement's entry at the surface. The ramp was empty at the moment, but would hum with activity when a shuttle arrived. It would bring a tide of arriving passengers down the ramp, and then take the departing ones who were waiting in the hall away.

Post seven was the first-level entry to the settlement, the most likely to see action from disgruntled or frustrated foreign visitors who didn't understand all the restrictions that came with travelling to Hedron. She'd been on post seven for four days in a row. That couldn't just be bad luck either. The command was doing it on purpose to test her, to get her to make a mistake that would lead to her retirement.

Wouldn't it be nice if they could just bring themselves to say the reasons out loud? *Returned service personnel are too cocky, too aggressive, too impatient. Once they've been away, they don't fit into our structure anymore.*

She'd heard it before, and never believed it would apply to her.

Well, guess what?

At the top of the ramp, there were two sets of sliding doors beyond which darkness loomed. The first door opened at her approach, letting her into the heat trap: a small area of quickly circulating warm air. Her footsteps clanged on the metal grate in the floor and the corners of her jacket stirred in the hot air. The second door let her out of the settlement into the darkness of Hedron's eternal night. She clamped down her visor, to shelter her face from the stinging cold and dry air.

The airport's landing field was a square piece of compacted dirt, most of which invisible in the dark. The brightly-lit entrance to the access ramp created a half-circle of lit ground radiating out from the entrance, beyond which all was dark except for a few light markers that indicated important locations: the corners of the field, the security zone and the direction of the flight path. Overhead was nothing except murky, dark purple sky with a few lighter-coloured swirls.

The guard station post seven was directly outside this entrance, and consisted of a small cubicle that held the scanner set in front of a single-room station. A fence surrounded a waiting area, where people who were not locals and didn't have an earring with an ID chip were assessed for further processing.

The guard on duty waited behind the scanner in Pose 1, with her hands behind her back and her legs slightly apart. She was one of the Green group, Green Twelve, the helmet comm informed Izramith.

Her head turned in Izramith's direction, but with the visor down, Izramith could not even see her eyes.

"Blue Forty-four reporting for duty," Izramith said to her own reflection.

The other guard bowed slightly and stepped back from her position. Her behaviour and manner gave nothing away, but Izramith thought she would have to be angry. She herself would be angry if her relief was late. That made her feel ashamed and angry in turn. Problems at home were no excuse to be late for duty and she would not let it influence the quality of her work ever again.

She would not give anyone a reason to dismiss her.

Green Twelve gave some brief handover instructions.

The Asto shuttle had entered the system and was expected to land soon. A few smaller craft may or may not be given priority to land first, or soon thereafter.

Izramith nodded and copied the information. "Thank you." And then she added, "Sorry for being late." It was not standard practice and personal contact between guards was not encouraged. Hedron guards were, above all, *anonymous*.

Green Twelve raised her visor. Gold-flecked eyes met Izramith's in a hard look. Then she turned on her heel and strode off.

Izramith took a few deep breaths.

Right. No more of this nonsense. She was not going to let Mother and Thimayu get under her skin. That wasn't worth the trouble.

She went to the scanner cubicle and pressed her comm unit against the screen. It lit up and showed her an image of the expected arriving craft. The Asto shuttle had been given priority, as expected. The craft was larger than usual. They were using a Rhion craft that seated about two hundred. There must be some sort of industry meeting going on.

She brought the passenger list up on the screen. There were a lot of people travelling alone, and a lot of them who listed their place of origin as Beratha, which was on the second continent of Asto, and a hot-as-hell industrial city.

In the public diary of the visitor section of the settlement she found that a meeting of metal workers in the conference centre started later that day. The passengers of that shuttle would be mostly engineers, mostly on their first trip here and maybe on their first trip away from Asto.

There went her hopes for a quiet shift.

A line of text sprang into her vision.

Blue Eighteen reported, *They got downlights on.* Judging by her coordinates, Blue Eighteen was at post two, under the approach flight path.

Blue Three, a section commander in the Exchange tower shot back, *Warning issued to the pilot.*

The faint whine of the engine was already audible.

She waited at the door to the cubicle, scanning the sky.

Bright lights from the shuttle were now coming over the horizon. Damn it, they still hadn't turned off the downlights. That craft coming down was a Hedron-built Rhion which was perfectly capable of landing safely without lights. Those lights interfered with the precision lasers of surface mining operations, and she bet the Exchange control room up there was getting some very unimpressed complaints about lost calibrations and missed production targets. So either the pilot was a self-righteous dick or inexperienced. Or both. The craft was from Asto after all.

The shuttle hovered to a mid-air stop above the stony ground, amid a cloud of grit and dust thrown up by the downward jets. The roar of the engines echoed over the barren and mostly unseen landscape.

The shuttle settled on the ground with a shudder, and not much later, the doors opened. A crew member in Pilot Guild uniform climbed down the steps and operated the mechanism to extend the ramp.

The Blue guards Seventeen and Fifty-two materialised out of the darkness where Izramith's visor had shown them standing. They took up their positions on either side at the bottom of the ramp. The Pilot Guild crewmember didn't look at them and didn't acknowledge them, but scurried up the ramp into the craft.

That was typical Asto Coldi behaviour, which was all about

self-preservation to avoid triggering of the *sheya* instinct that could lead to damaging and unnecessary fights.

The crew of the ship would be a complete association with the pilot at the top, co-pilot and communicator below that and one or two layers of crew below that: one layer of four and possibly another of eight. The crew would not interact with any other Coldi person unless properly introduced by whichever pilot stood at the top of the pyramid.

It was always creepy and alien to see this system at work. Fancy not being allowed to even greet another person. Coldi from Asto were impossible to work with.

The craft was now fully powered down.

A light in her visor screen showed the location of Blue Twenty-six who had gone to the cargo door to oversee the unloading of luggage and other items.

In the glow of the cabin lights inside the cabin, passengers were moving. First off the craft was a father holding the hand of a little girl barely old enough to walk. He carried a big pack in one hand, and the girl carried a toy. They were cast in silhouettes and their shadows extended all the way down the ramp and onto the stony ground. The girl walked in big, important-looking steps as if she were the ruler of the world.

Thimayu would never walk like that with her son. Cold and dark and uninviting as it was, the boy would never experience the surface unless he escaped his captors. He would never travel, and would be a prisoner of the Respite Illness Centre for the rest of his life.

And people called that the best way of dealing with him.

While watching the pair make slow progress towards her, Izramith tried to repress the feelings, but couldn't stop them. Her eyes clouded over. She had expected a bunch of rowdy engineers, or just regular passengers. Except passengers had children. She had never noticed the children that much, but now they seemed everywhere.

Now that she knew she could never have any.

Behind the pair came another couple of civilian travellers.

Text scrolled over the side of her visor. Blue Seventeen and Fifty-two stood at attention on both sides of the ramp, sending through anything they observed. A man in a black jacket *looked nervous*. A woman with a large bag—needs checking.

Izramith acknowledged this. People smuggled the most ridiculous things.

The man and his little daughter had arrived at the checkpoint. The light revealed them to be locals, dressed in Hedron's lilacs and purples. The man was probably some kind of administrator. The scanner registered their entry via the chip in the man's earring, and they went on their way down the ramp, the child pointing and babbling.

Izramith couldn't stop looking at them until a mass of other people blocked her view of the pair.

Oh, damn, she'd missed the man who was nervous, and the woman with the bag. They were already on the ramp into the settlement. All locals, since any locals on board came off first and could walk straight past.

There were indeed visiting engineers on board, a whole group of them, and they stood in the check-in queue at her scanner booth, talking and laughing in Asto accents. She knew the types of men. When they were out with mates, they tried to be smart and funny. Trying to show off. Since none of them wore earrings with ID chips, they had to be scanned manually.

She asked for the first man's ID. He passed. He was talking to a colleague while she scanned the colleague's ID. He passed, too, but he could produce only the one piece of luggage out of the two marked on his ticket.

"My mate has the other one," he said, and she had trouble understanding his accent.

The mate in question was at the back of the queue and had to be brought forward. Yes, he had the bag, but despite being told to keep each bag's contents the same at check-in and arrival, there was a weight discrepancy. Apparently, he had brought something for another associate, a piece of surveying equipment, which he located, she examined and passed.

As the line shuffled forward, people grumbled about why this mattered anyway. Several complained that they were cold.

When getting their tickets, they had been given information that the waiting area was outside. They knew Hedron had no sunlight. Why did these dumb people ignore all communication they had been sent through the Pilot's Guild with their bookings?

Similarly, the engineers had all given different reasons for coming here, while they were here for the same purpose and had applied for entry as a group. They would have been told to streamline their entries, and they had ignored those instructions. On purpose or not, it was always the same.

Damn, she hated dumb people who didn't stick to instructions.

All their luggage had to be checked and could not be processed until it was reunited with the owners. The men in the queue waited and complained.

It seemed like the meeting was some kind of trade fair. Many of them had brought lots of items of tech equipment. Unpacking took ages. What the hell was up with all these rolls of wire? The men's irritation was palpable. And no, Izramith could *not* just let them pass as some suggested. Some of the bags contained illegal technology, which she took inside, unpacked and placed on the table inside the guard station room.

"You will have to leave these here," she said to the merchant who had claimed ownership of the offending items.

"But I need those for my demonstration."

"The rules to entry state clearly that you cannot take long-range transmitters. That would have been a condition to buying your ticket. Our mining equipment uses long-range frequencies. Our ventilation units, our transport units, our *reactors* use them. You do *not* want to be on a train that gets stuck between here and the northern shafts because your equipment disrupts its communication back to base and disables the ventilation to the tunnel. And do I mention you'll be sitting on top of our largest reactor?"

The man gave her an angry eye.

"You're in luck. I'm kinder than most of my colleagues. They wouldn't explain, but just take the equipment off you." In the past, she would have done that, too, but Indrahui had changed her. At Indrahui, what civilians carried were the only things they owned. At Indrahui, a simple roll of wire or a half-broken piece of equipment, no matter how illegal, could make the difference between having money to feed your family or not. But her temper was quickly heating up. The insufferable idiots. Did they even look at what they signed?

The man grumpily agreed to have his machine disabled until he left the settlement. And then the group could finally leave. Izramith watched them go with anger building in her. If this behaviour was anything to go by, she wouldn't be surprised if the guards would be called a few times during the conference to break up fights of these men with security or deal with loutish behaviour. Asto thought they owned the universe.

Well, guess what?

The hold-up with the conference delegates had caused a log jam in the processing area. At least twenty more non-local passengers stood waiting in the dark. They must have come on smaller shuttles that she hadn't even noticed landing.

There were a couple of private people, mostly merchants. Two from Asto, but they were regulars. They had all their permits in order and she waved them through without much fuss. Next was a Trader.

He stood in the queue waiting calmly, reading something on a pad that lit his face with a soft blue glow.

Not just any Trader, a Mirani Trader, and those were usually trouble. Acted like they owned the world. Like the father and son team she had inspected a few days ago—on the day her sister's baby was born in fact—who had tried to conceal and smuggle a whole case of undeclared electronics out of the settlement. She had no idea where they even got the material, because certainly no local resident would give this sort of stuff illegally to Mirani Traders.

When she called the next traveller forward, he lifted his head. She met his eyes, which were so light blue as to be almost colourless. His hair, almost white, was tied at the back of his neck with a blue ribbon. It was, most un-Mirani-like, decorated with coloured ribbons and plaits. One of them dangled free when he moved his head. A couple of trinkets tied to the end made a soft tinkling noise.

A pretty boy.

He wore a thick Mirani fur cloak—and as such was the only traveller who had come prepared for the wait. When he stepped into the light of her booth she noticed that underneath his cloak he wore a uniform that she had never seen before.

The shirt and trousers were light blue and the ornamental jacket was turquoise and made of the thinnest sheer material that had to have cost a fortune. It was fastened on his chest with golden clips.

The Trader Guild registration on his medallion was 1101. The scanner told her that was the number of a major Mirani Trading family, except the uniform he wore was not Mirani—and to her surprise the helmet comm visual showed his ID in the place where only Hedron residents would display an entry.

So, what? He was going to be a mysterious enigma, right?

He bowed when he came to her booth. Not in a subservient way, but very patient and politely.

For some reason, that annoyed her even more than the Asto engineers' ignorance and petulance.

She asked him for his ID and he patiently gave her the black card. She shoved it in the scanner and it told her that he was from Barresh. Did they even have Traders there? Why did his details come up in the scanner? He wore simple hoop earrings without tag, as far as she could see, but he had to have a tag somewhere, and one that was synchronised to the Hedron system to boot. Where was the damn tag? Who had authorised it?

"Your business at Hedron?" she said in the curtest voice she could manage.

"I have a personal item to be delivered to a resident. It's confidential, urgent and time sensitive."

He held up an envelope which was bare on the outside except for an Exchange tag. Since when did Traders do delivery jobs?

"Leave it here with instructions and it will be delivered."

"I would prefer to deliver this in person. The recipient is a good friend of mine."

"Have you got a personal invitation?"

"I understand that the confidential tag should let me in."

Not that she had heard. Izramith took the envelope from him and passed it over the scanner. It was addressed to Trader Amandra Bisumar.

"Is this the person you want to visit?" What the fuck was someone with such a Mirani name doing at Hedron anyway?

"Correct."

Izramith turned the envelope over once more. Then turned to her scanner.

Amandra Bisumar turned out to be a Mirani Trader who had changed her allegiance from Miran to Hedron. Changed colours, Traders called this. According to the system, she had lived in the settlement for a number of cycles.

And now another Mirani Trader who had also changed colours wanted to speak to her personally. Never mind that Miran and Ceren, the Mirani homeworld, was often referred to as *the next Indrahui*, presuming the war at Indrahui was ever going to end. Her suspicion grew. The Traders they had caught trying to smuggle equipment were *Mirani*. There might be a connection.

She might have missed the man who was nervous and the woman with the bag, but she sure as hell wasn't going to let this guy pass without checking.

"What's in this document?"

"It's private, approved by the Exchange." He pointed at the label. Yes, she hadn't missed that, but what were those Exchange guarantees worth anyway? The Hedron Exchange hadn't approved this, and other places couldn't care less what happened at Hedron.

The rule at Hedron was: no entry into the settlement unless by personal invitation.

"Open it up." She tried to make her voice as threatening as possible.

"I don't think that's necessary. This matter is of a personal nature—" Still, he showed no sign of being intimidated or of an intention to back down.

"Those are our rules. If you want to enter the settlement, I need to see the contents of that letter." Especially if it was from one Mirani Trader to another. Commander Blue would have her head, especially after that episode with the smuggling a few days ago. Mirani didn't allow foreigners into their cities either. And when foreign people did get in, they were likely to be murdered on the streets.

"Do you have authorisation to demand this?"

"Open the fuck up." She shifted to position three, which involved sliding the gun out of its bracket and holding it pointed at the ground in front of the target's feet.

Meeting her eyes, and then looking at the gun, he shrugged. He slid his fingers under the closing flap and ripped the paper. Then he opened the envelope and gave the contents to her. His face still showed no sign of emotion.

The document was a single-page letter, written in the strange blocky Mirani script. Izramith engaged the translator of her helmet comm and read.

The letter was an invitation to some kind of party.

What the actual fuck? "This is private? You make a fuss over a fucking party?" She let the letter drop to the table.

"I make a fuss over principles. I asked and got a promise of confidentiality. These people—" He gestured at the sheet. "—are refugees who have had their lives threatened multiple times. I was assured by the Mines Board that I would be allowed in the settlement with a document bearing the seal of the Barresh Exchange." He pointed at the seal. He was oh so restrained in his anger.

"They did not tell me anything about that."

"Have you entered the number?"

"Don't fucking tell me how to do my job." But she manually entered the number anyway.

A line in her helmet visor said, *High level: approved.*

Oh, fuck. Was it even possible for her to do anything right today?

She slid his ID in the scanner and hit *approved.*

With a trembling hand, she took his ID card from the scanner and gave it back to him. "Get the fuck out of here."

He nodded politely, collected his letter and his small travel bag, and left. He didn't smile, or sneer or shout that he would complain. That behaviour would have given her satisfaction. This utter calm did not.

Private and confidential? What the fuck? Which idiot approved of two Mirani Traders meeting each other privately in the Hedron settlement? What had gotten into the Mines Board while she was at Indrahui?

Times have changed, Commander Blue had said on her first day back. *We need to become more accountable to visitors. No more threats. No more roughing up.*

Indeed.

4

———————

IZRAMITH STRUGGLED to get through the remaining visitors and then spent the rest of her shift standing at the booth staring into the darkness. Because Hedron was such a long way from the other settled worlds on an outlying and ancient arm of the galaxy, arrivals always happened in batches, because the Exchange network needed to line up eleven jumps from most other destinations and that happened at most twice in a shift so it got very busy for a short time, and the rest of the shift was mindlessly boring.

So she stared at the sky and counted the gas clouds that people called moonwhirls, since they were disturbances in Hedron's gas cloud cloak caused by the planet's many moons. She counted twelve today. There were seventy-two in all, and the path they described through the sky was called the skyway in the old stories.

Hedron's twin planet Veynu was low over the horizon, a giant fingernail in the sky.

The first time in her life that she'd come outside, the sky had been almost black, but ever since she started working for the guards, it had become more purple with the glow from the distant sun. Already, it was light enough for her to make out the ragged hills that surrounded the airport.

Day by day, the terminator crept over the planet's surface. The sun would soon clear the horizon. At this distance, it would not be more than a pinprick, which no one on the surface could see because of the gas cloak surrounding the planets and moons, but it would bring out the colours in the sky, the purples and blues and pinks and reds. The sun would stay above the horizon for the rest of her life and that of the next generation.

Nothing ever changed quickly at the surface of Hedron.

While she stood there, watching her breath steam in the light, there was no getting away from her demons. She was finished with this job. After her tour to Indrahui—where *real* people fought *real* wars—this border patrol job was just a licence to be a pedant about rules.

There had been a time, when she first started as guard, when the guards had been feared by all who visited Hedron. There had been stories about foreigners unwilling to believe that all guards were female. There had been tales about chases of smugglers trying to find ways into the Hedron settlements through entries other than the airport. Tall tales of shoot-outs, stand-offs and occasions where real enemies of Hedron had been apprehended.

Not anymore. The Mines Board had become soft, insisting that the emphasis should be on commerce and good relations with all other entities. Basically, the guards were not allowed to frisk anyone anymore, because it might upset relations. Visitors had become *customers*. What the fuck.

Instead, Hedron lent guards to peacekeeping efforts.

Like Indrahui.

Huh. As if the two sides would ever stop fighting there. The authorities insisted that the rebels disrupted the peace, and the rebels insisted that the authorities repressed them. Except there hadn't been a peace to disrupt for hundreds of years, and yes, the ruling class repressed the rebels. It was in their interest to keep the rebels poor and uneducated so that the landowners could have a supply of cheap labour.

But it was the ruling class that paid for help from outside, so she could either shut up and be paid, or speak out and be declared an enemy. From Hedron's point of view, the exercise was not about peace—what did they care about distant, basket-case Indrahui anyway? It was about arms deals and the sale of weapons. In addition to that, she had very strong suspicions that Hedron not only sold expertise and soldiers to the ruling class, but sold weapons to the rebels as well, so that it could sell even more expertise to the ruling class.

It made her sick.

No. Indrahui was a lost cause. She didn't want to think about it. But out here standing in the cold and dark with nothing else to do, her demons found her anyway. Dead men on the prairie, their bodies blown off below the waist. Drops of blood raining from the sky. The stench of burning flesh. She was sweating under her layers of uniform, and struggling to remain standing motionless in position.

Up there in the Exchange tower, Commander Blue would have a minion watching her. To check out her "suitability" for her job.

She hadn't expected to move back into her previous position. For one, it was occupied by someone else, but this hostility was a mystery to her. Yes, she didn't want to extend her contract, but she did want to complete her current employment honourably.

And then . . .

Was there anything for her now that she knew that she carried the *zhadya*-born gene? Was there anything she could do for her nephew?

Her thoughts went around and around.

As soon as her shift finished and the relief from the Yellow shift arrived, Izramith sprinted to the change room where she left her anonymous guard personality behind and became Izramith again.

On the civilian side of the cubicles, a group of women sat illegally talking on the benches in the change room. They fell quiet when Izramith came out of the cubicle and crossed the floor to hang up her uniform.

The women were all from the Blue shift and a mix of old and new faces. One of them whispered in another's ear and that woman glanced sideways at Izramith.

"Really? How many did it say again? More than a hundred?" She stopped at Izramith's glare and averted her eyes.

She must be a recruit joined at the most recent intake, because Izramith didn't know her. The other, older, woman of course was Nayani or Blue Eight, who never had anything nice to say about anyone.

The women remained quiet while Izramith put her heavy guns in her locker, shut the door with a clang and walked to the entry.

"The rumours are wrong, by the way," she said standing at the door into the security lock. "There were a thousand."

She opened the security lock's door, stepped in and closed the door again.

Leaning against the side wall, she closed her eyes while the scanner traced her body. Instead of a single beam of light crawling over her skin, she saw a flaming aircraft plummeting from the sky. She heard soldiers screaming. Once again, she was overcome by horror when she realised that the craft would crash in the rebel camp. And she could do nothing to stop it. It fell and fell. A giant chunk broke off. Voices around her cheered. Someone clapped her on the shoulder, but she stared at the unfolding horror, wanting to stop the fall, wanting to move away all those people who had done nothing except to be born to the wrong parents—

The light came on in the security dock. Izramith wiped sweat from her face. She must try harder to keep these awful memories away. Indrahui was in the past, gone, finished. She would never go back there.

She opened the door into the arrival hall, brightly lit and almost empty. Too normal, too civilised.

While waiting for the lift, a glass wall to the side allowed her to see into the conference centre. One of Hedron's chief civil engineers stood at a dais. The Asto engineers she had processed earlier sat in the audience, a bloc of blues and maroons amongst the greys and purples. On the far wall hung a banner that said *Guild of Service Engineers*, and a table to the side held a variety of equipment in boxes and tubes that would—she guessed—have something to do with power and water supplies.

~

Izramith and Thimayu shared the same father, a man called Deomor who had been contracted by their mother to provide her with his seed and stay the hell out of her life.

Typical of her, Thimayu had no interest in him, but Izramith visited him sometimes when she wanted to talk to someone. He was a relaxed, easy-going man, a crane driver in the steel works.

He lived on the second level in the new settlement behind the shops, where he shared an apartment with a group of other men all of whom worked in the steelworks.

"Izramith." His smile when he came to the door was genuine and his expression welcoming. "I didn't know you were back."

"Haven't been back long," she said and cringed. She didn't care so much about not having told Indor, but her father should have been told. "Do you have a moment? I want to talk."

An explosion of laughter came from the hall behind him. He glanced over his shoulder. "Sorry, me and my mates have just come off the shift, and they're in a goofy mood. Let's go for a walk, eh?"

She nodded and he came into the corridor, shutting the door on the laughter.

"Anything happened? I heard some stories coming out of Indrahui. You weren't close to that massacre, weren't you?"

It was not a massacre, it was an accident, and if you really have to know, I caused it. She shook her head. Indrahui was *finished*.

"You know that you're a really bad liar?"

"Have it your way."

Izramith glanced sideways. In the time that she had been away, the lines around his eyes had become deeper and the white streaks at his temples more pronounced.

They walked on in silence.

Not far from the apartment, the artificial corridor ended in an archway, where it continued as a natural tunnel, formed ages ago when, after the collision between Hedron and Veynu the earth turned liquid and water was turned into ice by sheer pressure of the surrounding rock. A path in the middle of the tunnel had been paved, but the sides and walls retained their natural glory. Delicate stalactites made from coloured salts hung from the ceiling, dripping water into multi-coloured ponds. Glittering leaf-crystals encrusted the side walls. All those structures were products of water-diluted salts. Dark moss grew on patches of the wall that were soft or rough enough to provide anchorage for roots. A colony of brown mycelioids spread its hairy fronds into the passage.

The tunnel sloped down to where it came out into a cavern. A few strong spotlights in the ceiling cast a ghostly blue glow over a pool. The water was as smooth as a mirror except for when drops plinked from the ceiling. The disturbance made in the water caused schools of silvery fish to start and swarm away. Their flanks reflected the light in flashes.

It was absolutely quiet in the cavern, except for the dripping of the water, rippling of the fish and the clicking noises they made when startled, and the faint sound of water running across rocks on the far side of the cavern.

"Did you know that a Damarcian company has asked for permits to bring visitors here?" Her father's voice echoed in the cavern.

"Visitors? Like, *tourists*? Are you serious?" This was not the Hedron she knew.

"Yup." He nodded.

"What the fuck . . ."

He laughed. "What the fuck indeed. The hide of them. They

wanted to bring exo-biology students *to study life as evolved under unfavourable circumstances.*"

"How do they even know about this place?"

"Guess a Trader might have told them?"

"Would have to be a foreigner." No native from Hedron bragged about Hedron's fragile and subtle nature.

Only outsiders called Hedron's nature one of the wonders of the universe. Natives thought differently. Hedron's nature was like Hedron people: it had survived where no one thought it would. No one had wanted to help Xiya Ezmi and his band of desert rebels—refugees from Asto—when they first arrived here, lived on the surface and starved and froze to death. People had watched the Ezmi clan struggle for survival, until they found their new world's metal resources. And now they were all over Hedron because it was suddenly a rich world? Pardon the hypocrisy.

Izramith and her father came to a platform overhanging the creek. On one side, water pooled in a still pond, on the other side, a small stream burbled down a couple of rocks.

Big stalactites of pink salt hung from the ceiling, backlit by a spotlight.

Izramith leaned on the railing, staring into the dark depths of the pool. A couple of fish glided through the water, swimming in relaxed positions. With all their sensor hairs extended they looked like giant balls of hair.

Her father came to stand next to her. "You wanted to talk. What is wrong?" She turned to him— "No, don't look at me like that. You only ever come to see me when there is trouble."

"Sorry." She let a short silence lapse and added, "Mother doesn't like me seeing you."

"You're an adult. Why do you still listen to her?"

Izramith shrugged. *Because I want to care for her and I want her to care for me?*

"How was Indrahui?"

"All right, I guess."

"I've never heard anyone use the words *all right* in the same sentence as Indrahui."

She shrugged. "I made it home safely. That's all." She seriously didn't want to talk about it. Because inevitably, the discussion would get back to that crash, because everyone had seen it. Surely he could imagine what it was like to see human figures on fire running towards you in so much agony that they fell on their knees, pleading for you to shoot them. Maybe he could even imagine what it felt like if that awful scene had happened because—like—you had shot the pilot of the aircraft.

"Izramith, horrible things happen in wars. It is OK to talk about it."

"I don't want to fucking talk about it."

"Maybe not now, but when you do—"

"I don't want to talk about it. It's over. I'm home." And the Indrahui rebels and the stupid government could all go to hell as far as she was concerned.

She clasped her hands together and sank into silence. Fuck it. Now she was angry. This was not why she had come here.

Before he could continue about the subject, she said, "Thimayu has had a baby boy."

"That's nice for her."

"It's not so simple."

He gave her a sharp look.

"He's *zhadya*-born."

"Shit." He stared ahead, showing no emotion.

"Thimayu has given him to the Respite Illness Centre. He's two days old." She found it hard to keep her anger out of her voice.

"That's the latest advice. What else should she have done?"

Izramith shrugged. "I don't know. Have you ever been there?"

"I'm guessing you have been to the second level corridor in the old settlement? Tell me which is worse." His gaze was unusually penetrating.

"But he is a baby!"

"It's better this way. He'll be in the care of experienced people."

"And what? Be a prisoner all his life? I can't imagine growing up in that place. It must be—"

"Izramith, why are you telling me this?"

She whirled at him and spread her hands. "Because he's your fucking grandson. Because I was hoping that maybe you know a way to keep him out of that horrible place." Because she was hoping that he cared, but she sensed that he didn't, because he'd gone all closed-up and defensive.

He turned and met her eyes. She knew that her voice sounded too desperate, and if she wasn't careful, he might say things about her to his mates, and those things might reach the authorities, and somehow that sort of information—personal instability, they called it—had a way of finding its way to the guards.

"Don't ask me." His voice held a strange intensity. "I don't know how to help these unfortunate people."

"But he's just a little boy. Two days old. There's got to be a better way—"

He shook his head, his lips pressed together. "There is not. Believe me."

The tone in his voice gave her the chills. "Why? What—"

"I couldn't even save my own brother."

"Brother?" He had a *zhadya*-born brother? Why did no one know about this?

He folded his hands and leaned forward on the railing, pressing his lips together as if repressing emotion. In the light from the side, he looked old. He was silent, and just when she thought he wasn't going to tell her, he said, "His name is Reyar. He was born with this condition. We were great mates when we were young. I didn't see him as different, he was just my brother. He did my schoolwork and I protected him from bullies. I taught him how to behave. We made pacts and promises. And one day, he betrayed me and when I confronted him, he tried to kill me." His expression was distant.

"Is he still alive?"

He turned his head abruptly to her. "You're not going to talk to him. He's dangerous."

Izramith said nothing. She could decide that for herself. Also, her father had just given away that his brother was still alive. In the abandoned second level corridor probably. Hence his earlier remarks about it.

"Don't be stupid. I can see what you're thinking by that look on your face. Listen to me, for once. Of all the times I've told you to do things, I've never been more serious. He can't help you. I don't want you to be harmed."

"I can look after myself. I've been into that place many times."

"Izramith, please. He can't do anything for a baby. He can't even look after himself." His eyes were wide and pleading.

"I have to try. I want to talk to him, because if there is anything that I can do to help that little boy, only another *zhadya*-born would know. Do you think anything could be worse than never interacting with normal people? Being labelled a potential criminal from the moment you're old enough to understand it? Being told every day that you're undesirable, useless and a threat to safety?"

Her father sighed and let his shoulders sag. He spread his hands, started to say something and let his hands drop by his sides.

Guess not.

5

I ZRAMITH HADN'T been to the second level corridor since the early days of her service with the guards. Before she was sent to Indrahui as part of Hedron's effort for the peace process, she used to be on the Yellow shift, but before that, she worked in Internal Security, and those were the guards that went into that place. It was where she had learned not to be disturbed by blood and guts.

This old part of the settlement had been derelict ever since Izramith could remember. Mother would sometimes talk of having lived in the crowded corridors when she was young, but she had moved out with the others when the Mines Board shut the section because of outdated infrastructure.

Izramith now found herself in that corridor, having walked past the broken seals and the warning signs about leaving the company-controlled area. Right now, the corridor was empty. Intermittent lights burned along the walls, showing ages of dirt and grime on the floor and walls. Grit and sand crunched under her feet. She walked slowly, trying not to make any noise, while feeling exposed without her veil and guard uniform. Her only protection was a comms device and a small gun.

She tried to listen out for sounds of approaching trouble, but the air vents in the ceiling clicked and hummed and made all sorts of rushing noises. The ducts were clogged from poor maintenance and the airflow swelled and ebbed when it started backing up and resonating. The air was stale with a faint tang of human waste and sweat.

Things scurried inside the air supply tubes. Once, she spotted a desiccated carcass of a small creature, most likely one of the eyeless rats that found their food purely by scent and that would start nibbling at anyone who remained still for long enough.

Years of neglect had stained the walls, which, since her last visit here, ingenious residents had attempted to cover up by painting murals in rust water.

It looked pretty, with delicate designs of abstract curls. In her mind, she saw a little boy with a paintbrush. He looked just like a normal child save for his dull black hair and pale skin, except when he put his brush in the rust-stained paint and started working, he was the most amazing and precise artist.

While she walked past decorated and scuffed walls, she remembered the times she'd come here as guard. A man had killed himself in that service alcove over there. There had been blood all over the walls and the floor. So much that passersby had walked through it and made a multitude of tracks on the floor. Nobody, apparently, had cared about the victim, because none of the footsteps showed that anyone had stopped to check the man.

And she remembered that one of those apartments to the right housed a couple of men who used to regularly have big screaming fights. Izramith remembered one time in particular when she was on night shift and one of them had welded the door shut from the inside, locking himself and his mates in the apartment.

The other two men wanted out, but the apartment's main inhabitant wouldn't let them go. He was screaming at them, and they were screaming back, all the other inhabitants of the corridor gathered around the door, hurling abuse at the guards for failing to turn up earlier, failing to keep these freaks out of their area.

Izramith and her colleague had bashed down the door and dragged the men off to the guard station. After that, she had lost track of what had happened to them. Presumably, they'd been freed and returned to this corridor and resumed their behaviour. That was what usually happened.

She started when a door opened to her right. A man came out, frowned at Izramith and walked the other way. He was not *zhadya*-born, but wore a very non-standard colourful outfit of a bright yellow tunic and multi-hued cape that looked like it was made from insulation fibres from the mines' huge power cables.

A woman—also not *zhadya*-born— came out of another door and looked down both sides of the passage as if she was expecting someone. Her eyes met Izramith's and she retreated inside and closed the door—which had been painted with a decorative pattern of swirls.

The sound of children's voices drifted into the passage.

Two young men walked past her. These were both *zhadya*-born and they wore long robes in pale blue. They went into a doorway further down the passage, taking no notice of her.

Talking to any of these people would not be easy. They distrusted people from the main settlement, and with good reason.

She came to that part of the corridor where she remembered some of the *zhadya*-born living.

The layout of the corridor was old-style, with a straight passage and plain doors on both sides. At some point in the past, ideas about what made a good artificial living environment had changed, which had been one of the reasons that this section had been abandoned. New sections no longer had straight passages, but were a string of communal living spaces, a maze with parks, playgrounds and eating-houses.

It looked like the old corridor's illegal inhabitants had attempted to break the dull monotony of the straight corridor by knocking out the wall to the front entrance of an apartment to make a kind of porch. A carved stone arch held up the ceiling of what used to be the apartment's hallway.

The arch was made from salt-plains sandstone with its typical yellow hue and white bands. This stone couldn't be found locally —the settlement was in basalt territory—and had to have been brought in from the salt mine basin. Someone had put planning and thought into this modification.

Izramith stopped to study the stonework, which displayed carvings of leaves and flowers of plants she recognised as being native to Asto.

The Mines Board had long ago decreed that all official displays of flora or fauna should be only of native wildlife— mycelioids, the many types of eye-less rats and the typical hairy fish of Hedron.

This artwork was in defiance of that policy. Was that because it was old or did it mean something? Her time at Indrahui had made her sensitive to this sort of thing. The display of a single flower could mean the difference between a fight and a welcome.

The door under the porch was made from polished stone and must weigh an incredible amount. It stood slightly ajar.

She knocked—it made a hollow echoing sound—but nobody answered. She pushed it open a fraction and peeked inside, but it was extremely dark, and she didn't trust herself to go in alone. Whoever lived in here might have seen her coming and it might be a trap. Being alone, she had no way to deal with traps other than not to walk into them.

So she walked back down the corridor into the intersection. A man dressed in bright orange came out of a doorway at the far end, but he disappeared into another door before Izramith could get close enough to speak to him.

A bit further down that passage, a young Coldi man came out of a door in front of her. Not *zhadya*-born, but perfectly normal, just like any young man who worked in the mines.

"Excuse me, I'm looking for someone called Reyar."

He turned. His eyes met Izramith's and a wave of irrational anger welled up inside her. Oh shit.

His expression reflected what she felt. In a flash, he lunged for her.

She didn't think, but instinctively grabbed him by the shoulders and pushed back. He tripped and hit the wall, expelling air from his lungs in a loud *oof*. He kicked her knee, but she shoved her leg against his so he couldn't find purchase.

"What the fuck!" she yelled in his face. "What did you do that for?"

"Hey, hey, I've done nothing!" His eyes were wide.

"Nothing? You attacked me."

"I . . . only wanted to know. . . ."

"Know what? Whether I'll bash your face in if you attack me? Well, guess what?"

"Sorry, sorry, sorry."

"Don't play with me." She blew out a snorting breath, exhaling tension.

She let go of him, wiping her hands on her overalls as if to wipe away that uncomfortable wave of anger that had taken possession of her.

He backed away, looking down, avoiding her eyes. He held his head bowed and his arms by his sides.

That was a submissive pose, like they did on Asto. He'd attacked her; she'd won, and now he wanted to serve her? That's what they did in Asto's *associations*.

"Stop doing that." She wasn't having any of that crap.

"Doing what?"

"Act like I'm going to hit you or something. I'm not a bully." Because that was the truth behind the Asto *associations*. The people at the top of the loyalty pyramids had to treat the ones below them like slaves to get them to obey.

That was why Xiya and his fellow Outer Circle poor people had come to Hedron in the first place. Because they wanted freedom from this system, and they didn't want to be treated as slaves by those in the higher circles.

He looked up, uncertain, flighty. He took a step back. "Sorry. I don't want trouble."

She shook her head. She didn't want trouble either, but this just proved how jumpy she was, and it had all started with that damn Trader during her shift. Even her father could tell that she was tense.

"I'm looking for Reyar. Does he live here?"

"I don't know. I said I don't want trouble." He backed away another step.

"Please. I need him."

A door opened nearby and a woman came out. "What's happening here?"

She glanced from the man to Izramith. "Xashya, you're getting into fights again?"

He cowered visibly.

Izramith felt like dragging him forward, telling him to straighten his back, speak up when spoken to.

"What's going on?" the woman yelled at him.

The man shook his head and darted into the open doorway.

The woman eyed Izramith with a curious expression.

"I did nothing," Izramith said into the silence.

The woman shrugged. "Never mind my brother. He's really odd, this is normal for him."

But it wasn't, Izramith knew that. Her brother might be odd, but something had clicked when he'd looked at her. The same thing that happened when she looked at Thimayu, only worse.

She swallowed hard. Fortunately, she had no reaction to the woman at all.

She said to the woman, her heart still pounding, "I'm looking for someone called Reyar. I've been told that this is the place where he lives."

"Not anymore, it isn't."

The panic again clamped Izramith's heart. "Then where is he now?"

"They left, the whole lot of 'em."

"What do you mean?"

"All the freaks. Used to live over there on the other side." She flapped her hand in the direction of the corridor where Izramith had just looked around. "They hollowed out and joined up all the old apartments. The guy you mention was their leader. But they're gone now."

"When?"

"Could be yesterday, could be a while ago. I don't know, I didn't see them go." She gave Izramith a *why do you care?* look.

"Where did they go?"

"I don't know." The woman shrugged. "Like they'd ever tell me. Likely, it's a secret and we'll never hear from them again. I hope so. Good riddance with the lot of them. Creeps."

Izramith stood as frozen. She wanted to grab the woman by the front of the shirt and slam her into the wall, but that was not going to get her an answer.

"Is there any way I could find out?"

"Maybe. Why do you want to know? You don't look the type." Her expression said that she suspected Izramith was a guard.

"It's . . . for retrieving a debt." It was rubbish, because no one lent *zhadya*-born any money, but the woman seemed to buy it anyway.

The woman turned around and yelled inside, "Hey, where did Eynor say that Reyar and his bunch of loons went?"

A man's voice replied inside, but Izramith couldn't make out his words.

The woman turned back to her. "He says Ceren. There you have it. Mind you, I don't know if Eynor is right. He tells stories every now and then. More now than then." She laughed.

"Ceren?"

"That's what he said."

Izramith didn't understand. "What would they want on Ceren?" Ceren was the second world in the Beniz-Yaza system. The other world was Asto, where it was too hot for the *zhadya*-born.

"I don't know. They would never tell anyone like me. But those people came here sometimes."

"People?"

"Yeah, the golden-haired ones. Pretty boys." Yes, the main entity on Ceren was Miran.

Her heart thudded. "Traders?"

The woman laughed. "I don't know. They didn't tell me."

She turned around and went back into her apartment, leaving Izramith to scratch her head in the corridor.

Ceren? Was that why so many Mirani visited here?

Apart from land at the north pole covered in ice and useless for pretty much anything, Ceren consisted mainly of ocean. A few islands, and one large continent that consisted mainly of inhospitable highlands. Almost all of this continent belonged to the nation of Miran, stodgy, traditional, old-fashioned, and even less likely to let in people from outside than Hedron.

Miran was mentioned a fair bit in the news right now. Izramith understood that for many years they had been playing a game with import restrictions for all non-local produce. For some reason which she had forgotten—some sort of conflict—the issue had come to a head, and the *gamra* assembly had instated boycotts. No entity was to buy Mirani goods and no one could export anything to Miran. The Mirani council had no money, no support from outside, and they hated anyone who was not pureblood Mirani. From what she remembered, the nation had suffered a silent coup from some crazy military general who was slowly bleeding off and driving out his councillors so that he could rule alone. No way a group of *zhadya*-born men would go there.

Then where?

There were a few other entities on Ceren, the most important one of which was Barresh—where that damn Mirani Trader had been from.

But Barresh was at war with Miran. And there were rumours that Barresh, which was very small, got direct support from Asto, which probably wanted to secure its food imports from Barresh. A war between Asto and Miran would get very ugly. Asto had the technology, Miran the stubbornness. Why would anyone go there voluntarily?

Izramith returned to the abandoned corridor. Stopped at the arched porch with the stone door that mocked her by being ajar.

In the narrow strip between door and doorframe, there was only darkness. If the group had left this apartment, she could probably enter safely. She pushed. The door moved slowly, with a great creak that echoed in the space beyond, a space that sounded much bigger than a regular apartment.

She stepped into the darkness.

The floor was dusty and grit crunched under her boots. Her footsteps sounded hollow in the large space. She flicked on the light from her comm and it produced fitful glow that didn't even reach the walls of the place. The floor was covered in coarse tiles made from a type of stone she didn't recognise.

She directed the light at the ceiling and found it surprisingly high up, also with carved arches of yellow sandstone. The walls were adorned with paintings of green scenery and flowers. Not Asto, because it wasn't green at all save for the land in the aquifers, and it didn't look anything like this at all.

What then? Ceren?

She studied one of the paintings, but didn't recognise any of the vegetation. She knew about mycelioids, not plants with leaves. At Indrahui, the bushes had been grey and featureless with small, needle-like leaves. Those bushes provided places to hide, since there were no rocky outcrops or anything taller than waist height near the camp.

From the large foyer, a hallway led further into the apartment. The air smelled stale here, and only one vent—modified to sit in a side wall rather than the ceiling—thrust out infrequent blasts of air.

Doors into rooms off the passage stood mostly open.

The place was huge. She had never seen pictures of any apartment like this, didn't know apartments like this existed, and she presumed that the inhabitants must have built this by joining up a number of old apartments.

A thought went through her mind like a flash. *This is not the work of madmen.* The craft was beautiful, well designed. The workmanship was immaculate.

The corridor even had pots with green *plants*, those that the

Hedron Mines Board no longer wanted in the corridors. Sadly, these particular specimens been standing in the dark for some time, and most looked sad, with drooping blackened leaves.

She went from the passage into another room constructed by joining smaller rooms together. The ceiling here was low, supported by carved pillars.

A few old couches stood in the middle, and shelves along the wall held glasses, plates—all neatly organised—and some books. Nothing of value, or nothing that told her where the men might have gone or why. She wandered through one abandoned room after another. There were dormitories still with the beds made, dormitories where all bedding had been removed. The place was tidy but covered in a layer of dust that felt greasy to the touch.

How long had these men been gone?

Had no one noticed or cared that they were missing? The thought made her feel sick. These people were someone's brother, someone's son, and because they were *zhadya*-born, no one had missed them. No one had checked up on them, not even the people who lived in the same corridor.

That was typically Hedron. Impersonal, distant. Work was more important than family. It wasn't customary for children to even live with their complete family most of the time.

And one thing was very clear to her: for her little nephew, life with these men *had* to be better than the prison of the Respite Illness Centre.

6

"BLUE, FORTY-FOUR."

The guard came to Izramith after the end of the shift, when she had just handed over her position to the Green guard. Izramith acknowledged her colleague with a short bow. Blue Eight, a senior leader, and one of the guards of whom Izramith knew the identity. It was hard to hide the vengeful personality that was Nayani. She could never wipe the sneer entirely from her face, or make the tone of her voice neutral. Some people couldn't be anonymous, no matter how much they tried.

"Commander wants to see you in the office."

"Acknowledged."

Blue Eight/Nayani turned on her heel and made back for the brightly lit entrance to the settlement.

Izramith cringed inside. This was going to be about missing that woman's bag the previous day, or not checking the man who had been nervous. Or about snapping at a colleague at the start of the shift she just finished.

And Commander Blue would have things to say about fitting into the command structure and listening to superiors, and about not being in a war zone anymore.

Damn it.

Damn it, damn it, damn it.

Izramith said the words in time with her steps while she made her way across the stony ground of the airport. Down the ramp, into the arrival hall, into the guard post and the large control room where veiled women sat at workstations collating data collected by their colleagues on the surface. One screen showed a map of the surface in intricate colour and detail. It would have been sent by one of the many satellites.

In the office off the main control room, Commander Blue sat at her desk in full uniform, purple jacket, hood and veil that showed only gold-flecked eyes and the surrounding skin, with distinct wrinkling. A purple-gloved hand gestured at the seat on the other side of the desk. "Sit down."

Izramith sat, her back straight. It was not particularly warm in the room, but sweat collected on her upper lip. It tickled, but it would not look good when facing a superior to rub her veil over her face or worse, put her hand underneath.

Outside the room, behind the closed door, a number of guards walked past. Their feet scuffled over the floor. Voices grew softer, the door to the control room hissed and then were gone.

Commander Blue touched her glove to the desktop, which displayed a schedule of some sort.

"Blue Forty-four, I remember saying a few days ago that I didn't want to see this sort of complaint again."

"Again, Ma'am?"

"We discussed the new visitor policies, did we not?"

"Yes, ma'am."

"I gave you some time to acquaint yourself with them. Can you cite rule 64-2?"

"Um—" She had been given the information, but because of the situation with Thimayu, she hadn't looked at it.

There was an uncomfortable silence.

Commander Blue said, "Rule 64-2, if I have to jog your memory, is that *the guard will accept a decision by the central Exchange in Damarq as final and will not contest its validity.*"

"I understand that, ma'am."

"You do?"

"I do."

"Then what business did you have interrogating a foreign Trader who was clearly in possession of the right documentation?"

Shit, this was about the Mirani cool fish. He'd gone to the Hedron Trading office to complain?

"I thought the matter was worthy of investigation."

"You thought. You are not employed to think. Rule 64-2 says that *we accept a decision by the Exchange,* so you are to fucking accept a decision by the fucking Exchange."

"It was only some kind of invitation."

"I don't care. If the Exchange decides that there is reason for the document to be confidential, you don't ask the carrier to open it. You don't open it yourself. You sign it off. You approve it and allow the carrier into the settlement, especially if he is a registered member of the fucking Traders Guild. You understand?"

"I do."

"Again, I don't think so. Because I don't want any more fucking angry complaints from Ydana on my desk."

Ydana? The head of the Hedron chapter of the Trader Guild? What did he have to do with a Mirani Trader?

"In case you still don't understand, the document was addressed to Amandra Bisumar. I thought you would have had the presence of mind to know that she and Ydana live in the same apartment."

Oh shit.

Suddenly it became too hot in the room.

Ydana sat on the Board and had connections all through the important places where important decisions were made at Hedron. He'd be in regular contact with Edyamor, the Mines' ultimate boss.

"So, what have you got to say for yourself?"

Izramith looked up and met the gold-flecked eyes that held not a skerrick of friendliness. She could find nothing to say.

"Your behaviour recently has been very strange. You apply to be released early from your Indrahui contract for a family matter. We accept it, because you've never used that provision before. Ever since you've been back, you've been neglectful. Most importantly, you still seem to think that we operate under the old ways. Just to spell it out for you: we are not to scare the shit out of our visitors anymore. We are to become a more open, more successful enterprise. Hedron has grown up. We are no longer children sitting on our toys and hitting anyone who looks at them. All that has been communicated to all personnel, even those serving offworld, but you obviously chose to ignore this."

Izramith stared at the edge of Commander Blue's desk.

Commander Blue sighed. "I respect you highly, but this has been happening too often for my liking. I don't know what kind of problem you have in your head, but clearly there is something and it needs sorting out. It's affecting your work and judgement."

"Yes, ma'am."

"And don't just sit there nodding, I want you to do something about this, and behave. I can't have people on my shifts who are unreliable. It's not just the incident with the Trader. We've caught you letting a bag go unchecked, failing to act on a colleague's warning. I'll let this go just once, because you've never caused me any trouble before."

"Thank you, ma'am." Suddenly, tears were very close to the surface. She wanted to scream *You try to do your job while worrying about your family*. But guards didn't, ever, talk about personal matters. In fact, they never talked at all about anything, except for brief exchanges about work at shift handover. Most of their communication went via the helmet comm.

"You can go now, but I'll be keeping an eye on you. I expect better work of you in the future. I want you to contemplate how you might solve this. I am going to advise the upper command that you take a posting somewhere else. Your work and ethics might benefit from some time away from the border patrol."

"Ma'am? To the northern shafts?" That was the only other

airport. A lot of freight craft came there. Less risk of confrontations with offworld visitors. A demotion.

"This is up to you. There are various positions you can apply for. Northern shafts, the main mines, offworld contracts, they are all possibilities. I cannot work with frontier people who are unreliable and make unforgiveable mistakes."

Izramith found it hard to breathe. Please, no. She couldn't leave her family. She needed to sort out something for the boy. Maybe her father—

"You're dismissed. You get five duty cycles to pick a spot to transfer."

Izramith stumbled from her seat. She wasn't sure how she left the room.

In the main control room, the Green shift was well underway and the atmosphere hummed with activity. A workstation in the aisle close to the door was not in use.

Izramith sat down and entered her guard number. She called up Amandra Bisumar on the residents' menu. The screen displayed a picture of her wearing the lilac and purple uniform of the Hedron Traders. Her licence number, 1123, was distinctly Mirani, so she had definitely changed colours. She was a woman past middle age, her white Mirani hair cut to shoulder length in very un-Mirani fashion. Her pale eyes looked intelligent. In the picture, she sat on the armrest of a chair. Head of the Hedron Traders Ydana sat in the chair, with his hand on her knee and an indulgent smile on his face. They each wore one earring with an amber stone—the Ezmi colour—and one silver hoop with a little trinket dangling off it. Contracted partners. Damn.

On either side of them were two children, one dark-skinned Indrahui boy with typical bronze hair in tight ringlets and lively green eyes. The other was a Kedrasi girl, old enough to wear an apprentice Trader uniform.

A happy family.

Coldi didn't breed with other races and neither did Mirani Endri, but it seemed that even those could make their own family.

So what did that make her own fucking dysfunctional family?

Izramith wiped the happy picture off the screen with an angry gesture. She checked the available off-site postings, but her eyes were too unfocused to register anything beyond the regular places. The northern shafts, the Outworld Mine—how was that for a dreadful posting. There wasn't even a nice underground settlement in that place.

Each of those postings was a demotion and a disgrace. It was where you went to gain points for a better posting or for punishment. Her colleagues would look down on her. She wanted out, but she had nowhere to go. If you walked away from the guards, that went on your record. She might as well join the *zhadya*-born in the abandoned corridor because there would be no support from the Mines Board.

In the change rooms, she took her clothes out of her locker and went into a change cubicle. She shed the many layers of her uniform, with the cold air making her shiver. She hugged herself, running her fingers over the initiation scars on her upper arms. Being in the guards was her life.

Feeling utterly empty, she left the guard station and walked down the ramp into the settlement. People around her laughed and talked, but she felt nothing. Nothing but hatred and anger. Her family was flawed. Not just her little nephew, but she was flawed herself. The fight that had happened in the second level corridor yesterday proved it. In fact, all the time she'd been a guard, she'd been enjoying this game of lording it over people. If they weren't intimidated and scared, she grew angry until they were. Seeing fear in their eyes gave her satisfaction. She had always tried to justify it as *another part of the job* but that didn't hold. There was something wrong with *her*. She was just a nasty person, a mass killer who didn't fit in the new Hedron.

At home, she found Mother and Thimayu in the kitchen talking in relaxed fashion as if nothing had happened. The crib in the spare bedroom was already gone.

She didn't speak about the boy, because they didn't care. As far as they were concerned, the problem had been taken care of. Whatever happened to him now was none of their concern.

Izramith went to her room and threw herself on the bed.

She hated what Hedron had become. She hated her family for being stupid. Her mother, Thimayu and her father were all the same: they didn't care. She hated herself for failing to keep her nephew safe. For being the guard at Indrahui that everyone knew about. Killing people, for what? Enemies were people. They had families and loved ones. When she'd seen the picture of Ydana and Amandra and their protégées, she felt nothing except anger.

Happy-fucking-families.

Everyone had a happy family, except she was stuck with a bunch of idiots who didn't care.

What would happen if she grabbed her gun, went outside and shot everyone?

And herself?

Gradually, her anger dulled and her mind turned to more manageable problems. The order to find another placing would not go away, and if she didn't do anything about it, Commander Blue would allocate a position and she would be stuck in a posting even duller than border patrol. Dullness brought out her bad side. Lack of patience, being contrary and argumentative, picking fights with people who had done nothing wrong were all things that had gone on her record at times. She needed a *busy* posting.

She had the choice of positions at industrial settlements, all of which were boring . . . or she could sign up for another offworld posting. Much as she didn't want to become involved in another war, there might not be a better option. What the hell, she might as well become a gun-wielding fucking mercenary and make her transition to evil complete.

She heaved herself from her bed, dragged her comm reader off the shelf and sat down in the easy chair in the corner.

The *internal opportunities* section in the guard directory gave her a list of offworld contracts. She flicked through the jobs.

Communications Specialist, based at Pataniti

Back to Indrahui. To the warlords and their irrational scream-ing. To the endless plains of Pataniti that were soaked with the blood of thousands to die in this pointless conflict. No way—she shuddered.

Next.

Communication Officer, Relay Station

The relay station was interesting, an Exchange relay in the middle of non-settled space between Hedron and the nearest settled world, but why would she want to go on a collaborative space-based posting with Asto personnel? That could only end in disaster.

Next.

Security Specialist, special event, Barresh.

Hmmm, what was that about?

She tapped the screen. Barresh wanted someone trained in combat communication to oversee security operations during a special event which involved a street festival. The contract was for two solars local time, however long that was.

Security officer. How hard could *that* be?

Reference for the job: Daya Ezmi.

That was a Hedron name and one she recognised. The founder of the Hedron Mines, Xiya, had two children. One of them, Edyamor, now headed the company. The other, Seveyu, created a huge stir by going into a partnership contract with a headstrong young man on Asto—whom she had met at a *gamra* gathering while representing the fledging member entity of Hedron. The young man was part of the Asto delegation and had gone on to become Chief Coordinator of Asto.

In anger, Xiya had disinherited his daughter and that should have been the end of it. But the couple had a son, Daya, and as per Asto's tradition, he inherited his mother's clan name. His parents stayed together for much longer than was customary, and their son got himself into trouble with his father.

By this time, Xiya had passed on, and Edyamor reached out to the boy, who left Asto for exactly the same reasons that the original settlers came to Hedron: he could not live with the rigid class system on Asto.

Edyamor reinstated his sister's part of the company to his nephew. Daya sat on the Hedron Mines Board for a while, but something happened and he left again. Rumours about him were a bit strange, as if a vital piece of information was being left out.

Izramith looked up Daya Ezmi in the local register. The system showed a picture of him at the table of a Mines Board meeting, dressed in lilac and wearing the company logo. He looked quite young. He had soft curly hair and deep black eyes, and a finely featured, pale-skinned face.

In one instant, everything dubious she had heard about him made sense: he was *zhadya*-born.

She laughed out loud.

Asto's Chief Coordinator had a *zhadya*-born son. Imagine how much of a stir that would have created in the precious Inner Circle of Asto. Would the Chief Coordinator have tried to deny that his own son was one of those freaks that were only born to people in the fringes of the megacities? People of whom it was said that they brought on the condition by failing to educate their children, by eating the wrong food, or by being of inferior stock, or all of those factors?

Because that's what people usually said when others were cursed with *zhadya*-born children?

Like Thimayu?

Like Asto's Chief Coordinator?

The job in Barresh was starting to sound like a good idea already.

She looked up Barresh.

It was a city-state on the edge of the Mirani continent, a former Mirani protectorate, independent since the Two-Day War when the Mirani army was ousted. Well, if their only war in the past *three hundred* years had lasted only two days, then it would be a heck of a lot better than Indrahui, where the only time of peace in the last three hundred years hadn't even lasted two days. And you could make that Ceren years, not *gamra* years.

The population of Barresh consisted of two local races, keihu and Pengali, and a good number of guest workers and semipermanent visitors, including Mirani, Kedrasi, Coldi, Damarcians and others.

The city-state was governed by a council which consisted of predetermined seats, based on family or elected representatives. Hmm, she disliked elections. Candidates always seemed to be voted in on such silly criteria, like popularity, which meant that they did silly things to maintain that popularity. Damarq had a fully elected council, and what good did it do except trying to stifle the commercial success of the Master Builders Guild?

But that was another discussion.

The Chief Councillor of Barresh was Daya Ezmi. Fancy that. Who said *zhadya*-born were always incoherent and mad in adulthood?

The main problems of the tiny entity were the continued troubled relationship with the behemoth of Miran and street crime. None of which involved Hedron, or, for that matter, a street festival and parade.

She stared at the information for a while, and couldn't see any bad things about this job.

But there would be some for sure. Other entities didn't ask for security help if they had no problems to begin with.

One thing was clear to her: of course this was where her father's brother had gone. An entity under the leadership of one of their own. The first ever *zhadya*-born to lead a government?

This was a place that could offer safety to her nephew.

7

I ZRAMITH WENT into the guard station early so she could send her expression of interest before starting the next shift. The approval came before she had even made it out of the change room, a personal note, written by Daya Ezmi, welcoming her to Barresh and instructing her to travel as soon as possible and not to bring anything.

A shuttle for Barresh would depart later that day, so she went to Commander Blue asking to be released from her shift.

Commander Blue eyed her over the top of her veil, looking from the screen to Izramith.

"Barresh. That's an unusual choice." Her voice sounded hesitant.

Izramith's suspicion went up a notch. She knew there had to be a catch somewhere. "Is there anything I need to know about Barresh that's not widely-known? I had a look at the contract yesterday, but apart from tension between Barresh and Miran—which is unrelated to the contract—I can't see any problems."

"No, Miran has been fairly quiet recently. They practically own Ceren, and make a point of demonstrating that they're not afraid of Barresh. There is only one thing you need to know about Barresh: it's Daya Ezmi. You know who he is, right?"

"Barresh's Chief Councillor? Edyamor's nephew? Thania Lingui's son? *Zhadya*-born. Anything else?"

"That's the main gist of it. You've worked for Internal Security. You know what the *zhadya*-born are capable of. You would have seen it many times."

"I know." But the man had sat on the Mines Board recently. He was Barresh's Chief Councillor, for crying out loud. Seriously, this stuff against *zhadya*-born was getting old. Like, stinky kind of old. Fine, if the person in question actually displayed signs of instability, but why lock them up before that time? And while she was at it, why had no one looked for something that might cure these people?

Commander Blue folded her purple-gloved hands on the desk. "Daya is a very special case, and I don't mean that in a good way. He was born on Asto, and wasn't supposed to live until adulthood, but did anyway, and then he started a life of drifting. Fell out with his father, came here to work for the board, but had serious disagreements with several board members. Went to a few other places, and now it looks like he's using his inheritance share of the Mines to prop up Barresh. He can deny it however many times he wants, but I don't believe for one moment that his father has nothing to do with this new project of his. Barresh is a tiny enclave surrounded on all sides by Miran. Asto wants an inroad into Miran, and Barresh is the way to do it. So there it is: Daya Ezmi, trouble spelled out in a name. Don't trust him. It's a pity that you have already accepted. If you'd have asked me before you applied, I would have said don't go."

"The job is to provide security for a parade, a street festival, and doing checks of the route and looking at security." She respected Commander Blue, but this sounded all kinds of wrong to her. It sounded like Commander Blue had a personal vendetta against him.

"Hmm, let's hope you'll be all right. Try to stay out of the games of politics, though. As with Indrahui, you'll be on loan, privately, and not through the guards officially."

"I have no intention of becoming involved in anything that's none of my professional concern."

"Good."

Izramith nodded and rose. She had her hand on the door handle when Commander Blue said, "Just one more thing."

Izramith turned back to the desk, and leaned on the back rest of the chair. This was it. The real problem was about to come out.

Commander Blue folded her gloved hands on the table. "Nobody knows much about this, and it's all been hushed up in a we-don't-talk-about-this way, but I think you should know. When I was younger and working as junior guard in the Blue shift, Daya came to Hedron as an angry adolescent. The bust-ups between him and his family were legendary. Sometimes we'd have to go in and rescue Edyamor's children from the terror he'd inflict on their family. We'd take him to the Respite Illness Centre and help the family clean up his room. The floor would be littered in countless empty bottles of zixas. Sometimes, the furniture would be smashed. Even at that age, Daya was a legendary drinker."

She shrugged. "He'd escape from the hospital, always by talking someone into letting him go. As far as we know, he never offered anyone money for his freedom, but talked them around with sheer manipulative power."

And Edyamor let him sit on the Mines Board?

"Yeah, I know what you're thinking. It gets better. Daya had been here a while when my commander at the time asked me to check out what it was that Daya was doing in the hills on the other side of the airport, where, apparently, he went every couple of days. The comm tech at the Exchange had noticed interference with their transmissions whenever he was there. So I kept an eye out and noticed him one day, coming out of the settlement entrance at the time a shuttle arrived. Passengers were going down the ramp and he was going up. I was given a floating position just so that I could check him out. He went across to the far corner of the airport, climbed over the fence and disappeared in the darkness up the hill. I followed a bit later, using only my infrared visor because it was too dark to see otherwise. He wasn't wearing one."

Izramith gave a small shudder, hoping Commander Blue didn't see it. Those hills were treacherous, littered with sharp columns of the fossilised remains of ancient vegetation, interspersed with hidden sink holes and hot vents which were hard enough to spot with an infrared visor and impossible to see without.

"He went up the hill and down on the other side, where there is a valley with a large open steam vent at its lowest point."

Izramith nodded. Sometimes if you were in position at that side of the airport, you could hear the vent thump like a giant beast that lived in the ground. Mostly, the vent leaked clouds of steam, but when it thumped, it would release great jets of it and spray the surrounding area with boiling water.

"He descended all the way to the vent and disappeared into the steam. I couldn't see him from the top of the ridge, so I went down the hill, and found that he'd jumped into the vent. There is a tongue-like protrusion in the opening. He was standing on it, with steam coming up all around him. I ran down, ready to yank him out if that thing started blowing steam, but then it did that very same thing. I was too close, and I had to retreat." Her eyes met Izramith's over the top of her veil. Izramith knew her as a middle-aged woman named Desani, a committed and dedicated guard, whom she respected greatly. "Rest assured, there was a great amount of swearing involved on my part. I scrambled away on my butt, wet and singed all over, and groping for my comm— which didn't work. The backup didn't work either. And meanwhile this thing was spewing steam and our big boss' nephew, the one he seemed to have made a personal project to turn into a functional person, the one we'd busted our backsides keeping alive, was in there being cooked."

Except, obviously he hadn't been cooked, because he had just signed Izramith's application to come to Barresh.

"And then the thumping stopped and the vent calmed. And Daya stood on that rocky protrusion like nothing had happened.

Except he showed up bright white on my visor. So hot, he should have been dead. He jumped out onto the edge of the vent and . . ." She shuddered visibly. Izramith stared at her. Guards never showed any emotions.

Commander Blue continued in a softer voice. "I don't know where it came from, but there was a huge explosion like thunder— I presume, having been at Indrahui, you're familiar with thunder?"

Izramith nodded.

"Daya was standing at the edge of that vent, with crackles of lightning all over him. I'm pretty sure that he didn't know I was there. And I was punching my comm, but it wouldn't work, and you know I've never told anyone, but I was too scared to move, while bolts of lightning flashed over my head, the ground rumbled and the air rushed with shockwaves. I've been in fights, seen people murdered. I've executed prisoners when we still had the death penalty. I've never been as scared as I was then. I had no idea what he was doing, but I'm sure that he was doing it."

She wiped her veil with a gloved hand.

"Anyway, eventually the thunder and flashes stopped, and it got quiet. He must have been long gone when I finally dared to come out. I reported it to my commander, but she didn't believe me until I managed to record another session, well hidden behind a rock this time. The recording was filed in a classified area. I've just sent you the code to get in. I recommend that you watch it and know what you're letting yourself in for. Daya has taken himself off the Hedron Mines board and gone to Barresh where he can do whatever he pleases by throwing money at it. He may buy our services, but you should never forget what he is."

"What did you think the flashes and thunder were?"

Commander Blue shrugged.

"Did he have a weapon with him?"

"No." The look in her eyes was intense. "I asked my superior at the time, but was told to file a report. My reports went all the way to the board and Edyamor put a gag order on the information. We were never told what happened. Edyamor visited the base personally, and said that whatever went on in that valley was better off happening outside than in his house. He was angry, as if we'd been wrong to investigate—don't tell anyone else that I said this, because he'll kill me if he finds out."

Izramith nodded. You did not criticise the Board. You had avenues of appeal and could bring decisions before a tribunal, but once the authorities had dealt with it and handed in their findings, you did not keep talking about it.

Commander Blue continued. "We were never called to his house again, and Daya was instated as member of the Board not much later. He still came to the valley, but the guards' upper command instated an exclusion zone. He even started to pick times when the Exchange was quiet. No one ever asked him what he did there, and no one ever asked Edyamor the question what he would do when his nephew had one of the explosions of anger that are so common in *zhadya*-born. What he would do when Daya killed someone."

"Did he ever have a fit of anger in the Board meetings?"

Commander Blue shook her head. "Not that I've heard. But the man can do some really weird shit. Highly dangerous weird shit. With that, and his *zhadya*-born temper, he should never have been on the Board."

Izramith nodded to acknowledge the warning, but inside, she drew a different conclusion. Daya had not suffered any further fits because whatever he did helped control his inner demons. He might still be dangerous, but, this far into adulthood, he could never have sat on the board if he didn't know how to keep the madness at bay. In fact, judging from the story Commander Blue told, it seemed that he'd been sliding into madness, but had recovered enough to sit on the board.

That was worth going to Barresh for.

"I will be careful."

"And take it easy at first. Your adaptation will knock you around a lot."

"Hey, I've been to Indrahui. I know about adaptation." She

hadn't suffered too badly from those few days that her body temperature adjusted to a new level.

Some people had a lot of trouble. Not her.

Izramith booked a spot on the shuttle and went home to pack up, but, having barely unpacked since arriving from Indrahui, there was not much packing to do. The apartment looked abandoned, and the doors to Mother's and Thimayu's rooms were shut. Mother was probably at work in the uniform factory and Thimayu might have gone to see one of her frivolous friends.

Izramith had no great desire to personally say goodbye to either of them.

Just the thought of the empty room opposite hers made her angry. She played with the thought of just leaving and not letting either of them know where she had gone, but relented. That wasn't her kind of behaviour. The fact that Mother and Thimayu behaved like pricks didn't mean she was justified in doing the same.

So she wrote a note to Mother on the internal system, trying to explain where she went and why, but each time, she saw what Mother's face would look like when reading it. And she almost heard Mother's voice.

Thank the stars, she is gone.

Or *why didn't she say where she was going, I could have asked her to bring . . .* and then mention some kind of frivolous item.

Or some other thing to show that they truly didn't care.

Because they didn't.

It made her angry just thinking about it, so kept the note short without mentioning where she had gone, because she certainly didn't want any stupid messages while she was away.

She shouldered her bag and left her room.

What seemed like ages ago, she had shut that same door behind her to go to Indrahui. She had been excited and keen to *help solve an old conflict*, not knowing that the conflict couldn't be solved—certainly not by her or any others of the Hedron guard. If anything, their presence made things worse.

She'd come back wiser and more disillusioned.

This time, she might not come back at all.

She walked through the underground maze of passages, courtyards and meeting areas to the special wing of the hospital that was the Respite Illness Centre.

It was tucked away in the furthest corner of the top floor, where the influence of cold air sneaking in from outside was strongest, and where any foul air accumulated if there was a problem with the ventilation. The walls were scuffed, a number of lights were out, the floor was worn and in one place there had been a fire judging by the black marks and molten plastic on the floor.

She found a kind of reception desk at the end of the corridor. It was empty, and behind it was a set of double doors that did not open at her approach. She had to ring a bell, and a woman came to ask who she was here to see. She seemed surprised when Izramith said she was here for a baby, but told Izramith that the children's room was at the very end.

At the door to the room, a nurse would not allow her inside, because *we discourage family from getting close to the children. It only causes harm.* Izramith made a show of leaving, only to hide in an alcove that held mops and brooms. When the nurse passed, she ran into the children's room.

The ward held at least twenty beds and on the side closest to the door, they were occupied by young patients who were genuinely sick. The rest were *zhadya*-born of ages varying from babies to toddlers.

Her little nephew was asleep and didn't wake up when she came to the cot. It was a simple metal structure with a bare mattress and plain sheets. None of the soft comfort and cute toys that people normally placed in their baby's cots. No scented pillows, no fan to keep the air fresh.

She stroked his hair, trying not to see the faded stains in the sheets and the dent in the side of the cot.

The slate at the end of his cot merely said "Male" and his date of birth.

He needed a name. A strong name that would be his light in dark days, a name that was honest and good. Like Shana. She checked the population register on her comm reader to see if the name was taken. It was, but Shada was not. *Shada, Shada, Shada.* She repeated it a few times to get used to the sound of it. Yes, that was a good name.

She used the end of her sleeve to wipe *male* from slate. A pen lay on a shelf against the side wall. She used it to write *Shada* above his birth date.

There. That was better already.

There were a few other young boys in the room. These would be his peers, enemies and friends when he grew older. He would spend the rest of his life in this place.

Unless . . .

Unless she could find him a safe place, a place where he could be free.

She bent down and kissed the top of his head.

"Shada," she whispered.

He twitched and his mouth curved into a smile before relaxing again.

Yes, she would do her best.

8

I ZRAMITH WENT from the hospital to the airport.
The shuttle wouldn't come for quite some time, but she
had no reason to hang around. She'd wait in the departure
hall and might even catch some sleep. Or watch that recording
that Commander Blue had given her access to.

It was still quiet in the settlement's entry hall, although the
shuttle to Barresh was listed, and the single employee at the
counter could already accept her confirmation. With the formali-
ties done, she sat down in the waiting area.

She pulled her comm reader out of her bag and finally
watched the recording made by Commander Blue.

Daya looked quite handsome as a young man. He was very
tall, as *zhadya*-born usually were, lacked the chunky and muscled
shoulders of the Coldi, and the typical associated heavy build. As
a male fighter at Indrahui had told her once, there was nothing
dainty and elegant about a Coldi woman and nowhere was this
truer than at Hedron.

The recording showed Daya walking up the ramp from the
entry hall—the walls painted in a disgusting light yellow in those
days—across the bare field of the airport. It shifted to infrared
view, showing him as a light grey figure scaling the fence and

climbing the hill. It showed the valley on the other side, with a bright white spot where the thumping vent was.

Daya walked right up to the vent, jumped onto the protruding rock in the opening and waited. The geyser went off and turned the section of the screen bright white with its heat. After the burst, a white figure climbed out of the vent and positioned himself on the edge.

Then the screen flashed white.

At first, Izramith thought that something had gone wrong with her reader's screen, but it slowly turned light grey and vague shapes materialised out of the murk. Daya stood in the middle of the valley for a bit longer before walking back up the hill. By that time, the surrounding valley had faded to a mid-tone grey.

Izramith stopped the recording and replayed the last section. Daya coming out of the vent—flash—slow fade.

What the hell did he do?

The hall had filled up with passengers for Barresh. The screen behind the check-in desk flashed that the shuttle was about to arrive.

She put her reader in her bag and rose. They weren't calling departing passengers yet, but a few people already stood at the gate. She joined them, impatient to be out of this place. After the surge of arriving passengers, they were allowed up the ramp.

The guards stood at their usual and familiar positions, most in Pose 1, with their arms by their sides. They were women of the Blue shift, which had been hers for quite a long time. They wore full gear, so she had no idea of their identities. They would see her, of course, and would recognise her. Some might like to say goodbye in their own, distant way, but they were not allowed to move a finger.

A fitting farewell from a place where no one cared about her.

The fellow passengers filing onto the shuttle were a mix of merchants and private people. Most wore thick clothing against the stinging dry and cold air, which they were now taking off and stowing cloaks and coats under seats and in luggage racks. Walking through the aisle, she scanned the passengers for soldiers, any sign that she was going into another war zone. She saw none. In fact all passengers were decidedly civilian.

In front of her was a passenger carrying a big bag and before that two merchants, men both, in colourful garb. They were not locals, both of them rotund and short, with dark curly hair. They spoke to each other in loud voices in a language she had never heard. Izramith knew a bit of Mirani, and they didn't speak that. She knew some Kedrasi and Indrahui, and it wasn't that either. She knew the ghastly Trader Coldi dialect, that very often didn't even sound like Coldi to her ears, but none of the languages fitted what the men were speaking. It had to be keihu, the native language of Barresh.

Her seat was about halfway down the central aisle. Her duffel was not nearly as big as some of the other passengers' bags. She didn't need much, she didn't have much, because she always wore uniform, and had only packed a few sets of her utilitarian grey trousers and shirts. She wore her only pair of boots and her bag contained only a guard-issue toiletry set and two towels.

She sat down, feeling naked and exposed without her uniform and all her gear. When she went to Indrahui, the contract had told her to bring her gear. The Barresh contract told her specifically not to bring anything.

Many of the passengers eyed her sideways. She caught a man in garish merchant garb staring at her arms. Her short sleeves covered her initiation scars, but her lower arms were bare. When she moved her hands, muscles tensed visibly underneath the skin. Her right arm bore a fresh scar from a shrapnel strike sustained on the Pataniti battlefield. The skin was still paler than the surrounding skin, and puckered.

Something hit her in the face. She turned aside to see some sort of long grey thing waving in front of her face. Two women were trying to squish many bags into the seats on the other side of the aisle.

"Hey." Izramith grabbed the grey thing and wanted to push it away, but it *moved*. And it was hairy. Damn, what sort of animal was that? "Hey, it looks like your pet is escaping."

Since when where animals allowed on flights anyway? Didn't they have quarantine at Barresh?

The woman closest to her turned around, giving her an indignant look. Her eyes were huge, with almost no whites and dark brown irises.

Izramith pointed at the grey thing. "Sorry, does this belong to . . ."

The woman's lips pursed. She had grey skin, with darker markings on the sides of the eyes and into her neck. In fact, the markings were the same colour as those on the grey thing, which now hung in the aisle, moving ever so slightly.

Damn. She had a tail. Izramith let go of it as if it had burned her hands.

The woman gave her a hard stare, and Izramith looked away, her cheeks hot. Yes, she should have remembered about the Pengali people of Barresh who had tails, but still . . . Maybe she shouldn't wave her tail in other people's faces.

The door to the cabin shut with a thud. Crew ushered the last passengers into their seats. A Pilots' Guild employee in his fancy uniform set the security panel next to the door. Lights blinked.

The crew went to their own seats at the front of the cabin. The floor already rumbled with the vibration of the engines that swelled until it drowned out conversation in the cabin.

With a lurch, the craft left the ground.

After a few lights had gone past, Izramith couldn't see anything out the window except darkness. The light in the cabin was off, with only small blue pinpricks showing the positions of major features like the aisle, the back of each seat and the doors.

The craft hit an air pocket and immediately after that a downdraft, and another air pocket throwing it sideways. Air rushed past the windows. Then they hit three violent bumps in a row. It felt like riding a mining train down the tunnels. Everything in the cabin shook. No one spoke, but a child started crying.

This was normal for Hedron, Izramith told herself.

All the pilots complained about how rough flying into

Hedron was. The plentiful hot air vents and hot gas clouds caused violent updrafts, and then there would be—

Whoa!

The craft dropped sharply, in freefall for a few heart-stopping moments.

The child cried louder. One of the crew attempted to get out of his seat to attend someone who had called for assistance. He had to rely heavily on the cable attached to his harness and a railing on the ceiling.

The two men next to Izramith got excited by the view out the opposite window of a delicate purple fingernail that was Veynu, Hedron's twin.

But that was short-lived when the craft pulled into cloud. The craft rocked sideways. Up became down as the pull of gravity eased and vanished.

Some people were sick. The two women on the other side of the aisle had produced a small light—on a chain around one of the women's necks, and were looking at samples of fabric spread out over the furthest woman's knees, completely oblivious to the jolting and rocking of the craft.

And then the sky turned black with many pinpricks of lights. A bright band of millions upon millions of stars scored across the sky at an angle: the swirls, and worlds, and star nurseries of the galaxy.

A child squealed, "Look, stars!"

Sickness and discomfort were forgotten. Passengers chatted and took pictures. If you'd never left Hedron, you'd never seen the galaxy in its full glory. Not even the people living on worlds closer to the centre would have seen this. This was beauty in its most powerful and primeval form.

Izramith was still admiring the view when a light started flashing at the front of the cabin. The first of thirteen jumps coming up. A silence came over the passengers. Clearly many people shared her feelings about jumps. Not pleasant. Then there were numbers. Seven ... six ... five ... four ...

Izramith clamped her hands between her knees.

Three ... two ...

A child started crying.

One ...

The world dissolved in a flash of white. For a moment, she felt as if she were floating in nothingness. Then vision returned, in separate colours which slowly joined and overlapped.

The vision out the window was clear, and showed nothing except stars of deep space.

That was the first jump.

By the time the shuttle had gone through three more jumps, the process was getting old. She leaned her head against the window, and fell asleep.

~

Izramith woke up with a shock when the floor vibrated. Ashamed, she looked around to see if anyone had noticed her sleeping. But no, the cabin was flooded with light from outside and everyone was looking out the window, where she could see a blue sky, and something else people from Hedron would never have seen in their lives: sunlight. Izramith remembered sunlight from Indrahui. It was bright and hot and impossible to look into. It was so bright that the glare hurt her eyes. Much brighter than the light room in the settlement. Much brighter than lights in the large agriculture hall.

And worse than at Indrahui, because this system had two suns.

The craft banked, bringing a large body of glistening water into view. More water than all of the underground reservoirs in Hedron put together. The glistening silver mass disappeared over the horizon with only a few dark islands breaking the silvery surface. White puffy clouds floated just underneath the craft.

The craft kept turning, now bringing a view of a landmass rising from the water in a steep cliff that stretched away on both sides as far as she could see. Banks of grey clouds sat atop the cliff. The ground at the top was dark and looked like it was covered in hair, but they were still too high to see—

—To see pretty much anything, because the view outside turned brilliant white, and then grey. Drops of water tracked over the windows—

—and out of the cloud again. The underside of it was dark grey and jagged.

A couple of islands protruded from the water between the craft and the dark mass of land.

Surrounding the islands, there were signs of human activity: walled-off fields full of brilliant green. Vegetation growing in rows. Little vessels moving over the water.

The islands themselves had human-made structures on them —houses, and other buildings. Streets.

It was just like pictures and simulations she had seen of Barresh.

And those huge things between the houses were trees?

Of course she had seen pictures, but she hadn't realised how big they were.

The craft descended rapidly now, and the glide became bumpy. On a little island where there were only trees, a plume of steam rose into the air. Hot springs. At least there was something familiar about this place.

Fields, boats, a jetty all passed underneath in quick succession. The floor rumbled with the power of the downward jets.

The craft touched down and settled with a few thumps. The crew unclipped themselves from their harnesses. Doors opened. All windows had completely fogged up.

Passengers got up, took their bags and lined up in the aisle. Some thunks against the outside of the craft indicated that the ramp was in place. People moved, and Izramith moved with them. She presumed that someone would be here to meet her. A faint breeze came in, bringing with it a waft of heat. Commander Blue had warned her about it.

It's not Asto, she had said. *I went to Asto once and my body took about ten days to get up to the right temperature. I don't think I've ever been so sick in my life. Barresh is not Asto, but it's much warmer than Hedron, and it's a lot hotter than Indrahui, too.* Indrahui was warmer than Hedron, but still considered to be a cool place with a small and distant sun.

Izramith had shrugged off the remark. Adaptation, when her body temperature rose or fell depending on the climate, hadn't worried her when she came to Indrahui and she couldn't see why it should worry her in Barresh.

But shuffling towards the exit, her head became more stuffy and dizzy, and she was beginning to feel like that had been an exceedingly dumb assumption. The air that wafted into the cabin was hot and sticky and the light was so bright that it made her dizzy.

Come to think of it, nobody she knew at Hedron who had visited Asto had shrugged off adaptation. Everyone spoke of how sick it made them.

Izramith was never sick, and she had never been in a truly warm place. This was going to be such a lot of fun.

In the open doorway the full force of the heat struck her. Sweat broke out all over her body. Her head was pounding and she had to do all she could to stay upright.

She stopped on the bridge between the craft and an open-sided building. Sunlight beat down unmercifully. People walked past her talking as if the heat didn't bother them.

She waited, holding the railing with white-knuckled hands until that horrible feeling that she was going to spew had passed. Her head cleared a little. She made it across the walkway into the building, where it was cooler. A breeze blew across her sweaty skin, making her break out in goose bumps. She followed the tail end of the passengers off the shuttle through a modern hall to a counter where, after inserting the ticket chip, an automated system of trolleys went to retrieve her luggage. It was a neat system, but the lines for the manual document check were very long. Her stomach was doing backflips, and she became certain that there would be spewing in her immediate future. Hopefully after she'd made it outside.

Hell, if they would only hurry up. Why did they have so few counters in operation? Why was no one using the furthest part of the hall?

There was a fence on the other side of the counter. Beyond the fence, the floor was bare and there were piles of building materials on the floor. A group of workers sat in a circle, eating. The smell of food drifted on the air. With a typical tang of *meat*. Coldi didn't eat meat. Her stomach churned.

Hurry up.

She shuffled in the line, dragging her duffel across the floor. At this point, her vision had contracted to the back of the person in front of her. Sweat ran down her back.

One person would go through the gate, show ID, walk through a glass cubicle which opened on the other side when the person's parameters were approved. Then the next person would go in. Sometimes the gate didn't open, and the person was taken aside into a booth.

The line shuffled closer, agonisingly slow.

Then the man in front of Izramith went in. He was one of the rotund merchants that were probably locals. His ID scanned. The guard waved him into the cubicle. He walked through and an alarm started flashing.

With a clang the cubicle doors closed.

Guards went in.

The passenger protested loudly and held up his hands. Guards took his jacket and patted him down. He was taken into one of the cubicles on the side, still protesting loudly.

And they said that Hedron security was crazy?

Then it was Izramith's turn. She took a dizzying step forward and handed the guard her ID. He entered it into the scanner— and it came up with a flashing light.

Damn.

The guard called another, and he said something in reply, all in a strange language that reminded her of the sound of water gurgling down a hole.

A third guard came out of one of the interview booths behind the barrier. He took Izramith's ID and beckoned for her to follow him. They bypassed the glass cubicle.

All the waiting passengers watched her. Izramith didn't like being watched while not on duty and unveiled. Her stomach gurgled and she hoped she could hold on to its contents until she was no longer in view of all these people.

They entered a room where another guard sat behind a bank of screens. He took her ID from the other guard and scanned it again. The text that flashed over the screen was in a script she had never seen before. The man spoke in his strange language. His non-Coldi voice sounded very deep and strange to her ears.

"I'm here to work for Daya Ezmi," she said. She had no idea if they understood.

One of the guards gestured for her to sit down, so she sat, leaning her back against cool metal. The guard left the room through a back door.

"Look, how long is this going to take?"

The guard gave her a blank smile.

Izramith clamped her hands between her knees. Did anyone here speak Coldi?

Hurry up, hurry up.

9

THE DOOR at the back of the room opened, and in came a woman dressed in a black uniform with five-pointed star embroidered in gold on the chest. A Coldi woman. "Ah, here you are."

She crossed the room and bowed in a subservient pose with arms limp down her sides, palms facing backwards. "Welcome to Barresh. I hope you had a good journey." Her accent was from Asto, and she used formal pronouns of the type hardly anyone used at Hedron.

There was an awkward silence. Clearly, the woman expected some kind of response.

Izramith rose. She'd seen Asto Coldi greet each other in this way, but never had anyone displayed this behaviour to her. This was the part of Asto's society that was a mystery to people at Hedron. Izramith didn't know how to perform the superior greeting, but it involved a touch to the shoulder, so she did that, but she felt like slapping the woman's cheek and telling her to cut this crap. This was why she hadn't wanted the contract on the space relay station, because of the Asto Coldi's stupid insistence on ramming this association stuff down her throat.

The touch on the shoulder meant that the inferior party was

allowed to look the superior in the eyes and the woman did just that. Izramith was surprised at her young age, at her sincere expression, like she really believed in these silly habits.

"They really don't do *nimiya* greetings on Hedron, do they?" Her eyes were wide.

"No, they don't." It probably sounded too angry, but damn it.

"Then, when you meet a new person, how do you know what your relationship is and whether you or the other person is superior? How do you even survive?"

"We do." *How do you survive?* Easily. People at Hedron didn't need a superior to tell them what to do. They did much better with less rigid structures.

This was stupid. Why send an Asto Coldi to meet her and make her feel like she was an exhibit while her head was swimming and her stomach unsettled?

She barely managed to follow the woman out of the hall—over a fenced path between piles of building materials—and into a glass lift cubicle. She leaned against the glass while the woman pressed buttons on the panel. On the other side of the glass, a moving ramp took passengers to the building's ground floor.

"You don't look so good," the woman said, in her distinct Asto accent, and started digging in a pouch that she wore on her belt. "Here." She held out a hand on which lay an orange pill.

Izramith met her eyes. The woman's face floated in and out of focus.

"Take it. It's your adaptation playing around with you, isn't it? Come on, take it, don't be silly."

"Silly?" No one called a Hedron guard *silly*.

"Well, whatever." And she was still smiling that annoying innocent smile. "It's that pride thing, isn't it? Like, *no one is allowed to see any emotion or any outward sign of distress*. That kind of thing. That's not necessary here in Barresh. We'll still respect you if you're sick."

What the . . . What did this girl think she was? She hadn't even introduced herself yet. Was it any wonder that Asto and Hedron didn't get along?

"Come on, take the pill. This helps, believe me."

Izramith wanted to tell the woman to go fuck herself, but a wave of nausea washed over her, so she took the pill. Put it in her mouth. Tried to swallow it. Her mouth flooded with saliva. Shit, she was going to spew. She swallowed hard. The feeling abated a bit. Coughed. The damn pill was gone. It wasn't on the ground. Maybe she swallowed it. That brought another surge of acid. She coughed again and managed again to push down that puking feeling.

The lift doors opened and she followed the woman into the hall, drenched in sweat.

There were eating houses on this side of the building, and further constructions were still underway. At a completed part people sat at tables. Izramith held her breath while walking past so that she didn't have to smell any food.

The world around her had been reduced to a blur of sounds and colours.

"Does that feel any better?" the woman asked.

Izramith nodded, not trusting herself to speak. The woman walked at a pace too fast for her queasy stomach, but Izramith followed, tensing every muscle in her belly so that it wouldn't feel like a water bag with sloshing contents. *Pride thing?* She'd show the meaning of pride to this fake-cheerful, dumbwitted bimbo.

"I know, adaptation is awful. First time I came here I was so sick, you wouldn't believe. It gets better with time, and the more often you do it—"

Izramith glared. *Stop. Talking. About. Being. Sick.*

She babbled on, "It will take you a few days to get back to full health. Seriously, I mean it. Your body will take some time to adjust to the temperature. Even when I go back home, I have to allow for extra time. I've never been to Hedron, but—"

Stop. Fucking. Talking.

"—I've been to Rayasha, and that was pretty bad, especially coming back home . . ."

Then she turned to Izramith. "I'm getting this all wrong, aren't I? My name is Dashu." The stones in her earrings were pink.

"I'm Izramith." Through the fog of heat and nausea, she tried to remember what clan that colour stood for. The amber stone in her own earring was the only thing the refugees had retained from their history on Asto. Amber meant Ezmi clan. And Hedron had the best amber of all the worlds. They wore the amber with pride. Pink was . . . Omi clan? They were builders, factory workers and drivers. Not smart, according to the jokes.

Just so that she would shut up, Izramith asked, "Are you a guest of the council, too?"

"No, I work here, in the security branch. I've been here for most of the year. It's very busy and a lot of fun. Most people are young and they're from all over the place."

"You came from Asto?" She remembered Commander Blue's words about Daya having ties with Asto. In the Security Branch?

"Yes, my family lives in an agricultural settlement to the east of Athyl. It's really boring there. The only other young people are ones who work on the farms and they're just so dumb—"

"Are you working *for* Asto?"

"You mean, like a spy or something?" She laughed. "Oh, no. No way, I'm not important enough for that. I came because I was bored at home. Daya will employ anyone who wants to work. So, we're kind of the same, huh? Guest workers. I came here for the adventure. What about you?"

"Yeah. Adventure." *Adventure with fucking guns and standing pretty at fucking parades.* Just her type of adventure.

They had come out on the other side of the building into a large open area, where an insane amount of building activity was underway. Paving had been ripped up to make place for digging apparatus, metal frames—made from Hedron steel, recognisable by its purple sheen. The heat made the air above the pavement shimmer, but that didn't seem to affect the workers. Many of them were of the small and tailed Pengali that she had also seen on the shuttle.

Her guide went into lengthy explanations about what each building site was going to be when completed. A new airport hall, with offices and maintenance and service halls, and commercial space and—

"The Exchange?" It suited Izramith to direct the subject of the discussion to something other than herself.

"No, that will stay across the square, but it is being done up, too. The building is more than three hundred years old, and the council is very attached to the typical Barresh architecture."

She went on about domes and ceiling windows and pentagonal designs.

Izramith stared at the building's domes, arches and stone walls, some restored, some in all their faded and flaking glory. Nothing in Hedron was older than a generation.

Xiya and his rebels had come to Hedron about a hundred *gamra* years ago, and the first passages of the settlement had been built about eighty years ago. Nothing was older than that. "Wait, do you mean three hundred *gamra* years or local years?"

"Local."

And that was almost twice as old again. Izramith could not get her head around that. When this building was being built, Hedron had been a lump of undiscovered and uninhabited rock. No wonder the building looked as worn and tired as it did.

"And the trees, how old are they? They're massive."

"Most trees would have been planted at the time the building was completed."

"That old?"

She just could not comprehend it. They were huge, spreading things with majestic trunks and rustling leaves. Indrahui, or at least the part where she'd gone, was devoid of tall vegetation. Most of what she'd seen was prairie, with endless golden plains undulating out of sight.

They went past that building, into a fairly busy street, around a corner into a more narrow street where there were not so many trees because one side was taken up by an elaborate but rusted metal fence and behind that a sprawling building with domes. Dashu led Izramith through an open gate, across a courtyard with mosaic paving and carefully clipped bushes, up a few steps into a dome-shaped foyer.

Dashu turned and met Izramith's eyes. "Still feel bad?"

Izramith had to think about that for a bit. The immediate nausea had abated, but now she felt sticky and very tired. "Better, I guess. So, where are we going?"

"Oh, did I forget? The council wants to see you for a briefing."

"Right now?"

"Yes. You're going to be pretty much wasted for the next day at least, so Daya wants to see you quickly."

Oh crap. She didn't feel like that now.

"Don't worry, you don't have to say anything. You'll just get your specs and docs and you can read them for the next day or so. This is a pretty important event, and there is quite a bit to do."

"I thought the party was not until next solar."

Dashu smiled at her. "You do feel better. I know, because you're talking and noticing things."

"I guess." *Noticing things is my job.*

"Beware, it will come back. Adaptation has a nasty habit of biting you in the butt when you're tired. It really does take a few days. Now, while we're here, you should really look at the old painting on this wall . . ."

Under this waterfall of words, she led Izramith from one hall to another, explaining why some were restored, and some not, and some in the process of being restored. Via a magnificent hall —with coloured glass in the ceiling—and corridors in various stages of renovation, they went up a wide set of stairs and came to a high-ceilinged hall that smelled of new materials.

The only furniture in the huge room was a single chair and two couches surrounding a low table.

Four men sat on the couches. One of the men rose. He was skinny and tall with pale skin and dark hair in loose curls. This man Izramith recognised from pictures as Daya Ezmi. Compared to the recording Commander Blue had made or the picture from the Hedron database, he looked older, with lines around his eyes and a few strands of white in his hair.

His eyes were the blackest she had ever seen. It was impossible to tell where his irises stopped and pupils started. It gave her the chills.

Just what had he done with that flash of light in the valley behind the airport?

The three others were men also, with olive skin and dark curly hair. Locals, she guessed, of the keihu race.

Daya bade her to sit, so she sat in the single chair.

He said, "Thanks, Dashu."

"Do you want me to wait downstairs?" Dashu used *chya* pronoun forms to address him. How quaint and formal.

"Yes, please."

Dashu made a submissive greeting and left.

He settled back into his seat.

Izramith found it hard to stop staring at him. All *zhadya*-born she had seen were deranged men in filthy clothes with blood on their hands. Daya's hands were delicate and cultured. His dark blue tunic was very classy, his hair combed and clean.

So this was the famed crazy *zhadya*-born known for repeatedly smashing up his room in his uncle's house? He seemed nothing like the adult *zhadya*-born men in the second level corridor. Heck, here he sat at the table with a couple of people who trusted him to be in charge of their town. How did he keep the madness away?

While she stared at Daya, Izramith was the subject of the unashamed stares of the other three men. She nodded a polite greeting at them.

All three were dressed in elaborate robes, with embroidery, piping at the collars and shoulder panels in different colours. One of them wore so much jewellery that Izramith wondered why he didn't collapse with the weight of it. The man next to him wore an orange robe of a shimmering, metallic-looking fabric. All of them had olive skin and curly dark hair.

Daya said, "Since we're all here now, I'll start. This is Izramith Ezmi of the Hedron guards, who has kindly agreed to help us with our security." His voice was clear, deeper than that of Coldi men, and he spoke with a curious combination of Asto and Hedron Coldi. "Izramith, these men are some of my trusted councillors who are helping me to oversee the logistics for the event. This is my right-hand man, Vice Chief Councillor Jisson Semisu."

This was the man who looked like a walking jewellery shop. He met Izramith's gaze with deep-set beady eyes under a heavy brow. His eyebrows were dark and thick with hairs that sprouted out at odd angles and some of which obscured his vision. Many of his springy curls had similarly escaped his ponytail.

He nodded, business-like. "Welcome to our great city." He had a strong accent and he probably meant *niya* to indicate a place of beauty, rather than *niyia* which was an archaic form that was only used in combination with the names of great heroes of ancient wars.

Daya indicated the other two men. "This is Emron Emiru." This was the man with the orange robe. He had a coarse-skinned round face with flushed red cheeks. He had a big blob of a nose with a distinct groove vertically across the tip. He nodded, too, but didn't say anything, while squinting at her. Oh no, she didn't think he agreed with her being here.

"And this is Merilon Damaru, who runs the Exchange."

This man was not as thickset as the others. He looked older, with a fair bit of white in his hair and wore classy dark blue.

"Had a nice trip?" He also spoke with an accent, but grammatically correct and he even dropped the troublesome pronoun.

Daya continued, "Welcome to Barresh, and welcome to the council. This building houses both the council offices and the Exchange, customs and quarantine departments. I trust Dashu has given you the tour?"

His voice held a playful tone.

Izramith nodded.

Her stomach gurgled and she really didn't feel up to dealing with these strange people and their strange interpretation of her customs. When arriving at Indrahui she'd gone straight from the airport to the camp and had been shown gear and weapons. She'd been fighting that very day.

Daya now faced his councillors. "I'd like to mention that Izramith's appointment is funded by me, and you are not to speak of the details with anyone, either here or in correspondence or discussions with family at home. Izramith, I presume that because of your regular occupation and previous contract, you will be familiar with restrictions like these." His voice carried a warning. His pronouns were imperative.

Izramith nodded. Her head was starting to throb again.

"All right then. The specifics of the job. In one solar, we celebrate the long-awaited wedding of Rehan Andrahar and Mikandra Bisumar. They, and the extended Andrahar family, have lived in Barresh for a number of years and have become valued and prominent citizens who not only give Barresh credibility but employ many locals. Of course, as you can tell by the names, they are Mirani. The Andrahar family did not leave Miran in a friendly way. They had a serious disagreement with the Mirani council and the Mirani chapter of the Trader Guild. The issues are too complicated to go into right now, but the short version is that they spoke up too loudly about the Mirani import regulations. Also the Lady Mikandra exposed a scam that Miran was running in order to bring the Barresh council into disrepute. This runs back to the conflict referred to as the Two-Day War, in which Miran was ousted as protector of Barresh.

"In their time in Barresh, the Andrahar Traders have become symbolic for the fight against the restriction of freedom in Miran. The family encompasses three brothers, all three Traders, and Mikandra, who has recently obtained her Trading licence as well. The rest of the family consists of the matriarch Isandra, who is vocal and politically active in our council, as well as the wife and three children of the youngest brother, Mikandra's mother and her younger sister. No doubt you will meet with the family later."

No doubt indeed. She had no intention of trying to protect them blind.

"According to Mirani custom, high-profile weddings include a parade of the couple through the streets of the city and a celebration for the people hosted by the family. Your task, and that of the security team you will lead, is simple: the family has got to be alive and unharmed at the end of the festivities. Now, I understand that you may be uncomfortable with working under your name and displaying your face, but the knowledge that I've employed a serving member of the Hedron guard is not to become public, so I will use your name and you will not wear uniform of any kind. I will supply all your gear. At this very moment, you'll be sent all information that you need for this job." He picked up a comm reader from the seat next to him, and touched the corner of the screen.

Her comm pinged. The screen showed *message received*.

"These councillors here will be your liaison to the council. Jisson is the one to go to if you have any questions about the council operations. Emron is familiar with the activities of the builders and street cleaners and other operations of the council services. Merilon, of course, can help you with communication, and can help you with access to Exchange records. Other than these three, no one in town knows who you are or why you are here."

The men nodded each in turn.

"You will meet your assigned team here tomorrow morning. You will find all the details in the information I've sent you. You can go to your guesthouse now. Mention my name and the guesthouse staff will know what to do. Rest well, and do not let your adaptation knock you about too much."

He rose. "Any more questions?"

Izramith shook her head. She did want to ask where he thought the risk was coming from, and oh, did he know someone called Reyar and why was he so in control and unlike the other *zhadya*-born she had fought, apprehended and thrown in jail?

But she was dizzy, sweating all over, and she desperately wanted to get out of here. Fresh air, or the opportunity to lie down. Most urgently of all, she needed to find a place where she could puke.

Izramith stumbled from the room, past the councillors whose faces passed in a blur. At the top of the stairs, she realised that she'd been too out of it to remember the way to the entrance. Fortunately, she could follow a breeze through the building to the nearest exit. Her head throbbed so much that she barely noticed the people around her. She had to get fresh air.

But of course when she made it outside, the air was not fresh but muggy, and it smelled of unpleasant things. She ran to the shade of a tree in the courtyard, and could not control her stomach any longer.

10

W HEN IZRAMITH had just about puked her guts out,
someone behind her put a hand on her shoulder.
"Hey, I almost lost you. I must have been waiting
at the wrong door. You were in a real hurry, huh?"

Damn. Dashu.

Izramith wiped her face with her arm. She wanted more than
anything to be alone, not to have to keep up her appearance for
her employers. Dashu would tell someone that she'd been sick,
and that would reach Daya or the council. No matter what Dashu
told her, they would start to question her ability to do the job.

"Come, I'll take you to the guesthouse. Daya is always like
this. He goes like, *I'll give you this map and you sort it out yourself,*
but I don't think you're in any state to find your own way there."

Izramith hated to admit it, but Dashu was right. Her steps
were so uncertain that Dashu put an arm around her shoulders,
and Izramith was glad for it. She didn't think she'd ever felt this
awful.

The walk to the guesthouse felt like an eternity. There were a
lot of large trees in this place, and a lot of people in colourful
dress. Gibbering, yelling, laughing people who made her want to
shout *Can you all shut up?*

The street paving was uneven and she tripped a few times. Worst of all, there were *steps* going into the guesthouse and her vision had gone all wonky. Her stomach was again making weird noises.

Dashu led her up to a desk and spoke in keihu to the guesthouse matron, a woman with a ridiculous hairdo that looked like some animal had built a nest on her head. The woman gave Izramith a disapproving look before turning to a cabinet on the wall behind the desk. Her butt was huge and wobbly. She handed Dashu an access key.

Dashu took Izramith through endless courtyards and more stairs.

Izramith's room was at the very back of a first floor gallery, a huge room bigger than her entire family's apartment at Hedron. There was an oval bed in the middle, rugs on the tiled floor, windows without glass but with ceiling-high lace curtains, and a bathroom with a large steaming bath that was filled from water flowing in from a hot vent.

She dumped her bag on the floor, where it resembled something ready to go out with the garbage collection.

Dashu left her a small supply of the short-working orange pills.

"They're not that good for you, and you can't take more than three per day, but they give a bit of relief. I'll come back later and tomorrow to check on you."

Izramith nodded weakly, standing in the middle of the room, and went to find the bathroom as soon as Dashu left.

The rest of the day and the night were not pleasant.

By the time Izramith could finally convince her stomach to accept some food and keep it there, the light was bright outside. She dozed on the large bed when the door opened and Dashu came in.

She wore her black uniform again, with a five-pointed star

embroidered on the chest. Her hair was, Asto-style, tied back in a tight ponytail. She bowed before the bed and proceeded to unpack several items from a bag. Something made out of cloth.

"What's that for?" Izramith asked, raising herself on one elbow.

"Your clothes. You can't go about the streets looking like you've come straight from Hedron."

"I *have* come straight from Hedron."

"Yeah, well, you still can't walk around looking like it. People will put the two together and figure out that you're a guard."

And no one liked having Hedron guards around in a visible way. She let herself fall back on the bed. This place was so plush and sophisticated, full of history and pretty things, albeit aged pretty things. So they weren't used to a woman who looked like a fighting machine, huh? Well, what did they hire her for anyway?

"Come on, we've got a meeting. You need to have a bath."

Damn, yes, another damn meeting. And what a way to say *you stink*. And what was worse, she'd fully intended to read Daya's information and be prepared, but she'd been far too sick to remember.

Izramith pushed herself off the bed. Whoa, that felt . . . not good at all. The world spun around her.

"Are you going to be all right?"

"Yeah." *Quit fussing, I'm not a weakling.* She grabbed the clothes off the bed and made for the bathroom.

But her first steps were very uncertain and she bumped her shoulder painfully into the doorframe. She was just about well enough to remember how much she hated being sick.

Someone had been in the bathroom to clean the mess she vaguely remembered making in the dark. All the jars in the basket that had fallen off the shelf next to the bath were back in their position. The soaps and powders that had spilled on the floor had been mopped up, and the stack of towels that had tumbled into the bath had been fished out and replaced with dry ones. Any—um—substances that had missed their intended places had been cleaned up.

Damn, had she been that much out of it? She had never even heard anyone come in.

She stepped out of her Hedron-issue grey nightclothes and slipped into the warm water. The jars and pots in the basket carried labels in various languages, including Coldi, and she selected one that said *hair gel* and hoped it would clean her hair rather than oil it. The stuff smelled unfamiliar and oozed cold over her head. Riiiight, not sure about this.

"Are you all right?" Dashu came to the door. She stared at Izramith's upper arms. The opposite wall was one big mirror and Izramith glanced at her reflection, including the crosshatched initiation scars on her upper arms, which were about twice the width of Dashu's.

"Yes, perfectly." Seriously, what was it with the snooping? Couldn't a person even have a bath in peace?

She rinsed off her hair by ducking under the water and climbed out with a feeling of regret. How she'd love to sit there a bit longer. But she wasn't here to laze around.

She dried herself and grabbed the clothes Dashu had brought. The trousers were calf-length and fitted well enough, but of the two tunics, one was too small. The other strained around her upper arms in a way that made the little frilly bits on the hem of the sleeves stand up. It looked . . . stupid. And yellow. Seriously?

Feeling like she could barely breathe in the tunic, she returned to the main room.

Dashu looked her up and down. "That looks better."

"It's too tight. I can barely move." Izramith turned around and held her arms in front so her shoulders strained against the fabric.

"Hmmm, yeah. I think you may need to get a men's shirt."

"You have any . . ." *less ridiculous* ". . . other colours?"

"What about the blue one I brought?"

"It doesn't fit at all. Can't I wear a uniform like you?"

"You're not in the official employ of the council."

"Then I want to wear my grey tunic."

"You're meant to look like a visitor."

"Even visitors can move their arms. I would wear my grey things if I were visiting." Seriously, was there anything more stupid to argue about than what to wear?

Dashu let the argument hang in the air. She didn't say that she would bring other clothes or ask Daya what she was allowed to wear.

They left the room via the gallery and navigated the guest-house's many courtyards to the main courtyard, where the guest-house's patrons sat at pretty metal lacework tables with pink tablecloths. There were plates and cups on the tables and wait-resses walked around with trays of food.

A Pengali waitress showed them a table. Dashu pulled out a chair for Izramith, and went to get her tea—which was pink—and a plate with a couple of slices of curious bread with a dark swirl inside. A group of Damarcians on the next table raised eyebrows at the pair of them. They were two elderly couples, the four of them dressed in rich clothing. The men both wore lots of rings, and one of them had a fortune of diamond studs in his ears.

Izramith remembered the first meal she had in Indrahui, or rather, the first meal she had missed out on because she turned up too late in the hot and dusty mess tent.

There had been none of this genteel business, no one waiting on her. Seriously, how could she tell Dashu that it was annoying and she could look after herself?

And she hated the way the damn tunic restricted her move-ments. Why couldn't she wear a black shirt like Dashu?

At least while she ate, the last feeling of sickness subsided.

"Feeling better?" Dashu asked, her expression anxious.

"Much better."

"Beware, because your adaptation is not settled yet, although you may feel fine now, it can come back with a vengeance."

Izramith snorted. Pampering was for weaklings. "I'm ready to do work." *Show me something I can work with*. Guns, spying equipment, anything as long as it wasn't more talk or stupid frilly yellow clothes.

They finished the meal in uneasy silence, and left the guest-house for the council building, where, according to Dashu, the team was waiting and *thrilled to meet her.*

Good grief.

They entered the building through the back entrance in the alley behind the Exchange.

In the near-empty foyer three people sat on the couches.

Facing her was a young man from the local keihu race. He was unusually lanky for his kind, had a heavy brow which gave him a serious look, and wore his curly hair in a ponytail. His eyes were kind and brown, and it was a pity about the ugly keihu nose —broad, with a longitudinal groove across the tip—because otherwise he would have been quite handsome. He wore the same black uniform as Dashu, with the council emblem of the five-pointed star.

The other two people had their backs to her. Judging by the black hair with the metallic sheen, one was a Coldi man also in council uniform, and the other had the typical bronze hair of an Indrahui.

At the same time as they looked over their shoulders at Izramith, Daya entered the room through a door on the other side.

"Ah, you're all here." He clutched a reader and some docu-ments to his chest. "Sit down. We have a lot to discuss."

Izramith walked around the couch with the Coldi and Indrahui man to the empty spot next to the young keihu man.

Daya had sat in the single chair and shuffled his reader and a couple of folded up papers on his knees.

Izramith sat down. Looked up—

—Met the gaze of the Coldi man.

Her cheeks flushed with heat and her mind flooded with insane impulse thoughts: he was an upstart, needed to be put in his place. He was here to make her life a misery, to contest everything she said. He was Asto Coldi of course. There was absolutely no way she wanted him on her team.

She clamped her hands between her knees. Blood roared in her ears. What the fuck? The man hadn't even introduced himself and had done nothing to justify this reaction.

With great difficulty, she kept herself calm by looking at his knees instead of his face.

Daya had started talking. ". . . are the people I told you about yesterday, a small confidential task force and specialists in the field in which I want you to work. First, let's introduce each other. Izramith, this is Eris Havaru, the head of Barresh's newly instated special security branch." The keihu man nodded. "Eris has worked as security officer at the Trader Guild headquarters in Kedras. His family are merchants and he has many commercial connections." The man looked much too young to have any of that kind of experience.

"One member on your team who isn't here but you will already know is Dashu Omi. She's your tech specialist and is taking delivery of some equipment right now, and may join us later."

Izramith nodded, still feeling flustered and hot and not quite alert. Her stomach was also squirming a bit, as if it was still deciding what to do with the weird breakfast she had eaten.

"This here is Wairin." The attention shifted to the Indrahui man, a giant with the characteristic skin that was so black that it had a green sheen. His bright green eyes met hers in that typical emotionless look that Indrahui did so well. He wore typical Indrahui fighters' garb: trousers and shirt made from tough brown fabric. What the heck was he doing here, fighting someone else's war while his own world was torn apart with conflict?

Daya continued, "Wairin has a lot of experience in undercover operations in conditions of war." Yeah, she bet. "He has seen active combat duty and is handy with traps and hidden explosives."

Did he know that she'd served in his native land? "You're from Pataniti?"

He shook his head. "I'm from Makitan."

At least that was far enough away from the blood-soaked plains for them to have never run into each other.

Explosives specialist, huh?

Daya continued, "The last member of the team is Loxa Azimi. He's one of the guards in—"

Izramith looked up again, and the heat was back, more ferocious than before. Her heart was pounding with it. The rest of Daya's words drowned in the roaring of blood in her ears.

Loxa similarly grabbed the armrest of the couch with a white-knuckled hand. The muscles in his legs strained under his trousers. She didn't dare look into his face. The breeze brought a waft of a musky scent that said *fight me.*

And she wanted to do just that, hang the consequences.

Daya reached over the table and broke the line of vision between them. From the corner of her eyes, she saw that Loxa brought his hand to his head and rubbed his face. He stared at his knees.

Izramith unballed her fists and tried her very best to calm herself.

This was ridiculous. She didn't even know him. He now leaned back into his seat, pointedly not looking at her, but his cloying scent drifted all around her.

She could only look as far up as his knees. His hands twitched as well.

This is not going to end well.

She could ignore this feeling when facing Thimayu, but this was so much worse. She wasn't going to spend time working with him like this.

Daya was still talking as if he noticed nothing, ". . . will be in liaison with the brother of the groom. As bonus, he has the best knowledge in town about Mirani security."

Damn, he was now talking about the Mirani family, and she had missed their contact's name.

Pay attention, stupid.

Daya put his reader on the table, touched a button and a projection sprang in the air. It was a map of the streets of the city. It looked like a builders' plan, and indeed the emblem of the Damarcian Master Builders Guild hung over the projection.

"The wedding parade is to follow the route marked here." Daya pointed at a circuit that lit the streets in blue. "This is what we have done so far: along this course, we have identified points of risk where someone with ill intent can hide, with or without knowledge of the owners of the property in question. These places need to be made safe before the parade. The families in the houses have all been visited by our team and have agreed to cooperate. They will all be given passes."

The young man Eris nodded.

"On the day before the parade, we'll set up an exclusion zone where only those with a pass can come. This work is all pretty straightforward and agreed-upon by the council."

He paused and looked around the room. Those eyes gave her the chills.

When he continued, his voice was softer and more intense. "The problem is the large guesthouse on the corner of the Main Square and Market Street, as you will have seen in your brief."

Izramith nodded, too ashamed to admit that she'd been too sick to read it. She swore she'd do it as soon as she had a moment.

"The guesthouse is a large, rambling old place where anyone can stay cheaply and without presenting ID. Most of the time, the owners have no idea who stays overnight in their rooms. Many are itinerant workers, usually labourers. There are also a fair number of ex-soldiers from Miran, who live there long-term. They hire entire dorms and sub-let beds to their friends or whoever pays. The guesthouse has been linked to much of the smuggling and criminal activity in town, and much as we'd like to think that we're making inroads on that front, there is a lot of work still to be done. As you can see, the route goes past the guesthouse, around the corner into Market Street, exposing the parade to danger on two sides."

Izramith said, "All right, so if the guests are all short-term visitors, why don't you simply close the place for those days? Or give permits only to people whose ID checks out?"

"Two reasons. The most important one is that Barresh is short on accommodation. If we close the guesthouse, there would be hundreds of young workers, perhaps as many as a thousand, without anywhere to stay."

"There wouldn't be, because you let them in when their ID checks out."

"I understand, but that will still leave lots of people who don't have ID, don't want to be checked or whose ID has expired or has been stolen—or who entered the city on stolen ID in the first place. There is a hard-core group of long-term residents at the guesthouse. We've only had border controls for about seven years. Before that, we were a Mirani protectorate and Mirani ex-soldiers would come back here after completing their period of duty. When the Mirani army was withdrawn from Barresh, they stayed behind. Most of them have lost contact with their families. They don't have ID, have no money to leave, or pay for another place to stay and have not taken up our repeated offers for new ID. If we toss them on the street, they'll create trouble."

All right. "Was that the second reason?"

"No. The second reason is more delicate. A local family owns the guesthouse. It is registered in the name of Risan Semisu, who is a direct cousin to Jisson Semisu whom you met yesterday."

The councillor with all the jewellery.

"The Semisu family is well-respected, and is not under any suspicion. I would count Jisson Semisu as a friend. His cousin, however, is a strong supporter of freedom from what they call *institutional prying* or *corporate espionage*, so he has refused council access to the building on principle. His guests, he says, are poor and disenfranchised Mirani ex-soldiers and refugees and low-paid workers. We haven't had anything to fear from them in six years, so why should we now?"

"Doesn't that mean he's got something to hide?"

"I'm pretty sure that the guesthouse *does* hide things, but I'd be surprised if he knew about it. He bought the place with the view of redevelopment and takes no commercial interest in the running of it. For him, it's merely a placeholder business until he gets the go-ahead from the council to refurbish the place."

"But he won't let you search the place?"

"I suspect *he* would, if presented with the right arguments, but a bit over a week ago we tried to conduct an audit of the population with the view of making it secure, and the manager denied us access. Not only that, he took the matter to the people's forum session of the council and presented the arguments in such a way that the council voted in his favour."

"Why would they do that?"

"Many councillors were already uneasy about access given to guards to climb on their roofs and search their gardens. They wanted to see proof of our claims that searching the guesthouse was necessary."

"Illegal people aren't enough reason?"

"Not if they've been illegal for seven years or more. You must understand some of the local sentiments. A fair number of Barresh natives take pride in not having ID and being illegals in their own town. It is not because they have anything to hide but because they dislike all forms of external control. Privacy and freedom have a very strong history in this town. It goes back to the time of the hero of Barresh, Omarion Baku, who was stripped of his ID and his Trading licence and still continued travelling and his Trading business."

"As pirate."

Did she imagine it or was there a sharp intake of breath from Eris? Everyone looked at her, including Loxa, whose eyes focused on her knees.

"Yes." Daya nodded. "Except don't say anything bad about Omarion Baku in the presence of locals, unless you're keen to get into a fight."

"So, as I see it, you and a few others on the council have wanted to clean up the guesthouse for a long time, and the wedding is a cover for us to do so?" No wonder he'd said nothing about this yesterday.

Daya gave her an intense look. "I would appreciate if you were not to repeat that outside this room."

In other words: yes. The look in his eyes chilled her.

"So. We can't go into the guesthouse with a full search party in uniform, but it's a very open place and nothing stops people going in separately for whatever reason they think will pass scrutiny. Maintenance, deliveries, laundry, anything. You can also watch it from the street and you'll have access to any communication made from the guesthouse to the Exchange. You can scan those records for the identities of guests and the content of their messages."

He met Izramith's eyes with another intense look. "But—you will not have an authorisation from the council to do this. Many in the council do not agree with your being here because of the reasons I gave earlier: privacy and freedom. They don't want outsiders prying in their business. I could only get your appointment through the council by assigning you general security duties. You will do routine security work. The rest you will do without authority, outside council hours."

She nodded, although she felt less easy with every word he spoke. She functioned well as a hired gun. Dancing around delicate politics was not her thing. "Any indication what we might find in this guesthouse? Is there a real threat to the family or is that a front, too?"

"Oh no, there is definitely a threat. The Andrahar family is well off and have been regular subjects of harassment from Mirani sources. They will inform you about those when you meet them later."

More fucking meetings. Even if it was necessary for the job, she didn't like it. It wasn't how she operated. Daya did realise that he'd let a killing machine into his dainty town, didn't he? To be honest, the stupid yellow frilly shirt was probably a sign that he didn't.

She'd thought there was a catch to the job, and this was obviously it. Her contract didn't involve anything serious; it was to support Daya's politics and play a game of one-upmanship with some political adversary on the council.

Oh fuck, she hated this.

She met Daya's eyes and held his gaze. His serious expression told her that he knew what he was doing to her. This was the point at which she could still back out.

Of course, she was in too far already, and going back home was not an option, or at least not one that wouldn't result in her being sent to the most boring and remote mining post. Being familiar with Hedron and the guards, Daya would know that, too.

So that's how you play games with people, huh? Bring it on, buster.

11

AYA WENT ON to describe the route and how the parade would progress. First the drummers, then the flower bearers, then the couple and the family, then the dancing party, and musicians.

While he spoke, Izramith struggled to concentrate. She'd had little sleep last night and while that alone shouldn't disturb her, being sick didn't help matters at all. The strength of Loxa's smell had faded, but a whiff of it clung to her like a foul odour that remained in a room no matter how often it was cleaned.

The Indrahui man Wairin had said very little during this meeting. He kept looking at her, too, and because she couldn't look at Loxa, she kept meeting his eyes more often than she wanted. She kept wanting to pull down her sleeves, but they already covered her scars adequately. The action was futile; they already knew that she was a guard and there was no way he could tell that she was the one whose action had resulted in the death of many of his fellows. Moreover, was his tribe supportive of the rebels or government? He looked like rebel to her.

Crap.

She didn't know his history, but could almost hear him say, "I had three brothers, but they died in that camp crash in Pataniti."

Crap, crap, crap.

Daya was finished with his explanation. He rose, and as he was saying that there were refreshments in the foyer, and he'd leave the group to discuss their work plans, Izramith was thinking how she could ask him about her uncle and noticed Loxa getting up from the couch.

She turned. Their eyes met. The heat returned in full force. His smell was everywhere, filling her lungs with every breath, making the blood roar in her ears.

Izramith sensed someone coming into the doorway with a tray, but the next moment Loxa charged for her. She ducked out of the way. He missed her by a hair's width and went careening into the staff member. The woman screamed. The tray went flying. Glasses bounced over the tiles. Tea went everywhere.

Loxa rolled, sprang to his feet—

People shouted for him to stop. Someone even tried to restrain him, but he just batted the man out of the way.

"Leave them," Daya ordered, in a curt voice.

People retreated to the edges of the room. Someone shifted the fallen cups out of the way.

Izramith crouched in a defensive pose.

Loxa's eyes were fixed on her, unfocused like a madman's.

He came at her like an angry beast, and while she ducked out of his way, she grabbed his arm and pushed him back while sticking out her leg. He tripped and fell, pulling her with him. She tumbled over him, not letting go of his arm. He pulled her back by that arm and tried to pin her to the ground by rolling on top of her.

He was strong, but had poor technique. She twisted by swinging her legs, gained purchase on one knee, and rose while he was hanging onto her back. She grabbed his collar and swung him over her hip. He fell flat on the ground with a thud, and she dropped on top of him, pinning both his wrists against the ground.

"I win." You did *not* argue with a Hedron guard.

He looked up at her, panting. Really looked at her, without the clouded expression of anger in his eyes.

It was noisy in the room. People talking in raised voices, having run in to see what the racket was about. Izramith didn't even hear what language they spoke. The roaring in her ears slowly subsided. Neither she nor Loxa moved. They just looked each other in the eyes.

Loxa's muscles relaxed. Sweat pearled on his forehead.

Slowly, Izramith let go of his arms.

"You win, right?" He grinned. With one finger he lifted up the sleeve of her tunic. From where he lay on the ground, he would be able to see the crosshatched initiation scars she had there. "Yup, it's true. I fought a Hedron Guard and lost badly."

The breeze coming in through the open balcony door carried a whiff of cool air and blew away the last of his confusing scent.

Izramith sat back on her knees, looking at all the horrified wide-eyed faces of the people in the room. The mist in her head had cleared.

Damn, what had she done? What was wrong with her? It was only her first day here. She'd wanted a clean record, and now she'd start a complaints file less than a day after her arrival. And for what purpose?

Dashu's cheerful voice behind her said, "Good that you sorted that out. And for the better, too, Loxa. Imagine what a mess we'd be in if you won. Now, get up and let's do some real work. All you've done so far is talk."

Loxa rose. Eris held out a hand to help him up, but Dashu motioned him away. What was she? His girlfriend?

Izramith also jumped to her feet. Loxa faced her, not meeting her eyes, and made the Coldi subservient greeting, with his arms limp by his side, looking down.

Oh crap. So that's what it was about? She'd won the fight, and now he considered her his superior, huh?

She grinned, uneasily. "We don't do *nimiya* greetings at Hedron. To us, all people are equal."

"You're kidding. You're going to be difficult about this?" Dashu spread her hands, rolling her eyes. "What have you been taught about associations? That they're evil and the root of everything that's wrong with Asto?"

"Associations are unnecessary. We don't have controlling leaders. We don't need that kind of structure."

"If you believe that we're all so primitive because we fight for positions in our associations, why did you take part in the fight?"

"He attacked me."

"And what did you do to provoke that?"

"Nothing."

"So you had no flush of irrational anger when you saw him first? It was purely self-defence?"

Izramith glared at her.

Dashu snorted. "You may know a lot about security, but you have a lot to learn about how to relate to your own kind."

She made to leave, but Izramith grabbed her shirt and pulled her close until their noses almost touched. "Don't you fucking start that kind of talk to me."

"Yes, I will. That's what I'm for: to annoy the crap out of you so you can get unwrapped from all the insulation you carry and start acting like a normal person."

"And a normal person is someone who acts exactly like you?"

Dashu spread her hands and rolled her eyes. "Damn, you make it hard! All I'm trying to do is make a connection, making you fit in our team, but I might as well be talking to myself for all the two words you say."

"Did I ask you to talk? Are you afraid of silence?"

"Can't you think of any questions to ask when you're just arrived in a place? Is that how you relate to your colleagues? Giving them the wall of silence?"

"Fuck off."

"Thank you. I'll do just that." She marched off.

Oh crap. And yes, that was entirely how colleagues at Hedron related to each other. *Ignore it and it will go away.*

Next moment, a strong and warm arm looped around Izramith's shoulders.

"Dashu can be pretty rude," Loxa said. "She did that to me, too. But she is a really good sort. You'll learn. You're not used to any of this, right?"

Izramith eyed his hand on her shoulder. He had to know that Hedron Coldi didn't touch a lot and she wondered if he'd get the hint.

He didn't. "It's all right. We're our own little association now. Only three of us, but we'll show them what we're worth, right?"

Dashu turned at the door. "There's no need to coddle her. She'll work it out. Eventually. They're ice-cool at Hedron, but they're not stupid." Then she was gone.

"Yes, she's rude," Loxa said. "But that's all right. She hasn't yet done anything to harm me and I've been following her around for years."

Crap. They weren't lovers. She was part of his association. Except Dashu had been subservient to her, and Izramith had beaten Loxa. But Loxa had followed Dashu around. What did that make him to her? Subservient? And what position did Izramith now occupy? The one at the top? Damn it, no. She didn't understand this association business. That system was rigid and unworkable and primitive.

Fighting for positions of dominance was stupid and now she had herself roped into this situation that would never work.

She wanted to explain that this was all a horrible mistake, but Dashu was already at the door, taking liberties with the contents of the new food tray, brought in by the staff member with tea dripping down the front of her uniform. She grabbed a couple of cakes and stuffed them in her mouth as she went into the corridor. She was still talking, but her words didn't make it around the cake in an intelligible state.

"Let's go," Loxa said, and went in the same direction. He also grabbed a few cakes from the tray, and two mugs, one of which he passed to Izramith. She wasn't hungry. In fact, she felt like she might be sick again.

In a small room off the hall stood a couple of tables pushed together and barely visible under a mountain of electronic equipment. Lights blinked, data scrolled over screens and cables went everywhere over the floor and into the corners. Dashu sat on a chair in the middle of this chaos, munching her cake.

"Whoa. You've been busy," Loxa said.

"Better busy than sitting in meetings." She brushed crumbs off her lap. "Sit down. We got a lot of work to do." She flapped her hand at a chair that contained a tottering mountain of electronics. "Just put the stuff on the table."

Izramith picked up a bevy of electronics and dumped them on the table. The pile contained Hedron-made equipment, but also stuff from Asto, and Damarq, and some of which she had no idea where it came from. She had never seen so much different technology in the same place. In the control room at the guard station they only had Hedron-made equipment, because it was all neatly integrated with each other.

Eris remained standing by the door, clutching his cup.

Dashu said, "Sit down, all, because I have quite a lot to show you."

Wairin came in, carrying three chairs for Eris, Loxa and himself, and placed these around the tables with the equipment. Wairin sat directly opposite Izramith, Eris behind her.

He tapped Izramith on the shoulder. "Hey, do you know that there is a rip in your shirt?"

"Where?" She reached with her hand to the shoulder closest to him. Her fingertips met skin where there should be fabric. Damn.

Stupid frilly shirt.

Dashu was ready to start. Had she even noticed the rip in Izramith's shirt? "All right. I'll give a brief overview of what we've done so far. Since we're not allowed to send a party into the guesthouse, there are other ways of finding out what goes on there. First of all, I've asked the Exchange for any communication they have originating from coordinates that are within the grounds of the guesthouse. As you can see . . ." She hit a control and a projection of a building sprang up.

The façade of the building looked like so many other buildings: two storeys, an arched entrance and arched, glassless windows at the top floor. The entire complex spanned half the block and twelve two-storey wings and four courtyards.

"As you can see, the place is huge. At any one time, up to a thousand people could be staying there. We expect it to be full for the celebrations. Whenever there is a party, people flock to the city. That should give us a fair bit of communication data. Secondly, we've installed cameras to monitor who goes in and out of the place. We run those recordings through a face recognition program and match it up with known names, mostly from guard records relating to small offenses. We already have a list of more than four hundred names. Third, but not last, we have Wairin staying in the guesthouse. Of course he can't pry around too much or behave in a way not expected from a guest worker, but he has installed a few bugs in strategic places and he hears and sees things that bugs can't."

She touched another button and a block of text was superimposed over the projection of the building.

"So, what have we found so far? As expected, the communication logs from the Exchange have been pretty ordinary. They cover the usual things, people sending messages home. The only remarkable thing I can say about them is that there are not as many communications as you would expect from a place of this size. With the number of people in that place, and the number of convicted criminals, you'd expect there to be a lot more communication. It could be because the people who stay in the guesthouse are from the poorer parts of the population and they don't have much money to spend on communication."

Dashu turned to a different device. "So the communication didn't give us much to work with and between ourselves, we're not happy with that. It almost seems as if someone knows we're listening and they're communicating in a different way. I've been to the Exchange myself and obtained frequency scans of the area, and there just isn't that much radio communication into the place. It's strange and puzzling. The bugs, however, are a lot more interesting."

Another projection sprang up, a fuzzy and grainy image that Izramith recognised as an infrared recording. It showed a group of people going up the stairs carrying bags and boxes. Then it cut to the view from another camera, showing the same group sitting at a balcony talking.

Dashu halted the projection and pointed. "This man is the manager of the guesthouse."

The quality of the recording didn't show much more than that he wore a loose robe—the infrared projection didn't show true colours of course—and his curly hair in a ponytail.

The projection had frozen at a point where another man was handing a bag over the table.

"The contents of the bag that he's receiving is probably cash for bribes. The other men aren't guests." The projection only showed their backs.

This was some kind of evidence? "Why would he receive bribes?"

"It's for keeping secret illegal people." Wairin hadn't said much in the course of the morning and everyone turned to him at the sound of his deep, heavily accented voice. "I hear people talk. Manis sort it out. Manis keep you safe from guards because guards don't come in guesthouse."

"And this Manis would be the manager?" Izramith asked.

"Yes. Is not a good man. Wants money."

"So. What is this supposed to mean?" Izramith spread her hands.

Everyone looked at her.

"I'm still unsure of our mandate and parameters of the job. My contract says that I'm here to provide security for a wedding, but now it turns out I'm not. I'm here to secretly clean out this guesthouse for a political purpose with no official mandate, and, if things go wrong, no support. Forgive me for being cynical, but I'd like to see the task sheet for this job."

Eris looked at her as if he wanted to say *what's a task sheet?*

Loxa said, "This isn't *that* kind of job."

"In my language, everything that pays me is *that* kind of job, even if to cover my own arse. Where do we fit, who do we report to, who are our feed-ins, who are our moles and what is the fallback plan? For that matter: what is our primary plan? Who are our first-level and second-level priority sources and what are triggers to disregard either? What is our level of autonomy?" She had to stop to draw breath.

No one said anything, and the fuck, it seemed like none of them had a clue what she was talking about.

Seriously! This wedding was in how much time? Was she expected to set up this whole structure from scratch?

Dashu said in a small voice. "All those things are what we have associations for."

"And what about Wairin and Eris? They're not in an association."

"They are."

Izramith stared at both men. Neither of them confirmed this. They didn't deny it either. They weren't even Coldi. How could they understand the concept if even she didn't understand it? "So . . . how does this work, then? Loxa is your superior, and—"

"Loxa is my *zhayma*." Her equal. "You're our superior. Eris and Wairin are *zhayma*s."

"And who is their superior?" That was how it worked, wasn't it?

"Braedon Andrahar, the groom's brother. You haven't met him yet."

So, a Mirani, a keihu and an Indrahui pretending to understand an Asto Coldi custom. Stranger things might have happened, but she hadn't heard of any. Hang on— "Then you're saying that this Mirani guy is—"

"Your *zhayma*, yes."

This got weirder all the time. "And who is our superior?"

"Daya."

Seriously? They had to be kidding. Were they so blind to the fact that other people didn't understand *sheya* at a very basic level?

And there were so many things wrong with this arrangement

from a security point of view, she didn't even know where to begin.

One, you did not include your employer in the job.

Two, you did not rely on informal information for a job description.

Three, you did not include your financial sponsor in a job.

She could go on and on.

Well, if they weren't going to give her one, *she* would make a task sheet and they would come to appreciate the clarity about who did what and where the information went and who had access to it.

First she should read Daya's information before she asked anything else. She rubbed her face with her hands. Her eyes felt gritty with lack of sleep.

"Are we doing anything further today?" she asked Dashu.

"I'm running a few further scans. Tomorrow, we go and talk to the family and we'll start our regular checks. You're tired?"

Izramith shrugged. Admitting to being tired would be considered a personal weakness with the guards. You were never sick, or tired, or heartbroken, or excited. You came in and did your job. You didn't speak about personal matters. You made no excuses. You were expected to protect anonymity and that of your colleagues. If criminals knew who you were, they would use it against you.

Dashu said primly, "It's all right to say so. I rather work with someone who's rested. Judging by the state of your room, you would have had to be up for most of the night."

And was there a need for her to mention this in front of the rest of the team?

Izramith pointed at her shoulder. "You might have noticed that I need to get changed into another shirt."

Great. Now she was officially mega-annoyed.

12

WHEN IZRAMITH arrived at the guesthouse, she remembered that of course she had no other shirt, since the second shirt Dashu had brought was too small and she was not to wear her Hedron gear. And she sure as hell wasn't going back to remind Dashu of that fact.

She had in her bag in the guesthouse a sewing kit, but the only thread in the kit was dark purple. Even her neatest stitches contrasted horribly with the dainty yellow of the shirt, but, as she sat cross-legged in the middle of the room, she felt a calm vindication. If they didn't want her to stand out, they should supply her with clothes that fitted.

If they wanted her to do a good job, they should supply her with the information to do so, and until they did that, she would write up her own parameters.

She finished sewing, tried the shirt on and found that it restricted her movement even more.

Damn.

Well, that was unacceptable. Maybe it was time to go to the shops.

She rummaged in her bag for her waist strap, lifted her shirt and looped it around and did up the fastening, then she found her small gun and clipped it into the holder. The shirt went back over the assemblage. She wasn't happy with the way the shirt bulged at her waist, but there was no way she'd go without her trusted weapon, no matter how much Daya said she was supposed to use only what he supplied her.

She grabbed her reader and—

No, maybe she should try to look less like a guard.

In the bathroom, she undid the tie in her hair and let the locks tumble over her shoulders. Like that of many Hedron Coldi, her hair was not entirely straight and the light coming into the bathroom reflected in the metallic surface sheen to highlight the waves. She ran her fingers through it to tease out the I-lost-my-hair-tie kink, draping her hair over the fixed seam in her shoulder. She had never considered herself to be particularly attractive, but looking in the mirror with her face lit side-on, she was glad not to be cursed with the course skin and hideous nose of the keihu. Her nose was broad and quite flat and did not stick out like a glowing beacon.

But damn, that purple thread on her shoulder really did look ridiculous.

Ah well, it would have to do.

The street that ran past her guesthouse was called Market Street and it was quite busy at this time of day. The light had turned golden and many families strolled in relaxed fashion in the dappled shade of trees. Behind the trees, ornate walls lined both sides of the street. The occasional open metal work fence gave her a glimpse of the mansions beyond: huge two-storey affairs surrounded by delicate gardens with bushes clipped into shapes and burbling fountains.

While she walked, Izramith turned on her reader and finally opened up Daya's document: it was a map of the route of the parade, with names and notes superimposed over the top. At each house, it listed the owner and the owner's function. Almost all of them were councillors of Barresh. Wow, they had really big families here. And why were there so many adult women in each of these houses? Did they live with partners and partners' sisters, or were they servants? Or did the owners rent rooms to other families because the houses were so big and the island crowded?

She ran her finger along the length of Market Street, looking at the family names. Semisu, Semisu, Damaru, Emiru, Damaru . . . on so on. The houses in Market Street were owned by just a handful of families, and all of those had representatives on the council. In the other streets along the route of the parade, ownership was a bit more varied, but not a lot more.

While she walked, the mansions on both sides of the street made way for eating houses where people sat at tables and chairs amongst the gnarled and rough tree trunks. Strings of lights that hung from tree branches dispelled the darkness, although there was still enough light for the glowing pinpricks to look feeble.

A couple of shops sold clothing, one of them sturdy gear with lots of pockets and straight, simple cuts. No frills. She liked that.

Except when the shop owner came to help her, it became clear that she lacked another very important item: money. He wouldn't take credits. Neither would other shops, judging from his rudimentary Coldi and hand signals.

Damn.

Most clothing at Hedron was free, and so was the food and other essential services. The few remaining services or personal items could be traded for vouchers or put on an account. No one had physical money at Hedron. They had no separate currency, no coins or similar clumsy things. The company had money, and it distributed wealth fairly across all workers.

Double damn. And she wasn't going to ask Dashu or Daya for help.

Time for a radical solution. An *Izramith Solution* her father would call it when she did these crazy things that sometimes got her into trouble, but sometimes worked.

From a rack at one of the shops, she selected the shirt she liked best—a plain and sturdy off-white number. Dust and a faded sign made her think that these shirts weren't exactly the most popular things in this shop. She asked the merchant if she could try it on.

It fitted well, and she made sure that she went out into the shop to look at herself from all angles in the mirror. A young man she presumed to be the merchant's son stood talking to another customer, but he ogled her arms and shoulders.

When she was certain that the merchant had seen her in his shirt, she changed back into the yellow shirt, which was getting rather smelly with the heat and the tight fit.

"Is it not to your liking?" the merchant asked, nodding at the white shirt draped over her arm.

"Yes, it is, but—um—unless you take credits, I can't take it. I don't have any money on me right now."

"We don't. I'm sorry."

"Then I can't buy. I really like this, and would like to get two. Look, this is the only shirt I have." She turned so that the ripped shoulder faced his way. "Is there something I can do for you in exchange for the white shirt?"

He fingered his lip with a hand laden with rings. "Hmm, I don't think—"

His son said something in keihu, and his father stopped speaking. He replied to his son. The son nodded.

"You carry heavy things?" the merchant asked Izramith.

"Anything you want." *Bricks, smuggled goods, dead bodies.* Well, he probably wouldn't appreciate the humour in that. People at Indrahui never did. They were way too serious.

"Come." He preceded her into the shop, where it was too dark for her to see properly, so she stumbled between racks of clothing and tripped over something stacked in the aisle.

"These ones here," he said.

By the glow from a fitful light against the back wall Izramith could make out a pile of boxes.

"These go upstairs."

"Sure." Izramith picked up a box. Oof. Whatever was inside weighed a lot. That and gravity was stronger here than on Hedron.

"My son go with."

The young man gave her a coy smile. He preceded her out of

the shop, across the street to a building taller than the surrounding shops.

It was an ugly rectangular thing, with three levels of balconies, each with rows of doors leading to businesses units. The areas in the shade of the balconies were starting to go dark, and lights burned in a couple of windows.

An open staircase led up the side, barred by a metal gate, a flimsy construction, which the merchant's son unlocked. It creaked when he pulled it open.

The windows in the first floor gallery were all dark, and so were those on the second floor. The top floor's layout was slightly different, with a partition blocking access to the far end of the balcony.

The merchant's son walked past offices with darkened windows. Some of them were dirty and the space beyond empty, the doors with peeling paint or scratches.

At the point where the partition stopped access further down the balcony, a breezeway cut across to the other side of the building. Another balcony ran past the back of the building and the merchant's son opened a door here.

When he'd flicked on a light, the room turned out to contain stacks of boxes, huge crates containing rolls of fabric, a large table, many different types of sewing gear, thread and pieces of equipment that were probably sewing machines.

"Put here." He indicated an empty spot against the wall. "Get other boxes."

Izramith did, and shook numbness out of her arms.

She followed him back down to the shop and then back up with another box and this she repeated, under increasing darkness, until all boxes were gone from the shop.

Phew.

She wiped sweat from her face. The ridiculous yellow shirt stuck to her shoulders and arms. While carrying loads up the stairs, she had heard fabric ripping again. Now to go down and collect her reward.

She fumbled with the light to turn it off—you had to push a

lever up that broke the contact between the light pearl and the metal holder—and walked along the gallery at the back of the building.

From up here, she could look into the yards of a number of the rich families' mansions. Light spilled out windows and the sound of chatter and children's voices drifted up to where she stood.

Oh, boy, those gardens must take some work. And why the heck would anyone want a glass room in climate as hot and sunny as this?

A couple of blocks down, a taller building protruded from the mix of roofs and trees. If she wasn't mistaken, that was the back of that infamous guesthouse. Hmm, that place was much bigger than it looked from the street.

She walked through the breezeway to the side of the building that faced the street. After passing a section where the dense foliage of a tree hid the street, she was rewarded with an excellent view of the shops, the eating houses, and a fair bit of the street in both directions.

She leaned on the balcony railing. This would be an excellent place to set up a sniper position. The townsfolk strolled down Market Street below her, well-lit by strings of lights strung in the tree branches. A fabrics merchant stood at a table piled high with rolls of fabric, showing various types to a Pengali customer. The black and white banded tail was never still while the man spoke. From up here, she could shoot both men and they'd never know what had hit them.

A skilled sniper would have a rope ladder at the back of the building to escape after firing the fatal shot.

Izramith was about to go back down when the sound of male voices came from somewhere close. Arguing voices, accompanied by the sound of footsteps coming up the stairs and then people walking along the balcony. Two men, arguing with each other in loud voices.

Izramith ran back into the breezeway and ducked into one of the alcoves, squeezing herself behind a rubbish bin.

The men had stopped at the entry to the breezeway and from where she sat, she could see their silhouettes backlit against the city lights. The argument was getting heated. One of them pushed the other against the wall, yelling in his face in keihu. The other man replied in a sneering voice and backed the other into the balcony railing. The man's back arched, making him lurch dangerously over the side. He shouted, his voice no longer angry but a frightened squeal.

The attacker held him there for long moments. Izramith balled her fists, ready to intervene, but he slowly pulled the other man back to the safety of the balcony. The two continued into the breezeway in silence.

The man who had been dangled over the side was heavy-set. His hair was tied in a ponytail and he wore a loose robe similar to that worn by merchants. The attacker was taller, with shorter hair and he walked with a slight limp. They walked past Izramith to the back of the building and entered one of the doors further along the gallery. A glow of light spread from the door, which they left open.

Izramith waited, but the men had settled in the room. Their voices drifted on the night air. She waited, but there were no more arguments and she had a shirt to collect, so she snuck back to the stairs and down to the street.

Back at the ground level, she returned to the shop to claim her shirt. The young merchant's son grinned when he gave her the soft package. Walking out of the shop, she noticed that he had given her two identical shirts. That was a bit odd, but oh well, it suited her. She had probably just done a job that would have been his.

Izramith sat on a bench under a tree and called up Daya's map that listed the tenants of the tall building. The unit where the men had gone was rented in the name of the Semisu family.

Jisson Semisu, who was one of Daya's trusted councillors she had met on her first day.

She was still sitting there when the two men came back down the stairs. The one with the limp was a golden-haired Mirani

Nikala in a khaki-coloured tunic, the other man a keihu local in a merchant robe, quite young, she thought. She used her reader to capture the men's faces, but they were too far away and the lighting was too poor for the face recognition to get a fix on them. The two turned right to the residential and much less busy end of Market Street.

Izramith pushed herself off the bench and followed the two at a good distance. They stopped to talk at the gate to one of the houses. Izramith walked past, casually eying the two men. One was definitely a young keihu man, but she wasn't so sure about the other one being Mirani. He seemed tall for a Nikala, which were usually fairly short people, but most of all, his voice wasn't Mirani. As Hedron guard, voice was often all you had to go by so she had become accustomed to telling people apart by voice. She could tell if someone was Coldi, Kedrasi or Damarcian or other types not just by accent, but by tone of a voice and this man did not sound Mirani.

She couldn't linger to listen, of course, and couldn't understand the keihu the men spoke so she walked until she found a side street and stopped around the corner. A couple of townsfolk walked past, chatting and laughing and when they had passed, the two men were gone.

Damn.

She ran back to the dark shade underneath a large tree opposite the house. The gate stood open a fraction and through its bars, she had a clear view of a path with a fountain. A male voice drifted out of the house's open door.

She checked Daya's file: it belonged to a branch of the Semisu family, a brother of the councillor and the young man she had seen was likely the brother's son.

Where had the man with the golden curls gone?

13

IZRAMITH RETURNED to the guesthouse not much later. By this time, she felt so sweaty that she had another bath. She sat enveloped by the soothing warmth of the water, breathing its faint scent of sulphur. A single glow bulb on a shelf cast a fitful light over the surface. Ethereal curls of steam rose and evaporated.

If she sat very still and held her breath, the water would go smooth as glass, with only occasional ripples from where the bath was constantly being replenished through the aqueduct that came into the room through a square opening in the wall.

If she held her breath, went under water, and stayed there long enough, the surface would forever be still, and her soul would be at rest in the depth where the light didn't reach. And Daya would simply write to the guards and hire someone else. Mother would shrug and say *Well, she was never much good for anything* and Thimayu would ask *Can I have her room?*

She stared at the water. A normal person would cry, but she just felt empty. Whether she cried or not, no one cared. They wanted her to kill people so they didn't have to do it themselves. They didn't want to hear the stories of the war. They wanted it neatly packaged, out of the way. They wanted someone to use weapons so that the factories could go on making new weapons and employing people.

Nobody cared about people who fought.

Nobody cared about people who came back against the odds.

Nobody cared at all.

Izramith didn't know how long she sat in the bath, but the skin on her hands and feet had gone funny by the time she came out. She lay on the bed in the too-luxurious sheets, looking at one of Ceren's two little moons track through the sky.

This place was getting her down. She couldn't stand this hanging around doing nothing and going to fucking meetings.

With her reader on her lap, she sat in the oval bed. If Daya wasn't going to give her a task sheet, she'd make one. The mission's overall aim went at the top.

To make sure no one is harmed during the wedding parade.

That part was easy. The next one, *likely source of hostile action*, was not. *Miran* or *the guesthouse* would not do. She skipped that part. Maybe it would become clearer by the time they'd seen this Mirani family.

For feeder sources and outgoing information, she could only enter Daya's name. That was a problem. A good plan and work ethic had more than one contact, preferably two for incoming, two for outgoing, different people. What was more, as Daya was their financier, any information going to or coming from him wasn't external, and wasn't even attempting to be objective.

So she arrived at the real problems:

Fall back position: none.

Secondary command: none.

Secondary sources: none.

Well, crap.

This was not a plan, it was nothing more than a work sketch. What was more, she lacked the information to fill in the missing parts.

～

Of course Izramith couldn't sleep. Her stomach was churning and gurgling again.

And the same images re-played in her head. A fireball. Screaming people. Burnt bodies in the sand.

It was still dark when she had enough of staring at the ceiling, got up and dressed in her grey gear. The guesthouse's courtyard was deserted. Great. No one to stare at her or complain about what she looked like. She left through the entrance arch, into the street and settled into a jog, slowly at first. The humid air was unfamiliar and sweat had already broken out under her shirt. Slowly, she increased her pace and in her mind, she raced over the plain at Indrahui, jumping over tussocks of vegetation. Abbasi, her local training partner, would be behind her trying to keep up—which he couldn't.

That was in the days after she first arrived, before the siege, when she had no idea what was in store.

She jogged down Market Street and over the square, where merchants and couriers were carting deliveries to the markets. The next street down was Fountain Street and she ran the length of it, turned around where it ended in an area full of trees and walled mansions and ran back. By now, people had started coming out of their houses, most of them Pengali house staff. She almost collided with one of them, so she thought to cut back to Market Street through a quiet alley.

It was narrow and wound behind big houses with large walled yards on either side. Huge trees grew in the middle of the path, their roots pushing up the pavement. Over the roofs of the houses on her left, she could see the dome of the council building catching the first rays of light—

Hey what was that?

At the base of a tree, between the trunk and the high wall of a yard, lay a dark, disturbingly *human* shape.

Izramith stopped. Yes, someone lay on the ground. Dark curly hair, dark clothing, his back to the alley. She had seen homeless people sit in the streets yesterday, but this seemed a really odd place to sleep.

"Um. Excuse me."

There was no reaction.

She inched closer. A breeze stroked her sweaty skin, making her shiver. The man lay much too still to be asleep, his back facing her, his head uncomfortably hanging down. And where his side touched the ground a dark stain seeped into the paving.

She crouched next to him. On the side facing the wall, his clothing was slashed, blood-soaked. His cheek was slashed open so that she could see his teeth. His eyes stared unseeing into the distance. They didn't blink or move when she touched his shoulder. Various creatures crawled over his face, leaving bloody trails.

Damn.

This was not the same man she'd seen dangled over the balcony last night, was it? She didn't think so. This man looked skinnier, and he couldn't possibly have lived with any of the rich families, not wearing that tatty robe and scabbed arms. In fact, he looked to have been in poor health even before meeting his grisly fate.

She grabbed her comm. Let Eris know. He'd know who to notify.

Eris answered, sounding sleepy.

"I'm sorry to disturb you, but I'm in an alley between Market Street and Fountain Street and there is a dead body here."

"What?" That was the end of Eris' sleepiness.

He told her not to touch anything and wait until the guards turned up. So she waited in increasing daylight. A Pengali man came out of a gate and walked past, merely glancing at her and the body on the ground. She used her comm to take pictures of the dead man's face, but the face recognition didn't know him, probably thrown off course by the slashed cheeks. Face recognition never did a good job on dead people.

Not much later, a couple of guards in black came into the alley. They asked her questions, but didn't speak any Coldi, and she didn't speak any keihu, so that was the end of their conversation. She repeated Eris' name a few times and hoped they understood that she'd tell him what she knew—which wasn't much.

When they looked like being in control of the situation, she went back to the guesthouse, changed into one of her new shirts, and met Eris not much later at the entrance to the council building. He looked clean and crisp in his council uniform. "Sorry that you had to experience that."

They turned into the entrance. A lot of other people were going in the same direction, most of them wearing robes or other forms of formal clothing.

"Is that sort of thing common?"

"Not a lot. At least not when there's keihu involved. More common for Pengali."

"Did you know him?"

He hesitated. "He didn't have ID on him. No one seems to know who he is . . ."

"But?"

They started walking up the stairs.

"It's strange. He reminds me of a boy who used to live a few houses up. He went funny when he hit adolescence and I stopped playing with him. Then, after a while, I realised that I hadn't seen him for a long time. I asked around and apparently he fought with his family, left home, lived on the streets and then went missing."

The familiarity in that story chilled her. "Was he living in a bad part of the city?"

Eris spread his hands. "I'm not sure. I was only a kid and he was a few years older than me. I remember a huge search party gathering at the gate to his house. There were rumours about how much his father spent trying to find his son. Then again . . ." He shrugged. "I was a boy. It was years ago. This man is probably someone completely different. He just . . . reminds me of him. His name was Jaris."

His expression was distant, mourning for a friend he wasn't sure he'd found. "You speak excellent Coldi, by the way."

"Thank you." He gave a small smile.

Upstairs, Daya was in the large foyer, talking to a man who was at least as tall and lanky as he. Apart from his height, his most distinguishing feature was his shoulder-length silver-white hair. A Mirani Endri. When Daya noticed her, he gestured her to come over.

Izramith did, while Eris went into the communication room.

Both Daya and the Mirani man were a head taller than her. The Mirani man's light blue eyes met hers in an intense and sincere look. His face was narrow, his nose straight and his mouth curved and more expressive than she would have expected. Strangely familiar.

From the back she hadn't seen that he was wearing a Trading uniform, light turquoise blue and made of thin material, with on his chest the medallion that bore the emblem of the Trader Guild. Licence 1101.

Crap. She remembered that. And she remembered the calm way in which the man had dealt with her inappropriate questions at the entry booth into the Hedron settlement. But had gone to Ydana with his complaint anyway.

Daya said, "I'd like you to meet Braedon Andrahar, the brother of the groom. He will be your contact with the family."

Oh, crap. The one considered by Dashu as her *zhayma*.

And the invitation he'd come to bring to Hedron, the one she opened against regulations, that would be for the wedding party that she had come here to protect.

Crap, crap, crap.

He bowed and Izramith returned the greeting, feeling like her face glowed strong enough to give off light in the dark. "I'm Izramith Ezmi."

Of course he wouldn't recognise her without the helmet and veil. Just as well that other people were not as attuned to recognising people by voice as Hedron guards.

"Pleased to meet you." His expression remained distant. Seriously, whoever still used the formal *chi* form of the second person pronoun? Coldi had enough pronouns without all the archaic ones being kept alive.

"Braedon is here because there has been a development

overnight." Daya's voice sounded grave. "I understand that you and your team were going to talk to the family today?"

Izramith nodded. At least she thought so. Dashu had said something about that, but her head still felt woolly, and days and nights mashed into one continuous stream of memories. And dead bodies in the street.

"I suggest you wait until the others are here and go with him straight away."

"Sure."

An uneasy silence followed, in which she wanted to ask him about the *zhadya*-born but couldn't because of the Trader.

Daya said, "I have to go. The council is sitting this morning and I've got to be there. We're voting on the next lot of reforms." He left Izramith and the Trader facing each other in the foyer in awkward silence.

He eyed her new shirt. A small frown passed over his face.

Izramith had never seen Mirani Endri hair in daylight, and his looked like a waterfall of silver. She wondered if it was as soft as it looked. And because it was kind of embarrassing to stare at his hair, she said, "So, that's why it was so busy downstairs, right, because of the council?"

"Correct."

"You don't have to attend?" She used the *chya* form of pronoun to address him, and even that sounded far too formal to her ears. At home, she didn't even use that to address Commander Blue.

"Our mother occupies our seat."

She nodded, unsure what else to say. As a highborn, privileged rich boy he couldn't have less in common with her had she tried. She couldn't decide if he spoke so formally because that was the way Traders spoke or because he thought she was a speck of dirt. Both, probably. At Hedron, everyone used informal pronouns, even when speaking to Edyamor and his family. And now she started to wonder whether she should have addressed Dashu and Loxa in *chya* forms as well, and if the fact that she hadn't done was part of the reason why she felt so uneasy with them. Why couldn't the Asto Coldi be sensible and, like the Hedron Coldi, drop the stupid pronouns?

He flicked his eyebrows. "Nice shirt."

"This? I got it at a shop last night, I—" Wait. There'd been a joking tone in his voice.

At that moment, there were voices and footsteps on the stairs and the rest of the team emerged, Dashu and Loxa in front, followed by Wairin.

"Hey, Braedon," Dashu said, smiling. She held up her hand and he slapped it, palm against palm, and grasped her hand in a brief grip.

Oh. So the standoffish behaviour was only reserved for her.

Typical.

Loxa came up from behind and put an arm around Izramith's shoulders. She stiffened. He was not going to fight again, was he?

"Hey, you got a new shirt," Dashu looped her arms around both of them. "What do they teach you at Hedron, huh? To be afraid of another person's touch? Come on, if you're going to be polite, you're supposed to touch us here." She brushed the part of Izramith's cheek near her ear with her fingertips.

Who said that she *was supposed* to do that? She'd come here to do a job, not to take part in silly schemes.

Over Loxa's shoulder, she spotted Eris and Wairin talking to each other and Braedon, and she wished she could be with them, but because she was Coldi, Dashu and Loxa seemed to think that she needed to take part in these rituals.

She almost wished for her clear, if blunt, brief when she arrived at Indrahui: here is a gun, there are the bad guys. Shoot.

Dashu retreated with an irritated sniff. "You have a *lot* to learn." She used informal pronouns that one would use to a boss.

"Let's go," Braedon said. His eyes met Izramith's and while she felt glad that he defused the situation, she didn't want anyone to rescue her, especially not a Mirani rich boy.

She just wanted to start the actual work, instead of all this talk.

They left the foyer for the stairs, into the passage below,

where people now queued up to get into a set of double doors that stood open at the far end.

"Council chambers?" Izramith asked Braedon who walked next to her.

"Correct."

"What are they discussing?" Daya had said it was important.

"Barresh only became independent a few years ago. The council is still working to align the constitution with *gamra* requirements so they can step up from provisional to full member."

"Do they have to make a lot of changes?"

"They're dealing with two overall issues. One is equal rights and treatment for the Pengali. Traditionally, Pengali have had few rights, have never sat on the council and have worked in keihu households as housekeepers, but have never received regular pay or had rights of employment."

More like slavery, she had heard. Izramith understood rights of employment. Hedron hung together with those agreements.

"This means that we now have Pengali councillors. It's not easy because Pengali don't treat ownership in the same manner as the keihu section. They function as group, not as family unit. The group owns property or ideas or businesses. The groups are not well defined, and some Pengali insist on maintaining tribal law rather than council law. It's a big mess."

"And the other issue?"

"Polygamy."

What the heck did that mean?

"Sorry. It's where one gender, in this case the men, can legally marry more than one partner. For years, most rich keihu men have had multiple wives."

More than one contracted partner at the same time? But that was disgusting.

The corner of his mouth lifted at her expression. "Polygamy is disallowed under *gamra* law, and no entity whose laws allow it can be absorbed into *gamra*."

She nodded, feeling sick. "So that's why their houses are so big." And why there were so many adult women listed per house.

"Correct. Every disadvantage has an advantage." His blue eyes met hers, as if he was issuing a challenge.

Thought he was smart, huh?

She knew that saying. "Coldi proverb, most often used, appropriately and inappropriately, by Xiya Ezmi."

He smiled in a way that reminded her of a teacher's smile to a student.

They left the building through a side entrance that looked like it could be used as exit only into Market Street. They came out under the trees directly opposite the large guesthouse. Its stained façade was still in shadow and the arched entryway deserted.

Eris came to walk on Braedon's other side and the two started talking politics. Izramith was quite happy just to listen, but Braedon insisted in explaining the workings of the council to her. Apparently, there were three sections in the council assembly: one for keihu, one for Pengali and one for non-natives. Daya was Chief Councillor, and had an inner council of eleven.

Apparently, the current structure had only come into place after the Two-Day war, and before that, the council had consisted only of keihu heads of family.

"None of my family," Eris was quick to assure her. "We weren't important enough."

Dashu said from behind, "Eris, every single member of your family is too mangy to sit in the council. You'd get lost in the seat."

Eris, Loxa and Dashu all laughed loudly. Braedon's eyes met Izramith's and his expression said, *inappropriate and crude joke.*

Izramith didn't understand why they thought it was funny.

"It's because the old keihu councillors tended to be a certain —um—size," Braedon explained. "All the seats are wide to accommodate the dimensions of their backsides."

Oh. Was it funny? People always made fun of the size of the women guards. She was still waiting for Dashu or Loxa to say something about her ripped shirt. Admittedly her shoulder size was not related to laziness, but she had grown very tired of those not-jokes.

They arrived at the house.

As soon as Braedon opened the gate, he made a strange and sudden movement and grabbed something out of the air that flew over their heads.

A boy stood on the porch holding the handle of a flat piece of wood. Braedon spoke some stern words to him in Mirani. The boy's cheerful expression sagged from his face. He went inside, dropping his piece of wood with a clang on the veranda. He was followed by a second boy who could have been his mirror image.

"Sorry, just my brother's sons being reckless," Braedon said. He tossed up the ball he had plucked from the air.

Izramith followed Braedon through the yard, past a fountain and clipped bushes and a bench underneath a creeper growing on a wire frame. The vine's big and floppy pink flowers had fallen all over the seat and the surrounding ground.

They went up a few steps to the veranda and through the front door, which led into a huge two-storey hall with a shallow pool, all paved in white stone. Coloured light fell in through the ceiling window and sparkled in the water, where a toddler was playing. The little girl wore nothing except a curtain of silken white hair. A young woman sat at the edge of the pool with her feet in the water. The twin boys looked on from the upstairs gallery.

Braedon led the group into a living room on the ground floor. Closest to the door were a couple of couches and low tables. Behind those, a steaming in-ground pool, its sides covered with a coloured mosaic of tiles.

The far wall of the room was made entirely from glass and looked out over the marshland between the shapes of three aircraft as Izramith had seen last night. Closest to the house was a low, matte black Mirani craft, behind that a utilitarian Asto-made model, and next to that, a craft she recognised well: a Hedron-made Gazion. At Hedron these were used only by Edyamor and

Ydana and a few other people on the board. Some people had entirely too much money.

Izramith glanced at Wairin, wondering what he made of this opulence in contrast to the stark destruction and poverty of his home world.

But he was staring at a cupboard on the right-hand wall, where lights blinked and a screen displayed five lines, four of which said, *status: home* and the fifth *status: leave.*

What the fuck, they even had their own hub.

A couple of people sat at a table at the far end of the room. Two were in Trader uniform: a tall man with a strong and angular face. He wore his white hair in local style, cut in sections of different lengths, with plaits and silver beads. The woman's hair was shorter, unadorned, but her neck bore a green tattoo.

"Sit down," Braedon said. "While the rest of the family arrives. This is my brother Rehan and his bride-to-be, Mikandra." They both wore Trader medallions displaying the same licence number, 1101. These two, and Braedon, accounted for three of the "home" reports on the screen.

Another man entered the room, also in Trader uniform, followed on the heels by the twin boys and a woman Izramith hadn't yet seen, carrying the toddler girl.

"This is my younger brother Taerzo and his wife Calliandra, with their sons Miruhan and Iztho and their daughter Aleyo."

A thin middle-aged woman came in followed by the young woman who had been in the hall, who was perhaps younger than Izramith had guessed.

"The lady Mikandra's mother, and sister Liseyo."

Izramith's head was reeling by now. All these people in one family? This was not just a Trading family. These people were a powerhouse of Traders.

And then an older woman came into the doorway.

"I am going to be inconvenient and leave you," she said in stiff Trader Coldi. "My attendance is required at the council."

"This is my mother, Isandra," Braedon said.

Izramith met the older woman's gaze across the room. The

family matriarch. She came into the room and eyed Izramith up and down. "So Daya has sent you to protect us, right? I hope you guards are really as tough as everyone says."

Braedon said, "Mother, she's just arrived. Can't you at least say welcome, or something nice?"

"Nice words are stinking salves on festering wounds."

Coldi proverb. Izramith knew that one. "Neyma Palayi." A historic warmongering Chief Coordinator of Asto. She gave Braedon a determined look.

"Hmm," his mother said, clicking her tongue. "If she knows her Coldi proverbs, she's got to be good."

"Mother!"

The woman laughed and as her eyes met Izramith's, they twinkled with mirth.

Izramith said, "Sure. The leader who knows the back streets of the town, knows the people who live in it."

The woman added, "Zhyara Ezmi, brother of Xiya."

"War and peace are nothing more than rearranging priorities."

"Thiya Palayi, Chief Coordinator of Asto."

Taerzo spread his hands. "Can you stop it, you two?"

Izramith said, "Your friends are the ones who stay after the end of the party."

Isandra frowned. "Hmm. Can't remember that one. You win. Anyway, I have to go now, or be late." She vanished into the hall.

Braedon frowned at her. "Who is that one by? I don't remember that either."

"It's something my superior used to say. It only needs another nine hundred and ninety-one uses to be eligible to become a proverb."

"I heard that," Isandra came back from the hallway. "That's cheating." Then she squinted. "By the way, is that an old Mirani army shirt you're wearing?"

Was it? "I don't know . . . I bartered it with a shopkeeper . . ."

But it made far too much sense that the shops would have gotten their hands on old stock left by the occupying forces.

Damn, the family had fled from the Mirani army and here she was wearing an old uniform? Was that why the shop owner had been happy to let her have two shirts for a bit of work?

That was utterly . . . embarrassing. Was there anything she could do right in this place?

A big-bosomed older woman had come into the room wheeling a trolley that had carafes of cold drinks, cups and a few plates of food. She proceeded to put these on the table and talk to the family, scolding one of the boys who ducked under her arm to grab something off the plate. He giggled while running out the door.

"As I said, my brother's sons are rascals in need of discipline," Braedon said.

His younger brother laughed. "Ha. We'll see how you do if you have kids."

"If." Braedon glared at his brother. "Ever."

Everyone settled around the table with a drink and a few sweets from the tray. Izramith sat next to Mikandra, tall and elegant, with her back straight. Taerzo's woman sat opposite her with the baby girl, who had taken to stuffing cake in her mouth with both hands. Her eyes were huge and blue, and stared unashamedly at Izramith, while casting more dubious glances at Wairin, next to her.

She was so incredibly cute. And then a painful thought: her nephew would never have a loving family like this one.

14

BRAEDON CALLED for silence and all faces around the table turned serious. The twins scurried out of the room, whispering and carrying a supply of cake.

Braedon began. "You will have gathered that these people are my family and the ones who will be at the head of the parade and will have to be protected during the event. As Daya already told you, there has been a worrying development overnight."

But he hadn't said what, so she still didn't know whether it was even worse news, or something she'd actually been trained for.

"We've been taking part in an experiment run by the Trader Guild where our hub communicates with a communication satellite owned by the Guild, which accesses the Exchange network through its own automated node. The purpose of this is to increase security, enable encrypting of transmissions and in no small part, to alleviate the ever-growing strain on the civilian network, a lot of which is generated by Traders. Ever since we've set up this satellite connection, there has been interference on the frequency. Clearly, someone else in town is using the range and not aware that we're using it as well. The Guild has not advertised its activities, so in some way this doesn't surprise me."

"Lemme guess," Dashu said. "You are using a frequency higher than the range covered by the Exchange."

"Correct. The Trader Guild is very specific with frequencies we can use. All day yesterday we had problems with interference. For most of the day, we heard just noise. The signals were regular bursts of noise, weren't very strong and we thought initially that we were intercepting an automated satellite beacon. Anyway, last night, we intercepted a clear, unencrypted signal." He gestured to the wall. Another Mirani man, this one a Nikala with golden curls, operated the controls at the hub. After a hiss of static, a clear man's voice spoke a few sentences in Mirani before the transmission was cut off.

"Thanks, Jocassa," Braedon said.

The man smiled in a jovial *no worries* kind of way.

Everyone in the room had gone quiet. Izramith met the lady Mikandra's eyes across the table. The expression on her face chilled her. The lady's mother held her hands clasped to her chest.

Braedon continued, "For those who don't understand Mirani, he said, '*If you marry the traitor, I will come after you and hunt you down wherever you are. You cannot hide from me.*' " His eyes met Izramith's and Izramith turned to Mikandra.

"Your father?"

Mikandra nodded, her face tight. Her sister let out a tiny sob.

"My father is high councillor under Nemedor Satarin. He ... has changed a lot since I first left home. It started when I was accepted into the Trader Academy and he didn't agree with it. He didn't agree with women becoming Traders and he didn't agree with Traders. He made threats, he said he'd never pay for any of my education, he said I was ungrateful. I left anyway, and lived in Barresh for a while, and while I was gone, Mother and Liseyo also left him. He blamed Mother for my stubbornness, for failing to give him a son, for failing to raise us as slaves to the men of the family, for ..." Her voice had grown louder as she spoke, and now she had to stop and swallow.

"I still don't think he's a bad man." Liseyo wiped her cheek with the back of her hand. "He just . . . wanted to care for us in a way we didn't want to be cared for."

Mikandra continued in a lower voice, "He is angry. He blames us for ruining his reputation. And he cannot stand that I've completed my course and am proving him wrong with every day that I live."

"He never stop," her mother said in heavily accented Coldi. "He hurt, he hit, he scream." She shivered visibly.

It felt like a cold breeze went through the room. Izramith shivered. Her family might have been uncaring, but at least neither of her parents had ever hurt her.

"I hate to say it about my future father-in-law, but Asitho Bisumar is bad news," Rehan said.

"How likely is he to act on this threat?" Izramith asked.

"More likely than he's ever been," Mikandra said. "It seems like he has gone completely mad with anger. It's like . . . I don't know my father anymore. He was never a very warm or understanding person, but this . . ." Her face looked haunted.

"What would he be likely to do?"

"Oh, it wouldn't be just him doing things. He's Nemedor Satarin's second and he has many people at his disposal. He's probably already behind all the things that have happened to us over the past year."

"What are those things?"

Braedon asked, "Didn't Daya tell you the circumstances of our departure from Miran?"

"He only said that you'd left and it wasn't voluntary."

Braedon snorted. "You can say that again. They would have killed us given half a chance. They almost did kill Rehan." Braedon's expression went distant in a way that gave Izramith the chills.

"We woke up in the middle of the night, and a mob was in the yard. They'd set fire to our house. We were trying to save ourselves and the children, while trying to fight back and escape the house. We couldn't find Mother, so Rehan went back into the house to look for her. The mob was throwing flaming torches on the roof and we couldn't do anything except run."

He took a couple of breaths while staring off into space. "The house was completely burned. Ever since, the Mirani council has tried everything to disown us. We have only recently tried to retrieve some of our possessions from the ruins of our house, but looters had been through the site and stolen everything they could clean and sell. We found some of our tableware for sale in the second-hand markets as collectable trophies. The Mirani council is pressuring us to sell the site, but we are not going to give in to them. We're not selling the office in Miran either. As long as we own the site in the middle of the Endri quarter and the office, they are nervous, because we're a Foundation family and we have every right to return to Miran. Most likely, they are keen to shut us up, because we offer a way in for people wanting to influence Miran. But they try to sabotage everything we do."

"We probably can't use the new satellite connection anymore now that they have access to it," Taerzo said. "It worries me what other conversations they've listened to and what they know about us."

"We've had deal-poachers grab a substantial portion of our contracts," Mikandra added, her voice angry. "There is no way anyone would have known about those deals if they didn't have access to the Trader system. They found out about the deals, went in, and undercut our price. Goods went missing from warehouses and never turned up. We've had aircraft damaged, family members harassed."

"The lady had her apartment broken into at Guild Headquarters," Rehan said. "They never stole anything, but went through all of our documents, most likely looking for entry codes."

Izramith asked, "Did you ever catch any of these people?"

Braedon said, "No, but they'll be hired muscle, sent by our ex-colleagues from the Mirani Chapter of the Guild or people sent by Nemedor Satarin, or both. Because we support free trade in Miran."

Rehan added, "They've probably been lying in wait and

getting into position for this wedding parade, waiting to strike at the heart of what we're about. I am the family's heir in absence of our oldest brother, and I have taken the biggest Trading business of the entire Guild out of Miran into a town Miran doesn't think deserves the business." His voice vibrated with anger.

The biggest Trading business of the entire Guild . . . That rankled with her. Did he have an inkling of how arrogant he sounded? Izramith used her detached guard voice. "What do your enemies actually want? Simply harass you and make your life miserable or is there a specific reason?"

Rehan missed the sarcasm in that remark. He said, "Other than to shut us up—which we never will—we know what they're after. It's the reason they looted our house in Miran and turned over every burnt scrap and the reason they've been trying to break into our house here. Mikandra?"

The lady dug under the neckline of her tunic and pulled out a finely made silver chain with a stone dangling on it, a very plain and not particularly pretty river stone. A little silver eyelet was fastened at the top where the chain went through and a band of silver went around the widest point. There was something inscribed on the silver, but it was too far away for Izramith to read, and she didn't read Mirani anyway.

"The Foundation stone," Rehan said, with a pompous tone to his voice. "There used to be five of these, each belonging to one of the Foundation families, but the other families all misused their right at some point, and their stones were taken. This is the only one still in the hands of the original family. If the rightful holder of the family's council seat comes into the council wearing this, he has the right to veto any council decision."

A single stone with all that power? And Rehan had said *he* has the right? What was it with the preoccupation of governments on this backward planet to leave women out of their decision-making? "That's rather . . ." *Silly* came to mind, but she didn't think he would appreciate that. "Um . . . If this particular law bothers the Mirani council, why don't they just change it?" That seemed a lot easier than trying to steal the stone.

"It's not a law. It's written in the Foundation agreement."

Oh. Did that make a difference?

"The Foundation agreement is thousands of years old. It is the basis and lifeblood of Miran. No one can change it."

Right.

And this evil enemy of theirs was going to hold himself to these strange and archaic rules while illegally pursuing the family? That made no sense to her whatsoever. Were they seriously willing to murder people and start a war over something as ridiculous as a river stone?

And she had been thinking that the war in Indrahui was senseless and stupid.

Good grief.

"One thing I don't understand: if this . . . stone is what they want, why would they try to steal it during the parade? There will be a lot of attention on you."

"It's not just about the stone, but about everything it represents, and everything we represent. They won't steal the stone, but they'll kill those who can legitimately claim its powers. Which would be me, primarily."

Oh, the pompous arse. "And if that's what they were planning, why should they warn you?"

Rehan frowned.

"By sending you that message. Professionals would never let their subjects know that they're listening or that they're being targeted. They would not warn of a potential strike. They would carry it out. Warnings are for amateurs and politicians."

And she was reasonably certain that because the warning was delivered by Mikandra's father, this meant that there wouldn't be an attack, or at least not from that direction.

This could be a diversion for another planned action or a front for something else.

"Could you possibly play that recording again?" she asked. Something had bothered her about it.

Rehan said, "Sure. Jocassa?"

The man pressed a few buttons and the Mirani voice again sounded through the room.

Izramith listened with her eyes closed to concentrate on the sound.

"Is there anything we're missing?" Braedon asked.

"I'm not sure. Let's say that in my . . . work, I'm used to listening to things I can't see, either over the airwaves or because my colleagues wear face covering. Two things stand out about this recording. It's not spontaneous. It sounds like a pre-recorded threat."

Mikandra was nodding on the other side of the table. "He's reading this out."

"Also, the source of this transmission is not far from here. They don't use the satellite, and they probably have been listening in to your other conversations."

"That's just fucking great," Rehan said. He rose from his seat and started pacing around the room. "That means we have to return to using the Exchange, and it isn't secure either. The Guild let us take part in the trial because we needed secure communication. Now what are we going to do? Send fucking couriers for every single message?"

"Whatever else you do, I'd like you to keep using this system."

He turned around and glared at her as if she had gone mad.

"Pretend you don't realise that they're listening and let us set up a tracking scanner to see if we can see where it comes from."

ERIS AND WAIRIN stayed behind in the house to set up the logging equipment, and because they were needed if the group was to start on the audit of the guesthouse, they decided to delay that expedition until tomorrow.

They went back to the security room in the council where Izramith spent some time staring at Dashu's lists of people confirmed to be in the guesthouse. She studied the recordings of conversations made by guests, but they were all pretty ordinary messages to family or friends or minor business transactions, expressions of interest in work positions, that sort of thing. Insanely boring stuff that almost put her to sleep. The amount of recorded communication was quite small. She had thought that it was odd for such a large place to have so little activity. Was it really because many of the guests were poor? They did have money to travel here in the first place, after all. Or did Barresh pay the fares for any who wanted to come and work for them, as they had paid hers?

Izramith rubbed her face. Her eyes felt scratchy from having had so little sleep.

Loxa touched her arm.

"You're tense. You should come with us after work. We know a nice place to go for a swim. You should come with us and relax."

Izramith made some noncommittal response. A swim sounded nice, but swimming involved taking off her clothes. It meant showing her scars. She was officially still in active service, so her scars were only to be seen by other guards. More importantly, this whole association business worried her. Clearly, Loxa and Dashu both expected something that she didn't know how to give and she had enough of pretending to go along with it. She had no intention of finding out if there was any truth in the rumours that relationships in associations involved intimacy. Dashu's greeting this morning had been uncomfortable enough. She didn't like being touched. She didn't like public intimacy and certainly not with another woman.

They could all fuck off as far as she was concerned.

Dashu and Loxa sat next to each other facing the table with all of Dashu's equipment controls, talking and laughing with each other in low voices.

Damn it.

She was hot, she felt sick. She was angry.

She took her comm reader and left in search of a place to work in peace, or more likely, to have a snooze.

The ground floor corridor was deserted. A single young man in black council uniform stood at the closed door to the council assembly hall. He said something in keihu.

"Sorry?"

He said something else, and gestured at the door.

Izramith turned to him. "Is the council still sitting?" Must be a long session; they'd been talking since she went to the Andrahar house.

The man gave no indication of having understood her, but opened the door for her. What the heck.

She started to protest that she had no intention of attending the meeting, but that was going to be pointless, because he couldn't understand her. Also, she might learn something, so she thanked him and went through the door.

It was dark in the hall beyond. The warm air and sounds of murmurs that spilled out suggested that the hall was packed with people.

The huge chamber was an amphitheatre in which stepped rows of seating sloped down to a well-lit central area in which there was a table where councillors sat. Everything about the hall's design was pentagonal: from the tiered seating to the floor space, to the table and even the ceiling lighting.

Izramith waited for her eyes to become used to the dark and felt her way to an empty spot on a nearby bench, a seat that didn't require asking an entire row of people to get up. Still, she managed to miss a step and almost tripped.

She sensed several people looking over their shoulders at her.

In the middle of the room, a man was speaking at a dais. She had seen him before: he was Emron Emiru, one of the councillors she had met on her first day. His curly dark hair hung to his shoulders, with little plaits and silver trinkets that glittered in the light. His face was red and sweaty, and he constantly wiped his forehead in the middle of his talking. His nose was large, with a groove down the middle, and he wore a wide rust-coloured kaftan with embroidery down the sleeves, which glittered when he gesticulated, which he did a lot.

Izramith fiddled with the translate function on her comm reader, knowing that it wasn't up to translating informal speech. When translating from Mirani or Kedrasi, the modules had become good enough to at least produce something that made sense, but the keihu module made no such claims. The result was an unintelligible passage that might be grammatically correct Coldi, but made little sense to her. Apparently, he was talking about a *fortitude of attributes* and *error is better than the seat of your pants*.

Seriously? What the fuck.

Never mind clever technology, it never did half as good a job as a person. She could learn a lot more by watching.

The spotlights in the ceiling made the sweat on his forehead glisten. He spoke passionately, waving his hand about and occasionally he hit the microphone. His voice sounded angry at times.

The rest of the councillors sat at the pentagonal table in the middle of the room.

Daya sat immediately facing her, and the Andrahar family matriarch next to him. The spotlight made her hair glow like silver fire. Daya was reading something on the screen in front of him, and she watched the speaker, a frown on her face, fingering her top lip with her right hand. Whatever he was saying, Daya didn't care and the Andrahar matriarch didn't like it.

On the other side of Daya sat a Pengali councillor, a man with greying hair who the reader's face recognition told her was a Pengali community elder called Sheida. His duties, besides being a councillor for the Pengali, included being major-domo at Daya's house. He owned several apartments on the city's second island.

Two more Pengali members sat on his other side, both women, whose huge eyes burned with enough anger to start throwing daggers at the speaker. At one point it looked like one of them was going to interrupt the speech, but the other put a hand on her shoulder and made a *leave it* kind of gesture.

So, let's get this right: there were three sections in the council, the keihu, the Pengali and the others. They were supposed to represent different interest groups in the city and should by rights be independent of one another. Then how come one member was employed by someone from a rival section? Didn't that breach a whole swathe of regulations? Conflict of interest, for starters? Was this even allowed? At Hedron, members of the Mines board would scream *branch stacking* at anyone who put people related to them in any way on the board.

Emron Emiru finished talking. People applauded, but, judging by the level of the sound, not as many as there were spectators in the room. A man at the councillors' table cheered loudly. He was dressed in dark green and the reader revealed him to be a nephew of the councillor. Jisson Semisu sat at the side, his face impassive and his arms crossed over his chest.

So, right, now we had fucking *family members* on the council.

The people not clapping were the Pengali in the audience and some of the keihu—mainly younger women. Two Kedrasi on the bench immediately outside the brightly lit area were talking to each other, also not applauding.

Daya spoke, also in keihu. For someone unfamiliar with the language, he sounded quite fluid. He remained at his seat, yet his voice carried through the entire hall. All whispered conversations stopped. What did he say that was so captivating?

Izramith tried the translator again, but it didn't translate Daya's keihu any better than it had translated Emron Emiru's. Something about *rightful natives* and *the firmament of wandering stars*. Yeah. What the fuck. Someone needed to do something about this useless program.

When he finished talking, the applause was more enthusiastic than for Emron Emiru, even though his speech had been much shorter.

Someone at the councillors' table—a woman with her back to Izramith—made a remark that sounded sharp.

Emron Emiru responded, equally sharp. He stepped away from the dais and made for an empty chair at the table.

A Pengali councillor woman rose and made a second harsh remark.

Emron Emiru responded—

Daya slammed his hand on the table—

A keihu woman on Emron's side of the table rose and barred his way.

He tried to get around her, but she stepped aside. He grabbed her by the arm—

Someone shouted. A Pengali man got up from the table. Another jumped down from the audience gallery and a third came running from the other side of the floor.

A keihu merchant rose to pull the Pengali away from his colleague.

Within moments, the scene descended into a fight. Shouting and screaming. Black-and-white banded tails going everywhere.

Daya hit the table with a thud. He had remained calmly

seated throughout the fight. He spoke in an authoritative, commanding tone.

People retreated to the edges of the brightly lit spot on the floor. Guards came to usher Pengali from the audience back to their seats. But a couple of them started yelling at the councillors, and some of the younger keihu joined in. Daya again thumped his hand on the desk several times, but a woman kept yelling.

Then another more harshly accented voice spoke up. Isandra Andrahar rose from her seat. As Mirani Endri, she was tall, and her age had not bent her back. She spoke while walking back and forth in front of all the people who'd been in the fight and now lined up around the pentagonal table. Her voice was sharp and admonishing, its tone rich and mature. It vibrated with experience. No one interrupted her.

When she stopped speaking, a raucous applause erupted, and another fight started on the side of the floor where Izramith sat. Guards rushed forwards. Spectators climbed over the barriers separating the audience from the councillors and joined the fight.

People in the audience were shouting, adding to the deafening cacophony. Very soon, they'd start killing each other. What the hell were they talking about that made them so angry?

Izramith rose and went back up the stairs. At the door, she looked over her shoulder back into the hall. Daya was the only person still seated. Jisson Semisu and Emron Emiru were arguing with a group of women, two of them Kedrasi. Isandra Andrahar was attempting to drag a Pengali man away from the central table. People in the audience stood in their seats, yelling.

The foyer outside the hall was deserted except for the single black-clad attendant who was standing in position at the door, showing no signs of wanting to go in to help his colleagues. He bowed to Izramith when she came out, smiled at her and shut the door again. Wait—he wasn't curious to see what was going on inside the hall?

"They're almost killing each other in there," she said, but of course he didn't understand her.

He smiled and nodded and took up position with his back to

the door. So—was this a normal state of affairs at a council meeting?

That was a disturbing thought.

Izramith didn't feel ready to go back to the security room and the question whether she should go swimming with Loxa and Dashu, so she wandered down the corridor to see what else she could learn in this warren of a building.

Through a succession of corridors that had already been restored, she came to a modern-looking part of the building, with new fittings, electronic door panels and rooms of equipment. In this section, she found a large room—and seriously, why were all these rooms so dark? Definitely not designed for Coldi eyes— with in the middle a holographic projector surrounded by a circular bench of control panels.

This setup she recognised from the way the same service worked at Hedron: it was the town registry. The room smelled of new paint and new equipment.

She sat down on the seat facing the circular bench. The touch of a button brought up a holographic projection of the two islands of the city.

It was a nifty piece of modern technology, enlargeable to the extent that it showed the designs of features in back yards and curls in the metal lattice of fences. Clicking another button brought up superimposed info boxes for each street and house. She was surprised at the amount of information the council collected in this backward-looking town. But this was clearly where Daya's information had come from.

The man she had just seen speaking at the dais, Emron Emiru, lived on the corner of Market Street and Island Street. He was married four times and his youngest wife was barely out of adolescence. The entry for his family included a field for "official partner" and "companions", but nothing had been filled in there yet.

The old Chief Councillor, Jisson Semisu, had no less than five wives. His house, also in Market Street, was huge, and included the glass room in the back yard which she had seen from the top floor of the commercial building.

She scrolled over all the houses and their occupants. Nowhere were the *official partner* and *companions* fields filled out.

Hmm. So, in anticipation of the changing laws against men having multiple women, they had to make a choice about which of their wives was their official partner?

That could lead to interesting situations in those families.

Izramith glanced at the door, and, seeing the corridor empty, entered "Ezmi" into the search field. The registry came up with a single entry: Daya Ezmi. He lived in Sunset Street immediately next to the airport. The Andrahar family were his neighbours. He lived in a house with a woman, Anmi Kirilen Dinzo—what sort of name was that?—and three children, all boys. She thought *zhadya*-born didn't have children?

She entered "Reyar", but the registry only came up with someone called Itreyara Assa who was obviously both female and Damarcian.

But she noticed that whenever someone's name came up, a small field told her the person's origin, so she entered *Miran* in that field, and the registry came up with a long list. A very long list. At a quick glance, most of the names looked Nikala, and she recognised some of them from Dashu's list of guesthouse patrons. But she was more surprised at the number of Mirani who did not call themselves visitors and who lived in regular houses on both islands of the city. Izramith understood that Far Atok was where the workers and less rich families lived. She hadn't even been to that part of the city. How did one get there? Was there a train?

Someone grabbed Izramith by her shoulders. "Hey, I thought you'd escaped."

"Dashu!" Shit, she'd gotten such a fright. Her heart was thudding against her ribs.

Dashu looked at the map. "What are you doing?"

Loxa had come in behind her. The glow from the projection lit his face, but his dark clothing made the rest of him disappear into the background.

"Seeing what I can learn about this town."

Her heart was still thudding loudly.

Dashu nodded and studied the projection. "Suppose they could put a sniper on that roof." She pointed at the house opposite Daya's, which still displayed all of Daya's personal details. Crap.

"Yes, and almost every roof along the route. I climbed to the top of the commercial building." Izramith changed the focus to that building. "From up there, you have a great view of the street."

Dashu nodded. "Eris has an army of people lined up to check all those places on the days before the wedding."

"They'll only be checking the roofs and gardens."

Dashu looked at her sharply. "Would you want to search the houses as well? These are Barresh's major respected families. Many are on the council. They'd be extremely offended."

"These people are also coming to blows in the council meetings. I just went into the council assembly hall, and people in there are physically attacking each other."

Dashu shrugged. "They're keihu. They've always been like that."

"Not what I heard," Loxa said. "I've been here longer than you. Before the Two-Day war, council meetings used to be more quiet."

"But the council had no power then."

"True."

Izramith said, "Back then, the council had also consisted of only keihu heads of families."

"Also true."

Both Loxa and Dashu stared at the projection.

Loxa met Izramith's eyes. His face was broad and reminded her of her father's. "I don't think you need to worry about keihu antics in the council. It's pretty normal that they have big bust-ups. It's a thing they do, like we fight for positions in associations."

Izramith could hardly call that normal either, but she said no more. Maybe she was too naïve to expect that members of councils always behaved politely towards each other. Maybe that was a Hedron norm.

No matter what he said, she was definitely going to keep an eye on the people she'd seen behaving badly, as well as the young keihu man she'd seen involved in the fight at the top floor of the commercial building. He was an Emiru, too. Some of these families had a lot of influence in this town.

Dashu said, "So, are you going to come swimming?"

16

DAMN IT, there was nothing for it.

Izramith convinced Dashu that she wanted Eris and Wairin to come as well—since they'd be talking about work. Strangely, both men hadn't come back from setting up their equipment at the Andrahar hub.

Dashu said that it shouldn't have taken them that long, so they went back to the Andrahar house to check what was going on—

To find both of them, and Braedon, Taerzo, Liseyo and the twins, playing with the ball in the garden.

Eris yelled, "Hey, guys, come join us. We need more people on the team."

All right. That was better than swimming. Dashu and Loxa joined the team with Taerzo, Wairin and one of the twins. Izramith joined Braedon, Eris, Liseyo and the other twin.

Braedon explained the game. "You're in the batting team. Someone is going to throw the ball at you, and you stand here, in front of the planter box, and you have to defend the box with the *bat*. The ball is not allowed to hit the box. Instead, you'll whack it as far away as you can. You get more points the further you hit it.

If you hit the ball and someone from the other team catches it, you're out."

Izramith said, "That's a very unusual game. Where does it come from?"

"Anmi, Daya's wife, grew up on a non-*gamra* world and she says they used to play it all the time. She brought the *bat*, and said it was given to her by her adoptive father. The game is called *cricket*."

Izramith sat on the bench next to Braedon while Eris started with the *bat*, a length of wood with a flat side and a handle. He turned out to be quite deft with it, dispatching the ball into the garden beds with a loud *thwack*. But after a few hits Taerzo caught him out. Next was Braedon, who also did quite well, obviously having done this before, but he was eventually caught by Dashu, who dived into a garden bed to catch the ball.

Liseyo was up next, looking really awkward. She was holding the *bat* wrong and standing wrong with her feet. Taerzo threw the ball. She swung the *bat*, missed the ball and it bounced between her legs to the planter box.

"Aw!" She threw the *bat* down, and marched across the garden to sit on the lovers' bench under the creeper with the floppy pink flowers. Izramith felt sorry for her. She'd been surprised when she discovered that the women of Indrahui never learnt how to fight. Clearly, the girls of Miran never learnt to play games.

Miruhan in her team was next. He did quite well. His brother was tallying the score—and it was quite a complicated system based on how far into the garden the ball went. If it rolled under the veranda, that was good for six points.

Wairin caught him out.

Then it was Izramith's turn.

By now, the light was starting to go golden and the house cast a long shadow over the yard. Standing just outside it, she had to squint to see. The handle of the *bat* was wound with some kind of material with little holes in it. Something was printed on it, in a script she had never seen before. She weighted the wood in her hands. It was a bit on the light side to make a good swing, but it would do.

"Come on, you do better than me," said Miruhan in curiously accented Trader Coldi.

"I'll try. Six points under the veranda, huh?" Getting up from the bench had brought an attack of dizziness. She stood with her legs slightly apart, and made a couple of practice swings to loosen her shoulders.

"Ready?" Taerzo asked, with a tone of apprehension in his voice. "Be careful of the house."

She grinned. "Ready."

Taerzo threw the ball, much harder than he had done with the others. Izramith was back at guard training. Heard the Training Commander's voice. *Concentrate! Watch your opponent! Focus your anger!* Her vision narrowed until it included only the fast-approaching ball. Oh, she was angry, at everything. Her family, the heat, this chaos of a town, her inability to function normally, Dashu and Loxa and how they kept pushing her.

She swung the *bat* with all her pent-up anger. The ball connected with the wood with a loud *thwack!* and it flew high. And flew and flew, into the bright sky above the roof, all the way over the house.

Everyone stared.

"Wow!" Miruhan said into the silence when the ball had disappeared from sight.

"I think that's worth twelve points," Braedon said.

Taerzo grinned, and added, in a more serious voice, "Let's hope it hit none of the aircraft."

Crap. She had completely forgotten about those. "Um. Sorry."

"I think we'll declare that a win for us," Braedon said. "Let's go and get the ball."

Izramith put the *bat* down, feeling stupid. She shouldn't have done that. She was reminded of how Commander Blue said that showing off was never a good thing. "If there is any damage, I'd—"

"There won't be. Those craft can take micrometeorite impacts. A ball is not going to do anything to them."

She followed him anyway over a path of smooth sandstone past the side of the house, into the long shadows of trees where the air was humid and cool.

The path opened out to an area with low vegetation that sloped down. The house was at their backs, with balconies and huge windows. By now, both suns were very low over the horizon, bathing the back of the house in golden light.

The water of the marshlands looked like silver. A couple of boats moved in the cleared channels, with someone standing in the back with a long stick to push the boat forward.

Braedon continued downhill to the paved area where the three aircraft stood. The ball had rolled under the Asto-built craft.

Braedon ducked to get it, while Izramith admired the gleaming surface of the Gazion. It was a newer model, slightly larger than the standard build, and would have been made to order not long ago. The panel near the door displayed the Andrahar family crest and licence number.

"It's Rehan's," Braedon said, while coming to stand behind her. "Very nice. Amazing craft."

Amazing price tag, too.

He jerked his head at the Asto-built craft. "This workhorse is Taerzo's. He does all his own maintenance." And she'd heard pilots say that the Asto craft were easy to maintain.

That left the Mirani-built craft as his, an older model with a few scratches where the ramp had retracted into the recess and the panel that covered it had scraped over the outside.

"Yeah, I know," he said. "I should replace it. There's hardly a place to service it here, and most technicians do a poor job. It's hard to get the fuel, too."

"But?"

He shrugged, sighed, and shrugged again. "We're here under sufferance. If Miran could just get rid of the tyrants that run the council, we should go back. Rebuild the house."

She eyed him sideways. Homesick?

"I had a successful business and was respected. I traded medicines to the hospitals. The surgeons liked me, I liked them and we had good and interesting relationships. Here . . ." He signed again. "I have to start all over again. It's not easy. There are few services. The hospital is in a mess. Unlike my brothers, I've retained my Mirani citizenship, but a lot of my contacts still don't want to have anything to do with me out of fear of being labelled a sympathiser of rebellion. Anyway." He tossed the ball up and caught it again. "I shouldn't complain. Daya has done his very best to help us, but there are a lot of other things that he has to look after. I can't blame the local families for demanding his attention. It's just . . ." He shrugged again. "Not easy."

He let a silence lapse.

Then she asked, "I'm wondering, do you know of any local families who have a problem with your presence here? Like some of the older keihu families may feel that your presence threatens them. I mean, you're successful, have a lot more money than they do, have more power outside Barresh—"

"Not openly, no, but I wouldn't be surprised if some said these things in private. I know Rehan carries on about our successful business and that Barresh should be grateful to have us, but that's just . . . Rehan. There are people in Barresh who don't want us here. He knows that."

"Do you think these people could possibly plan to disturb the wedding?"

"Possibly, yes, but likely, not at all. Many of them hire out services. Never underestimate the capacity of a Barresh merchant to be swayed by the language of money."

An animal produced a loud screech and a black winged shape flew over the yard, up to the balcony of Daya's house next door where the creature latched onto the railing. It dangled by its feet before hauling itself on the top bar of the railing with much flapping of wings. Its fur was dark brown, with light brown wings that folded on its back.

A door opened on the veranda and Daya came out, carrying a

bowl. With loud squawks, at least twenty more of the creatures came from nearby trees. They landed on the railing, on Daya's arm, in his hair. One clung to his back.

Daya scratched furry backs and between ears. A creature climbed up his shoulder and licked his face. Daya's laughter drifted on the evening air.

It was a strange, unguarded private moment, and not at all Daya as she knew him: distant, aloof and cool. A breath of warm air made her shiver.

Daya's arm was completely invisible under the crawl of furry bodies that occasionally flapped a wing to stop falling off while trying to get to the food bowl.

"What are those things?" Izramith asked, her voice low.

"They're called *meili*. Usually, a whole horde of them hangs around here until he comes out. I've no idea how he's been able to tame them. They're quite wild and I swear every local has warned us at least once that they bite."

This was the third time she had seen this now: when Daya spoke, people were quiet and animals were tame. When he was angry, the air was cold. When he was happy, this place seemed like the best place to live.

Manipulative, smart, controlling, temperamental: was it all part of the *zhadya*-born plan?

In her mind, a white flash blinded the screen and slowly the outlines of the valley near the Hedron airport returned. A shiver of goose bumps went up her arms.

"Can I ask a question? Are there any more *zhadya*-born in this town?"

Braedon turned to her, his expression serious. "Before you say anything else, try not to use that term here. It's offensive to them. The proper name is Aghyrian. They are survivors of an ancient race that used to live on Asto before the meteorite strike."

"I'm not talking about a race, I'm talking about the unusual people sometimes born from Coldi parents. They . . ." She'd been going to say *They're mad*, or *They usually end up in jail*, but she couldn't very well say that about Daya, who was considered the hero of this town. "Daya is one of them."

"I know. They're Aghyrian. Yes, there are others in Barresh."

"Where are they?" Her heart thudded.

"Daya's wife is one of them, and all three of their boys."

"Their children? I thought the . . ." She almost said *zhadya*-born again. ". . . They didn't have children?"

"You've been told that they are defective, mad people." His eyes met hers, intense.

Izramith didn't reply.

"Aghyrians lived on Asto before the Coldi existed, before the meteorite. If a person combines enough of the original genetics, he or she will have the distinct Aghyrian look. They're tall, often very pale with usually vivid hair and eyes, very black, or vivid green or vivid blue. The Aghyrians were the rootstock of all humans and all of us have some of the blood in our veins. You'll probably have heard about the claims they make about the history of the Coldi."

"You're talking about the people who say that the Coldi are an artificial race?" That was one of the weird stories that circulated at Hedron, and apparently there were people on Asto who believed this.

"It's a bit more than people talking and making claims. Daya has gathered a big group of people to work on this. He has collected the best researchers in genetics from all over the settled worlds. There are very clear answers coming out of that work right now. The Aghyrians are the original people. Distinctly different races, like Pengali, split off a long time ago, Kedrasi and Damarcians much later. The Coldi and the Mirani Endri are much more recent. If you want, I can take you to the labs. They're in Sunrise Street. That's where you will also find the other Aghyrians. Daya is putting as many people as possible through the testing procedures to see if they have any Aghyrian blood."

He shrugged. "Whether you believe the part about the artificial race or not, Coldi do have a strong Aghyrian line. It comes out in the people you call *zhadya*-born, but the line also exists in other modern races. In some, the blood is buried very deep, but it can be traced and bred out. Daya has developed a quick test for Aghyrian blood, and any people who test positive are invited to come to Barresh. He wants to resurrect his people."

"Are there any people from Hedron here?"

"I wouldn't know, honestly, but there might be. Rehan might know. He's quite involved with them. Or ask Daya."

A door opened at the back of the house and someone yelled into the yard.

"Come, let's go. It's dinner time."

"I guess I better leave."

"No, you're staying. Everyone is in the kitchen already. Anyone who is at our house at dinnertime eats with us. That's Mother's rule." One corner of his mouth curved up. "We have plenty of food, and our house is always one big noisy chaos anyway."

"Thank you." Izramith was at a loss for something to say. She sometimes went out to one of the eating houses with her father, but she'd never been invited to dinner at anyone's house. Braedon led her up a set of stairs at the back of the house into a light and airy kitchen, with benches and basins around the side and in the middle a huge table set out for at least twenty people. Some were already there. The family matriarch Isandra sat at the head of the table, Rehan and Mikandra next to her. Loxa and Dashu were on the other side of the table with Wairin and Eris. The twins were running around the table, and Taerzo with his woman and little daughter came in after Izramith. She and Braedon ended up across the table from a boy she hadn't seen before: with golden hair much darker than the near-white hair of the family. The boy's eyes had a very unusual sandy colour.

Isandra nodded at her when she took her seat. "Here we are again. I believe you have met everyone here except my grandson, Vayra."

"Nice to meet you," the boy said, in Hedron Coldi complete with the Hedron *micha* pronoun form. The tone of his voice was not Mirani.

What the?

"Vayra is the son of my oldest son, who's not here."

Everyone sat down and the big-bosomed Mirani woman came around the table with plates. Mirani food was said to be bland, but Izramith didn't mind the thick soup she served and the bread that came with it was quite nice. She didn't feel quite so dizzy anymore and her stomach had settled. The twins wolfed their food down, scolded by their mother, and the boy opposite her was much more reserved.

She kept meeting his eyes across the table. From what she understood of Mirani law, the oldest son of the oldest son was the family's main heir. Rehan had spoken of the people who had the rights to claim the Foundation stone's powers. She bet that this boy was high on that list. Why had no one mentioned him to her before? Why was he not listed as an inhabitant of the house? Where were his parents?

"How was the council meeting, Mother?" Rehan asked. No doubt they spoke Trader Coldi for her benefit, because the conversation at the other end of the table went on in Mirani.

Isandra snorted. "That was the most useless meeting ever. Spent the entire afternoon fighting over ridiculous and pointless details. I don't understand why those old fat idiots are trying to obstruct all decision-making. For the sake of what?"

"Mother, I don't think you can call them fat in front of our guests," Braedon said.

"I can call them whatever I want in my own house. Most of our guests have been at our table before, and the ones who haven't—" She met Izramith's eyes. "—are no doubt used to much worse language."

"I was at the council meeting," Izramith said. "Although I didn't understand much of it. What were you discussing?"

"Hah! Because Barresh has applied for *gamra* membership, they have to do away with the ridiculous laws that guarantee the lazy keihu heads of families an easy life in return for doing nothing. So they're upset now that they can't have more than one woman. Heaven knows they should never have had that many in the first place. A woman is not some thing of ownership. We want them to appoint women to the council as members of the keihu faction and they will not. It's like they made a point of being stubborn and holding onto their precious way of life that denies most of the population an existence."

"They're afraid," Braedon said. "People don't like change, especially when it's being forced on them from outside."

After dinner, there was tea, and much talk and silly games by the twins. By the time Izramith and her team left, it was too late to go swimming. She pretended to be sad about that.

Dashu and Loxa walked off to their home. Apparently they rented rooms in the same house from a local family. Eris went to his family and Izramith and Wairin walked together into Market Street. The presence of his silent form next to her brought memories of the smell of dry grass, of sitting in the sun all day, clutching a gun and staring at the haze at the horizon. And knowing that somewhere in the hideout behind her was another fighter with a gun whose body would keep her warm when the sunlight faded.

"Big family, hah?" he said, and even his accent reminded her of Abbasi.

Izramith nodded. A big, funny, bickering, slightly crazy but warm and protective family. Maybe that was why Hedron people who weren't on the Mines board hardly ever made a name for themselves. Many at Hedron didn't have supportive families. Edyamor had a large family, and he was successful. Ydana had made his own family and he was successful.

Wairin said, "I don't have much family. You?"

"Same."

"I grew up with aunt. She never want me, but my father was gone to war and my mother die. Aunt is annoyed with me. I become a mercenary. Can look after myself."

Izramith turned to him. "Why did Daya hire you?"

"He wanted explosives man, so got one."

"You did mostly explosives detection?"

"No. I blow things up. But can also find explosives. I do a lot of checking before big day."

"Doesn't it bother you that we seem to be here for political purposes?"

Wairin shrugged. "I'm a mercenary. I do job. They say blow up, so I blow up. Don't ask questions. It's tiring. You got to be in it for yourself."

Yes, a mercenary would. And that was why she'd never make a good one. She asked too many *questions* about inconvenient things like right or wrong. And procedures, and accountability.

Damn it, what was she going to do when this contract finished?

Wairin was staying in the large guesthouse at Market Street, so Izramith continued her walk alone past the shops and big houses, where there were still a lot of lights on.

Even the outside lights at the council building were still ablaze.

And the door was still open, too. Hey, what if she went back to the register to check on that place in Sunrise Street that Braedon had mentioned?

Izramith turned into the street at the back of the building to the main entrance of the council section. All lights were on here, too, even though she had no idea why. The corridors in the building were deserted. On her entire way from the guard at the door to the register, she saw only one other person, a keihu woman, walking the other way and paying her little attention.

The register room was quiet and looked exactly the same as it had earlier in the day. Of course it had no windows.

She sat down and activated the display.

Trying out a few of the buttons on the panel in front of her brought up the query field. Ah, that was useful.

She found Sunrise Street. As Braedon had said, it was on the other side of the island, and quite a trek. She would have to plan an expedition there for a time that she had nothing planned after her work in the security room.

The street ran right along the edge of the island, like Sunset Street, only on the opposite side. Most of the buildings lining the street were keihu family houses. There were parts where houses stood on both sides of the street, and sections where only one side of the street was built on.

In one such place, the land sloped gently to the marshland. There was a low hill and on top stood a group of interlinked buildings surrounded by a wall. This had to be the complex Braedon was talking about.

The info field for this group of buildings mentioned that it was an educational building, and brought up a list of names, none of which meant anything to her. There wasn't even the usual supply of Emirus and Semisus. A lot of the names looked Pengali.

Reyar's name was not on the list.

"You seem to have a special interest in who lives where in this city," said a male voice behind her.

Izramith gasped and turned around.

Daya stood in the doorway, leaning against the doorframe, with his arms crossed over his chest. How had he known she was here?

"There are cameras everywhere in this building," he said.

Shit, it was like he knew what she was thinking.

She forced her voice into a professional tone. "I'm still trying to assess risks posed by every building along the route."

He looked pointedly at the building displayed in the projection. "The parade won't go past that street."

"I got distracted." In the horrible silence that followed, she shifted the projection's focus elsewhere. "You have a lot of information stored here."

She'd been snooping and he knew it. Moreover, the nature of the building in Sunrise Street was none of her business.

"We try to be open about who we are and what we do."

Really?

He crossed the room silently and sat down on the bench next to her. Crap, every time Izramith forgot just how tall he was.

And no, she hadn't imagined it, the air surrounding him did feel cold. It brought a shiver to her bare arms.

There were hundreds of things she wanted to ask him. About her uncle, but he was obviously not in Barresh. About how Daya had stopped his slide into madness, but that seemed rude to ask. About his relationship with Hedron, or with his father, or why she was employed here, but all of that seemed exceedingly dangerous questions and this was a dangerous man.

What had he done with that explosion of light? How could he stand in the hot air vent when it blew and still survive?

"The Aghyrian compound is a school and institute of research," he said, his voice flat and icy. Those eyes gave her the chills. "I'm not sure why you are interested in it, but I am well aware of what you and your peers think of what I am. You can spy on me whenever you like, and whatever you find you are welcome to share with your employers at the guards. We are not mad. We are not outcasts. Just remember who is paying you."

17

W ELL, PHEW! Izramith wasn't sure how she got out of that room alive.

During her walk back to the guesthouse, she grew both disturbed and angry with herself for being disturbed. Since when did a man, and especially a thin and bookish one like Daya, frighten her?

But the fact was: he did.

Every time she met those fathomless eyes a chill went over her. She had seen the *zhadya*-born men with that expression at Hedron. Wielding a knife, blood on their hands, or peeling off blistered skin from the victims they had burned.

He looked calm and in control, but every time he spoke, people froze and listened. People in this town worshiped him, and didn't know of the dangers. Most *zhadya*-born betrayed their families. What if he was going to betray an entire city?

Braedon's words that the *zhadya*-born were a people in their own right only justified the town's behaviour towards him. He was an outcast, they saw themselves as outcasts, and considered him a soul mate. They adored him because of his money, but no doubt he was using the money to earn himself more money, no

longer shackled by the communal shareholder regulations at
Hedron.

He was a *zhadya*-born who had learned to control his
madness and used his intellect to play games on the big stage.
Owning half the Hedron Mines, he was a huge economic player.
Now he was trying to resurrect his people?

But why this town? Because it was the only one that would
have him?

When she arrived in her room she sat down with her reader
on the oval bed and checked her mail. She had messages from
Commander Blue and one from Mother. Her courage sank at the
third message, which was from Indor.

She opened the one from Mother first, but it was only a question about some invitation that had come to the apartment. *Do
you want me to accept it?*

Seriously, Mother, did it hurt so much to ask *How are you?*

Commander Blue sent her official release notice, just a simple
document with no personal note or inquiry about how she was
getting on.

Indor on the other hand, wanted to know when was a right
time to visit Barresh *so we can get acquainted with each other before
the start of our contract.* Good grief. The only way he could be
more blunt was to say *hey, babe, I want to get laid, how about it?*

Izramith closed all those messages without replying to them.
She wanted the rest of her life to go away. Hedron was an empty
shell where no one cared for her.

What reason was there for her to go back home after this
contract finished? Mother didn't want her, Thimayu didn't care
for her, and there was no way that she could see Indor again. By
now, he probably would have heard about Shada, and would be
waiting at her door as soon as she set foot in the settlement to
sever his contract with her.

And her life would be wasted, her wishes unfulfilled, her
home empty of children's laughter.

The Respite Illness Centre would never release her nephew to
her, and she didn't know how to stop him sliding into madness

anyway. And the only person who knew frightened the life out of her.

She never used to be frightened. She would enjoy frightening hapless merchants who didn't have their permits in order, and watch how they weaselled and cringed their way through the interviews.

And then she went to war and everything changed.

She lay staring at the ceiling deep into the night.

By the time Dashu came into the room, daylight was bright.

Izramith had been fast asleep on her stomach. She pushed herself off the mattress, sweaty and feeling disoriented. Nauseous again. Seriously, how long was this adaptation crap going to last?

"I've brought some new shirts," Dashu said, and proceeded to lay them out on the chair. Because, you know, one couldn't possibly wear old Mirani army shirts around town. The two shirts were plain, khaki-coloured and quite wide. "These are men's. I'm sorry about that, but the women's don't come in sizes that fit big shoulders." Dashu's pronouns were all professional today.

"Thank you." Izramith pushed herself from the bed. Her stomach was still gurgling like mad. She grabbed the shirts and stumbled to the bathroom.

Oh, this was not going well.

Not well indeed—

And another puking session.

Oh, for fuck's sake.

What did these people say about adaptation when visiting Asto? Ten fucking days?

She washed her face and quickly dipped in the bath. The khaki tunic fitted much better than anything else Dashu had brought so far. Izramith could even strap her gun underneath so that no one could see it.

Back in the main room, Dashu sat on the couch. She gave Izramith a rather sharp look when she came in. Izramith tied her hair in front of the mirror. To her surprise, the skin on her arms had darkened where it had protruded from the shirt she had worn yesterday.

In silence, they went to the courtyard where breakfast was being served.

Izramith drank some tea, but didn't feel hungry. She took a few nibbles of the bread with the dark swirls inside, but had trouble swallowing them.

"You do know what associations are for, don't you?" Dashu spoke in all accusatory pronouns.

"We help each other," Dashu continued when Izramith didn't say anything. "We are always there for each other, to make a stronger team. That's what Daya wanted when he put us together. Because that is what Coldi people do."

Izramith sipped her tea.

"So, if you're sick, we're here to help you."

"I'm fine now."

Dashu rolled her eyes.

Izramith said, "I'd prefer to keep this professional. That's why I'm here: to work. As long as my personal situation doesn't affect my work, there is no need to discuss it." It was private. Next thing, she'd want to know about her family and about what she'd done at Indrahui. No way. Just, no way.

"Suit yourself."

Another uneasy silence.

Then Dashu spread her hands. "How can you work like that? I mean, you have the *sheya* instinct, otherwise you'd never have fought Loxa, or you would have called the guards. You clearly won. Now he's all confused about what his relationship with you is. Why do this to him? Why do this to yourself? *Sheya* is not something that you can turn off. It comes from inside. You can't stop it. When someone looks you in the eye, you have to react to it. You have to know who is superior. When it's settled, you're both fine. *Sheya* is not a subject of shame. It's why we have such a strong society. It's why we don't get involved in wars—"

"Shut the fuck up." Now she was probing about Indrahui.

Hedron was not involved in the Indrahui war. It simply hired out specialists.

And she was not going to discuss that with someone whose agenda was to show how right she was and how wrong Hedron was.

Just. Not.

∼

Most of that day was spent securing the parts of the route considered "safe" to honour Daya's promise to the council.

Izramith took a team of Eris' council workers and ordered them to cut bushes, move bins and restore lids to drains so that no one could hide in those places. A couple of the team spoke to the owners of the houses. Children came out to watch what was going on, bothering the workers.

One of the council workers explained in rudimentary Coldi that it was annoying that the children had nothing better to do. Izramith asked, to fish for information, if the building in Sunrise Street was a school, why didn't they go to it? But his command of Coldi was not good enough to understand.

They spent all day checking gardens, balconies, windows and roofs of houses. The work was routine and hot. Izramith worked through the fog of heat haze.

As per Daya's directions, they could not visit the guesthouse in the time they worked for the council, so they planned the trip for that evening.

The cover was to visit Wairin, who had gone to the markets and bought food. Being a local from a moderately well-off family, Eris didn't fit in their plan, and he stayed back to monitor any transmissions picked up by the bugs he'd set at the Andrahar hub.

It was only a short walk from the council to the guesthouse, but the streets were busy. A couple of musicians had set up just outside the guesthouse entrance and a crowd had gathered to watch.

Young people were going up and down the stairs, greeting each other. Izramith, Dashu and Loxa followed them into the arched entryway. Unlike the guesthouse where Izramith was staying, there was no reception desk and there didn't seem to be anyone controlling access to the building.

The courtyard was full of people and more music. The air was heavy with the smell of cheap food and sweat from many different people. A couple of Pengali women hung around under the overhang of the upstairs gallery, as if waiting for something.

Dashu led the group in single file through the crowd and up the stairs to the first floor balcony. More Pengali girls stood here, leaning against the wall and measuring up everyone who came up the stairs. Their huge brown eyes reflected the light. Not all of them had tails, but those that did waved gently at knee height.

Wairin sat on the upstairs balcony, where there were a couple of tables and mismatched chairs. The parcels of food lay on the table.

They all sat down. From Izramith's position, she could see into a dorm room off the balcony, where at least twenty beds stood in rows. Bags lay on the floor in the aisles with clothes and other items spilling out.

Wairin unwrapped the parcels, which released a strong waft of fried food. By the look of things, he had bought some of the dishes from that Coldi woman at the markets.

"Ooh, you bought *leishya*." Loxa dug into one of the parcels and extracted a handful of fried curls.

"You told me," Wairin said. "I know I can't eat."

"That means there is more for us."

They spent some time eating. Izramith was still not very hungry, and the curls looked greasy. It was, according to Loxa, *real Asto food*, and he said it as if he challenged her to eat it. She did—and the curls burned on her tongue.

She managed to swallow saliva that flooded into her mouth.

Damn it.

Meanwhile, the courtyard on the ground floor was filling up with people. Most of them were a lot younger than in the guesthouse where she was staying. Many of them were Mirani, but there were also Kedrasi and Indrahui and the occasional Coldi, all of them from Asto.

In the gathering darkness, the crowd blended into an indeterminable mass of bodies. Light pearls under the overhang of the balcony did little to illuminate the scene. Tables were moved aside when the musicians from the street outside joined the party.

Pengali girls danced with Mirani men. A stream of couples went up and down the stairs on the other side of the courtyard. Mostly Pengali girls and Mirani men. They'd go up arm-in-arm, and come down separately, the men always first.

Oh, she saw. At Hedron, some of the establishments like the Traveller's Bar had companion girls. A lot of those were classy, intelligent, slender Damarcians because the patrons of the Travellers' Bar were mostly upmarket merchants and other professionals. Rumours went around about how much the women got paid just to share dinners with customers, let alone spend any time with them in private.

There was also a bar where the male waiters were all tall and muscular and mostly Indrahui. No one at the guards spoke about it—to be found with a man was cause for a strong warning—but many of the women went there after coming off duty. If you asked the muscled barman, you would find that most of the men were for hire, and if you asked the bar's owner nicely, she would let you into the back section of the establishment and the less said about what went on there, the better.

They talked about small, insignificant things, pretending, but probably failing, to be a group of friends, while observing the goings-on in the courtyard downstairs.

Izramith had insisted on making a task sheet, and in the morning Loxa had outlined the three-pass plan he and Eris had drawn up to audit the guesthouse's population. It was all pretty much standard security operations, like checking communication, putting bugs at the entrance and hauling the results through face recognition and cross-referencing the results with existing databases, most of which left Izramith wondering why these things had never been done before. If the lady Mikandra's father had hired thugs or snipers to disrupt the wedding parade, this method would catch them. However, looking into the courtyard, she worried at the stream of people coming into the entrance. Why couldn't they simply lock this place down for a few days?

When the pile of food parcels on the table had been reduced to a collection of empty wrappers, Wairin took the group for a tour to check for points to put up bugs. Through an arched passage, they entered another courtyard with a pool amongst trees with spreading branches. They walked casually around the gallery, lit by intermittent pearls in holders. The floor was uneven and their footsteps sounded loud.

A couple of young men sat in the pool on the ground floor. Their voices and laughter echoed in the enclosed space.

A group of five Mirani men came the other way. They were all short and curly-haired Nikala, talking and laughing. A strong smell of liquor lingered in their wake.

At the far end of the courtyard, a passage led to another gallery at the back of the building, looking out over a yard with bins, clothes lines, tables and benches. A wall indicated the perimeter of the yard, and beyond that were surrounding houses, most of them two-storey mansions. The group spread out, pretending to be guests relaxing in the warm evening.

While Loxa and Wairin leaned with their backs against the balcony railing, Izramith stared over the yard with the lines of washing. Sheets rippled in the breeze. A few petals rained from a flowering tree in a pot in the middle of the yard.

From this position, and across the courtyard, there was a passage to the alley behind the walled yard, closed off with a large fence: a metalwork structure set into the wall. The bars were ornate, curved like flowers.

On the other side of the fence was an alley and across that a wall surrounding a typical council family's residence. Was this the back of one of the houses on Fountain Street? She'd have to study the map to be certain. She pulled out her comm and scanned the yard. The screen caught the low sunlight that just peeped over the roof of the house to the right. It made a brilliant reflected spot into the shadowed yard, but the image came out all black and useless. She had to scan a few times. The screen kept flashing and reflecting, and in the end, it would only work when the last of both suns had dipped under the line of the roof.

Sunlight, she concluded, was very annoying.

The comm took a while to compare the scan with the map. Izramith waited.

Wairin and Loxa were chatting to each other a bit further down. Their voices carried in the courtyard. Dashu had disappeared.

From the balcony she could see between two mansions on the left, across a couple of yards to the blocky shape of the commercial building and the top floor balcony where she had stood on her first night in Barresh.

A light flashed briefly on that balcony, a series of short bursts. The balcony was still in sunlight, and Izramith thought it was a reflection, but then another flash replied from the roof of a house ahead.

She signalled to the others and they came over. "There's people signalling to each other with lights. One up there on the top floor, one on a roof somewhere over there."

Just then, the light on the top floor of the commercial building flashed again.

"Damn, you're right."

"Hey, guys, have you seen—" Dashu came onto the balcony.

"Shh. We got a few people giving light signals," Loxa said.

Now the light on the roof flashed again.

"Crap," Dashu whispered.

"Do you know whose house that is?" Izramith asked.

"The Emiru house's observatory? Loxa? Do you know—"

—a click sounded in the yard below.

Izramith didn't think, she pushed Loxa and Dashu away from the railing, and dropped flat on the boards.

A crackling beam hissed overhead and hit the wall where

Loxa had been a few moments earlier. Someone yelled downstairs and this was followed by the sound of running footsteps and rustling.

Izramith swung herself over the balcony railing and let herself drop to the ground floor. Oof. Damn gravity. She unclipped her gun and crouched, all muscles tensed.

"Come out if you don't want to be shot."

Bushes rustled and branches cracked. A small human figure detached itself from the bushes and bolted across the yard to the metal gate that led to the street and climbed up on the bars. Izramith sprinted across, but tripped and went down on her knees.

The man swung himself over the top of the gate, jumped down on the other side and ran into the alley. Izramith went up to the gate, hauled herself up. Into the alley. It was narrow and flanked on both sides by tall walls. There was no one in sight.

She ran down, but found no gates or any sign of where the fugitive could have gone.

Damn it, she should have worn her infrared gear so that she could see in the dark. She wouldn't have tripped and could have caught him.

There were shouts in the guesthouse building, thumping of footsteps down the stairs, and Wairin, Dashu and Loxa ran into the courtyard, meeting Izramith while she climbed back over the gate.

"Did you see who it was?" Dashu asked, still panting.

"Couldn't see. Too dark. Possibly Pengali." Damn it. She was still angry for missing that step. At Hedron, she wouldn't have had any trouble with catching that man. But the higher gravity and that constant tired feeling played havoc with her.

Damn it, damn it.

Loxa said, "It could be one of the residents—"

Something beeped.

Dashu glanced at the screen of her comm reader.

"Shit. It's Eris. He's found something."

18

I N THE DARK, they ran back to the council building, and found the security room shrouded in semidarkness with only a few lights blinking over the projection of part of the city. By now, Izramith recognised the guesthouse.

Eris sat on the chair in the middle of the room, his face illuminated from below by greenish light that made him appear like a ghost.

"Come in, have a look at this."

The team gathered around the projection.

Izramith managed to get entangled in leads because she didn't see them in the dark. She almost took a piece of equipment down, but thanks to Wairin's quick reflexes, managed to avoid disaster. Damn, why was it so fucking dark in all these rooms?

Eris moved his hands over the control panel, and the image of the city buildings zoomed out. Another touch of a button and a bright glowing spot appeared. At the top of the commercial building.

Izramith asked, "This is a transmission in a frequency outside the Exchange range?"

Eris nodded.

"When did you record this?"

"Just now."

Izramith told him quickly what had happened at the guest-house. "We interrupted them signalling to each other. The person at the guesthouse fled into the garden before we got to the balcony, but couldn't warn his mates, so they continued to flash their signals for a while. My screen reflected the sunlight, so they mistook that for their mate signalling at them."

Loxa nodded. "It seems so."

There were nods all around.

"So it also seems that there is little communication activity from the guesthouse via the Exchange because they use other signals, and they use high frequency transmissions from the commercial building. That is starting to look like a highly organised operation. Do they use a specific office?"

Eris shook his head. "Just the balcony in front of an office."

"What about the house where we saw the person replying?" Izramith reached over the controls. "May I?"

"Go ahead." He shifted aside, so that she could reach. She rotated the projection until the viewpoint was almost at ground level. She found the balcony at the back of the guesthouse dorm, and turned the view so that it was the same as that from the dorm. She pointed, the projection distorted over her arm. "Some-where over there, about two or three houses away."

"Hmm." Eris moved the projection to the group of houses in question. "The house with the observatory tower in Fountain Street belongs to the Emiru family. It's not their main residence, but a cousin of Emron's lives in it. The unit on the top floor belongs formally to the Semisu family, but it's been more or less vacant for a long time. One of the sons started a business that didn't work out, and as far as I know, nobody has used it for a long time."

"I think we should go and have a look," Izramith said. She told the team of the night that she'd climbed up there and had seen the two men deliver boxes to the unit. "One of them was golden-haired, but not Mirani. The other was a local and walked with a limp."

Eris frowned. "Skinny fellow?"

"No. Quite big, in the usual keihu kind of way. He went into one of the Semisu houses further along Market Street."

"Ah, that was Jorin, a cousin twice removed of the councillor. He has a limp. He's the official owner of that office."

"Why would the golden-haired man threaten him?"

He shrugged. "Jorin tends to get himself involved in dumb situations. We've had to rescue him a few times from dubious characters."

"Do you know who the golden-haired man could be?"

He shook his head. "All the golden-haired men I know are Mirani. Did you follow him?"

"He disappeared before I could see where he was going."

"There's not that many places to hide in Market Street."

"I know. One moment he was there, and the next he wasn't. I think we should check out this unit."

"It's private property. We need approval from the council to investigate."

"We don't have time for approval. The moment you ask for approval, everyone in town knows about it. Everyone's related in this part of town. I say we should go now."

"I agree with her," Loxa said. "We should check it out tonight. They might still be there."

Eris didn't agree with it, but it was one against four, so he packed up some of his surveillance equipment. Dashu and Loxa strapped on guns. Izramith waited, leaning against the door-frame. She never went anywhere unarmed and needed no preparation.

Even this late at night, the eating houses in Market Street were still doing good trade. Many people sat at the tables underneath the trees, and the sound of their conversations drifted through a large area surrounding the commercial precinct.

Izramith and her team kept to the opposite side of the street, mostly in the shadow of the trees.

The ground floor of the building held a guard station and a few shops, all closed. The group walked past in single file. Eris reached the stairs first, but then stopped.

"There is a gate here. I don't think that's legal."

"I don't worry if it's legal, only if we can open it." Izramith remembered the merchant opening it for her.

Eris protested. "They should have applied to the council to put this gate here. We may need to get in for security or emergency services."

"I think they preferred to run the risk rather than have homeless people sleep up here and breaking into offices," Dashu said.

Izramith extracted her comm unit and by the light of the screen, studied the door. It looked sturdy, but the door locked in only one position. She dug in her belt pouch where she usually kept a thin strip of metal just for this purpose. When she stuck her hands through the latticework and pushed the metal strip into the space between the gate and the frame, it hit something that wouldn't budge.

Damn.

"I can blow up," Wairin said.

Sure, he could, but she preferred to use that option only if there truly was no other way in. For one, everyone would hear the explosion.

Izramith grabbed the bars in the gate and pushed. There was a surprising amount of movement in the frame.

Maybe . . .

"Stand back."

The others retreated a few steps. Izramith kicked the gate. It bulged inwards, but didn't budge. She kicked again. A small metal object fell out and bounced down the stairs. She kicked again. Something in the lock broke with a snap. And again. The entire door fell inwards. She caught the metal framework before it could slide down the stairs and alert the entire neighbourhood.

"There."

She set the broken door against the wall where it slid sideways until it leaned against the remaining gate structure.

Dashu led the team up the stairs to the top balcony. All the windows in the units were dark on both sides of the building, including the one where Izramith had spotted the two men. A board covered the inside of the front window.

Loxa shone a light in through a narrow gap between it and the window frame.

"Can you see anything?" Dashu asked.

"Just a lot of mess," he said, his voice muffled against the window.

"I can break the door," Izramith said.

"No," Eris said. "We can remove illegal fencing without a problem, but we can't break into private property without good reason."

"Isn't the suspicion of involvement in something and the illegal use of transmission equipment good enough reason?"

"We don't have authority from the council."

"Fuck authority. Either Daya wants us to do something or he—"

"You don't have to live in the same town as these people."

"Then Daya should have appointed only local people. If he wanted us for show, he shouldn't have appointed a Hedron guard. If he wanted someone to stare themselves blind on his precious fucking guesthouse making pretty lists of people he doesn't like ... what's his point anyway? He's trying to score points against the family that owns the guesthouse because they won't submit to a full audit? Is that why we're here? To prove some sort of political view? And we aren't actually meant to discover anything, just to frighten the pants off Daya's local enemies? Well, he's chosen the wrong person. Permission or no, I'm going to bash this door in."

Eris made a strangled noise, but no one else protested.

Hmmm, that was a sign.

Izramith put her shoulder to the door and pushed hard. The wooden frame splintered.

"There. Not very secure, isn't it?"

The inside of the unit smelled musty and unused. Lines of boxes were stacked up against the walls, covered in dust. Wairin poked at a box.

"Heavy," he said. "I open?"

Eris' face looked dubious. "Don't know that we can. We'll get into an awful lot of trouble. The Semisu family owns a lot of businesses in town."

Dashu snorted. "Aw come on, we've broken into the place now, might as well finish what we came for."

"Your legal system is not the same as ours."

"We're looking for criminal behaviour. Since when have they ever stuck to the laws?"

She ripped the top off a box. Eris' face showed horror, but said nothing. Seriously, what was all this shit about rules? She had enough of trying not to offend the locals.

"What the heck's this?" Dashu had lifted a small bag out of the box. She ripped the top and upended the contents on her palm. A couple of round objects, each the size of her fingertip, fell out.

"Oh, I remember those," Eris said. "It's some sort of game that's popular on Kedras. Jorin Semisu was trying to sell them."

"Hmph." Dashu put the bag and contents back in the box.

"Are these all like that?" Loxa said. His voice held disappointment.

Izramith was sure that this was the unit where the two men had gone with their boxes. All the stuff in this room looked like it had been here for a long time.

An arched doorway led to a second room, where it was pitch dark without any light. She used her comm unit to find her way.

This room was also full of boxes of the same type as the ones in the front room. Yes, she saw why the business hadn't been successful.

A couple of boxes had been pushed together to make a table in the middle of the room. On top of the sheet that covered them lay a few pens, the empty case of a datastick, and a timer. Not the ocarion type which Traders used and which told dates and times for all known entities, but a cheaper version. When attached to a comm unit, as they usually were, the device kept track of conversations and, most importantly, the location of those conversations.

A few commands brought a list of past connections on the screen. Most of the coordinates Izramith recognised as being in the city, but one outlying point came up quite a few times. The owner of the unit had communicated with that location as recently as early in the evening.

"Come and check this out." She held up the unit.

"Where is that?" Dashu asked, squinting at the screen.

"I'll check." Eris entered the numbers in his scanner as she read them out. His screen displayed a map. "It's not in town, but at the edge of the escarpment."

"What is there?" Izramith remembered seeing the escarpment: a sheer rock cliff with forest at the top and marshlands at the bottom.

"Um. Nothing. Forest."

Izramith met Wairin's eyes across the dark room. She saw in his dark face an expression she recognised. This sounded very much like some organisation's secret base, set up in a way similar to the Indrahui rebel camps. Those rebels communicated through a network of illegal satellites, and, like the Andrahar transmitter, independent of the Exchange.

19

IZRAMITH JERKED awake at the sound of splashing water. She sat, leaning against something that poked into her back, on a hard surface that turned out to be the bottom of a boat, with her knees drawn up to her chest.

The boat glided through marshland, water interspersed with clumps of vegetation and the occasional tree. Ahead, golden sunlight hit the sheer cliffs of the escarpment.

She rubbed her cheek, sweaty from where it had leaned on her left knee, and a trail of wetness ran down her leg. Great. She'd been drooling on herself.

Eris and Wairin sat in the front of the boat, talking in soft voices while playing some sort of game.

Braedon kneeled in the pointy end, bent over and trailing something in the water. She remembered the preparations for this trip. They needed someone trustworthy who knew about the routes to get to the location and about camping out. Braedon said he knew and offered to come.

A glance over her shoulder revealed Loxa standing at the back of the boat pushing off the bottom with a long stick. His strong, rhythmic movements created a gentle rocking motion.

Dashu sat on the bench behind her.

Izramith stretched, working kinks out of her back. "How far away are we?"

"Should arrive just before dusk," Loxa said. She wondered if he had been pushing the boat all the way. The escarpment looked close on the map, but reality was different. They'd left from the jetty close to the airport this morning and had been sitting in this damn boat all day.

"Do you want me to take a turn?" Her butt felt like it was made of stone.

"If you want." He pulled the stick up. The boat slowed.

With the rhythmic forward movement gone, the boat became wobblier. Izramith stumbled to her feet and awkwardly clambered over the benches to the back.

"You stand here." Loxa indicated a platform wide enough to stand with feet apart. "This bar is for bracing yourself so that that you don't fall off." A faded and frayed cushion was tied to the metal, presumably for comfort.

Izramith took the stick, which was surprisingly heavy, and plunged it into the water. At first she moved awkwardly, afraid to upset the boat or lose her balance, but then she got the hang of it. She was taken back to her youth, when she and a friend had made rafts and punted down Hedron's underground streams and their wondrous caverns filled with pale mycelioids with fronds that hung down like curtains and made your face slimy when you touched them.

Her friend's mother got extremely angry when she heard of these trips and had forbidden her daughter to go. Typically, Mother had never cared much whether Izramith lived or died, so she'd gone alone, ridden the streams until they met with the hot vents into the steam-filled caverns. Getting back upstream wasn't always easy, and it was probably where she'd developed her penchant for bodily punishment, in the hot, steam-filled caves where you either used your strength or died.

She settled into the rhythm. Splash—push—pull—heave —splash.

Fancy all the times that she'd come home with bruises from

being bashed by her own raft in rapids, or scalds from too-hot water.

Mother had never asked about any of those.

Splash—push—pull—heave—splash.

And she had never wondered where Izramith had been, and why Ennathi never came around to their apartment anymore.

Splash—push—pull—heave—splash.

No one else had a stupid family like hers. Just look at the Andrahar family. One big rambling group of people, laughing and talking, always helping each other and anyone who stepped through their gates. Look at Loxa and Dashu, sharing little jokes while they sat on the bench in front of her.

Splash—push—pull—heave—splash.

None of these people would ever understand her.

Braedon yanked at the string he'd been dangling off the boat's stern. A silvery fish flew from the water into the boat, threshing violently. He slammed it against the side of the boat and held it up.

"Looks like we'll have something for dinner tonight." It was still twitching.

The animal was much smoother than Hedron's hairy fish. It also had a pair of prominent orange eyes.

"You have to do better than that," Wairin said. "One tiny little fish is not enough for us. I could eat that by myself."

Dashu pulled a face. Like most Asto Coldi, she didn't eat meat of vertebrate animals.

"The reeds are getting too dense." Braedon rolled up his fishing line and joined Wairin in playing his game, because Eris had abandoned his position and was watching the sky. He had pulled the receiver on the bench next to him, and from where she stood in the back of the boat, Izramith could see it looping through all frequencies. The line on the screen remained flat.

"Anything going on?" She asked him, over the heads of Loxa and Dashu, who looked up.

"No. Just being cautious. We're entering Pengali land. They

should know that we're here, but should doesn't always mean that they do know, especially their scouting parties."

As to whether Pengali used radio equipment, she let that question go unasked. Obviously they did, even though their traditional dress suggested otherwise.

She'd been warned not to underestimate Pengali use and access to technology.

"So, being on Pengali land is a big deal, huh?"

"If you think being killed is a big deal, yes, it is. The area where this signal comes from is in a disputed border section. The Pengali main settlement is to the south of here. This is where visitors are most likely to go. During Mirani occupation, there were bands of Pengali who used to roam the forest and round up anyone who wasn't supposed to be here. They'd get paid by the Mirani to deliver those people to the city. Because the main tribe shunned them, because they didn't agree with any engagement with the occupying force. At first, there were only groups of young and angry men, but they took away some women and now there is a second village up there somewhere to the north. The salt baths area, where we're going, is considered to be the border of their territory. All Pengali value and harvest salts, so there are often disputes."

Great. It was starting to sound familiar.

She said, "We'll just go in, check out this spot where the transmissions come from, and leave again."

Wishful thinking. Things were never that simple. Glad they'd brought Braedon who apparently spoke some Pengali.

The boat glided closer and closer. The dark mass at the bottom of the cliffs dissolved into individual trees. A lighter patch turned out to be an area of rock. A veil-like waterfall trickled into a lagoon, which was separated from the marshlands by a sand spit that curved all the way around the lagoon.

The closer they came to the beach, the more imposing the rock formation. From the water, you could see over the top to the forested slope and the cliff face, now golden with the light of the low suns. But close up, the rocks and forest restricted the view to just the lagoon. For one used to living in corridors and underground passages, it surprised her just how claustrophobic this made her feel. Rock walls at Hedron didn't provide opportunities for enemies to hide like the forest did. It was not like Indrahui, where she could count on enemies being visible from far away and attacking with fairly primitive weapons. Pengali were quick, strong and, with their huge eyes, saw much better in the dark than she did.

The boat glided across the still, dark water and hit the beach with a crunch. Eris and Loxa jumped out to pull it up. Loxa studied the wall of forest at the back of the beach, his hands held at elbow height so that he could quickly grab his gun.

The air was still, with not a breeze ruffling the trees. The only sound was the tinkling of the waterfall at the rock formation. A faint whiff of sulphur hung in the air.

"It's best to set up there," Braedon said, with a wave towards the rocks. "There is a cave where we can shelter."

"But we can't see anything coming from there." The thought of sleeping in the open without being able to see all around gave her the creeps.

"If we're in the cave, they can't see us either. If the rogue Pengali decide that they want us out of here, we'll have more chance to defend ourselves from that cave."

Eris nodded. "I'll set up the motion alarm and trips before we go to sleep."

They unloaded their packs and carried them across the soft sand to the overhang of the rocks. It was quite cool in the cave-like structure, and the rock wall was wet in places where water seeped through.

Loxa dragged the boat further up the beach. Then Eris and Dashu set out with a bunch of motion sensors and a large roll of invisible wire.

Izramith left the cave and climbed on the rocky outcrop to inspect the area where wisps of steam curled into the air. The slope was a terraced patchwork of pools. Steaming water ran from one pool to the other, across salt-encrusted edges that coated the rock like icy stalagmites. Water in the pools was orange, yellow or pink, each more garish than the next. The low sunlight made the salt crystals sparkle.

"Wow," she whispered.

"It's quite something, isn't it?"

She whirled around. She hadn't seen Braedon come up behind her. With his hair tied back and dressed in tough gear that probably came from the old Mirani army supplies, he no longer looked like Trader. He held his hands in his pockets, relaxed. The breeze blew a strand of hair over his forehead. "It's such a pity that this area is disputed and unsafe, because it would be great for day trips."

"Have you been here before?"

"A few times. Usually with the tribal Pengali. They show me natural remedies, and I buy various medicinal compounds off them. I like to see where those compounds come from, so I go into the forest with the Pengali, and I pick the leaves and dry them, and grind them up." He smiled. "Silly, right?"

She shrugged. He clearly loved what he did. There was nothing silly about that.

"I love it," he continued. "It's so beautiful here."

"Yes." *Different* from Hedron, but beautiful.

For a moment they stood in a strange companionable silence. Unlike with Dashu, Izramith felt no need to say something or defend or explain her behaviour. He didn't care about *sheya*, about who was highest in ranking or any of that Asto crap.

Eris and Dashu came walking uphill along the edge of the rock platform.

"Where are the others?" Braedon asked.

"At the camp," Eris said.

A look of concern passed between them.

"We set up motion alarms all around the area. We should be secure."

"Let's go back there," Braedon said. "*Should* is not a word we must learn to trust."

"Thania Lingui, current Chief Coordinator of Asto," Izramith said. And father of her current employer. "Seriously, is there that much danger in this area?"

"Pengali land is never safe, unless you have Pengali with you."

Dashu pointed towards the forest. "The location we're after is just uphill from here. There is a bit of a hill in the forest. You can't see it from here, but it would overlook most of the bay if it weren't for the trees. We might go and have a look."

They assembled at the cave, donned all their safety gear, armour and helmets and set out for the spot, led by Eris with the tracker.

Izramith soon discovered that forest was a very annoying thing. They had to push vegetation aside, and climb up a hill without making noise, while trying to keep in contact with the others whom she couldn't see if they were more than a few paces away. On top of that, her stomach started gurgling.

It was so unbelievably hot and she was still annoyed with herself for feeling this way. She was never sick.

How long would it take before she could finally function normally?

For now, her clothes stuck to her body with sweat under her suit. The helmet fogged up, and she was under constant temptation to rip it from her head, but then she would lose her communication.

There was no path, so she needed to jump from moss-covered stone to moss-covered stone. Hanging branches poked out at the most inconvenient spots, and the damn stones were slippery as hell, so she had to steady herself with her hands while holding onto branches, and she couldn't see well because of the fucking helmet. She tried the infrared scan, but it just turned the whole forest into a mush of grey and slightly darker grey.

They found the hill, cloaked in thick vegetation. From the

bottom you couldn't even see the top, let alone down to the bay. The hillside was covered in vines that dropped floppy strings of flowers when touched. She wasn't sure if flowers was the right word. The stems were very flexible, and covered in fluffy stuff, so that the assemblage looked like a floppy bug. It gave off a white powder that itched like crazy when one of the stems fell in the space between her suit and her helmet.

A bit further uphill, bushes threshed about where Eris and Loxa were making their way up. It was impossible to remain quiet in this impenetrable jungle. If there was anyone around, all they needed to do was hide in the trees with a gun and pick them off.

Someone on the comm said, "I can see something." It sounded like Loxa. "There is a structure on the top of the hill. Can't see any people."

"Wait approaching until we've caught up." She looked over her shoulder. Braedon was trailing behind. "Where are the others?"

"Can't see them, but I can hear them. Still coming up the hill."

"Yup, doing our best," Dashu said. She sounded out of breath. "Wairin's with me."

Braedon scrambled up a boulder behind her, meeting her eyes through the visor of his helmet.

"Anything wrong?" he asked. His voice sounded muffled. His armour had collected a number of green smears.

"Loxa and Eris have spotted something." It was annoying to have to speak inside the helmet instead of sending text. But: no Exchange coverage here. "They're waiting for us to get there."

But as she said that, she spotted the glint of Loxa's silver insulation suit a bit further up. They hadn't been so far behind after all.

Izramith clambered up a giant boulder to join them.

She peered ahead between the bushes but saw nothing except a tangle of vegetation. That damn stupid forest. She wanted to scream and blast it out of the way so she could see.

Braedon joined them on top of the boulder, followed by Dashu and Wairin. In the spots where Wairin's skin was visible, it glistened with sweat. He wiped his neck with the back of his hand.

Braedon detached the gun from his arm bracket, and Izramith did the same.

Slowly, they advanced up the hill, and in the light that angled between the trees, a primitive shack dissolved from the forest: two walls, one at the back and one at the left hand side, and a sloping roof, held up in the opposite corner by a post. It stood at the base of a large tree, which formed the support in the corner where the two walls joined. Under the shelter of the roof stood a makeshift table and two benches. A tangle of vines had made a carpet of green on the roof, which cascaded down the outside wall and crept into the covered space. A couple of vines trailed around the legs of the table.

Against the back wall stood a platform that could have been a bed and above that on the wall hung a shelf that was empty except for a few dead leaves and a single bright yellow piece of resin that looked like a cap for a plug or something similar.

The floor was covered in dead leaves, moss and creepers.

Izramith studied the yellow object without touching it.

"It's a cover for transmitter plugs," Dashu said.

"That means there's got to be a transmitter somewhere around here." She studied the ceiling. The corner of the shack housed an interesting arrangement of leaves and sticks woven together with what looked like dried slime. There were five oval constructions, about the size of a fist, each with a perfectly round hole at the front. Some sort of animal nest. "Where would they hide the antenna?"

"They could have brought in a portable."

"They'd have needed a decent dish to reach pretty much anything from here. There is no Exchange coverage."

"Yeah, and that's not equipment you can easily move." Dashu studied the ceiling and the interesting animal nests. "But unless you can see an antenna . . ."

Izramith stepped out of the shack and peered into the mass of green above. Leaves, branches, clumps of vegetation growing on the branches, things growing on trunks. Air roots and vines going everywhere. Where did one tree even stop and the next begin? You might be able to hide a satellite dish up there, and no one would ever find it. "How long ago do you think they left this place?" There were no signs of disturbance.

"Not sure. Doesn't need to have been very long. They might be hiding out close by. Maybe they only come here when there is something to transmit."

Which, apparently, there had been last night.

Eris dropped to his knees and studied the ground and the underside of the table. Wairin walked around the shack, studying the ground. Loxa and Dashu followed him, looking at the walls and up into the tree. Izramith studied the bed and the shelf on the wall, all made from crude timber. She found no remarkable features, and neither did the others.

They gathered back under the cover of the shack.

"Nothing," Loxa said, and there were nods all around.

Izramith said, "We'll do a search of the immediate surroundings and then we can go back to camp. Eris, can you set up motion sensors in this area, armed and wired?"

Wairin and Eris went back to the beach to get the gear, while Izramith, Braedon, Dashu and Loxa swept the area. The top of the hill formed a kind of platform surrounded on three sides by steep drop-offs littered with boulders and overgrown with tangles of bushes. No way anyone could easily get down that way.

Izramith's map had shown the geography, but reality made it so different. The position of the hilltop shack was quite defensible, as if someone expected trouble.

Wairin and Eris returned. They directed the others to string thin "invisible" wire around the top of the hill, they armed the wire by connecting it to the power supply and hung motion sensors in strategic positions in the trees.

After all that was done, they returned to the cave.

Since the area was now searched and secure, they took the opportunity to organise the camp and start thinking about dinner.

Braedon cut up the fish he had caught and hung it to cook in a cloth bag in one of the pools, but one single fish wasn't going to feed six people, and Wairin joked to him about it, so he got his line out again and went to the point where the beach jutted into the lagoon. He stood there, a tall silhouette against the darkening sky.

"You need to put something on the hook that the fish like," Izramith said, ambling up to him.

He turned. "What do you know about fishing?"

"We have fish at Hedron."

"Really?"

"In the underground rivers. I used to catch them sometimes."

"Is that true, huh?"

She sat down in the sand, but as she did so, spotted a few holes. Just like the worm holes she used to dig out at Hedron.

She stuck her fingers into the sand and dug. After a couple of scoops of empty sand, she came up with a small wriggly creature. It jumped from her sandy palm onto the sand and started to rebury itself, but she grabbed it and held it between thumb and index finger.

"Here is something for you."

Braedon withdrew the line. The end held a piece of fluff with a vicious hook inside.

"What is that thing?"

"It's a lure. Fish see it and think it's some creature that's fallen in the water."

"Oh. Fish at Hedron have no eyes." Izramith spiked the wriggling thing onto the hook. "So they go by smell and taste alone. You have to put something they can smell on your line, or the fish won't come. There you go." She let the end of the line go, and the wriggly thing swung back and forth over the water, still wriggling on the hook.

Braedon swung the line behind him and threw it back into the water as far as he could. It sank into the depth.

Not a moment later, the line jerked. Braedon pulled it up. A much larger fish jumped out of the water and splashed back in, scattering diamond drops of water.

"Whoa!" Braedon started rolling up the line, but it snagged underwater.

"I'll get it." Izramith jumped into the water and waded to the spot. With each step, she sank knee-deep in soft ground. The muddy bottom sucked at her shoes.

The fish was about the length of her forearm and it had tangled the line in underwater vegetation. When she pulled it up, the slimy skin slipped from her hands. It fell back into the water, threshing and splattering. Water went into her face.

Braedon shouted, "Watch out!"

From the corner of her vision, Izramith sensed something big making ripples in the surface of the water. Next moment, a huge thing reared from the water, a massive long-bodied creature, with a big spiky head and open mouth. The skin shimmered in the low sun. A vicious yellow eye glared at her.

In that one moment, Izramith knew she was dead. She'd survived the battlefield and siege of Pataniti to be eaten by a creature in Barresh.

She ducked.

A charge flashed overhead.

There was a moment of silence in which Izramith waited for the bite of teeth and then something very large splashed in the water, soaking her.

Crap.

Izramith raised herself on her knees. Her clothes dripped with muddy water. The fish she had been holding had escaped.

The creature that had attacked her lay on its side, a long body with a spiky head at an odd angle to the rest of the body. Its skin was dark grey and shimmery. Its eye—yellow and the size of her palm—stared lifelessly into the sky, while a trickle of dark fluid oozed over its neck. Shit. Even half in the water, it reached midway to her thigh. This thing could have gobbled her up in one bite.

Braedon stood on the beach, slowly letting the gun sink to his side.

"Good shot, buster." And she meant it. He fucking saved her life.

He tucked the gun in his arm bracket. "Well, I think we now have enough fish for dinner."

20

WHILE DASHU, Loxa, Wairin and Eris came running onto the beach, Izramith stumbled out of the water, her heart still thudding.

"What is that thing?"

"It's an eel," Braedon said. "I'm sorry I had to kill it." The latter to Eris, who nodded, his face grave. He waded into the water. "It's a big one." He placed a hand on the side of the creature's head and stood like that for a while. No one said anything. Eris faced away from the beach. His lips moved. A dedication? Death prayer?

Then he let his hand slide from the head and turned around. "Throw me the rope."

Together, they heaved the creature to the beach. You had to watch the spikes on the head, Eris said, because they were poisonous.

Loxa brought him a knife and he sliced into the flesh, peeling off the skin and cutting chunks of the white flesh underneath. Wairin wrapped these into the skin and piled them on the beach. Braedon took one of those parcels to the hot springs. Then Eris cut long strips from the remaining flesh. His hands dripped with blood and grease.

Loxa and Dashu retreated to higher up the beach. Dashu looked sick, and because no one else volunteered, and because it was getting dark and because it was her fault that the creature was dead, Izramith grabbed her dagger and helped cut the rest of the fish up. They worked in an odd reverent silence. Izramith frequently had to hold her breath, because it was foul work and the smell of dead flesh was making her sick.

Slowly, the piles of fishy flesh on the beach grew and the carcass was beginning to resemble the framework for a tent.

"What are we going to do with all this? We can't take this back with us." At least she hoped not, because sharing a long boat ride with smelly fish would not end well.

Eris turned around, wiping sweat off his face. "No, but if we leave it here on drying racks, others will use it. That is the Pengali way." Like this, with the low sunlight on his face, he looked older and wiser than all of them. Even though he had the typical keihu —extremely ugly—nose, he was not unattractive. He was yet to acquire the excess weight that so many keihu men seemed to carry and his eyes, soft brown, were intelligent and kind. Crazy as he was about rules, he had displayed a lot of maturity in the way he listened and considered the effect of his actions on others. In fact, if he had a little bit less consideration for others, he'd probably do better for himself.

Izramith carried the last pieces of fish up the beach, where Wairin had set up a drying rack. Loxa and Dashu sat on the beach, looking out over the lagoon. Dashu's face displayed the disgust Izramith felt.

"Not impressed?" Izramith asked while sitting down. She wiped her hands on the ground but sand stuck to the half-dried fishy juice that covered her.

Dashu said, "I've learned to eat fish here, but this is a bit much."

"We eat fish at home, but they're not big like this." Or messy. There was something satisfying about deeply agreeing with Dashu.

"Why don't they cut what we need and leave the rest?"

"It's an insult to the fish not to use it when you've killed it," Eris said, coming up the beach. "Pengali believe this and we live by it. These eels are not common. There are many Pengali legends about them."

Lucky me then, almost eaten by a rare creature.

"Don't pull a face like that. Wait until you taste it," Braedon said. He had retrieved his parcel.

They sat on the beach in front of the cave.

Eris had brought a light pearl and a stand on a stick that poked into the sand. By its light, they ate. Loxa and Dashu chose to stick to their dried rations, but Izramith tried some fish. It tasted very subtly of salt and herbs, and was very oily. Also very satisfying.

While it got dark and the group sat at the camp, Izramith kept looking at the motion-sensor's screen. If creatures like this lived in the water, what dangerous things would live on the land, in the forest where no one could see them hiding?

She felt incredibly tired. Now that she had dried herself, her neck was getting very itchy from where that furry flower had fallen. When she scratched, she could feel welts on her skin.

"You should look at that," Eris said. "Or it will become infected."

"I've got some stuff for it," Braedon said. He dragged his bag over, opened it and rummaged inside.

"That's not necessary. It's only itchy."

"Yes, but you've already broken the skin. Infections are nasty in this place."

She leaned back and let him wipe the spot with a piece of cloth soaked in fluid that cooled her skin and felt wonderful. He inspected the skin in her neck, close enough for his breath to tickle.

"What caused this?"

"One of those long fuzzy things that fell out of a tree when we were going up the hill."

"You've got little white spines buried in your skin all over."

Ew. "Can you take them out?"

He probed carefully with a finger and then rummaged in his bag again. He returned with a pair of tweezers and spent the next while removing spikes from her skin so thin they were barely visible.

Sitting there patiently with her head leaning back, Izramith couldn't help but be reminded of Abbasi and how she'd first become involved with him. He'd been teaching her about the kind of landmines used by the rebels, and standing so close to her that in the cold night air of Pataniti, she could feel his warmth on her skin. He'd asked if she was cold and when she said yes, offered her his jacket. The smell of it still hung around her: dry stone, engine oil, dry vegetation. The last time she'd seen him, he'd been wearing that jacket, ripped, blood-smeared and dirty.

She couldn't control an involuntary shiver.

"You all right?" Braedon said.

"Um. Yes."

A moment of panic. He was so close to her. Wairin and Eris sat under the light, playing a game. Dashu and Loxa had gone to the pools to bathe.

"Sit still. I've almost got them." Braedon shifted so that he didn't cast a shadow on her neck. He continued pulling out spikes with his cool and gentle touch, his brow furrowed in concentration. His hair was not as dead straight as Rehan's, but there was a gentle wave that made different parts reflect the lamp light at a different angle.

She'd never said goodbye to Abbasi. Presumably, his family had claimed his body and had burned it according to Indrahui customs. She'd been too upset to ask if there was a ceremony. She'd justified it to herself by saying that the relationship was never intended to be serious anyway, and it wasn't, or shouldn't be, because she'd signed with Indor and didn't want to explain to him about an Indrahui lover who probably wouldn't relate to her outside the context of war anyway.

And damn it, now this man was so close to her that she could feel his breath on her skin. He'd been oblivious to her insults, oblivious to her strength and oblivious to the fact that for all his scrawny body, he was not unattractive. Most of all, he was cool as a fish. Unflappable and devoid of hysterics or silly displays of emotion that she hated so much.

Damn it, she hadn't been near a man for so long that if he spent any longer breathing on the sensitive skin in her neck, she was going to flush. Already, her cheeks felt hot. "You finished?"

"Almost." He put the tweezers away and wiped her neck again. "There. That should be better."

He packed his things, still oblivious to the cause of her glowing cheeks, then looked up at her.

"Anything wrong?"

"No. Let's go to sleep."

She rolled out her mat and he did the same. Loxa and Dashu came back—walking awfully close together—and Wairin and Eris stopped playing.

One by one, they settled on their mats.

But of course as soon as Eris turned off the light, Izramith felt wide awake. She lay on her mat pretending to be asleep for a while, but gave up on that and sat at the entrance to the cave, her knees pulled up against her chest, staring into the darkness. She told herself that someone needed to stay awake for their safety and all these lazy bums were not going to do it. Look at Loxa and Dashu on the same mat, her arm draped over his waist. How could they be serious about their job when all they saw was each other?

She might as well admit it, she was jealous of the way these people trusted each other and the way they talked about personal things. And she couldn't stand why they were all sleeping peacefully while she was feeling terrible and cut up inside. Wanting to scream *I lost my lover, I lost my family and I lost my nephew and the chance to have a family*. Wanting to grab her gun and shoot things. Wanting to bash something into pulp.

She rose and clambered up the rocks to the hot water pools. In the serene light of Ceren's two moons, steam rose off the water. It was all too pretty, too peaceful.

She splashed through the shallow parts, disturbing that image of peace. She kicked the water so a great spray chased away the steam. At the base of a single gnarled tree that grew on the rock platform, she yanked her shirt over her head and flung it on the bank of the creek that fed the pools, and took off her long trousers.

In just her singlet and shorts, she jumped up to the tree branch that hung over the water, and pulled herself up, let herself down and up again. And up and down and up and down and up. Just like she had done for training.

The higher gravity made the muscles in her arms scream their protest, but she kept going. Up, down, up, down. Eventually, her arms shivered so much that she had to drop herself in the water, panting and shining with sweat.

The water was warm, and stank of farts.

Damn it, even the water was hot in this stupid place. Her hand found a rock under the water. She picked it up and flung it to the opposite side of the pool.

Wait—was that white spot over there the reflection of moonlight in someone's hair?

No, it was that damn Trader again. Why did he have to keep fussing over her?

"What are you looking at?" She didn't intend to make it quite as unfriendly as it came out.

"You should go to sleep. You're not well." He used colloquial pronouns.

"I can look after myself, thanks."

"So you've stopped feeling ill, and stopped vomiting?"

"Just mind your own business. I didn't ask you to come here and babysit me."

"I know you need no babysitting, but you can't do your job when you're not well."

She whirled at him. "You don't give up, do you?"

"Nope. I'm a Trader. Giving up is not part of my vocabulary."

They said nothing for a while. Izramith ran her hands through the water, spreading her fingers so that they sliced the surface. She felt like saying, *Remember when you came to Hedron, the guard who gave you a really hard time, well that was me,* but she didn't. She hadn't come out of that confrontation so well, had she?

Then he said, "You're really strong. I've never seen anyone pull their entire weight up so many times. Especially not on Ceren."

She hovered between wanting to run away and wanting to pick him up and bodily deposit him back at the camp. He was poking her, invading the space that she didn't want to share, trying to get a response out of her about subjects she didn't want to talk about.

Eventually, he spoke. "You seem very . . . angry, stressed-out."

"Didn't I tell you to bugger the fuck off?"

Again, he said nothing and didn't move. He said nothing about the language or about being polite. She snorted, and he met her eyes. His irises were eerie light-coloured. He wasn't afraid of her, like he hadn't been at their first confrontation at Hedron.

She sighed.

"Do you ever lose your temper?"

"I do. I just don't let it show."

"Part of the Trader ethic, huh?"

He said nothing and didn't move. She sighed.

"You are so angry. I can virtually feel the anger coming off you in waves."

"That true, huh? I can decide whenever the fuck I get angry."

"Yes," he said, and then he let another long silence lapse. Izramith was about to get up when he added, "War is not something that can be taken lightly."

"You tell me about war? Seriously? What do you know about it?"

"More than I care to remember."

He was looking ahead, his eyes distant.

Shit.

After a long silence, he said, "I killed a man, once."

Only once? Only one?

"More than one, but one in particular I remember. He was climbing over the wall of our house. We were hiding in the back alley from a bunch of people who had broken down the gates. All of us were in our nightclothes in the snow. Calliandra and the twins, and Mikandra and her mother and sister. It seemed everything was lost. Rehan had gone into the house to find Mother, and the house was burning. It was burning so much that the entire neighbourhood was glowing with it. And this man climbed up on the wall right where the family was hiding. He was a Mirani Nikala, probably a hired thug. I didn't think, I just shot him. He fell back in the snow. There was no blood. Every time when I think of war, I see his face. He looked . . . surprised."

She nodded, but said nothing and trailed her fingers in the water.

He made to get up. "We should probably try to get some sleep. Things could get hairy any time. I just wanted to make sure you're all right."

She didn't move. There was no way she could sleep. She'd slept badly enough recently. And she was not all right. All night, she'd be replaying her memories of the moment that the flaming aircraft crashed into the enemy camp. The aircraft that she had shot. Who ever thought of using non-impact proof glass in an aircraft anyway?

It was not her fault, was it?

"Coming?"

She let another silence lapse, her throat closing with emotion.

"Izramith?" It was the first time he'd used her name.

"You go. I'll just . . . sit here. Can't sleep."

"You served at Indrahui recently, didn't you?"

Izramith nodded.

He knelt in the sand, facing her.

Silence lingered.

Izramith's thoughts whirled. Commander Blue had suggested she go to the clinic. It was normal to feel upset after going to war, she had said. Get into the routine, and the pain will numb and the nightmares stop.

Except they didn't. Her thoughts kept getting tangled in webs of awful memories. Everything she did caused flashbacks. People with normal lives were too far away from her to understand. And she kept getting these horrible, nasty flashes of jealousy.

There was a time for "getting over" things, and a time to get help. The first was fast regressing and the second was becoming inevitable.

She said, her voice soft, "I worked as a contracted communication officer for the Indrahui consolidated army. At first I was stationed in Pataniti and would direct logistics and transport. But then the rebels attacked Pataniti and we were surrounded, and everyone was called up to fight. The rebels advanced on the town and captured an outlying community. They slaughtered families, killed the men, raped the women and killed their children before their eyes. We organised an attack to break out of the blockade. There was no other option, because no one seemed to care about liberating the town, and we were fast running out of food and water."

She shuddered at memories of the despair, of the dust, of the stink of garbage and unwashed bodies.

"We were ridiculously under-equipped. We only had our personal weapons, but little else. Many of us were Coldi, and we voted down the proposal to attack at night, because, you know— we can't see too well." Or at least not as good as others.

"So we attacked early in the morning. It was a mess right from the beginning. I saw three partners killed before my eyes. We had no time to even check if they were dead. You know, before you go to war, the supervisors drill into you: if someone falls, take their weapon and keep going. So that's what we were doing. I had about four or five guns. One of them was wet with blood. But we were fucked, basically. They had more weapons and more people. Then an aircraft joined their side. It was a merchant-style craft, a battered-up thing, but it had a large cargo door and people were throwing explosives on our line. I was doing tech at the back, and I'd just been unjamming this beast of a rocket launcher. It was an old-fashioned thing, no idea who owned it or where it came from.

I didn't know what I was doing, but I loaded the thing and fired at the craft. It was a dumb move, because the kickback would have hit the troops badly, but it happened to be unarmoured, and the craft exploded in a huge fireball . . ."

She had to stop talking to regain her composure.

"And everyone around me was cheering. I mean—if I hadn't done that, I wouldn't be sitting here now."

She let a silence stretch on.

"The worst thing was, that as it began to fall, I realised that it was going to fall in the rebel camp. And all these people inside the camp realised that too. I could see them running. But of course a barrier ran around the camp—to keep us out—and people couldn't get out quickly. So it fell, in a huge flaming explosion. I don't know how many explosives they had in the hold, but the ground shook and everything in the camp burnt. Tents, people, vehicles, everything. No one knows exact numbers, but they said there were at least a thousand people in the camp."

"Crap." That one word was full of understanding. Whatever he had done in his life, and however sheltered he had grown up, he knew about war.

"Yes. Crap. You know, you go to war and you expect to kill people. That's part of the job. I'd seen people killed and maimed many times. I thought I was used to it. But this . . ." Her eyes pricked. She wiped them with the back of her hand, but that did nothing. It just would not do. Guards did not cry.

". . . this was senseless. The whole war at Indrahui is senseless. They don't even remember what they're fighting for. It's just one warlord against another for the sake of old family vendettas, and if it suits them, they'll align themselves with either the government or the rebels. There is no point to the conflict. There is no way to solve it. There is no need for pointless deaths."

Her vision went blurry. She wiped her eyes again.

"It's all right." His voice was soft.

She shook her head, furiously. The tear escaped her eye and rolled over her cheek. "It's not all right. All those people are dead, and they'd done nothing to me. I know about war and all that, but not . . . not . . . this. Mass slaughter. Almost a thousand people died because I launched that rocket—"

He opened his mouth—

"No, don't tell me that a thousand different people would have died had I not done it."

Silence.

Then he said, "I was going to say that you cannot un-change what has happened. You have to learn to live with it." His voice was soft.

"But life is pointless. My family doesn't care. They . . ." *hate me. They don't even care about a baby.* Her voice caught. Her mind flooded with awful thoughts. Her family hated her because of what she'd done. They hated her because she always got into fights. They knew that she displayed some remnants of *sheya* behaviour, which was a character trait and not learned, and because of that, she was dirty, unclean.

She bit her lip. Her shoulders shook. Her breath jerked in a sob. Another tear leaked out of her eyes and ran down her nose.

"Shh. Come here." He pulled her out of the water by her upper arm, needing two hands to do it. She let herself be pulled into his warmth.

She turned into him and buried her face in his tunic.

And burst into tears.

She cried and cried, her body shaking.

He said nothing, asked her nothing. Just held her, the palm of his hand describing small circles on her shoulder blade.

Izramith had no idea how long they sat there, but slowly she calmed down, leaning into him.

"I don't know what I'll do when I finish this contract. I'll never again make a good guard." Her voice had gone hoarse.

"You'll make a better guard. There is nothing shameful about feeling like this over terrible things. It would be more worrying if you didn't have these feelings. Someone at the guards should have offered you and other returnees debriefing, but, knowing Hedron, I'm not surprised that they left you to handle it on your own. You'll probably find that most of you have trouble."

"I haven't seen any of the others since returning." Although that wasn't entirely the guards' fault. She hadn't wanted to be reminded of the war by serving with people who had been there —who knew what she had done.

"See? There you go. It is normal to feel like this."

His voice rumbled in his chest under her ears. All of a sudden, she felt so incredibly tired. She wanted to go to sleep and never wake up. He was still holding her and instead of her usual discomfort of being touched, it felt right. Because he understood. Because he had gone through bad things himself.

He smelled like fresh outdoor air, with a tang of sweat. A very male scent that made her cheeks glow again. Damn, this was not going to end well.

He shifted his arms ever so slightly. "We should go to sleep."

"Do you think you can sleep?"

"I'm not too bad with sleeping in odd places at odd times. I'm also not too bad with not getting much sleep. Comes with the job."

Wait—"What's that supposed to mean?"

"Whatever you want it to."

"Are you flirting with me?"

"Of course not. Every idiot knows it's dangerous to make a pass at a Hedron guard."

"You must be an idiot then."

"Yes." He reached out and stroked her cheek. "But I'm mad enough to run the risk."

Her cheeks were definitely glowing now. Damn, unless she went into the water to cool off, her hormones would run crazy and she was going to flush. After such a long time of not being with a man, her skin was so much more responsive that just a male smell would set it off. She could go to sleep and deal with it in the dark . . . or . . . she could just give in to it.

I'm not too bad with not getting much sleep. The hell, if that wasn't a blatant invitation.

She met his eyes. Her vision was already going watery.

He gave her an intense look. "You're flushing."

"Whose fault is that?"

He laughed.

"It's less easy to control when . . . with intense emotions . . ."

Hell. "It doesn't mean anything except . . ."

"You're attracted to me."

She laughed awkwardly. Her skin was glowing, and her mind was going foggy. She wanted him and no longer cared about anything else. And it was not as if when she left here she would see him again, or that there would be any consequences. Mirani Endri didn't breed with anyone else and neither did Coldi.

"You want to have a taste of what is normally forbidden?" Her voice was already going husky. Blood roared in her ears. There was no stopping it now.

She slid a hand under his tunic from below. His skin felt soft and strangely cool. All her flings had been Coldi except for Abbasi. She pulled her shirt up, but Braedon held it down.

"Um, maybe we should go to a more private spot." He gestured in the direction of the cave, invisible from here under the overhang of the rock. If anyone came up, this spot was the first thing they'd see.

Sure.

He took her hand and led her past the lower pools to the ones on the far side of the rock formation. The water here was still as a mirror, with faint wisps of steam rising off the surface. The moons had already gone, but the broad band of the milky way arced overhead and produced a faint glow.

Braedon stopped at the edge of the water. First he unbuttoned his shirt and then stepped out of his trousers and put both in a neat pile.

Izramith took off her singlet and shorts and tossed them into a heap.

He was already in the water when she waded in and sat next to him. And then neither of them moved for a long time.

The water was warm and smelled faintly of sulphur. The rocky bottom of the pool felt rough to the soft skin on her backside.

Boy, this was awkward. Asto Coldi had a word for this, *nethana,* intimacy without meaning, something that was common in associations, in particular between *zhayma*s, and also between other equals, like business contacts.

Braedon put his hand on her shoulder. His hand slid down her upper arm. She flinched when he ran his fingertips across the initiation scars, a series of crosshatched cuts that she should have kept covered. He retracted his hand. "It doesn't hurt anymore, does it?"

"No."

"We can heal wounds like that these days without scars."

"The scars are the point. My service will be forever inscribed on my body."

"Oh." He frowned. "Like initiation?"

"Yes. No one is supposed to see the scars when you're in active duty."

"You've not done anything wrong then. It's too dark for me to see them. I can only feel them."

True.

She leaned closer and put her hands on his upper arms. His skin was cool and moist with sweat. Did he want to back out? Was he just as nervous as she was?

She said, "We're grown-up. We understand. I know what I'm doing. I know what I'm asking. I know that there will be no rights or claims made on the basis of *nethana.*"

"I don't like that word," he said. "*Nethana* is old Coldi for 'whim'. A decision to give yourself to someone is never a whim. It's only called that when the results are not that good."

"You know what I mean."

"Yes." He said nothing for a while.

"All right," he whispered and bent towards her. "I'll settle for that. *Nethana,*" he said in the hollow of her neck so that her skin tickled.

His lips caressed the soft skin under her ear. A series of delicious shivers crawled over her skin. He knew how to make a Coldi woman crazy.

She pushed herself onto her knees while facing him. She swung her leg over both of his and curved her back so that the sensitive skin on her belly touched his. His skin felt cool against hers, his breath a warm spot on her chest.

"You're a crazy woman," he whispered.

"Not half as crazy as you."

"Might as well go for the big prize, huh?" His hands slid up her sides.

"Go for it."

He pulled her down onto his lap. What had been unremarkable during the day had grown to be quite impressive. Her heightened senses could feel him sliding into her all the way.

"A big boy, huh?"

"Only where it matters."

They settled in a rhythmic rocking motion. Not too fast because it made the water splash. Not too vigorous because already the flush was building. He clung onto her and she onto him like they were the only surviving people in the world.

The wave of the flush built and built. Her skin felt so hot that she thought she'd glow in the dark. The familiar tingling sensation started in the skin of her chest, spread to the soft skin of the underside of her arms, to her inner thighs and up to the most secret and sensitive of spots. All her sensations balled together in that one area. She had to clamp her jaws to stop herself shouting out. Braedon's grip on her tightened. His fingers dug into the soft flesh of her thighs. He let out a stifled moan, spilling his seed inside her.

And then there was only the roaring of blood in her ears, and Braedon's hands slowly sliding off her thighs. His chest heaved with deep breaths. "Oh crap, that was like . . ." He blew out a breath.

"Been a long time?"

"To be honest, yeah."

"Sorry if I caused any bruises," she whispered.

"If there are any, it was worth it."

She rolled off him, into the water, her mind relaxed and

calmer than at any time since going to Indrahui. Even encounters with Abbasi had always been hurried, since they had to be secret and there were few places on the Indrahui plain to hide. *Worth it* —Braedon's words.

They went back to the camp, without speaking a single word. Izramith fell asleep almost the moment she hit the mat.

21

I ZRAMITH WOKE abruptly when it was still pitch dark. There had been a noise, but it had stopped now, and she had woken up too late to hear what it was. Right now, all she could hear was her pounding heart and the roaring of blood in her ears.

And see nothing.

Except—

A faint thrumming sound made a continuous whisper in the background.

—a red light blinked on the motion sensor.

Fuck.

She crawled off her mat, bumbling around randomly placed shoes and bags in the cave, and activated her comm screen. The glare of it made her vision blurry. She blinked away sleep—

It was definitely the motion alarm. The screen said *activity detected.*

She switched to the infrared channel.

Most of the screen was dark grey, with a few lighter spots where boulders still radiated the heat of the day.

Amongst these boulders, something moved. It could have been an animal, but as she watched, the light-coloured blob clambered up a boulder, sticking out a leg for balance, and the figure was unmistakably human. Now that cleared her head.

She found her helmet with infrared sensor and panned the surrounding forest in greater detail than the motion sensor offered. All members of her team were asleep on their mats. Loxa and Dashu next to each other, Wairin on his back, Eris curled up in foetal position. Braedon faced her. The peaceful look on his face caused a small warm spot to grow inside her chest. It flowered briefly, and then it flickered out as reality set in. They'd agreed on *nethana*. She could only dream of ever being part in his world. It was too genteel, too sophisticated, too . . . surrounded by loving family members.

Damn.

Izramith crawled across the ground and shook his shoulder. "Wake up."

"Hmmm?"

She shone her comm screen light in his face. He raised an arm over his face, turning away from the light. "There's someone at the shack."

"What?" He took his arm away, squinting into the light. "Sure?"

"The alarm went off. I checked the scan and it's very clearly a person."

"Shit." He pushed himself up, looked around, and listened. "Just our luck. It's raining." He activated his lights to find his gun. The faint glow from his comm showed water dripping down from the overhanging rock ledge. Outside their shelter, the ground was dark and glistening wet.

Izramith went around the cave, waking up the other members of the team.

She donned her suit and body armour and checked her gear. The infrared view on her helmet showed her a mush of grey and darker grey. They would need every bit of gear in this awful weather.

Wairin joined her, his dark face serious. Eris came a moment later, followed Loxa and Dashu and Braedon. Izramith didn't meet his eyes. Inside, she was one ball of nerves.

The team gathered around her in silence. The rain pattered softly on her helmet. Already, the part of her suit around her neck was wet.

"All right, so this is what we'll do. We have no idea how many people there are or if they've noticed the wire. We'll go up that hill and we try to stay unnoticed for as long as we can. That's going to be really hard in that forest in the dark, but we have to sacrifice speed for silence. It's better if we split up into groups of two. You." She pointed to Braedon and he met her eyes without emotion. "Stay with me. Dashu and Loxa go up the left side. Eris and Wairin take the right side. We go up the middle. We try to make as little noise as possible. Keep your weapons ready. Stay in your position as we advance. Shoot anything that moves and is not in position."

"Stun or live?" Wairin asked, his voice dark. She heard echoes of the war on his home world.

"Stun, for now."

Nods all around. But their faces showed that they heard the implied threat in her words.

Helmets went on, connections were tested and they set out into the forest, walking slowly. Dashu and Loxa went first, and soon disappeared in the darkness. They showed up as light grey shapes in Izramith's infrared cam. Wairin and Eris strode past her up the other side.

Braedon walked slightly behind her. She wanted to say or do something that would acknowledge what had happened last night, even though they had agreed not to do this. But she could only think of Abbasi and how she'd tried so very hard to behave according to her Hedron guards' guidelines about relationships. Those regulations were why, that fateful morning, she had not spoken to him before he went out on the patrol. And why she had never spoken to him again.

Going up the hill was very slow going, even following the trail they'd left the previous afternoon. The vegetation was far too dense to move quietly and it was too dark to see much. Her pack kept snagging on trailing vines. Mossy boulders made for slippery footing. So much for being quiet. If there were any people at the shack, they would hear them coming from a long way away.

To make matters worse, the rain had intensified, an insistent soft drizzle not strong enough to limit vision but enough to make everything wet. The air was very humid. The higher they got, the more shards of mist drifted through the forest. Sometimes it was hard to see more than a few steps in front. Using the comm lights did not make much difference.

They were about halfway up the hill when the sharp crack of a branch echoed in the forest, followed by the sound of footsteps, just in front of them. In a split second, Braedon had taken out his gun.

Loxa's voice rang out. "Show yourself or I'll shoot."

There was no reply.

No one moved for what felt like a long time. Izramith listened, but heard nothing except drops of water falling from the trees, and Braedon's breathing behind her. She saw nothing except mist and the tree trunks immediately surrounding her.

Did she imagine it or was it starting to get light?

They started moving again, even more slowly this time, stopping for every tiny sound.

They caught up with Loxa and Dashu at the shack. They were dark shapes in the mist, bristling with antennas on the back of their helmets. As before, the shack was empty and there were no signs that anyone had been there overnight.

But it was on the other side of the hilltop where she had seen the human figure. After checking the coordinates off the motion sensor, all without speaking, Loxa and Dashu disappeared into the forest again.

Braedon fiddled with his belt. "This thing keeps getting caught."

Izramith sat down on the bench while he readjusted his gear.

By pure chance, she looked up to the underside of the roof, and noticed a glint of metal in the corner. That definitely hadn't been there before. She took off her glove and felt the branch that supported the roof. The object was smooth and cold. She pulled it from its hiding place. It came free, attached to a lead with a plug that snapped loose as she pulled it, leaving no visible sign where it had been attached.

The thing in her hand was just another part of an electronic connection plug. Had it remained behind because the owner had tried to pack up in haste? Moreover, where was that lead going?

She circled the shack, looking for cords or connections. The tree itself stood on the highest point of the hill. That would be the best place to set up a transmitter. But she couldn't spot anything unusual in the small patch of glow of her comm reader. The branches above her were a tangle of sticks and leaves. It would be easy to hide a thin cord in the cover of moss and little plantlets that grew on the trunk. With a bit of skill, someone could even hide a satellite dish up there. One of the team would have to climb the tree to inspect it. Climbing the tree wouldn't be too hard. She grabbed a handful of the mossy cover, pulled herself up—and a slab of moss ripped free.

Something glinted in the gap where the moss had come off. She pulled the surrounding moss, which came off quite easily. The surface underneath was metal. With her knife, she levered off another chunk. Damn, it looked like the whole trunk was covered in metal. She tapped it. The sound was hollow.

What the. . . ?

She tapped at a different place. Definitely hollow. And the surface was cold not because the trunk was wet, but because . . .

She ripped away part of the shack's roof where it attached to the trunk. The roof material came off, but the support beam was part of the tree. Just as she feared, this wasn't a real tree.

"Come and have a look," she said to Braedon behind her.

He did, running his hand over the trunk. "The whole thing is an antenna."

She was about to yell for Loxa to come back when a crack echoed through the forest.

Fuck. She pulled her gun from its holder. Braedon did the same, dropping to one knee and staring into the forest.

The early light rendered bushes, tree trunks and the debris-covered ground in featureless shades of blue. Shards of mist hung between the trees, cloaking the hilltop in heavy silence. Not a twig or a leaf moved. Her infrared visor showed no recognisable shapes. Damn, where were Loxa and Dashu? Where were Eris and Wairin?

An explosion rocked the ground, somewhere on the other side of the hill.

Izramith ducked under the shelter and behind the table just before the shockwave hit. Branches and other debris rained down on the roof.

Someone shouted but it was too noisy to recognise the voice.

She looked around the edge of the shack. All she saw was smoke or steam.

No movement. No Loxa or Dashu. Braedon raised himself from the other side of the table. He, too, held his gun ready to fire. The light on the side of the charge barrel was still blue for the stun setting.

Izramith turned hers to the kill setting, and when she looked at him again, his light was orange, too.

She spotted Wairin a bit further down the slope, taking shelter with his back to a large tree. No Eris.

Another shard of mist drifted by, restricting vision to no more than a few steps away.

When it was gone, Eris had poked his head up from between two boulders close to where Wairin stood.

Izramith jerked her head to the far side of the hill and the four of them crept forward, from tree to tree.

Wairin was to the right and just ahead of her. Eris further right.

Izramith hit a spot of level ground and prepared to sprint across—

—and noticed the faint shimmer of tripwire just in time to avoid hitting it.

Crap.

Braedon caught up with her. He dropped to his knees, following the wire to a nearby tree trunk where it was attached to an eyelet and a battery pack that sat in a hollow between a branch and the trunk.

Eris had discovered a section of wire on the other side of the tree trunk, too. "This is not where we strung it yesterday."

"This is not ours. It's Mirani army gear," Braedon said.

His expression was grave. Dashu and Loxa had passed here, and one of them had probably set off the wire.

Eris stepped over it carefully, holding his scanner. He walked slowly, holding the apparatus close to the ground.

Izramith, Wairin and Braedon waited.

Drops fell from the trees in increasing frequency. Water ran into her suit from her helmet into the neck of her armour. The growing wet spot made her shiver.

Then a patch of mist lifted and Izramith spotted Dashu behind a tree at the edge of the drop-off, peering into the forest ahead. No sign of Loxa.

Eris motioned that they could follow him. He led the group to Dashu in an agonisingly slow pace.

Izramith mouthed, "Where is Loxa?"

"I don't know what happened. One moment he was there and then he was gone." .

"Was that when the explosion happened?"

"No. Just after. I hit the trip wire and it went off. He said he'd check it out." Her eyes were wide.

Izramith's helmet-scan showed a tangle of bushes ahead, with the ground dropping off sharply.

"He might have fallen in between two boulders."

Izramith nodded, but she felt cold inside.

Her common sense told her that they were better off retreating and asking for backup, and she would have given that order if Loxa had been with the group.

"Let's go find him. I go first. You cover me."

It was unclear where the hilltop ended and the drop-off

began. The vegetation was so thick that some of the roots and branches formed shelves, some of which were supported by rock underneath, some not. You could slip and your leg would sink all the way into the hole. There was no way that someone could easily escape that way. Or take aim, for that matter.

Loxa could have fallen down there, especially with his Coldi poor eyesight in the dark. She peered between the gnarls of shrubbery, but saw nothing except tangled vegetation.

Leaves rustled behind her, and a weapon discharged.

Izramith spun around just in time to see a figure jumping from a tree. She raised and aimed the gun, fired—

The figure went down. Bushes threshed violently when he fell.

Izramith ran forward. Braedon and Dashu came out from behind the tree trunk. All three of them had just walked past this man and had missed him. How was that possible?

She pushed branches aside—

—and found a man in a grey insulation suit. The shot had hit him square in the back, where his suit had blackened and disintegrated. His helmet had fallen off and his head was uncovered. He had short-cropped, golden curls.

"Mirani?" Dashu asked. Her face was pale. How much actual battle experience did she have? Not much probably.

Izramith turned him over. His face was covered in mud, his eyes open. The irises were blue.

Then she spotted a device attached to his chest. She unclipped it and studied the unfamiliar screen.

"Braedon? What does it say?"

He took the device from her, his hands fleetingly touching hers. A flash of memory from last night jolted her. *Nethana,* huh? Keep acting like nothing has happened and ignore each other in daily life.

Braedon frowned at the screen. "It looks like it's some kind of communication device, but I haven't seen anything like this before." He turned the thing over. "I can't see how it transmits, if it does so. The text is all in code. A lot of numbers that don't mean anything to me."

"Take it? Leave it here?"

He looked up, his blue eyes meeting hers. The concern in them disturbed her. "It could give away our location."

Just as she thought.

Dashu shouted in the forest. Izramith dropped the device next to the body. She'd pick it up later.

Dashu had managed to clamber down through the tangle of shrubbery and was standing in a narrow gap between two mossy boulders, looking up.

"There is a cave of some sort here," she said.

"Natural?" Izramith asked.

"Seems so, but there are footsteps in the sand."

"Recent?"

"Looks like it."

"How far down does it go?"

"Can't see the end of it. Too dark."

Izramith stepped off the hilltop onto the tangle of vines, which supported her weight. She wriggled through a gap and slid down a large boulder. She landed next to Dashu.

The cave was a natural hollow between the boulders. A path worn smooth by the passage of feet led from the opening to a path zigzagging between the boulders downhill. That, clearly, was the easier way of reaching this site. Holding her gun, she peered into the opening, but as Dashu had said, it was too dark. She activated her comm light. The cave walls all looked natural, with places where the moss had scraped off with people passing. The floor was mostly rocky, but a patch of sand showed booted footsteps and the mark of something being dragged across. And dark spots.

She crouched and examined them. Braedon leaned over her. Izramith looked up and met his eyes. They said what she thought: *blood* and also *Loxa.*

Shit.

She directed her light further into the passage. It disappeared out of sight.

"What would they want with Loxa?" Dashu's eyes were wide. Izramith didn't feel the strength of the *zhayma* bond, but it was evident from the pain on Dashu's face.

Izramith wished she could say something positive, but this was not looking good.

She said, her voice grim, "We have to find him. I'm going in."

"I'm going, too." Braedon came to stand behind her, fiddling with the settings on his gun.

"I'm using my knife," Eris said, sliding it from his belt.

Dashu positioned herself at the front. Her face was pale.

Izramith asked Wairin to remain at the entrance. "Either these people are inside or outside. If outside, warn us if anything moves and retreat to a position you can defend."

He nodded, his face grave, then started taking some of his arsenal of explosives out of his pockets and placing them on a rock shelf. Guess they would know pretty soon if anyone turned up.

Dashu insisted that she wanted to lead the group inside. Izramith went second, followed by Eris and Braedon. The passage was quite long and winding. At first, they stumbled through a rough tunnel, but then the ground evened out and walls became smooth, showing up as hewn out into the stone by the light of their comms.

Dashu stopped. The passage ended ahead in two steps leading up to a closed door.

She went up the steps and listened.

"Hear anything?" Izramith mouthed.

Dashu shook her head. She heaved at the door handle, and it opened. The room beyond was dark. Dashu angled the light into the opening. The glow hit moss-covered walls, and another set of stairs going down into the earth.

As quiet as they could, they went down. The floor consisted of roughly hewn rock, covered in moss and slime.

At the bottom of the stairs they came to a low-ceilinged room which contained tables around the perimeter, carrying a bevy of equipment, none of it familiar, but all of it working and on despite the cloying humidity and trails of water running down the walls. Lights blinked in the gloom. A ladder in the middle of the room led to a hatch in the ceiling.

"We're under the shack," Dashu said, looking at her comm screen.

But where was Loxa?

The room had another exit, up a couple of steps and down a narrow corridor.

Dashu went first, followed by Eris, and Izramith followed them with Braedon bringing up the rear.

Izramith was studying her infrared scanner screen when Eris stopped suddenly and she almost crashed into him.

Dashu at the front said, "Shh." She switched off her light.

Eris did the same and Izramith held her scanner with the lighted screen pressed against her body armour.

They listened.

A faint sound of voices drifted down the passage. Izramith could make out not just two, but at least four different voices.

Very slowly, Dashu moved again, holding the grip of her gun in both hands. They went around a corner. The glow of light came into the passage from the other direction. Izramith raised her gun.

Male voices laughed in the room ahead. These passages echoed so much that it was hard to hear what language they spoke. It could be Mirani. Could be something else. Their voices were too deep to be Coldi.

She glanced over her shoulder. Braedon's face stood out like a pale oval.

Izramith quickly sent a message to Wairin, *Have found people.* They might need Wairin. Explosives were bad news in caves, but they might still need him.

At that moment, people were getting up in the room, pushing chairs over the ground. A silhouette came into the opening—

Dashu fired.

Men screamed inside the room. Furniture was pushed around.

Dashu ran forward, followed by Eris. Izramith went next. Into the brightly lit room, low ceilinged, but quite deep. There was a table at the far end and at the side closer to the door stood rows of beds. A couple of people—men, all, she thought—had been at the table and now ducked between the beds. One of them had been overturned to provide shelter.

The mattress hanging halfway on the floor was leaking smoke, probably from having been hit by Dashu's charge.

Izramith crouched behind the closest bed, pointing her gun at the other side of the room.

A man came out from between two beds and charged towards her. Izramith deflected his attack with her shoulder. She grabbed him under his arm and by the back of his clothes and swung him over her hip. The ceiling was so low that his feet slammed into it before he crashed into the ground flat on his back.

Braedon yelled, "Careful!"

Izramith hit the ground next to the man, while a weapon discharged over her head.

The man was a lot taller than her—that's why his feet had hit the low ceiling—and pale-skinned. His hair had an odd reddish tint and was curly like that of a Mirani Nikala.

A bit of blood trickled from the corner of his mouth and his eyes were half-open but didn't move. His head lay at an odd angle.

Damn. At least he wouldn't attack anymore.

Braedon stood at the door, firing over her head at the far side of the room. Two men went down, both hit square in the chest.

Dashu stood over another man who lay in a puddle of blood on the floor. The last man crawled under a nearby bed. In a few steps, Izramith crossed the room and lifted the whole thing off the floor. It was attached to the wall, but wood splintered and the structure disintegrated.

The man squeaked and backed away. Izramith pinned him to the wall and Eris helped her tie his hands behind his back.

Braedon came into the room, his chest heaving with deep breaths. His eyes were wide. He still clutched his gun with both hands.

"Was that all of them?" Even his voice sounded shocked. She remembered his story about killing a man that he had told her last night.

"Think so," Dashu said.

"Did you find Loxa?"

Dashu's face hardened.

Eris nodded to the other side of the room, the wall next to the door. With all the fighting, Izramith had not noticed that Loxa lay on the bed in the furthest corner. His suit was covered in blood, one of his hands hung limp off the side of the bed.

Braedon strode across the room and dropped to his knees. He undid the fastening to the neck of Loxa's suit, probed the soft flesh of the neck with his fingers.

No one dared move.

No one dared speak.

Braedon sighed and shook his head. He slowly heaved himself to his feet.

Izramith looked at Dashu, whose face was white and devoid of all emotion. She had known this. Izramith had no idea what to say to her.

She had failed Loxa and Dashu both. They had wanted her to be part of their association, but she had pushed them away, creating confusion, not just for them, but for her as well. Loxa was Dashu's *zhayma* and only last night had she begun to understand what it might mean.

22

DASHU FELL to her knees, leaning over Loxa's chest. Her cries cut Izramith inside. Memories took her to the aftermath of the Indrahui disaster, the dust, the smell of blood and decay, the lines of family members in front of the makeshift morgue. Tears were too close to the surface. She glanced sideways at Braedon, but he didn't meet her eyes.

Wairin came into the room, looking wide-eyed at the bodies on the floor.

"I discovered—" He swallowed visibly. "We seem to have stumbled across a major spying post. All the equipment back there relays to a Mirani satellite via a separate network that doesn't use the Exchange."

"Contact Barresh," Izramith said, trying to force her voice into an unemotional tone. "We'll want reinforcements and a pick-up."

Wairin nodded wordlessly and left the room again.

Braedon knelt next to each victim in turn. There were two Mirani, a Pengali—a woman in combat gear—and a keihu man too young to be involved in armed conflicts. There were four men like the one she had killed. Izramith had no idea where they came from.

The man whose wrists they had bound sat, pale and shivering, wide-eyed, propped up against the wall. A red welt bloomed on his cheekbone and a drop of blood welled from a cut on his lip. This man had bronze-coloured hair like Indrahui, but only loose curls, and pale skin. His eyes were vivid green.

When Braedon went to treat his cuts, he yelled something in Mirani that didn't sound friendly. Braedon calmly continued cleaning the man's bloodied face.

How did he even do that? She would have slapped the guy, maybe hard enough to kill him.

Wairin came back into the room. "They're coming."

No one said anything. Dashu still sat with Loxa, staring at his face, running her fingertips along the line of his jaw. Tears ran over her face. Eris sat on one of the beds, his head in his hands.

Izramith couldn't stand the tension. People were dead and it was all her fault. This was Indrahui all over again.

She went into the room with the transmitters and stood there in the semidarkness, staring at nothing and trembling. Braedon's voice drifted from the other room, but no one came to check on her.

She clutched the gun in her left hand.

How easy would it be to just shoot herself? There would be no more war, and no more guilt. No more pain or fear.

The thought scared her.

If she died, would anyone mourn her?

Her vision blurred.

More than anything, more than that nasty jealousy that kept popping up at stupid moments, more than her anger towards her family, she wanted some place to belong, someone to come home to who would be happy to see her.

Last night with Braedon meant nothing. *Nethana,* they had promised each other. He was a Trader and had his own life. He cared a lot for people, but not in particular for her. No one cared about her.

Why was she thinking this shit?

She was strong. She was a guard. Her nephew needed her. Like Ydana, she would make her own family.

Slowly, she relaxed and sank back into the awful truth.

Dashu was no longer crying, but when she spoke, her voice sounded hoarse and her tone empty.

Dead bodies, damaged equipment.

All the stuff in this room would have to be taken to Barresh and would have to be investigated. She sat on one of the chairs, in front of a screen that looked familiar. Sure enough, the Hedron guard used the same equipment for tracking aircraft in the area. She switched it on. Even the commands were in Coldi. She navigated through the menus and settings. Whoever had used this last had been using it at long distance, receiving a signal from elsewhere, a satellite or a stratospheric balloon, probably.

She swept the receiver around but it found no signal.

A few lines of Mirani text had appeared on one of the screens. She called, "Braedon, look at this."

He came in from the dorm room, his hands covered in blood and with bloodstains on his clothes.

Izramith gestured at the screen. "What does this say?"

He crossed the room and looked. "It says 'Initiate procedure 34.'"

The prisoner yelled in Mirani from the next room.

Braedon replied.

"What did he say?"

Braedon rose and went back to the dorm room.

Another line of Mirani text scrolled across the screen. Damn, this stuff was auto-communicating—maybe with a base in Miran, maybe just across the border. Barresh was only a small territory and maybe troops in Miran were even closer than the backup which was coming out of Barresh.

Braedon came back. "How long did Wairin say the transport would take to get here?"

"I don't care. We're leaving now. Back to the beach."

"What? Why?"

The prisoner yelled again.

"I think it may be a trap. We should get out of here to a defensible position. I don't know what this equipment does, but it's communicating with something elsewhere. Get everyone ready."

He nodded, his face serious and went back into the other room.

Izramith looked around the banks of equipment. If the equipment was Hedron-made, there would be a data storage hub somewhere. She rummaged behind the screens, under the desk, in the corner that held all the power boxes. A cabinet stood against the back wall—

Ah. Part of the back wall was a storage bank with blinking lights. On a shelf stood a couple of boxes with datasticks and other small electronics.

From the storage bank, she removed whichever tabs she could find. A couple of lights blinked red after she pulled the tabs out and tucked the data tabs in the pocket of her jacket.

Braedon entered from the dorm, followed by Wairin, forcing their captive in front by pulling the hair at the back of his head and pushing the barrel of his gun into the man's back. The man yelled what sounded like abuse.

Then Dashu and Eris, carrying a makeshift stretcher with Loxa's body. Dashu's face was distant and unemotional and didn't meet Izramith's eyes.

They trudged to the cave entrance in single file. The prisoner kept yelling.

They got as far as the cave entrance, only to find that they couldn't easily negotiate the boulders while carrying the stretcher.

Eris had to go between the rocks first so that Dashu could push the stretcher to him.

The captive said something in Mirani in a strained, almost desperate, voice.

"Tell him to shut up."

Braedon said something in Mirani. How come he always managed to sound friendly? He was such a softhearted person. Not full of bristle and anger, like her.

The soldier spat. The glob of spit landed on Braedon's leg.

Izramith grabbed the man by the front of his uniform. "You don't do that to any of my trusted people, especially not to him. Do that again and I'll bash your face in."

He met her eyes with a defiant look. Oh, he understood her well enough.

The scent that rose from him was strange and familiar, and one she had smelled before, on a baby.

She took in his narrow face with strong cheekbones, his weird green eyes, his curly hair, resembling Daya's, but sand-coloured.

She grabbed him by the collar and shouted in his face, "The fuck, what are you? Some sort of perverted *zhadya*-born?"

He retreated, eyes wide, and fell quiet.

Braedon gave her a sideways look. "Was that necessary?"

"Someone needed to shut him up. You're much too nice."

"My regular job is to make people better. I do not enjoy killing them."

"And what is that supposed to mean?"

He didn't reply.

The expression on his face remained emotionless. No doubt the irony would not pass him by that he was the person with the highest number of kills to his name during this expedition. The precision of his fire still chilled her. What were the things that Traders saw in the course of their normal work?

The feel of forest around her was suffocating. She couldn't see. Her visor kept fogging up. The humidity was so stifling that she couldn't breathe. Sweat ran under her armour.

Damn, fucking adaptation. Was this ever going to end?

"You want us to take our wire and motion sensors back?" Eris asked.

"Leave it for now," Izramith said. "Until we're safe. Until reinforcements have turned up from Barresh." Her voice sounded more strained than she wanted. The prisoner was nervous and that made her nervous.

The semblance of a path that led from the cave entrance faded pretty soon and then they were back to clambering over boulders, although this route at the back of the hill was definitely easier than the one they had taken. It was still raining and the moss was even more slippery than when they tried to climb up. The prisoner was carrying on in Mirani.

They finally arrived at the bottom of the hill where at least they could walk normally.

The golden sand of the beach and dark water of the lagoon peeped between the trees. Hopefully the backup from Barresh wasn't too far awa—

A bright flash somewhere behind them.

A rumble in the ground.

For a moment, the world stopped.

Wairin yelled, "Run!"

Air whooshed through the forest. Then the front of the explosion hit.

Izramith pushed the prisoner face first into the sand and fell on top of him. Debris flew over her head. A large tree branch crashed next to her, spraying her with leaves and crap.

Oh, shit. What the fuck was that?

She scrambled up and pushed the foliage aside, even though her ears were still ringing.

The area behind her was a tangle of fallen tree trunks and branches. Sunlight penetrated between bushes stripped bare and tree trunks snapped straight in half.

Wairin struggled to free himself from the snarl of vegetation. Izramith gestured *You're fine?* He nodded.

Eris, who had been in front of her, said, "Shit, we're lucky." His eyes were wide and mouth open. Trails of blood ran from a series of cuts in his arm, probably from flying debris.

The hill and the shack had been turned into a crater. Little bits of splintered wood lay scattered everywhere.

She hated to think what the explosion had done to the bodies, or what it would have done to them if they'd still been in the shelter.

Dashu was talking on her comm. Someone at the council guard station, presumably. "Yes, we're still here. Come quickly. I don't know what else will blow up."

She and Eris dragged the prisoner onto the beach where they hid in the cave. Blood ran down his face onto his suit and there were cuts in his leg, too.

Eris unrolled his mat and let the prisoner sit on it. He displayed no more bravado and had stopped yelling. His face was pale and he said nothing. Braedon dug in his pack to get the med kit.

Izramith went to stand at the entrance, holding the gun. Her ears were still ringing from that explosion. That had been a very, very close call.

"There they are," Eris said into the silence.

The stout shape of a short distance craft already showed in the sky, going slow. Its downward beam blew aside reeds and made trees thresh about wildly.

Not much later, it landed with a spray of mist and settled on top of the water. The door opened and someone slid a dinghy out the door.

A guard jumped into it. A second person handed the first one the engine. This went onto the stand, a huge jet-fan that would blow the craft forward. It gave a high-pitched whine when the guards started it.

With the boat coming towards the beach, Izramith ordered the group to grab all their gear. Eris, Dashu went in the dinghy with the stretcher that contained Loxa's body. Eris carried both Dashu's and Loxa's packs.

Izramith remained on the beach while the boat receded. She couldn't look at the long shape wrapped in cloth and couldn't look away. Dashu's eyes were still red.

"What about boat?" Wairin asked, waving a hand at the punt that they had taken here.

Braedon said, "Pengali will return it. They do it for money."

She said, "We haven't even seen any Pengali."

"They're around. They know exactly where we are."

"Does that mean they're in agreement with these Mirani spies being on their land?"

"They probably don't care, as long as they get paid. It's never been any different. Pengali care about Pengali interests."

The dinghy arrived at the shuttle and filled up with guards, all of them in full gear and armed and carrying duffels.

The boat charged for the shore and crunched onto the beach not much later. The guards streamed out.

The superior spoke to Eris in keihu and Eris gestured at Izramith and their prisoner.

"Mirani?" the guard asked.

"Not this man. He speaks Mirani, though."

From the corner of her eye, she noticed that the man flinched.

"You killed some?"

"There were eight in total," Izramith said. "Mirani and others. With spying equipment. We killed seven, before the hideout blew up. I managed to salvage a couple of data storage sticks."

"You've taken one casualty?"

"Yes." She hated how impersonal that sounded. Remembered the look on Dashu's face as if she knew, even before they went into the hideout, that Loxa was dead.

That kind of connection had to be special. That was the *zhayma* bond.

The guard superior ordered his team into the forest, and Izramith climbed in the dinghy.

She was broken inside. This was why she could make love to a man without loving him, without speaking to him afterwards. Braedon was busy helping the prisoner into the boat and didn't look at her.

Wairin, next to her, was also very quiet.

"Don't like blood," he said when he noticed her gaze lingering on him. The glare reflecting off the water silhouetted his outline. "Seen far too much of it at home. Death and destruction. War is never pretty, no matter the glorious stories."

She nodded.

War made ruins of people's lives like a deep burn. It hurt when it happened, but continued to do damage for much longer than that.

23

THE DINGHY arrived at the shuttle and Izramith climbed into the craft, a pretty basic cabin with two rows of seats against the side walls. The floor between them was a cargo space, where the others had put their bags, and the stretcher with Loxa's body covered in a grey cloth. The guards pulled up the dinghy. Dashu sat on the chair closest to the back, next to Loxa's body, hugging herself and staring out the window.

Izramith sat in a seat on the opposite side of the cabin. The whine of the craft's engines sounded like it came through a thick sheet of glass, as if it weren't part of the same world that she was in.

Braedon had his med kit out and sat on his knees to attend to Eris' cuts. Two long bandages went over Eris' forearm, stuck down with white tape. When he finished, he dragged his bag to Izramith and crouched next to her.

"Let me have a look at you."

"I'm fine."

He reached out and touched her face. His fingers came away covered in blood. "Not from where I'm standing. Do you feel fine?"

She nodded, but at the same time a wave of nausea washed

over her. Blood had also leaked onto her uniform. She hadn't even noticed that she'd been hit.

"Take off your armour."

She didn't argue. She undid the clips and he helped her lift it over her head. The underside of his arms brushed her hands very lightly, bringing memories of a time that seemed much longer ago than the previous night.

"Whoa, look at this." He held up the armour. The backplate had a big dent.

He massaged her shoulder with firm hands. "Does it hurt anywhere here?"

She shook her head. With her fingertips, she gingerly touched her cheek. Blood. She smeared it all over her face looking for a cut or injury. Where did it even come from?

"Let me do that." With gentle hands, he wiped her forehead and the side of her face and her neck. She remembered how his fingers had caressed her. His face looked serious. The pile of bloodied bandages grew. "You might want to get this treated."

"I'm fine." She still felt nauseous.

"You get this glued, all right? I don't like to see a nasty scar on your face." His eyes met hers and held her gaze for an intense moment.

Why didn't he acknowledge what had happened between them? Yeah, she agreed to *nethana* but that didn't mean he had to go all stupid over it?

Braedon rose and moved to the prisoner, who had been tied to his seat.

He tried to wipe blood off the man's face, but he'd run out of clean wipes, so had to use part of the man's ripped shirt.

Each time Braedon's hands came close, the man tried to retreat. His face had a sheen of sweat. In the light of the cabin, he looked younger than she would have guessed he was. Barely adolescent.

She recognised his behaviour. His earlier aggression came from trying to mask fear. And because he was scared, he could probably be broken. She pushed herself from her seat and crouched next to him. He gave her a sideways glance and stiffened ever so slightly.

Braedon continued cleaning his face.

"You speak Coldi, no?" Izramith said, her voice low.

His gaze flicked to her, and then went back to staring at Braedon's hands. Too intense.

"If you talk to us, we can help you."

He stared ahead. Those eyes were really the most unusual colour she had ever seen. In the cabin of the craft, the *zhadya*-born scent was even stronger.

"What were you doing with all these Mirani people? Did they treat you badly?"

He didn't move.

"I understand that you are from a group of people that has been treated poorly just about everywhere they live. At Hedron we call them *zhadya*-born, but he—" She glanced at Braedon. "—says that you don't like that name. I am really stubborn and I'm going to use it anyway, because that's what we call your people at my home."

There was no reaction.

"I don't think you're from Hedron. I've never seen anyone like you before, but if I'm right, you'll probably know some of the *zhadya*-born from Hedron. I'll tell you something. I'm here because the Barresh council hired me. I'm also here because I have a nephew who is *zhadya*-born. At Hedron, people put these children in the care of an institute. They will never see the surface, they will never work, they will never have a partner and never lead a normal life. I wasn't happy with that future for my nephew, so I found out that my father has a *zhadya*-born brother. I wanted to ask him if he knew of a way to keep my nephew out of this horrible institute."

She paused, aware that Braedon and Eris were listening in.

"But my uncle has gone missing. One of his neighbours said that she thought he went to Ceren. When I saw images of Daya, I thought of course he would be in Barresh. But my uncle is not here. Is he in Miran?"

The young man's eyes met hers. "You'll never see him again. Not after this." He spoke a curious mix of Hedron Coldi with a Mirani accent.

Yes! Once he'd started speaking, the information would flow.

"What do you mean by that?" But he had already admitted in a roundabout way that the Hedron *zhadya*-born were in Miran.

He didn't reply and looked out the window.

Izramith made a show of unclipping her knife from her belt. After the fight in the hideout, it was covered in dirt and other unmentionable substances.

He glanced at it. "I'm not afraid. Kill me."

Izramith raised the knife in front of her face. He didn't flinch. He really wasn't afraid.

She proceeded to clean her nails with the tip of the knife. "*Gamra* prohibits the execution of defenceless prisoners without a trial. I think I might be better off handing you back to Miran. I might be able to negotiate something for your release."

His eyes widened. "Please, no. Don't send me back. They'll kill me."

"And just a moment ago you wanted me to kill you?"

"I rather you kill me than be sent back for them to come and find me, like what happened to my friend. He escaped and was killed by soldiers in a back street."

Izramith's heart jumped. "When did that happen?"

"A few days ago."

"He was keihu?"

He nodded.

Izramith met Eris' eyes. The man who had been butchered in the alley that linked Fountain Street and Market Street. The man who was very similar to someone who had gone missing years ago, because he was someone who had gone missing years ago.

"Tell us about this person. Tell us about yourself and where you were held and why."

The man's eyes widened. "You have to guarantee that you'll keep me safe."

"We're almost in Barresh now. We'll be met at the airport by guards. If you're afraid of your captors, custody is probably the safest place to be."

The man was silent for a while, looking out the window as if he expected someone to be in pursuit.

Then he started speaking in a low voice. "I was born as Ridan in Miran of a Mirani Endri father and a keihu mother. I never knew my father, but my mother lived in the same building as me. With us were a group of people, thirty-five in total, some of us of the same blood, some from other races. Twenty of us were men, and fifteen women. All except me and a young boy were taken off the streets of various localities, but mostly Barresh. There were Pengali and keihu. They were mostly girls. The men were mostly from Hedron—"

"Do you know anyone called Reyar?"

He frowned. "Tall fellow?"

"Yes." Her heart thudded.

"He's in Miran. He does the communication for this whole plan."

"Voluntarily?"

He laughed, not in a funny way. "None of us are there voluntarily. We are prisoners. They killed my mother. My friend was keihu. He was abducted from the street during the midsummer festival. He had fought with his family and was living on the street. He was always talking about going back and when they gave him the opportunity to come here, he took his chance and escaped. Caught him, too."

"Who are these people keeping you prisoner? The Mirani council?"

"We had contact only with one: Nemedor Satarin. We're a private project of his and he uses privately hired guards to control us. He knows about Daya Ezmi and his group of people with Aghyrian blood and he's trying to set up a rival group, because he thinks that Daya is stealing Mirani genetic material, because the Endri are the purest Aghyrians of all the races, but they have fertility problems and—" He glanced at Braedon. "—sorry. The man is paranoid. He's keeping us in an old building that's been abandoned. It's old, with little pretty towers and coloured windows and everything. In the middle of town somewhere. He comes into the compound where we live with a couple of thugs and makes us strip down and stand naked in the courtyard for 'experiments'. Look." He slid his foot out of his shoe. The pale skin was marked with purple patches. "That's where I had blisters from standing in the snow."

"What are you doing in Barresh?"

"Nemedor Satarin wants to take back Barresh and he needs to find its weak points. He's using local people because they can blend in with the population."

"By local people you mean other prisoners captured from Barresh?"

"Yes, and people who live locally."

"Who are these people?"

"I don't know them. Nemedor Satarin has a big network of friends in Barresh. They look like rich families. We went into their gardens and roofs."

Izramith's heart jumped. "People who live along the main streets?"

He shrugged. "I think so. Don't ask me for names or anything. Most times I never saw who lived in the house. I just got told where to go."

Izramith couldn't help thinking of the golden-haired man she had seen with the young Semisu nephew. So, the two of them had been setting up spying equipment on the top floor of the commercial building when she witnessed their argument. Why did none of this surprise her?

"Did you send messages with threats to the Andrahar family?"

"Not me, but others did. Nemedor Satarin hates them. And there is this second in command who keeps talking about how his wife and daughters betrayed him and how they should come back to Miran with him."

Mikandra's father. "Is he likely to carry out his threats?"

"I don't know. You can expect anything from those lunatics."

Izramith didn't like the hesitation in his voice. Likely, he had some information he wasn't going to share. She gestured to Eris, Wairin and Braedon and the four of them moved to the front of the cabin.

"What do you think?" she asked them, meeting their eyes in turn.

"I don't trust him," Eris said. "He's much too upfront with the information. Who is to say that they haven't planted him to tell us what we want to hear?"

"He's young enough for me to think that he wouldn't have the maturity to lie so convincingly. I think a good deal of what he says is true."

Wairin said, "Local families involved?"

Eris shook his head. "That's rubbish."

Izramith said, "I'm not so sure about that. There is a rift in the council. I blundered into a council meeting and saw councillors attacking each other. Now this may be a regular state of affairs and you may have become used to it, but it is hardly normal. Some groups in town are very angry. The old councillors worked under the Mirani occupation for years. It made them rich and protected their status. Now they have to comply with *gamra* law and it tells them to do things they don't like. Give up some power to groups they formerly repressed, and their right to have many women at the same time. It's not hard to see why they would allow Mirani to come into their houses. Some of them will think that Barresh was better off under Mirani rule. For some of them, it might even be true." Like the merchant stuck with masses of ex-Mirani army clothing.

Eris looked disturbed. "But why would they do that? These people are Daya's friends. Since Daya has come, this town has never been so rich."

"The town, yes, but what about the traditional families them-selves? Everyone is joking about how lazy and decadent they are. Even you are doing it between yourselves. You know, that your family's butts are not big enough to fill council chairs." He opened his mouth, and closed it again, understanding on his face.

"I'm sure they can't be too impressed with that treatment. They were more respected and had more power under Mirani rule."

"But if that's true, then every old keihu family could have an interest in bringing down the Barresh council."

Izramith nodded. "And every house along that route could harbour a sniper. That's what I've been trying to say, but everyone is so fixated on that guesthouse that no one is listening. Yes, the guesthouse is part of the problem, but it's not the only problem, and not by far the worst problem."

"Shit," Braedon said, staring out the window.

After a silence, Izramith asked him, "Do you think your brother might postpone the wedding?"

He gave her a sideways glance. "Because of this?"

"Because the problem is more serious than we thought, and we don't know where else these people may have posts, we don't know how many of them there are, and there will be no time to search the entire city." In fact, she felt overwhelmed by the possibilities.

Braedon said, "We don't need to secure the entire city, just the streets along the route. That should be feasible. My brother is not the kind to back down."

Damn Traders. "Can I at least talk to him? He needs to consider all the facts before putting everyone else in danger."

He shrugged. "Talking does no harm."

24

S OON, THE FIELDS of green leaves became denser and the waterways more crowded with boats, and then the houses of the island passed underneath.

When the craft landed at the airport, a couple of guards were waiting for them and took the prisoner off their hands. He'd gone quiet and looked defeated, like a convicted man waiting for punishment. She wondered what sort of interrogation techniques Barresh used. At Hedron, there were a couple of guards who specialised in getting answers out of people. Izramith had watched their interviews sometimes. They never touched anyone, but had twisted ways with words that managed to break their spirits enough to make them spill their story. Izramith stood in awe of those women. Who needed torture when those people existed?

A couple of guards helped unload the stretcher with Loxa's body. Dashu went with them, in the direction of the new terminal building.

Izramith watched the sad group progress across the airport. What would happen to him? Would Dashu hold a ceremony? Would she be alone farewelling him? Would she have to notify Loxa's family? And then a thought: if she died here, would anyone know how to notify her family? In her application, she had left the next of kin field blank. Maybe that was a silly thing to do. Her father at least would like to know, and she would like her mother to know, even though she might not care very much.

Izramith, Wairin and Eris went into the council building, where she passed the datasticks she had taken from the equipment in the cave to the people who worked in security. Dashu and Loxa had been two of those people. Later, she would have to deal with replacing Loxa. Would she be required to find Dashu a new *zhayma* or could she just find someone else who knew about security? Someone who was not Coldi, preferably?

The question made her feel sick. What did she know about this? If *sheya* was an instinct rather than a taught behaviour, she might have some of it, but it wasn't strong and nothing told her what needed to be done for Dashu, who clearly expected her to have the answers.

Everything in the security room had Loxa's mark on it. The cloying atmosphere reminded her too much of Indrahui. Too much loss, too much death and destruction.

Eris caught her staring into nothingness seated in the chair in the security room. Dashu normally sat there, but she had not yet come back.

He leaned against the doorframe, his hands in his pockets.

"I know you haven't been getting along very well with Dashu and Loxa, but you should come this afternoon."

"Come?"

"The farewell ceremony for Loxa."

Oh. "Here in Barresh?"

"At the jetty where we left. You'll be welcome. I mean it. There will only be very few of us."

"He has no family in town?"

"They're all at Asto. Dashu has been in contact with them."

And that, by rights, should have been *her* job. Damn, she'd made a mess of this. She could still hear Dashu's voice *You have a lot to learn.* She did. Not about security, but about people. About learning to confide in people and learning to trust them.

And damn it, the tears were so close to the surface these past few days. She hated it. She hated herself and all the Hedron guard toughness. It was a front, and it didn't work. You couldn't be tough on the outside if you had a weak inside. Inner strength was not denying grief and doubt. It was acknowledging it and dealing with it.

"Can I . . . is there anything I can do to help?"

He shook his head. "It's all organised." His expression was sad and his eyes met hers for longer than necessary.

With the weight of guilt settling on her, she went down the corridor and asked to see Daya, but a council worker told her that the council was in session and he was not available until later. When she asked for a time that the session would be finished, he told her that he didn't know, but that council sessions often went overtime.

Just wonderful. Did Daya even know what had happened?

She left the council building again and walked to the guest-house to clean up. Her head was in turmoil. The implications of what the young prisoner had told her were still sinking in. There were few houses along Market Street that did not belong to the old keihu families. Most of those houses had top floor windows that looked out over the street, or roofs from where you could see over the boundary walls. If all those families were now suspect, there was a lot of work to be done and they had about ten days to do it.

In the hall of the guesthouse, a group of keihu people stood talking to each other and looked strangely at her when she walked past in her blood-soaked and dirty clothes.

She charged through the hall, up the stairs, across the gallery and into her room—and stopped. Why was her bag open? Why were her clothes on the floor? Who had searched through her belongings while she was away?

She slid her pack from her shoulder and flung it on the bed with such force that the bed slid across the tile floor with a scraping sound.

"Oh, fuck this fucking hellhole!" Fuck it, fuck it, fuck it.

They had no idea about proper security procedures, they hired her and ignored what she said. They were too stubborn, too stupid or too lax to listen, or too politically-motivated to understand.

She was *finished* here, in this horrible, hot, cloying, sticky place.

She upended her bag on the bed and went through her things a number of times, but couldn't discover anything missing. They'd found nothing because there was nothing to find. Then she scanned the room for listening devices, both visually and with her frequency scanner, but didn't see anything either. Neither did the door display any signs of breaking in.

And Daya was talking about trust and honesty, the hell! The guesthouse owners had allowed someone to come in here.

This place was worse than Indrahui. She understood fighting. Shooting enemies was unpleasant, but at least she knew who she was shooting at. War was awful, but the parameters were clear. These are the good guys, these are the bad guys.

This . . . was such a fucking mess. And she was supposed to work with these people and slash her way through political motivations, grandstanding and posturing. Meanwhile, everyone was trying to appease Daya and didn't see his *zhadya*-born manipulation.

To hell with keeping a low profile. The council would sack her, but she was going to give the people in this town a piece of her mind.

She left the room and went down to the registration counter in the hall.

The matron with the ridiculous hairdo was talking to an elderly Kedrasi couple, and glanced over her shoulder at Izramith.

Was she nervous? Good. She had better be.

When the couple moved away, Izramith came to the desk, placed both her hands on it, fingers splayed, and leaned forward. "Explain to me why you allowed someone to search my room."

Her voice was low, but the couple turned at the door and then quickly disappeared.

The matron retreated, her eyes wide. She had the gall to look surprised. "I did—what?"

"Why did someone search my room while I was gone? All my belongings were on the floor. Do you think I wouldn't notice?"

"But no one could have—"

"I have the key and took it with me. Who else, except you, can get into the room?"

"Our staff would never do that," the matron said, her face miffed. "They are all trustworthy people."

"There is no sign of a break-in. So if that doesn't scream foul play to you, I'm not liking your customer service."

She swallowed visibly. "Why would we search your room?"

"A very good fucking question. Why? Tell me! Because some lazy arsehole of a rich guy doesn't like me here and wants to find something to pin on me so he can force me to leave?"

The woman said nothing. Her massive bosom heaved with shallow breaths. "I . . . I don't like this sort of threat. I don't like your language. We're a quality establishment. We—"

"If you think this is a threat, wait until I make a fucking threat."

The woman retreated further, her eyes wide. "You stop this or I'll call—"

"The guards?" Izramith laughed. "I work for the guards. You'll get no sympathy from them for going through my stuff. Who's paying you?"

"I honestly know nothing about this. It must have been some . . . maintenance worker, or . . ."

"Rubbish. Someone went into my room to look for something. Who was it?"

The woman gave a tiny squeak. "I know nothing. I swear."

Izramith glared at her, but realised that the woman probably spoke the truth. Likely she had accepted a bribe in return for the key, but knew nothing more.

"I'll be reporting this to the guards and the council. If this happens again, I'll make you regret ever having accepted me in your guesthouse. You understand?"

The woman nodded, her eyes still wide.

Dressed in her dark tunic, Izramith went back into town and made for the other side of the square. An unpaved path wound past the side and back of the airport to the water. At the end of the path was a jetty, with a number of boats already moored there.

Dashu stood on the edge of the jetty, wearing the traditional Asto maroons. She stood so close to the water that for a moment Izramith was afraid that she might jump and drown. The eels would make short work of her.

In the water lay a boat made of bundles of reeds tied together with rope. A rather flimsy construction. On top of the flat bottom lay a human shape wrapped in white cloth, surrounded by pink flowers.

Izramith went to stand next to Dashu. She didn't look aside, but stared into the distance where the waters of the marsh bled into the horizon. "Apparently, there is a sea out there," she said, her voice empty.

"I've seen it," Izramith said. "When I came in."

"It was dark when I flew in." Dashu let a silence pass. "I think he will enjoy the sea." Her voice caught.

Izramith's vision became blurred. She had failed Dashu and Loxa.

Dashu wiped her face with the back of her hand. "Sorry."

"You should apologise to me?"

"You at Hedron don't like emotion."

"That doesn't mean we don't *have* any." It came out too angry.

Dashu turned and met her eyes. A look of understanding went between them. There was no hint of *sheya* or any of the Asto Coldi nonsense.

Izramith wanted to say how much of an absolute dick she had

been, and that she was at fault for Loxa's death, but words wouldn't come out. She did what Braedon had done to her: she hugged Dashu. The woman's body felt delicate under her uniform, her upper body shaking with cries.

Eris and Wairin had also arrived and stood like solemn statues.

She helped Dashu down the steps to the water and together, they untied the knot in the rope. The current tugged it from Dashu's hand, taking the boat with the tide towards the horizon. The reeds would get wet and it would sink. Loxa would be one with nature.

The sad group made their way up to the square in the last rays of dying sunlight. Looking over the square and all the building activities, the majestic and ancient building of the Exchange and the roofs of rich family's mansions, it was hard to imagine the level of betrayal in this town.

Izramith let Eris take care of Dashu. She had some serious talking to do.

~

It was late afternoon by the time Izramith arrived at the Andrahar house and the garden was bathed in orange sunlight. The place looked so idyllic that it was hard to believe that there was so much tension under the surface. That illusion proved hard to pierce.

There were no children playing on the veranda this time, so she crossed the yard, past the burbling fountain, the bench with the overhanging vine with its floppy flowers—they had fallen all over the seat—and up the steps to the front door. As seemed traditional in Barresh, it stood open and the sound of laughing children's voices came from inside.

No security whatsoever. At Hedron, even Edyamor had a guard at the door to his family's private residence.

In the hall, she found the twins playing in the knee-deep

water of the fountain with a couple of tailed Pengali kids and
their toddler sister, soaking wet and squealing with laughter.

Watching the kids was Braedon's younger brother Taerzo. He
sat on the stairs with a reader, his hair tied at the nape of his neck,
and wearing only his uniform tunic and trousers. Without the shirt
underneath, his upper arms and shoulders were bare. His skin was
pale, his arms thin but wiry and corded with lean muscle. In her
mind, she felt the touch of Braedon's soft skin under her palms.

She said, "I want to speak to all of you, mostly Rehan."

Taerzo greeted her and ordered the kids out of the hall. They
drooped off, making protesting noises.

He preceded her into the house's living room, where his
mother sat at the table with the golden-haired child and old-fashioned books on the table.

The boy's face was serious as he copied characters onto a
writing pad, his lips pressed together in concentration. The old
woman spoke soft words to him in Mirani, then rose from the
table.

"I'm busy teaching, as you can see. Is this urgent?"

"Urgent enough for me to come here."

Her pale blue eyes met Izramith's and held her gaze for a
moment, assessing her intentions and the seriousness of the
matter. "Very well."

The boy looked up. Isandra spoke to him, leafing through
pages of a book.

Taerzo bade Izramith to sit on the couch. From the back of
the room, he retrieved a tray with a carafe and glasses. Condensa-
tion pearled on the outside of the glasses.

The door opened and Rehan came in, followed by his bride-
to-be. They all sat down on the couches, while the little boy kept
working on his letters at the table.

"Is Braedon not here?" She had expected him to be, and
wanted to talk to him. Not that she knew what she would say, but
she just wanted to see him, wondering why he hadn't come to
Loxa's farewell.

"He's on a run to Indrahui," Rehan said.

So he'd come back from this emotionally exhausting trip and he'd gone straight to work in a violent war zone? "No time to sleep, huh?" She chuckled awkwardly, trying to hide her disappointment.

Isandra said, "He received an emergency call from the military hospital. My son always responds to emergencies." The way she said it sounded like Izramith had ticked her off about something.

She put her pad on the table and explained the problematic situation: what they had discovered, that the old keihu families were likely to be involved, and that many of them supported Mirani interests. She showed all the places along the route that now needed rechecking, and all the things that were currently unknown. Taerzo watched from the corner of the couch, Rehan and Mikandra next to each other opposite the table. They were both in uniform.

When she finished, Rehan licked his lips. "The council has assured me yesterday that there are no major issues."

"That was yesterday. This changes everything. This is not some amateur setup."

"You killed seven of them. That will have taken the heart out of their operation."

"We don't know that. The man we captured suggested that this is a large operation and that there are various people in town involved."

"She is right," Isandra said. "You can be foolhardy and go through with it, but we know what Miran is capable of. Can I remind you of a yard with a burned-out house?"

"I strongly advise you to cancel or change the route or length of the parade. We may not have enough time to sort this out. We may not have enough people. We're up against a group of people who will have formed a tight wall of protection around their group, and have probably been doing so for years. We have some of their data, but we're a long way off being in control of this situation. You can go ahead with the parade, but I won't be able to guarantee your safety."

"Do the best you can, and that will have to do."

"No, it won't. I was contracted to keep you safe. *That will have to do* is not in my job description." What the hell was she even doing here? These people weren't going to listen to her, a lowly guard. Maybe Braedon would, but he wasn't here and that showed how much he cared.

"Then we hire more security staff," Rehan said. "I'm very reluctant to let them win." But for the first time, he sounded rattled.

Good. He should be. This was a fucking mess.

Mikandra frowned at Izramith. "You said that these people you found have gone missing from the streets of Barresh?"

"Barresh and Hedron, and some other places. On the second day I was here, I found a man stabbed to death in the street. Eris said that he remembered this man as a boy who had gone missing many years ago. Apparently, the Mirani also hold Pengali prisoners. It's strange that no one has ever complained about this."

"People have," Mikandra said, her voice low. "But the council has never done anything. Mostly it was because they were too busy, but also because the Pengali that went missing were mostly people off the streets who didn't have family in the city, or people whose families live in Far Atok and who barely speak keihu, let alone have the confidence to report the disappearance to the council. The other group where young people have gone missing are keihu girls. There are rumours that their fathers sold these girls as whores to the Mirani army. Some even said that the men joke about how their girls would end up killing high-profile soldiers in Miran they're forced to sleep with, because they were mad. But in reality, none of the disappearances ever attracted much attention because either the vanished people don't make sympathetic subjects or the keihu establishment society feels shameful about having received money for them. It's awful."

Now *that* sounded familiar.

"How do you know all this?"

"I learned most of it when I lived in the big guesthouse in Market Street."

Wait— "You *lived* there?"

"Yes, I'd come to Barresh alone, but I was robbed. I had no money and no way to leave the place. Jocassa and his friends gave me somewhere to live." Her expression went distant with memories. "Anyway, one night a group of men came into the guesthouse, stationed guards at the exits. They took all the Pengali and keihu people out of the crowd and shone a light in their face. If a light flashed back, they would take the person."

Shit. This had been going on and no one had told her? "Who were these people?"

"Hired thugs. Some local, some Mirani ex-soldiers. No one knew where the people went. We've suspected that they went to Miran for a long time, but we never found any proof. I kind of . . . made it a personal project, with my mother . . . You know in Miran, women are taught to care for the sick, the poor and the fallen. It's how my mother feels most comfortable. But so far, we haven't had much success, because none of the abducted or sold people ever came back."

"The man we captured said they were held in a wing of an old building. He said it was an old building, in the middle of town. He said they were made to stand in the snow in a courtyard. They didn't have contact with other people."

Mikandra's eyes went wide. "The building next to the council hall?"

"He said there were pretty coloured windows and little towers everywhere."

"That's it. How many people?"

"Something like thirty."

Her expression went distant. "I know where they are." Her voice was soft. "I've seen them. You can look into the council compound from the top floor of the Trader Guild building. I was there, in one of the guest rooms and I saw these people in a building I'd thought was abandoned. I saw a fire burning in a room and people standing in front of a window looking out. The courtyard with the towers is on the other side of that wing."

"You didn't recognise any of the people?"

"The window isn't close enough to see detail of faces. All I saw were silhouettes."

"My uncle is with them."

"From Hedron?"

Izramith nodded.

In the silence that followed, she met Mikandra's eyes over the table. Here was another person whose personality she had completely misjudged.

The boy had gotten up from the table and now stood quietly next to the table, a little back from the conversation.

"Yes, Vayra?" Isandra said. "You wanted to say something?"

"I've finished," he said in a clear voice in perfect Hedron Coldi.

"All right then, run along home. Come back again in the morning."

"Can I tell Daddy about carrying the box?"

"Sure, go ahead. Hurry. Your mother will be wondering where you are." She stroked his head, her face tender.

"Bye, grandma." The boy hugged her and ran out the door. She smiled after him.

Izramith let a silence lapse.

"About that boy," she said.

They all looked at her, but no one spoke.

"He is your official family heir, isn't he? This oldest son of the oldest son?"

"He is," Isandra said.

"And he will be walking in the parade?"

"He'll be carrying the box with the arm bands."

"Don't you think he'll be at risk? They will be targeting him."

"We know. That's why we keep quiet about him. He's got enough on his shoulders for his age. We do what we can to protect him."

"He doesn't live with you?"

"No, he lives next door. Anmi, Daya's wife, is his mother."

Izramith didn't ask where the oldest son was. The family was so complicated that it made her head hurt.

Other than Rehan and his bride, this child would be a main target.

Wonderful.

~

Izramith walked back from the house seething in anger.

What was the point of hiring people and then undermining them in every way possible? Or giving them only half the information required to do their job?

Daya would have known about the boy, but he was a Hedron person through and through. Like others on Hedron, he didn't care about family in the same way other people did.

Family didn't matter on Hedron. Little else mattered either, except the company, being polite to each other, and *worker's rights*. People were all selfish and horrible. Emotion was bad. Too much emotion and you were considered unhinged. Everyone shut their doors at night. The way these people sat around the table and actually talked to each other would never happen at her house. It made her feel cranky and lonely. Seriously, how much effort would it take Mother to send her a message asking how she was?

She felt like kicking something.

And how the hell was she going to solve this security situation with a family that was too stubborn for their own good, without a huge force to lock down the city, without trustworthy support from the Barresh council and with Daya off in politics?

She had almost arrived at the guesthouse when she noticed a dark figure behind her. To be honest, someone had walked behind her most of the way down Market Street, but she had assumed this person to be just another shopper or someone returning home.

It was not.

She turned around and watched the street. The shops on one side, the apartments above the shops.

A man had stopped under a tree not far back. He was keihu, typically coarsely built, with a pudgy belly, big arms, dark hair tied back in a ponytail. He glanced aside, and his eyes met hers briefly. Then he took his unit from a pocket and turned sideways, too obviously studying his comm while still keeping an eye on her.

Wow, someone needed to get a lesson in shadowing people.

Izramith continued walking, casually picking up her reader. Her infrared sensor showed him just behind her. She slowed, and he came closer, then ducked behind a tree. She stopped and pretended to study something on the screen. He stopped as well, but not before coming even closer behind her.

She continued, walking slowly, still looking at her screen.

Then, when she was almost at the guesthouse gate, she turned around and charged for him. He was so surprised that he didn't move before Izramith pinned him to the trunk of the tree.

He squealed like an animal.

"Shut the fuck up." She pressed a hand over his mouth. He tried to bite her fingers so she clamped harder.

"Mmmmmmm!" His face went dark red.

"I'll kill you if you don't shut up. I'm serious."

He fell quiet.

"I'll take my hand away, but one shout and you're dead."

His eyes showed whites on all sides, but he nodded.

She removed her hand. His face was red where she'd clamped him.

"That's better. Now, what do you want?"

"Nothing."

"You were following me for nothing? I'll tell you, Mister. Nobody follows me for nothing."

He swallowed visibly.

He opened his mouth, but said nothing and closed it again. His gaze darted sideways.

Too late, Izramith realised that he wasn't alone. Two more

men appeared to her right side, and three to her left. They were all keihu, in dark clothing and no jewellery, but looked clean. One of the men pointed a gun at her from between the folds of his robe.

Shit.

He said, "Put your hands down. If you raise them as far as your waist, I'll shoot you."

THE MEN led Izramith back down Market Street. They surrounded her on all sides, solemn and silent like walking statues. A few nightly passersby gave the group odd glances, but most people took little notice, although Izramith by now knew that the Barresh rumour machine would be working overtime. The citizens pretended not to notice, but they saw everything. She had perhaps a day, maybe less, to get to the bottom of this before all the townsfolk knew of this excursion. She might not know the men, but those passersby all knew who they were and what they stood for. They drew their own conclusions about her being in their presence.

The commercial building had already come into view when the men turned off the main street into an alley that curved around and then ran behind the larger and more lavish houses of Market Street. One of the men pushed open a back gate and they went into a yard where bushes grew un-clipped into a wild tangle of vegetation. A fountain in the middle of the path was empty and paving broken and uneven. The house loomed on the other side of a pergola, dark, with all windows like gaping holes.

In the corner of the yard, under the pergola, was a square stone structure about knee-high, with a lid made from wooden

planks. The first man to reach it heaved the wood off to reveal a
deep hole in the ground. Some sort of underground passage or
drain. The first man climbed down.

Crap. That wasn't in the agreement. Up until now she'd felt
that she could escape if the right moment presented itself, but a
dark tunnel was not her thing. She couldn't see in the dark as
well as they did, and if it came to a fight down there, she would
be very much at a disadvantage.

The first men disappeared into the hole. Izramith could do
nothing but follow down the rusty ladder, finding the rungs by
touch. The air that wafted through smelled of mould and algae.
At the bottom of the ladder, she stepped onto solid ground slippery with slime. Some sort of stormwater drainage system. Probably highly dangerous in wet weather.

A man held up a comm unit light. Its bluish glow reflected in
walls glistening with slippery algae. They were in a tunnel that
disappeared out of sight in both directions. A stream of water
moved sluggishly through the lowest part of the tunnel.

They waited while the others came down. The last man
pulled the wooden lid over the opening again.

The group set off along the tunnel, all without speaking. The
man in front of Izramith carried a light, but in the shadow of his
broad back, it was pitch dark to her shitty night vision. Izramith
did her best not to show how little she saw. Without her infrared
scanner, she was nothing in the dark.

They walked like this for a good while. The man with the
light first, then Izramith and then all the others in single file. The
thug with the gun was behind her. The only sound was the
splashing of footsteps in puddles. The air in the tunnel was stale
and smelled of rot and other disgusting things. Izramith tried
very hard not to think of the corridors in the second level of the
old settlement. Or huge eels.

Most of the time, the group moved in pitch darkness, but
every now and then, an opening in the tunnel's roof would let in
fresh air and a smattering of light if there happened to be a street
light or a house above.

Izramith attempted to remember the turns they took, in case she had to get out in a hurry, but had no particular faith in her memory. If she had to flee, she'd be in big trouble.

Then the man in front of her turned right, up a set of stairs and through a narrow passage. The ground became dry here, and smelled of stone. He stopped at a door and knocked.

The door opened a crack. A warm glow and a smell of food spilled out, and the sound of a male voice. There was a short exchange of words in keihu and then the door opened further.

The first man went inside. The man behind Izramith said in a low voice, "Any funny business, and you're dead." As if to illustrate his words, the low light glinted off the surface of his gun's barrel.

She went through the door and came out into a large cellar room furnished as bar. Rows of stone pillars held up the low ceiling. Some of these pillars held wall brackets with light pearls. The feeble greenish glow from the pearls showed tables and chairs, many with bowls and plates, bottles and cups. At a quick count, she guessed there were at least fifty men in the room. The air was heavy with the scent of food, liquor and sweat.

When the group came in, conversations stopped, men turned in their seats.

At the far end of the room was a larger table with about eight men around it. The first of her captors spoke with one of the men. He was a rotund, grey-haired fellow and Izramith was going to assume that the younger man was his son.

The older man eyed her past the younger man's shoulder with downright hostile beady eyes. He didn't look familiar to her. Neither did the younger man look familiar now that he was in the light and she could see his face properly.

"Sit down," he said.

Two others at the table vacated their spots and retreated to the wide circle of onlookers—men only—that formed.

Izramith sat down, trying to take in the faces of those around the table. They were all keihu men, well-to-do heads of families in tent-like robes, wearing glittering jewellery and beads and plaits in their hair. It was a pity that their noses were so ugly.

The young men with the guns took up position behind her and for a while no one said anything.

Then a man with grey-flecked hair said, "We're waiting."

Another silence followed.

Waiting was fine with her. She stared at each man in turn. None could meet her eyes for very long. A low level of talk had returned to the other parts of the room.

A door creaked open somewhere. A pair of feet in sandals appeared on the stairs in the corner of the room. Then a wide robe, dark red, held out of the way by a pudgy, be-ringed hand.

Two men at the bottom of the stairs made a greeting.

The newcomer emerged fully from the stairs. With his bushy and curly hair, his broad face and shiny, pore-riddled skin, she had definitely seen him before: it was the councillor Jisson Semisu.

He strode across the room and sat down across the table from Izramith with a tinkle of armbands. He tucked a curly strand of hair behind his ear. A smile played on his face, but his red cheeks made him look flustered.

"Surprised, huh?"

"Well, yes." What did his presence here mean? That he was trying to undermine his own council? He was supposed to be Daya's advisor, not a supporter of men who kidnapped her.

He reached over the table and pulled a carafe and two glasses closer.

"Drink?"

"No, thanks."

"Suit yourself. It's safe." He poured one glass of pale orange liquid.

Izramith folded her arms over her chest. The uneasy silence lingered.

He took a sip from the glass, put it down on the table and met her eyes with a grin. "See? Not poisoned, huh?"

Izramith said nothing and let his attempt at levity hang there.

"What am I doing here?"

He put his hands on the table and joined the fingertips. He was trembling. "Well, it's like this—understand that Daya knows none of this, but since you captured Ridan—" He glanced aside. "And Ridan will probably have told you some of the story—and it's important that you understand our version of it—"

Just tell me the fucking story. I don't have all day.

He flinched at her glare. "Well, it's like this. You probably don't agree with any of it, but a keihu custom is that we—no I should say we used to—marry many times. Each time we married, a man would pay the woman's family an agreed amount of money. Which meant that having girls was valuable for parents. This meant that there were a lot of girls born. You know there are methods to . . . determine the sex before birth. There are methods so that each man only has one son and many daughters. This happened for years. Then one day, poof." He spread his hands. "Not allowed to marry more than once anymore. Not allowed to pay for it either. Many families had to rip up contracts and there was nowhere for all their daughters to go."

Probably just what they deserved.

"I see in your face that you think it serves us right, but tell that to the mothers who hoped to marry their daughters off well and use the money to live comfortably in their old age. Tell them that. Tell that to the people who were respected in this town and whose many years of work was thoughtlessly shoved aside because they spoke out in favour of the old customs. Tell that to the people who constantly have to hear that they're fat and lazy and only out for the money, who, for many years, made sure that the town didn't slide into outright war. Tell it to the fathers whose children are unhappy because everything they were promised they could be is no longer. The sons who can't find work, the daughters who can't find husbands. Tell them that."

His eyes met Izramith's eyes in a challenge.

"Anyway, so the girls stay at home. They're sad, they're bored. They get into trouble. So, one day a Mirani man comes and he says to a father: 'I want your girl.' The man is ex-army, but he now has a local business and is well known in town. He says, 'I got work for her, you'll get paid and she might even find a man.' What father of a heartbroken daughter wouldn't jump at that opportunity? So the man says: 'Your girl would have to come to Miran.' Normally, the father might have a problem with that, but at that time, he's so desperate, he just wants to see his girl do something useful. She's at home, she's slowly going crazy and he thinks every time she goes out to the baths that she'll drown herself. So, he talks to his daughter's mother and she says yes, because she has been dealing with a bored girl for much longer. And the daughter goes off to Miran."

It was so silent in the room that Izramith could hear footsteps on a tiled floor above. She said, in a low voice, "Except the family never hears from her again."

He met her eyes in a disturbed look that told her she'd guessed right.

"Why doesn't Daya know about this? Have you told him?"

"Oh, it's not *that* simple. It's a lot worse . . . to be honest."

Worse? Was that possible? People disappearing from three different places, forced to work for no money and forced to stand in the snow in their bare feet. What was going on?

"It gets worse because after she's been gone for a while, the father sends messages, which aren't answered, and tries to contact the man from Miran. He says the daughter is fine and he can deliver a message. He does, and the father receives a message back. It's written by the daughter and she says that she is happy and working hard. The father is happy for a while. But then he contacts the man again because some important day comes up like the girl's birthday. And he is told that the man will deliver a message, but it won't be free. The father pays, and the man takes the message, which is again answered by the girl. She says that she is happy and working hard, but doesn't give much more information than the previous time, so the father gets suspicious. Did she write the message or is it a copy of the first one? So he goes back to the man, and there is a problem. Because the Barresh council has passed laws that families can no longer be paid for girls, the man wants the money back because he doesn't like trouble with the council. He is, he says, going to be reasonable. The family can keep the money that the girl has earned already and will be paid in regular instalments for the rest as the girl works. At that point, the father has had enough and he says he likes to have his daughter back. But, the man says, 'Would you tear her away from a happy life? Because she is about to get married and there is no way she'll ever do this in Barresh.' The father knows all too well that this is true. There are not many boys of her age in Barresh. At that point, the Mirani man produces pictures of the daughter with a young man. The family can keep one of the pictures, he says."

Most of the other men nodded.

"The father caves in. The daughter should obviously stay in Miran. He says he can't pay the money back because he's used it, so the man offers a loan. The terms are terrible, but what is the alternative? So he agrees to the terms, but he doesn't tell his family. Instead, he shows them the picture. But instead of being happy, the girl's mother wants to visit her daughter. And the father says: 'But it's in Miran,' and she replies: 'They were good enough to rule our city for three hundred years and no one ever complained much about them then, especially not you, so why can't I visit Miran?' So the father goes back to the Mirani man to ask if a visit is possible, because, you know, if his daughter is really getting married, then the family should be invited."

He stared at the far end of the room. "At that point, there is another problem. There has been a foreigner murdered in Miran, and people are nervous. Would the father agree to house someone for a little while? 'But what about my daughter?' he asks. 'She's fine,' the man assures him. 'We'll arrange a visit when the situation is a bit better.' So the man accepts a stranger into his house. The visitor is young, male and dark-haired. He is barely ever there, so the father doesn't mind his presence in the spare room very much. The visitor stays for a few days and leaves. Before he leaves, he asks if it's all right if he leaves some stuff in the room. It's not a lot, just a few bags of clothes and personal belongings, so the father says all right, even though he knows that the women won't like it. But now at least all obstacles have been removed for him to see his daughter. By now, she's been away for over a year."

He looked aside and met the eyes of another man at the table. Their expressions were haunted; she had no other words for it.

"But when he comes to the man's house, the Mirani man is no longer there. The father hears that the Mirani business has decided to replace him with another, and this new man doesn't know anything about his daughter. He says: 'There are no keihu girls in Miran,' and when the father shows him the picture, he will point out how the picture is not real. At this point, the father will get angry and demand to see his daughter and if not, he will take the matter to the council and the guards, and the man will reply . . ."

Jisson Semisu swallowed. It had gone very quiet in the room. Few of the men watched him speak. Most stared at the table or their glass. Faces were grave and solemn.

"The Mirani man will say that if the father goes to the council or tells anyone, he will never see his daughter again. Also, because the father had the audacity to make threats to someone who's done him a favour, he is required to pay a big chunk of money to the Mirani man, or he will report the father to the Barresh council for treason, because the stuff that the visitor left behind contains spying equipment." His voice went quiet.

"The father runs back home and tips the contents of the visitor's bag on the floor, and he finds nothing. Then he investigates every part of the room. He finds bits and pieces of equipment stuck to the outside of the window and a roof ledge and on the balcony. He knows that his house is being used as a spying post, but there is nothing he can do about it."

A long silence followed. A few men nodded. One blew his nose.

"There you go. It's not pretty, but there is the story. It's happened to a number of us."

"So why are you telling me this only now?"

"Because they *would* have carried out the threats, especially to our daughters, but now you captured Ridan, and the Barresh council will find out anyway." He added almost in a whisper, "Because now there is hope."

"How many girls are we talking about?"

He handed her a piece of paper on which someone had scrawled names in the untidy and disjointed hand of someone right-handed trying to write Coldi. There were twelve names, and one Semisu girl, on the list. She met Jisson Semisu's eyes.

"That girl is my cousin's daughter. He owns the large guesthouse on the corner of Market Street. I don't get on with him very well, but he's been pushed really hard by these Mirani underworld people and doesn't deserve this. I've been trying to help him by telling him ways he can refuse an audit, even though I know how wrong that is, but . . ." He spread his hands. "He's still my family."

This was getting worse all the time. "What jobs exactly are these girls doing for the Mirani?"

"We've never been told. Daya himself should know more about it, because he only just managed to escape from Miran himself."

What?

"Please. Help us. We're desperate. We fear for our children. We fear for ourselves when the city finds out what we've done. We've lived here all our lives, and we've already been the subject of so much negative attention. If Miran finds out that we've spoken to you, they'll kill our families. They're on our roofs and in our back yards. We had to let them in. They're all over the city. They want to take out all of the Andrahar family, as well as Daya and other councillors. We've been ordered to mislead and obstruct the Barresh security operations, and we're too afraid to speak out as long as they hold our daughters."

26

IZRAMITH ASKED questions. When did they last see their daughters, who was this man who paid money in exchange for them, who was the last girl to disappear. Even if they didn't know what the girls did, what did they *think* Miran wanted with their daughters? The answers were many. To be whores, to marry mid-level officers. Some said it was to be test subjects for medical treatments.

"Because of the *gamra* boycott, Miran can't import much anymore. They're relying on their own methods and have to develop new science in a hurry."

In the end, no one could be certain about it. No one had yet been able to visit the girls.

"We don't even know if they're still alive," an older man said and several faces went sombre after that remark.

Izramith said that she would do her best to both help them and keep this meeting secret.

The room was very quiet while she walked out. She didn't look back or meet anyone's eyes.

When she was at the door, she let out a breath of relief.

Part of her oath to the Hedron guards stated that she should be prepared to die for her job. Her oath also stated that she would follow orders and never question. She already had far too many disciplinary notes on her records for questioning and disobeying rules. Some she probably earned since coming here. Disregarding Eris' concerns about breaking into that unit, bashing down the door, talking back to her employers.

It was time to step up the disobedience to a whole new level.

She'd been fucked over from all sides, especially by Daya. It was time to question.

She walked faster and then started running through the underground passage. Not from fear, but sheer pent-up anger. She found an access hole and leapt up the ladder. She came out in a street unfamiliar to her, chose a random direction and ran.

It felt so good to be doing something. This was what she had missed all that time. She'd been paralysed with fear after Indrahui. Too afraid to take action, to make decisions or assume responsibility. Too afraid to get angry.

At the street corner, she recognised the cross street as Fountain Street. She turned in that direction, towards the airport, came out in the large square, turned left, ran across the markets, where there was still plenty of night-time activity. People stared at her and scurried out of her way.

Into the street on the other side of the markets. Sunset Street. Daya's house was the first one on her right, next door to the Andrahar house.

She pushed open the gate. A guard came to look, but recognised her and stepped back. Up to the porch and into the open door.

Daya must have been warned, because he came out of one of the rooms under the gallery and stopped, staring at her.

"What have you been doing? What happened?"

She glanced down. Her clothes were covered in slime and mud, some of it caked in her ponytail. No doubt her face was dirty, too. She wiped her arm across her cheeks and it came away with a streak of blood. She didn't remember scraping or hitting anything.

"You have to call off the wedding parade." Because the

Andrahar family themselves were too fucking stubborn to do it themselves.

"Why? What's going on? Eris assured me that everything is covered."

"You and Eris and everyone in this town have had your hair pulled so far over your eyes by your own councillors, you've been too drunk to see what's going on."

His eyes widened. Having lived at Hedron, he would know what it meant for her to break ranks like this. Knowing his history, *drunk* was probably also a poor choice of words.

"You knew nothing of this scheme by Miran to force people from this town into slavery? You knew nothing of the fact that the people who make this town unsafe are right in the council? You knew nothing of the fact that they were unhappy with the way the town was going, that their daughters can't find husbands, that they're the laughing stock of everyone and that *of course* they're not going to sit back and take that treatment lying down and—"

"Whoa, whoa, slow down. Let's go inside." By the expression on his face, he seemed genuinely rattled. Well, he deserved to be.

He opened the door of the room where he had just come out. It was a library, a luxurious room with a soft carpet and beautiful furniture. A window at the far end looked out over the marshlands.

A set of couches directly opposite the door was empty, but a light stood on the floor in the corner and a woman and three young boys sat around it, the glow gilding their faces. One of the boys was the Andrahar heir whom Izramith had seen at their house.

The other two were younger, chubbier and both had the black hair and eyes of their father.

Wasn't it way past the children's bedtime? Whatever had they been doing?

The woman rose in a fluid motion while cradling a baby in the crook of her arm.

She was almost as tall as Daya and, dressed in a robe with many folds over a multi-layered dress, more imposing.

Izramith had never seen a female *zhadya*-born. Her eyes were fathomless black as Daya's, her face pale with prominent cheekbones. Her hair, straight and dark, hung past her shoulders.

"This is Anmi Kirilen Dinzo, head of Anara Teren, our research and education facility, and mother of my boys."

Izramith nodded a polite greeting. The familiar chill went over her.

The infant squirmed and raised two little hands. The woman turned him around so his belly leaned into her, patting his back. How old was this baby? He didn't look much older than Shada when she had last seen him.

"I'm sorry if I disturbed you."

"The boys were having a welcome ceremony for their little brother," Daya said. "He was born late this afternoon."

When she had been looking for Daya in the council building. Had no one at the council known this?

"I'm sorry, I didn't mean to be rude."

The woman's expression said *You're already rude.* Izramith cringed. Thimayu wasn't even fully recovered from the birth two days later.

"I *am* sorry, but I've made an important discovery."

The woman sat down at the chair at the desk, still patting the baby. She spoke to the other boys in a low voice, telling them to keep sitting quietly, judging by her hand gestures. The language she spoke didn't sound familiar at all.

"Now, what is the problem?" Daya asked. She could almost feel his annoyance.

Izramith told him as much as she dared to share of what Jisson Semisu had told her. She didn't mention names or descriptions of any who had been in the cellar. She named the prisoner Ridan as her source of data.

"So you did get some information out of him after all," he said. "Good. I heard about him, and intended to question him tomorrow."

Intended? Past tense?

"The guards found him dead not long after being locked in

his cell."

Shit. Was he that afraid of being handed back to Miran?

"What he said was clear: your betrayers are in the council. They sit opposite you at meetings and know everything because everyone trusts them. They are not even willing traitors, but they act out of despair and powerlessness."

"No one is powerless in this town."

"Maybe not, but they have less power than before. They feel unhappy and marginalised and powerless to change their lot. People laugh at them, how they'd been primitive, stupid and a lot of other things I don't need to repeat, but I'm sure you know. They provide inroads for the Mirani army. Or rather, were approached by the Mirani army. They allowed their property to be used. They are reluctant to act against Miran because their daughters are in Mirani control. Miran is holding twelve girls, and also some Pengali."

She took a deep breath and plunged in further. She knew how powerful this man was.

"The old councillors say that the council ignores their concerns, pushes ahead with reforms they don't support and that the new laws hurt their families."

"You do know that in the past, these men had many wives, often too young to be jumped on by an old man."

"I know, and I don't defend them, but I do understand what their problem is. We're standing in a town that's been theirs for hundreds of years. They feel like everyone is walking over them."

He said, sharply, "And have you seen what a mess they made of the place?"

He rose, went to the window and balled his fists against the glass. Breathed out deeply and came back to his seat.

He was quiet for a while. "This concerns all the old keihu councillors?"

"Lead by Jisson Semisu and his followers."

"Impossible!"

"Yet it's true."

"Nonsense. I would trust those men with my life."

"Well then maybe you need to re-examine your concept of trust." She'd said it before she realised what she had done.

In a few steps, he crossed the room and stopped in front of her. *Really* close. Shivers-down-her-spine kind of close. His face was hard and unemotional. The depth of his eyes whirled with anger. This was the man who, as an adolescent, had terrorised Edyamor and his family, smashed up his room, drunk himself into rages of anger.

This was the man who, when followed by Commander Blue, had climbed into a boiling hot steam vent, lived to tell the tale and unleashed a blinding flash across the valley. This was the man who, with those flashes, disturbed the Exchange reception at Hedron, and the man who was feared so much at Hedron that no one dared ask him how he did it.

Blue sparks flashed across his eyes.

Izramith retreated, but she was as good as dead already.

Anmi said something.

Daya turned his head to her. He said nothing, but the tension was broken. He breathed out heavily. Even his breath felt icy cold.

Izramith spoke slowly. "Why. The hell. Did you appoint me?"

Anmi said, "He didn't want to appoint you. I did." She rose and walked through the room with the grace of a hunting animal, while still carrying the baby. This woman had given birth this afternoon?

Daya snapped something back at her.

She replied in Coldi. "She deserved to know. I didn't trust those friends of yours as much as you did. And it seems I was right, wasn't I?"

Oh, for fuck's sake, that's all she needed, to be caught up in a spat between two halves of a powerful couple.

Daya sighed and balled his fists.

He turned to the window again and slammed his hand flat onto the glass. The smack startled the baby. The three other boys still sat around the light, quiet and subdued. Large eyes blinking in the low light. Had they learned to keep out of the way when their father was angry?

Anmi met Izramith's eyes, dark and penetrating. A corner of her mouth lifted. "You did well."

Daya snorted. He turned back to the couch and sat down.

He said nothing for a long time, and then he blew out a breath. "Jisson Semisu. Why did he talk to you?" The latter to Izramith.

"Because we captured Ridan, a bunch of the councillor's sons tried to silence me, so that I wouldn't tell you what he had told me about the councillors. But these men couldn't kill a fish if they tried. They are as unprepared for this sort of conflict as the rest of this town, so they took me to see him instead. He says he and his people are sick of being the joke of town. He says their daughters had no future, so Miran offered them work, and they paid for the girls in the way this used to happen in this town. He said you should know what work these people are doing for Miran, because you barely escaped from Miran yourself."

Daya came back to the couch and put both his hands on the backrest.

"It is true that Miran tried to kill me," he said in a low voice. "When I first came here. It's . . . a long and unpleasant story. You may hear it some day. Most likely, you will not. When I escaped, they tried to blackmail me. They wanted to hold me hostage because they thought my father was trying to insert spies into Barresh."

Izramith laughed, not in a happy way. "Since when have Coldi fathers cared about their *sons*?" Especially the *zhadya*-born ones. Coldi fathers cared about their daughters, because they continued the line of family inheritance—from father to daughter to son to daughter. "What Miran did had nothing to do with your father. It was because of what you are. Nemedor Satarin has a breeding program for your type of people and that's why he wanted you."

"Nemedor Satarin never stops expressing his contempt for foreigners. He would not actively encourage them to come to Miran."

"That's why he has no trouble treating foreigners like second-rate citizens. He's got people from Barresh. He's got people from Hedron, people like you. I have no doubt that he's got people from Asto, too. I suggest that you talk to your father. I highly suspect that people have gone missing from Asto, too."

This was like the escape of the Ezmi clan from Asto all over again, poor and disenfranchised people driven away from Coldi society. No one seemed to have learned anything.

Damn, she was near on fire with anger.

"Why wasn't I told about your escape from Miran? What good is it to me now? We've got this whole fucking mess, and not enough time to sort it out before the wedding. I've asked the family to postpone it, but they don't want to. The whole upmarket end of town have sold themselves to Miran, and Mirani spies could be in every house along the way. Seriously, how could anyone ever be so lax with security? Why weren't people told? Why do you have Barresh and Asto security running around and no one knows what everyone else is doing? Why?"

He said nothing.

Licked his lips.

Sighed and got up from the couch. He walked to the window and back. As he passed Izramith, a waft of hot air followed in his wake.

Anmi's dark eyes followed him. Her expression was one of interested curiosity. *Look at this crazy woman who dares to piss off my husband.*

Did she see a hint of admiration in her face?

Izramith didn't care what he thought of her or about his status. She no longer cared what the guards at home thought, or whether there was still a job for her at Hedron at the end of this contract. Fuck Hedron. She was going to sell herself as mercenary to Indrahui or something. And fight and shoot people for the rest of her life. She didn't even care if she lived or died.

Daya let another long silence lapse. Then he said, "Barresh has probably grown too quickly. Taken on too many projects. All the work we've done in this town has concentrated on construction, on meeting *gamra* requirements, on expanding our reach, being inclusive to the Pengali, educating them, righting the wrongs of the past."

"So, you've fucked up in the security department?"

"Essentially, yes."

"And in a couple of days, we have a huge public event that is a major security risk and any work I've done so far has not only uncovered far more trouble than my contract stipulated, but has increased that risk."

"It seems so."

"Great. We've been going backwards since I started here."

Daya said, "I don't think the risk is so great anymore. You've taken out the spy station and I think we're well-cover—"

"You don't think anything. You don't know anything about security. That's why I'm here, and I say it's a fucking mess. I have never seen such a mess, and I've served at Indrahui, and that is a shithouse mess. If you hold that parade, almost every house along those streets could have a sniper in it. I have no time and no people to comb the area. I have no authority to search the councillors' houses. They've just admitted that there are devices and people hiding on the roofs."

He spread his hands and rolled his eyes at the ceiling. "Then, miss security guard, what do you suggest we do?"

Izramith let a silence lapse, aware that every eye in the room was on her.

She said, "The main problem, why the council is reluctant to do anything, is because Miran holds these girls hostage. The councillors are afraid for their loved ones. As long as the girls are in Miran, you will never get their full assistance. You will never get the councillors to let guards search their houses. You will never get Jamis Semisu to agree to have the guesthouse audited because the missing Semisu girl is his daughter."

"Yes, you told me all that, but, sitting in my position, what would you do about it?" His voice was sarcastic now.

"Because Barresh is small, there is only one thing you can do: something radical. Something they don't expect."

"Sure." Daya raised his eyebrows. "Did you have anything radical in mind?"

Izramith grinned. "I belong to the radical clan."

His face twitched. All right, so he didn't appreciate that joke. As Ezmi having grown up on Asto, she should probably have suspected.

She said, her voice more serious, "I'd propose to lead a team of people into Miran to free these girls, the Pengali and any other prisoners we find."

Daya snorted. "Free them? By force?"

"By stealth. I know where they are. I need an aircraft, someone who speaks Mirani and can pass for a local, a few people who can handle a gun and a pilot." In her mind, her team was already forming. Wairin, Braedon as Mirani guide, Braedon as sharpshooter and Braedon as pilot. Dashu and Eris were optional, as long as they didn't whinge about rules broken.

He said, "It's a crazy, stupid plan."

"It would fix the problem in one swoop."

"Only temporarily. Make Miran angry enough and they'll retaliate. No one has ever accused Nemedor Satarin for being sensible."

Anmi was shaking her head, while regarding Izramith with a curious expression. "I don't think you give the man enough credit. He's blunt, but he's smart, or he wouldn't have been able to lure those people out of Hedron. He knows when to be nice if he needs to. He offered the Andrahar family help, too. Likely, he sent someone to Hedron under the guise of being a merchant, and offered personal invitations."

Izramith nodded. She had wondered why the number of Mirani visitors to Hedron had increased so much lately.

Back to the original problem. "So, what do you think? Are we going to do this?"

"It's crazy."

"Yes."

"We risk the situation blowing up in our face just before the wedding."

"There is no point in going ahead with the festivities if we can't secure the streets."

He nodded, his face grave. Then he said, "We do something *after* the wedding." His voice was intense. "That's my final decision. I'll see you tomorrow to discuss what needs to be done to make the festivities safe."

That was as clear a dismissal as any, and after that disappointment, Izramith had no desire to stay in that house for longer than necessary.

She left the room for the hall. Anmi followed her, still carrying the baby.

Izramith thought it was to see her out and make sure that she left, but as soon as the door to the library had shut, Anmi said, "Thank you."

Izramith wasn't sure what she needed to be thanked for. "I'm sorry for coming at such a . . . personal time."

She shrugged. The baby squirmed and started to make noises.

"Did you really hire me?"

"I made a very strong suggestion to Daya to appoint someone from outside Barresh and he said he'd only have someone from Hedron because others wouldn't understand him. He wasn't very happy about it. I was worried. The Barresh council all live in each other's pockets. We've tried to make it better but recently it has been getting worse. The guesthouse refusing audits. Threats made to the Andrahar family while they were in Barresh, threats that clearly came from within Barresh. Daya has been drawn into the culture of the councillors and their families. It's easy and comfortable if you're a man and if you have money. He's been under a lot of stress. And now this . . ." She stroked the baby's back, staring at some spot in the distance. "Our efforts to resurrect the Aghyrian race are in crisis, too. Since we started a few years back, twenty-three children have been born. They're all boys. He's . . . extremely disappointed to have yet another boy."

"I'm sorry." The poor little bundle reminded her so much of Shada. Izramith knew all too well about that kind of disappointment. "You know . . . one of the reasons I came here was to look for a place for my nephew to grow up. My sister put him in the care of so-called professionals. He was only two days old." A wave of emotion threatened to overwhelm her. "Especially because . . . it seems you know what to do to stop people like you . . ." She almost said *zhadya*-born. ". . . going mad."

"We do. We help a lot of people. Please, don't let Daya's outbursts stop you bringing your nephew here. He desperately wants girls for his program, but we care a lot about every child. When I'm . . . a bit better at walking, come to see me and I can show you around the school and what we're doing. It's important that your nephew learns how to let the energy escape from his body before the buildup does any permanent damage."

"Energy?" A white flash across the screen in Commander Blue's recording.

"It's called *avya*. When we're in sunlight or hot weather, our bodies are charged with energy. With no way to get rid of it, that energy will build in the body until it starts affecting the mind. Look." She held her free hand palm up. A tiny spot of light flickered into existence in the middle of her palm. "It won't always look as dramatic as this, but the majority of Aghyrians need to learn how to control it."

Izramith stared at the spot. It looked like the butt of a glow bug without the actual bug. "Does that . . . hurt?"

"If you leave that energy inside, it hurts."

"That's why people go mad and become crazy murderers at Hedron?"

"Exactly. And there is no need for that slide into insanity if the boys learn early enough. Bring your nephew when you can. I'm serious."

"I will. Thank you." And she felt like she had never meant anything more seriously. Then she added, "I hope you'll recover quickly."

Anmi smiled. "Giving birth is never again as hard as the first time. You'll find out."

27

BUT OF COURSE Izramith would never find out what it was like to give birth, because her contract with Indor was dead and if ever she got out of this mess, she'd sign up for some sort of mercenary position.

Briefly, just briefly, she'd tasted life as a woman with her own family, but now she had gone back to feeling sorry for all the twenty-three little boys, who, even though they were unwanted, would still have a life much better than her nephew.

For that matter, what did this dignified, beautiful woman see in an arrogant arsehole like Daya? Since when did a woman have to apologise for the actions of her partner?

She crossed the yard back to the street and hesitated just outside the gate in the shadow of the trees. Light still burned in the house of the Andrahar family. If she walked a few paces back and looked down the side of the house, she could see the glint of light on an aircraft. She thought she spotted a velvet-dark craft. So Braedon had come back.

She could go there and pretend to be checking something on the listening equipment. Except of course she had no idea what to check, because she didn't know more than the basic operations on the equipment.

Also the family were probably about to go to bed and wouldn't appreciate a random visit from a stranger, not even for a proverb-fight with their mother. The old lady would probably have gone to bed long ago.

So yeah, Izramith could just go to her guesthouse with the unfriendly matron and the luxurious but boring room, she could walk through the streets and freak out over all the old keihu family mansions and their unknown contents, or she could—

There was a noise a bit further down the street. A shuffle of feet on pavement, a sigh or repressed sneeze.

Izramith froze and stared into the darkness. The noise stopped, so she very quietly crept forward. She unclipped the gun from its bracket and turned on the infrared sensor on her gun. It wasn't as good as the dedicated one, and the screen was very small, but she didn't have her helmet. As she pointed the gun in various directions, the tiny viewfinder screen showed clearly that the house next to the Andrahars' was abandoned. It showed no heat source inside.

In the Andrahar house, there were light-coloured spots in some of the rooms. A few standing in front of the window.

Izramith picked up movement at the corner of the Andrahar yard. A narrow alley ran between the outer wall and the next yard.

She ran into the alley, weaving between bushes and piles of abandoned wood and other rubbish. Who left all this rubbish here? Did no one know the security risk of—

Her foot caught behind something. She fell on one knee and managed to recover herself well enough to avoid an embarrassing situation.

"What the fu—"

A wire ran across the alley. It went up the wall, through one of the ornate metalwork grates and disappeared there.

A *trip* wire. The same as the ones in the forest.

Going to the house.

Shit.

Shit, shit, shit.

She grabbed her comm unit and rummaged through her contacts.

Braedon, Braedon, where was—oh, there.

"Braedon!"

No reply yet.

"Braedon—"

"What's going on?"

"You have to get everyone out of the house now. There's trip wire out here."

"Wait, wait. Where are you?" A light flicked on at her side of the house and a silhouette appeared at the window.

"In the street outside your house. I can see you. Come down now. Tell everyone to get out."

Izramith climbed up using the ornate metal fencework on a grate set into an alcove in the wall. She jumped down on the other side of the wall and landed heavily on the paving. It jarred her knees. Ouch, higher gravity.

She directed her light onto the grate. The wire went to ground level, into a planter box with a clipped bush. At the base of the bush, a small device had been taped onto the stem. Something blinked there.

All she could see was the dreadful explosion of the hideout in the forest. Trip wire. Blinking lights.

Someone ran into the yard from the house.

"Izramith?"

She showed him what she had discovered by following the wire with her light.

Without a word, he dropped to his knees.

The wire stopped at the device, but clearly it was sending commands to elsewhere. But where was the main control box?

She needed Dashu here with her equipment, but there was no time.

"Go, go, get the family out."

Braedon ran off, and she pulled out her comms and called up Dashu anyway, but she would come too late. Maybe not, it was worth a try.

Izramith crouched next to the bush. From where the device sat, the range would cover about half the garden. Most of it was paved, except for the fountain and that planter box with the wire frame and the creeping vine with the floppy flowers which covered the bench underneath.

She remembered: a wire frame held up the bush. Holy crap. A perfect receiver.

She ran through the garden, yanked at the frame, uprooted it. It wouldn't come out, because the vine held it in place. And wires. She pushed the frame sideways as far as she could, dug into the soft earth underneath, her fingers following the wires into the ground by touch.

The sound of agitated voices drifted from inside the house. Someone—Braedon probably—ran through the yard back to the house. Then the children came out, and Isandra in a white night gown, all walking quickly towards the gate.

Izramith's fingertips found bristly wire ends. Ouch, that pricked. Underneath, her hands closed on another hard object. She dug away in the dirt, trying to get her fingers around it, trying to lift it out of the soil. It wouldn't budge. She dug, scooping handfuls of dirt onto the pavement. Sand clung to her sweaty arms.

Someone appeared next to her. The youngest Andrahar brother Taerzo. "I know about mine explosives," he said. He went to the other side of the basin and helped her dig.

They uncovered the box, lifted it out—it was encased in a metal housing. Taerzo ran off, she had no idea where to. She studied the casing, looking for a sign of what it did or how to open it.

Taerzo came back with a handheld tool that had a vicious saw blade at the end. He revved it up. Sparks flew while he cut around the top. The cover fell off.

A control device indeed.

Mirani-made. She had seen these types of things in her training. She had even looked at that information before coming here, because of the Mirani merchants smuggling them. But she had never touched this kind of device.

And her mind had gone blank on how to disarm it, except she remembered being told repeatedly that turning it off would set the explosive off immediately. There had to be a code. The time on the device was slowly ticking away. Of course this device was slightly different from the ones covered in her training. What was it about these controllers?

Izramith studied the screen. "What does this say?"

"It says it's live. Going off in thirty, twenty-nine . . ."

"Shit." She could smash the thing but that would only set it off.

Wait. Those timers could be disrupted by a strong external signal. She held her comm next to it and issued a message blast. All around Barresh, people would be waking up now from her messages.

She held her breath. The blinking light stopped.

Taerzo blew out a deep sigh. He sank down on the lover's bench, on top of the fallen flowers, his head in his hands.

Braedon's pale face looked in from the street through the metal latticework in the wall. There were voices in the street behind him, and a child was crying.

"I think we've got it disarmed," Izramith said. Her heart was still thudding.

"Damn, I hope so."

"I've got to find the explosives before anyone can go back into the house."

"Wait. I'll come and help you."

A moment later, the gate creaked and Braedon came back, together with Rehan.

"Is it safe to approach the house?" Rehan asked.

"I think so. The ignition has been disarmed, but don't touch anything, especially not items that can be moved, like furniture or plants."

Taerzo joined his brother up the path. A moment later, the light from Rehan's comm device lit up the dark space under the porch. He scanned the walls, found nothing and jumped off the porch, looking underneath.

"This is going to take a long time," Izramith said to Braedon. "You're better off taking the family somewhere else."

Braedon went back out the gate. People were talking out there and a moment later the gate opened again and someone tall with curly hair came in.

Daya.

He came straight for her.

"Need help?" He spoke in clipped Hedron Coldi. Very business-like.

"I've called Dashu and asked for Eris. He's got explosives and tech experience. He should be here soon."

Daya nodded and looked at the house, where Rehan and Taerzo were still examining the outer walls.

Izramith was wondering if he was going to say anything else. Something like *sorry for doubting you* or *I think you might be right* would do for her, but that didn't seem to be part of his vocabulary.

28

IZRAMITH REMAINED with Rehan and Braedon in the garden, assisting Dashu and Eris and other security crews when they arrived. When daylight came, Izramith left the house and walked back to her guesthouse room.

The markets were in full swing already, with a steady stream of people wheeling trolleys with produce from the local fields up the hill. There were tottering piles of baskets with leaves, nuts, fruit and fish. Also, bags full of flowers, which a couple of Pengali men were weaving into ornamental headdresses. Probably some festivity going on.

She came past the airport, where a number of private craft stood in the corner furthest away from the building. Two bored guards leaned against the gate.

Just a normal day in Barresh. No one cared much about the missing girls apart from their families. No one cared about the missing Pengali and the missing *zhadya*-born at all. Worlds were not so different from each other. They each had groups that were too distanced from the society norm to be truly part of that society. Governments didn't judge these people worth the risk of sparking a conflict. Their relatives didn't have the power or were too tied up in abusive structures to challenge.

She arrived in her room, and sat with her reader on the bed, flicking through maps of Miran. The city had a classic village structure, like Pataniti, but of course much bigger. The city's centre was a square, with the council buildings along the north side: a huge interlinking complex with a couple of different building styles and courtyards big enough to land an aircraft.

The more she thought of it, the more she realised that she would be the ideal person to mount a private action to free these people and the more she wanted to do it. Between maps and pictures of the council building complex in Miran and Mikandra's description, she could tell where the group was likely to be held. The Mirani Trader Guild headquarters were to the north-west of the square. A narrow street ran in between it and a part of the council buildings that, on the satellite image, were not marked as in use for anything. From the top floor of the back of the Trader Guild building, you would be able to see over the wall that surrounded the council complex, and you'd see parts of those wings.

She could go to Miran with a team pretending to be visitors of some kind. Over the days that she'd been here, she'd been surprised at how many shuttle flights still went to and from Miran. The borders were not entirely sealed. If Miran was like Hedron, shuttle crew had immunity from border checks anyway, as long as they didn't leave the airport. Merchants and private people still travelled to Miran, and they weren't all Mirani either.

With a bit of dressing up, she could pass for a merchant. She'd seen old bits and pieces of security equipment for sale in a shop. She could carry those along as "demonstration material", as long as the equipment in question didn't violate the boycott on imports into Miran.

A team would go in and climb the wall that surrounded the complex at night. They would take the people into the courtyard. The person flying the craft would then bring it and land it in the courtyard.

What would she need?

An aircraft, a pilot, a couple people handy with guns, especially when hanging out an aircraft, someone who spoke Mirani well enough to pass as local.

Getting the people . . . might not be a problem, although she doubted that any of the Andrahar brothers would be interested, but who would lend an aircraft for this mad mission? The brothers' Traders' Craft were all too small.

For the next few days, Izramith and the team spent a frustrating amount of time doing mundane work: checking out all the councillors' yards and overseeing the issuing of passes for the day. Every time when in the street, one of the councillors who had been at the cellar meeting walked past her, Izramith wanted to scream at him, *It's not my fault that no one is doing anything.* It wasn't entirely true that nothing happened. Rehan agreed to change the route so that it wouldn't go past the guesthouse or the commercial building. It would now go one block further to the north and go past the Exchange instead. Izramith didn't think it was enough, and would have preferred the parade to be cancelled in favour of a street party at the markets, but at least the parade no longer went past a number of houses in the hands of risk families. And the parade might yet be cancelled; there were some rumours about that. Even the larger security force was paralysed with indecision: there were those who agreed with Izramith and those, mainly older ones, who said threats and posturing by Miran was nothing new and the best response was to ignore it.

A middle-aged Kedrasi woman replaced Loxa. She was a good worker, but very quiet and Dashu didn't speak to her more than necessary. In fact, Dashu didn't speak much at all, except to announce publicly that after the wedding she would go back to her family in Athyl. Eris became withdrawn as well, but it took a lame joke about how he would have to develop a ceramic skin for Izramith to realise that there had been a lot more going on under the surface of her team.

"You not know?" Wairin asked her when she commented to

him about it. "Loxa and Dashu—they *zhaymas*. But Eris, he have stars in his eyes when she walk past."

And that made Izramith angry. Well, why the fuck would she get angry with Daya's ineptitude to judge people when her own judgement was just as bad?

She might as well face it: the team was broken and Izramith didn't know how to fix it.

They saw little of Braedon. He only came in for short periods of time, and Izramith got no opportunity to speak to him alone.

If she had, she wouldn't have known what to say to him anyway. All his actions showed that he was happy with their pledge of *nethana* and had moved on. Like most Traders, he probably visited companion ladies a lot and thought nothing more of their one-night stand.

But every time he did walk into the security room, or met the team in the street, the light became a little brighter, and the breeze a little warmer. Izramith tried to get to speak to him personally, but the one time she did, on the stairs leading up to the foyer, she clammed up and didn't know what to say.

She was standing there, her mind gone blank, looking into his eerily light eyes and all she could think of was seeing his eyes closed and the look on his face as he spilled himself inside her. The feel of his hair under her hands. The male scent of his sweat. Thoughts like that would normally set off a flush, and by now enough days had gone past that she could flush again. But no matter how much she wanted the flush to happen, it wouldn't come. See? Even her own body thought she was being stupid.

And Braedon said, "Well then, I'll go back to work." And went back to his job, leaving her to stand on the stairs, screaming frustration on the inside.

For fuck's sake, three simple words shouldn't be so hard to say.

I was wrong would have been a good starting point, not to think of all the other three-word sentences that she wanted, but was too afraid, to say.

So he left the building and did not look back.

~

A couple of days before the wedding, the pace increased. A small Rhion craft arrived from Hedron. Izramith happened to be at the Exchange and from the large window that overlooked the square, she could see Ydana and Amandra Bisumar come down the ramp, in the presence of their adopted children. They both wore the purples and lilacs of the Hedron Traders and, since the picture Izramith had seen of the couple, she had cut her hair even further so it was now short and spiked-up, like Mikandra's. She also wondered why, as Traders and with at least two aircraft between them, they'd use a shuttle, but on further inspection, there were a lot more small shuttles at the airport. The Andrahar family had probably hired them to bring their guests to Barresh. Some people had entirely too much money.

Izramith met a group of pilots later in the street. Laughing, talking, all dressed in Pilot Guild uniform. Her eyes met those of one of the female pilots. While as guard, she had seen most of these people before, this particular woman was different: she had also served at Indrahui.

She saw the Trading family later in the afternoon, too, when she walked into the guesthouse and they were coming out, talking and laughing like a happy family.

There were guards everywhere on the streets now, and Eris had his hands full managing them. From the security room, Izramith could now see along the entire route through cameras Dashu and her council workers had installed, and someone attended the station at all times.

It was Izramith's turn that night.

She sat in the chair in the middle of the room struggling not to fall asleep. The last few nights she had slept badly again. Seriously, that adaptation crap was supposed to have finished by now.

Darkness was falling over the city outside. Flocks of meili fluttered between the trees. She switched to the camera that stood at the back of the Andrahar house. Daya had just come out of the balcony door for his daily feeding ritual. It was such an oddly private moment for a man whose social awkwardness rolled off him in waves.

Izramith almost felt sad when the moment was over, the contents of the bowl consumed and the furry visitors had gone back to their trees. She returned to her regular program: Sunset Street, markets and square, Fountain Street—

Wait, what was that?

A golden-curled head in the citizens at Fountain Street. Not just anyone, but a familiar face: Ridan.

Eris was off-duty, but she called him anyway. He answered his comm with a lot of noise in the background.

"You know how we got the news that Ridan apparently killed himself in jail? Have you seen a death report?"

She had to repeat her question. He was, he said, at a family function and couldn't hear her very well.

No, he hadn't seen the death report. "But that's not unusual. It's not my job to look at those. Why?"

"Because he's walking down Fountain Street."

"You're sure? Wait for me, I'm coming in."

Izramith protested, but he said the party was boring anyway and was looking for a way to escape.

But when Eris had turned up, and they'd run the security camera recordings through the face recognition, the man turned out to be someone different. Moreover, Izramith began to think that this could be the man she had seen making threats to the young Semisu nephew on her second night in Barresh.

"Ridan said he was born from a keihu mother and a Mirani Endri father. There are obviously more of these people that look like him of similar parentage. Ridan might have turned against the Mirani, but others clearly haven't. We might have dented their plans, but we haven't killed them. Those people are even still walking around the streets. No matter what Daya says, I think we need to get the councillors' full cooperation before, and not after the wedding. They've admitted that there will be people in town who have sold out to Mirani interests. I know you've been through the wedding guest list extensively, but there are members of old keihu families on that list, and until we solve the problem of their girls kept hostage, we can't trust any of them."

Eris nodded, his face dark. "Believe me, we all know that you're right. It's just that right now, with as little time as we have, all we can do is instate a contingency plan."

"Or do something that no one expects." Like strike deep into Miran and free those people.

Except she still hadn't solved the aircraft problem.

Well, bugger that.

She leaned on an elbow, staring at the many recordings of the security cameras. People walking to the markets, people carrying their purchases home, people talking at eateries, a line of people walking from the half-completed aircraft building—

And then she had another crazy idea.

Silence fell in the room when Izramith finished speaking. It was late and the Andrahar house was quiet—no twins running in the hall, no voices in the kitchen.

Outside the large window everything was dark. She couldn't even see the outlines of the aircraft, only her own reflection, and that of Braedon's and Rehan's backs, in the glass.

Rehan regarded her with a serious expression on his face. She would have preferred not to have him here. He seemed too friendly with Daya. But Taerzo, whom she'd judged more inclined to agree to her plan, was on a business run and Rehan had opened the door and he had let her into the formal living room.

"So, essentially, you want to run a quick mission into the heart of Miran, free these people and get out again?" Rehan's voice sounded incredulous, sarcastic even.

"Pretty much."

"Whatever makes you think that crazy plan will work?"

"There are no guarantees, ever, that anything will work."

"No, of course not." In a don't-be-smart-with-me tone.

Izramith glanced at the clothes stand in the far corner of the room. On it hung a heavily embroidered dress with a sheer, see-through veil. It was pretty, but not elaborate enough to be the family's wedding costume, she thought.

"However," she continued in a lower voice, "It is something Miran won't be expecting."

"Well, that is true." He frowned and then met her eyes. "Does anyone know of this?"

"I proposed it to Daya, but he didn't like it."

"I'd say for good reason. This is the craziest thing I've ever heard." But he continued to frown and his voice had lost some of its sting.

"We don't need Daya's approval to do this. In fact, the less people know about it, the better."

"But—what is the plan? I haven't heard you talk about anyone except yourself. You're going to need help. There are at least thirty of these people, if not more. How do you expect to walk into Miran and demand their freedom. For one, you'd never get a visitor's permit, not in the current climate."

"I'm not demanding anything. We'll go up to the part of the building in question, and simply free them."

"I understand that part, but how would you even get into Miran?"

"Well . . . We pretend we're someone else, like a passenger flight. There happens to be a suitable craft I could borrow."

"One of the passenger shuttles?" Braedon's eyes were wide.

Rehan said, "Tell me the fuck you're kidding."

"Nope. I served at Indrahui with the pilot."

"Shit." Silence. "You're serious, right? You could lose your job."

"My contract is about to finish anyway."

Braedon gave her a glance of astonishment. "The crew could lose their jobs."

"We don't need a crew. We need a pilot." She didn't let her gaze waver from Braedon's.

He blew out a forceful breath and hid his face in his hands.

"The fuck you don't, brother," Rehan said. "Don't you go doing stupid things. One conviction and your licence gets suspended."

Braedon nodded slowly. He looked at his folded hands on his knees. "Yup. We know that from experience. It's much safer if we don't do silly things like that."

"Good. Then we're in agreement."

"However, I suspect that she will go anyway."

Izramith nodded. "Whether Daya agrees or not, we can't sit here and—"

"She is one of the Hedron guards and has no personal involvement in this issue—"

"—I do, actually—"

Braedon kept talking. "Miran is our nation. I've kept my citizenship because I hope that some time in the future people will see sense and get rid of this tyrant and his lackeys. However, that is not going to happen unless people see the truth of what sort of person Nemedor Satarin really is. In one way or another, we've known about these prisoners for a long time. Everyone's been talking about it, even at the Mirani chapter of the guild. They were always rumours denied by the council, but we know that anything like this that the council denies is likely true. We've stood by and let it happen, too busy saving ourselves. Well, guess what? I'm not busy anymore. Out of the three of us, my business has taken the hardest hit. I had a successful Trading business and now I don't. My business was reliant on Miran and the Miran hospital, where I can barely travel these days without someone attempting to stick a knife up my back. I love Miran, and one day hope to go back there. For that to happen, it is important that we get rid of the tyrant. Maybe we should stand up and see that their deeds are exposed. It's all very well to hide in Barresh, but if even someone who has no personal involvement—"

"I do. My uncle is in Miran."

Both Braedon and Rehan looked at her. Braedon's face was red.

Izramith said in a low voice, "So, the expedition is on?"

"I'll be your pilot."

Rehan interrupted. "No, if you're going, I will fly the craft. I know the procedures and routes to take. I can make it look like we're a commercial shuttle."

"You're not going, brother. They almost killed you last time you were in Miran, and you're about to get married. When I die, I will leave no one. I won't even leave anyone a business to look after, at least none to speak of!" His face had gone red again.

A tense silence followed Braedon's outburst.

Braedon pressed his balled fist against his lips. His nostrils flared and his chest heaved with deep breaths.

After a tense silence, he said, "I will go with her, because if someone will be kind enough to shoot me, I will die having done something useful with my life." He rose and strode across the room. He opened the door, and screamed, "Fuck it!"

His voice echoed in the hall.

He slammed the door behind him, leaving Rehan and Izramith behind in astonished silence. The door opened again, and Mikandra came in. "Was that Braedon?"

"It was," Rehan said. His voice sounded astonished or awed, it was hard to decide which. Braedon who never lost his temper, who had told her that it was part of a Trader's ethics to keep calm. Who had driven her mad by being calm.

Mikandra said, "What got into him? I've never heard him swear."

"I don't know." Rehan shrugged. "Ever since that incident in the forest, he hasn't been the same." He met Izramith's eyes. "Did anything happen out there that could have rattled him more than having shot a few men while we were escaping Miran?"

Izramith spread her hands. "It was violent, but no more than what he described to me about your escape from Miran. He's very good with a gun. He's very gentle and I'd never expected him to be such an ace. Maybe the thought that he kills so easily upsets him."

That thought made her shiver. Killing was surprisingly easy. It was the thoughts you had about it afterwards that were hard.

Izramith left, unsure what to do now. The Rhion was free tonight or tomorrow, but she would be missed at work tomorrow, and any moment they waited was a moment that someone could suspect what they were doing. She wanted to leave as soon as possible, but didn't see Braedon anywhere in the hall. Did this mean he was still coming? Was anyone going to ask him?

Rehan was definitely coming, he confirmed that. Mikandra glanced up the stairs a few times and before she could offer to come instead of Braedon, Izramith said, "That's his room up there?"

She nodded.

Izramith climbed the stairs. She didn't miss the first door on her right being ajar and quickly pushed shut and didn't miss the sound of children's voices. If one needed to know what went on in the house, those boys would know everything.

She knocked on the door. "Braedon?"

A moment later, the door was opened.

Braedon had changed out of his uniform into sturdy trousers, dark-coloured, and a jacket of the same fabric. Both had plenty of pockets. He wore a belt with a Mirani-style dagger and a Mirani crossbow over his shoulder. He carried a heavy-duty charge gun in brackets on each arm. He had tied his hair at the nape of his neck.

"I'm ready."

Their eyes met for longer than necessary. She searched for signs of emotion, but there were none. She wanted to say something personal, but had no idea what. She wanted to tell him that he didn't need to try and out-do her in toughness. She wanted to hug him and tell him it would be all right, even in his work, but there was no way she could be certain and she hated empty reassurances. She understood so well the difficulties of trying to get ahead while you couldn't, and while your friends and colleagues all went on as normal with their lives. And she understood the feeling when well-meaning people said, "Everything will be fine," and you knew that it wouldn't, and you felt that if one more person said that, you'd smash their face in.

So the only thing she ended up saying was, "All right then, let's go."

Izramith went to the guesthouse and dressed in her insulation suit. Over that she put her armour, both guns, her knife in a bracket, her rope, three comms, her infrared sensor and toolkit.

Dressed like this, she met Rehan and Braedon on the corner of Market Street. Wairin just came out of the guesthouse, carrying an ominous bag, the contents of which had probably best stay where they were. Rehan distributed thick fur cloaks. Izramith had some trouble draping it over her jacket. The weight of the fur made it slip from her shoulders.

Someone leaned against the wall behind them. Dressed in fur, with a dark-coloured jacket and trousers, guns bulging from the sides of armour and on his arm brackets. He was much taller than Wairin, and with loose curls.

"Daya!" What was he doing here?

In the gap between the two sides of his cloak, something glistened: he also wore an insulation suit.

"You're coming?"

"I am."

"I thought you didn't want us to do this?"

"I said that in my capacity as Chief Councillor of Barresh. After you left, I had a talk with Anmi about the things you said. It wasn't an easy talk, and you won't need to know the details. But she has instructions, the moment this craft leaves the ground, to send my resignation as Chief Councillor to the council, to become effective after the wedding. I will concentrate as advocate for the Aghyrians. So technically, that means the council doesn't know about this expedition, and can't disapprove of it."

Izramith's head was reeling. Things were changing faster than she could keep up with. And he'd resigned because of something she'd said?

"Well then, let's go," Braedon said. He was looking at his reader. "Our window to arrive in Miran on dusk is fast closing."

When they arrived at the airport, Dashu waited there with a group of about twenty people, mostly Mirani, mostly Nikala, and many of them wearing cloaks that weren't half as nice as Rehan's. "Who are these people?"

Rehan said, "We're a commercial flight. We need passengers, so I asked Jocassa to offer a bunch of his friends free tickets. One way only."

29

"THERE IT IS," Rehan said.

Izramith peered out the window against the glare. Her eyes were gritty from lack of sleep. For now, she couldn't see much more than mountains, mountains and more mountains. A touch of white stuff coated the mountaintops, but the lower slopes were blinding green, and the sky was unbelievably clear blue. Ceren's two little moons hung like cut fingernails high above.

Braedon pushed himself from the back seat and clambered over Wairin's legs. Having no capability to fly or operate any part of the aircraft, Wairin was still asleep, which, in the pilot cabin designed for a crew of four, wasn't an easy thing to do. Dashu sat in the corner with her reader. She had changed into the Pilot's Guild uniform, and she would be the one to "assist" the passengers off the craft.

The ancient city of Miran lay in a saddle high above the level of Ceren's sea. The city had been built there because the first settlers had feared attacks from other people, and Miran was fabled to have the best views of any settled world. From the front of the shuttle, Izramith had an even better view than on the ground.

She glanced sideways at Braedon, who was peering intently into the distance. Drops of sweat twinkled on his upper lip.

"See anything yet?"

"Not many craft at the airport. Do you have vocal contact with them yet?" The latter to Rehan.

"Not yet. Just the beacon."

"Is that a good or a bad thing?" Izramith asked.

Rehan shrugged. "Probably routine."

Izramith yawned so much that tears sprang into her eyes. All of a sudden she felt hungry, in fact so hungry that it made her feel sick. Did she have anything to eat in her bag? The stuffy air in the cabin did nothing to improve her alertness.

Braedon was looking at her, his eyes intent. What had he meant with that outburst before they left? She gave up the search in her bag and leaned back in her seat, her eyes closed. "I hope a visit to Miran includes breakfast."

Seriously, she was over this adaptation crap that kept rearing its head unexpectedly.

"We'll get some food," he said, again meeting her eyes in an intense look.

Why did he keep staring at her like that? For fuck's sake. She returned his stare, but where she expected her cheeks to get hot with a flush, this didn't happen. Her own body kept disobeying her. Was there anything else that adaptation could upset?

The city of Miran now came into clear view. Surrounded by walls and only with a narrow path trailing down the mountain pass, the main way in which people got here was by air. Yet the airport was surprisingly quiet.

Rehan landed the craft without problems and Dashu guided the passengers off. Now it was Izramith's turn.

She explained to the Exchange that the shuttle had a mechanical problem and needed a technician to deliver and install a part. Did they have any technicians capable of working on a Rhion? Which of course they didn't; Rehan already knew this.

Dashu then deflected a visit from a couple of Mirani guards

by not speaking Mirani, and Izramith asked if, now that they needed to wait for tech service to come from elsewhere, the crew could at least have passes to go into town and buy something to eat.

Passes were produced, much to the amusement of Rehan. "No idea it was so easy to get these."

"I work at an airport. I know the stuff that goes on at airports all the time. No one would be surprised being asked for any of those things. No one would suspect an ulterior motive."

But it worked. They were in.

As agreed, Rehan was going to stay with the craft.

When Daya opened the door, a breeze of icy air came into the craft. He jumped out first, after having pulled his cloak over his head. Then Izramith. The cold stung her face. Braedon, Wairin— looking more heavy-set than normal with his gear strapped to him— and Dashu also followed.

Rehan waved briefly before shutting the door again.

The group set off across the wide expanse of the airport. Directly ahead was a low building with windows overlooking an area where a few private craft stood, all of the black Mirani type. To the left, a meadow sloped up the mountainside, luminous green and interrupted only by patches of pink and yellow, and the occasional rocky outcrop—except on closer inspection, some of the outcrops weren't rocks; they moved.

The sky above was completely cloudless and deep blue. With the suns almost overhead each person walked in their own shadow.

With the air cool and thin and fresh unlike the heavy humid stink of Barresh, Izramith understood the beauty of the place, even if it left her feeling light-headed.

They arrived at the airport building, where everyone except Dashu and Wairin pulled their hoods over their heads. Dashu stumbled through the permit check. Her cloak hung open, clearly displaying the Pilot Guild uniform.

None of the bored guards objected.

Then they were in the city. First came the old gate in the city wall, and then stately old houses, streets paved in intricate patterns of natural stone, houses and shops with intricate stone-carved façades, houses with towers, statues, patterns in different coloured roof tiles.

Hidden in the hood of the cloak, Izramith marvelled at what she had thought would be a dreary, cold, forbidding place.

"It's beautiful," she said in a low voice to Braedon when he came to walk next to her.

"This city is history. Miran has the most complete written history of any place in all of the settled worlds. We can't let Nemedor Satarin destroy it."

Further downhill, the buildings became bigger and closer together and even more elaborate. Braedon pointed out the council building and the famous library. They entered the central square, which Izramith had only seen in pictures. The Foundation monument bathed in bright sunlight. A group of children sat in neat lines on the steps while a woman spoke to them. The sunlight made their hair shine like silver.

Then Braedon pointed out the dark windows above the shop on the corner, dull with dirt. One window had been broken and boarded up.

"Our office," he said in a low voice. "The Mirani council and various other businesses have offered us lots of money for it. We've retrieved all our possessions from the office and the house, but we won't sell either."

"Will you ever go back to Miran?"

"Maybe. Maybe not. Maybe some of us will go back. I don't think Rehan and Mother will. Taerzo might go back, and maybe Iztho if he feels he can be accepted as a musician rather than a Trader."

It was the first time she'd heard any of the family talk about the oldest brother. She'd heard rumours of Anmi's refusal to marry him.

"What about you? Will you ever go back?"

"It depends."

"On what?"

He didn't reply to that question.

They arrived at a big building where it was very busy.

"Markets," Braedon said. "Breakfast."

Inside the building were many stalls where merchants in fur coats sold their wares. Large fires burned at set intervals and people sat around eating and drinking steaming drinks. The smell of food and smoke hung in the air.

It was cosy and pretty. Izramith saw how people could love this place. There was pride in surviving harsh conditions. That's what people did at Hedron. These people were more in tune with the climate. They didn't hide, but lived, in the snow and biting cold, and they stuck a finger to the rest of the *gamra* entities. She could identify with that. For so long, Hedron had done the same. Shut out everyone who wasn't a local. The barrier to coming into Hedron was still huge. Hedron could easily have been Miran and faced the same sort of scrutiny. The two nations had a fair bit in common.

They found a table around one of the open fires, and Daya went to buy food at one of the surrounding stalls.

Dashu sat huddled in her chair with an I-hate-this-place look on her face. Wairin had his cloak's hood pulled far over his face. Braedon wore his loosely to cover his Barresh-style hair, but Daya had pushed his hood down and chatted and laughed with the food seller.

"He lived in Miran for a while," Braedon explained.

Not much later he returned to the table with a tray of bowls of steaming, lumpy sauce.

Izramith gave Braedon a questioning glance, not wanting to speak and give herself away. He nodded from within the hood of his cloak. Mirani ate yellow-coded food, so there was no safety issue, but what was this?

He gave her a spoon and started eating his portion.

Izramith tried the sauce. It was very salty and had a strange tang that she couldn't place and wasn't sure she liked. But it was warm and she was hungry, so she ate all of it.

Neither of them spoke. On the tables around them, men sat

talking and laughing. Some chewed leaves and sat staring into the fire. Their faces were rugged, with chapped and red skin from the cold. Sometimes they glanced at the group of assorted visitors.

The food merchant walked past, stopped and said something to Daya.

"He says to watch out, there are gangs about."

"We better move," Braedon said. "Let's check out the building."

They left the market building again for the bright and sunny square. The council complex was to the left, an impressive construction with a façade of a double row of columns. An open door between the columns offered a glimpse of a large foyer where people walked around.

Braedon led the group up the stairs, but instead of to the entrance, they veered off to the left, past the side of the building with the many columns. At the back, away from the square, it was attached to another building via a covered walkway. That second building was in a different, more elaborate style, with corner-stones of granite carved into flowers and leadlight windows with many-coloured panes. To the left was another building of two floors. The steeply sloping roof had many little towers. A gallery-style balcony went around most of the top floor. The windows at the front were dark and dusty, the front entrance closed off by a roughly built wall.

"It's this building," Daya said in a low voice. "Second floor, at the back. The Trader Guild building is the one on the other side of the street."

That building stood on the other side of an alley. A wall with only a few windows on the top floor faced the council buildings. Those windows were likely to be the ones from which Mikandra had seen into the courtyard.

The stone wall that blocked the building's façade left only one entrance, in front of an archway that led underneath the building to a courtyard. A uniformed guard stood there, feet slightly apart, a crossbow slung over his shoulder. The Mirani wore white and grey uniforms, which really stood out elsewhere, but blended in with the bright colours here.

"How do we get in?" Wairin said.

Time for another silly idea.

Izramith simply walked up to the guard. His frown grew deeper while she approached, until he could ignore her no more, and stopped her going into the entrance.

He said something in Mirani.

She mimicked eating, while looking past him into the courtyard beyond.

His face cleared. He said something else, pointing to the market building.

"Oh. Thank you."

She turned around and went back to the group. Dashu gave her a what-did-you-do-that-for look.

"It looks like the courtyard on the other side is unsecured," Izramith said. "If we climb the wall, there are no more obstacles that I can see."

30

THEY LEFT the building and walked past the markets to a commercial area with shops. Compared to Barresh, this area looked bleak. In Barresh, shop owners had crammed every available space of their rickety shops with wares, whereas many of these shops had little stock. Clothes offered for sale were sturdy and plain, furniture basic, and Izramith spotted only one shop that sold any technology. They did, however, pass at least three places to buy weapons. Heavy Mirani-style cross-bows with fearsome bolts. Big knives and clunky-looking charge guns that probably shouldn't be underestimated.

Braedon went into a bakery and came out with a bag of bread rolls which they took to Rehan at the airport.

In the cramped cabin of the craft, they studied plans and discussed their attack.

Braedon's supply of rolls vanished.

When the sky had gone dark blue, they donned armour and then the jackets and cloaks. Izramith strapped her guns on: one on the waist, one on her right arm, one on her left leg. She felt cold and hot at the same time, and her sweaty hands made moist marks on the gun barrels.

Daya wore an Asto-style silver insulation suit under his cloak, as well as armour. He carried just one gun, and also a Mirani crossbow slung over his shoulder.

Izramith grinned. "Use their own weapons against them, huh? I'm afraid that thing will only slow you down. If they have charge guns, what good is a crossbow going to be?"

"Wait and see."

Braedon gave her a look that said that perhaps this wasn't a regular crossbow, or that Daya had some trick up his sleeve.

All dressed up and armed, they left the craft again after checking and rechecking all the gear.

In single file, they passed the checkpoint again, where Daya spoke to the guards.

The guard chuckled and pointed at the crossbow.

"What did he say?" Izramith asked Braedon when they passed the checkpoint.

"Daya said that we're cold and going to find some blankets. The guard asked if the crossbow was to chase off the maramarang."

He explained that maramarang were the cousins of the Barresh meili, but much bigger and fiercer—scavengers who didn't care if their prey was dead or alive. Ah, so the crossbow was part of a disguise.

"They've become worse since we left." Braedon searched the sky. "Stay close to the walls."

The streets had not been very busy when they came here earlier, but now they were deserted. In the commercial quarter, shops had closed and the only windows that were not dark had heavy curtains that blocked most of the light. The whole city could have been deserted for all Izramith knew.

In the alley between the council building and the Trader Guild headquarters it was so dark that Izramith could barely see the ground. A broad ribbon of stars arced overhead with the brightest star a pink dot low on the horizon. Of course, that was not a star, but Asto.

They walked in single file along the wall of the Trader Guild headquarters, first Braedon and then Dashu and Izramith, with

Wairin and Daya behind. The orange glow of light radiated from an upstairs window, but didn't reach the ground.

Braedon stopped. "This spot will do. Once you're up there, make sure that you spend as little time as possible exposed on that wall."

Izramith took up position with her back to the wall. She linked her hands together. Braedon stepped into them and climbed on the wall.

"All clear." He heaved himself up, and vanished. The last visible part of him was the hem of his cloak as it jerked away when he jumped.

Next was Wairin, who was considerably stronger but needed more effort to get up. "You heavy bugger."

He, too, clambered over the top of the wall and vanished. Then Daya, and Dashu was last. She kneeled on top of the wall and extended a warm hand to help Izramith up. Her hand shivered.

"Damned freezing hellhole," she muttered at Izramith.

The top of the wall provided a view over a longitudinal courtyard that ran past the side of a single-storey part of the building, all shrouded in darkness. Good.

A light from a reader flicked on at the base of the wall, gilding Daya's face. He was looking at a map of the building.

Dashu slid down and Izramith followed, landing heavily on the ground.

Daya led the group across the courtyard.

At the far end, steps led into an arched entryway that ended at a door sagging on its hinges. A chain around the door handles held it shut, but when Izramith pulled, the door broke clean in half. The chain fell off, and she caught it before it could land on the paving.

They entered a corridor with a gritty floor that stretched away on both ends. Dusty and broken furniture stood stacked against both side walls.

Braedon mouthed *That way* and started off to the left. Their footsteps were the only sound disturbing the stuffy space.

Izramith made a mental picture of the building. She noted all side corridors and passages. Some doors stood open, revealing dusty rooms with more furniture.

They came to a door that led outside, this one properly locked. Daya stopped to examine the doorframe, looked behind him, drew his charge gun and fired at a little knob at the top of the doorframe. The charge left a black mark on the frame.

He opened the door. "Quick."

They entered a courtyard which looked like the one that Izramith had seen from the other side when talking to the guard. In the time it had taken them to get here, the sky had turned almost black. A light from a top floor window spread a golden glow through the courtyard.

Daya said, "Up there."

Wairin started across the courtyard—

The air moved.

Braedon yelled, "Watch out!"

Someone fired, but the shot missed the dark shape that swooped over the courtyard, rose sharply, looped back to Wairin—

"Get out of the way!" Daya shoved past Izramith.

A second dark shape fell from the sky and latched onto Daya's cloak. Huge wings flapped, the tips brushing Izramith's head.

"Run!" Daya shouted.

Braedon grabbed her arm and dragged her across the court-yard, while more dark shapes rained from the sky. Into an alcove. Wairin and Dashu were already there.

"What the hell are those things?" Dashu asked, panting.

"Maramarang. Don't stick a hand out. They'll eat you alive."

Izramith pressed herself against the stone in the alcove, clutching her gun. This fucking planet was full of things that ate people. "What about Daya?" She didn't dare fire into the court-yard or she might hit him.

Daya stood where they'd left him, covered in the black furry creatures. They hung off his shoulders and arms, one crawled on his head. Like the meili in Barresh, only much bigger and darker.

Daya patted fur, scratched wings. One of the creatures head-butted his leg. Daya crouched and scratched its head. It rolled over, exposing a grey furry belly.

Braedon gaped. "I've never seen anything like this before. Any normal person would be dead by now. They usually start by eating the hands."

But Daya wasn't a normal person. Did none of the others see the blue glow that hovered over his skin?

One by one, the creatures drooped off and once more took to the air with a great flapping of wings. Daya dusted off his sleeves and strode across the courtyard. His shirt was covered in hair.

Izramith turned her attention to the door in the alcove.

"This is the place," Daya said. His voice sounded haunted. A strange and vaguely unpleasant smell hung about him. "This is where they took me a few years ago. *Guest quarters* they said. The accommodation upstairs has all the luxuries, but the door remains locked."

"How did you get out?" Pushing the door didn't even make it move.

"Out the window."

"I don't think we have time to mess around trying to find a non-destructive way of getting in," Izramith said, taking her gun from its bracket. "They've already been alerted that we opened the other door." She pointed back at the door which Daya had just disabled. A tiny orange light flashed in the darkness of the porch.

"Stand back."

They did and she fired at the lock.

The material of the lock plate smoked and melted. The hole was big enough to stick a couple of fingers through—oh, fuck, that was hot. She pulled down her sleeve, jammed her fingers in the hole and felt around for something to push. The inside of the door was full of prickly metal things which moved under her fingertips.

No time to be gentle. Izramith pushed and pulled as hard as she could. Now the door moved in the frame. Good.

She took a step back and shouldered the door with all her strength. It creaked and moved a bit more. Again. Something snapped inside the frame, but the door still didn't open. She took a few more steps back and launched herself at the door with all her force.

A whole section of the frame broke. The door shot open, and Izramith stumbled into the dark space beyond, clutching her side from a sharp stabbing pain.

Oh shit. Did she just break something?

She was in a stone-paved hallway with a set of stairs leading up. Golden light shone from the top floor, and the faces of at least twenty people looked down.

"Are you prisoners here?"

None of them said anything.

But these had to be the people. At least half of them were *zhadya*-born men, the others keihu women, Pengali men and women and others she didn't recognise. Pale faces, sunken cheeks, hollow eyes. Many wore tattered clothes. Their arms carried red blotches from the cold. A man had only one shoe.

As she progressed up the stairs, the stink of unwashed bodies grew.

The people shrank back from her as if they were ghosts, or as if she were a ghost. In their emaciated faces, their eyes looked unnaturally bright and large.

"How many of you up there?" Izramith asked.

She'd come out in a large room with many sets of mismatched tables and chairs, where more people sat. There were women, there were children. One of the girls looked pregnant, much too young.

A fire burned in the hearth in the corner, but it barely did anything to raise the temperature in the room.

Faced with this misery, memories of Indrahui came back. She struggled to keep her composure. "Get all your clothes, we're taking you out of here."

"It's useless," said a wrinkled man with long greying hair. He was a *zhadya*-born with a strong Hedron accent. "We tried to escape many times, but they always catch you."

"Not this time. We got help from outside. How many of you?"

"There's thirty-four, thirty-five including the babe."

"Is Reyar here?"

"How do you know him?" said a middle-aged man in the corner. He was Hedron *zhadya*-born with long and lanky greying hair that hung limply down both sides of his face.

"I'm Izramith."

Silence. His eyes widened. He rose and came closer until he faced her. "Damn, I didn't think that sister-in-law of mine would ever come to any good." His voice sounded husky and clouded with emotion.

The fathomless depth of his eyes made her shiver. His shirt hung off him like an empty bag, dirty and torn. The light from an oil lamp lit his face from the side, bringing out canyons and crags in a ravaged face. A scab on his forehead looked infected.

There were also scabs and dirty bandages on his lower arms. Purple blotches marked his skin.

A wave of nausea threatened to overwhelm her.

The other members of her team had come up the stairs behind her, Wairin with a hard expression on his face, but Dashu pale and wide-eyed. Clearly, she had never seen anything like this before.

Daya said, "Come on then, quick, we need to get down. Rehan is coming." He strode across the room and disappeared through a doorway in the far corner.

The old man who seemed to be the group's leader, said, "Down the stairs? That's not going to be easy. A lot of us can barely walk."

Izramith said, "We'll carry any of you who can't walk. Get anything you want to bring."

Braedon was standing near the window, talking on his comm to Rehan. He spoke a rendition of Trader Coldi so full of jargon that he might as well have spoken another language.

Some of the residents already lined up, one of them the pregnant woman, who was also the mother of a young child. Izramith noticed the groove in the woman's nose: she was keihu. But she couldn't have looked less like keihu had she tried. Too gaunt, her hair too dull and too straight, her skin too pale. What happened to the chubby, cheerful, round-faced appearance that was normal for the keihu people?

Damn, how long had she lived, and been mistreated, here?

The older residents were slowest to get ready, and not just because of their age.

"We tried to get out so many times," a man told her. "We always failed. It's the punishment afterwards that gets you."

Dashu and Wairin were already helping people down the stairs. Izramith helped another keihu woman who had a bad leg. She was so skinny that it looked like a mere breeze would snap her bones.

"Didn't they feed you?" Izramith asked.

The woman didn't reply and obviously didn't speak Coldi, but clutched onto Izramith's arm all the way down into the hall. She shivered. Her hands were cold as ice. What the hell did Miran do to these people?

Izramith ran back up the stairs—

A window shattered upstairs. People yelled.

"They're already shooting at us!" That was Dashu.

Izramith ordered, "You and Wairin, go down and secure the courtyard."

Wairin and Dashu thundered back down the stairs. She ran up, meeting Braedon on his way down. "Got to guide Rehan to make sure he doesn't come to the wrong courtyard."

Then he, too, was gone.

Izramith entered the upstairs room. "All of you, hurry up. Collect anything that you would not want to leave behind, and get dressed in as many clothes as possible. Then come down the stairs as far as you can. Help people who can't." She found Reyar's face in the group. "Come on, whatever language they speak, tell them to hurry up, if they don't want to be left behind. Get your backsides moving. We've got a couple of very high-profile people with us, and they risk a lot by coming here, so if you want to stay here then fine, but everyone else, don't drag. When that aircraft comes down, I want everyone in the courtyard."

"Aircraft?" the old man said. "You are bringing an aircraft? Who are you?"

"Hedron guards," Reyar said. He held a near-empty cloth bag over his shoulder. "She's my sister-in-law's daughter. If my sister is anything to go by, this will be our best chance to escape, because she's stubborn as hell and doesn't stop until she gets her way."

That seemed to convince the few remaining people to move. The rest were on the stairs and in the hall.

But where was Daya?

She crossed the room and found that the door he had gone through led into a corridor with a number of doors to the side. Those were dorms, with rows of simple beds. There were no carpets here and no fires. The staleness of the air reminded her of Hedron.

"Daya?" She arrived at the end of the corridor and couldn't see him anywhere. She walked into one of the rooms that faced the courtyard.

"Daya?"

He stood in front of the window, trying to open it. Through the frosted glass, she could see both Wairin and Dashu in the courtyard, firing into an alcove on the other side.

"What's going on?" Izramith asked.

"The guards have discovered the security breech. Come, help me open this."

Izramith kicked the window. The frame bulged outward but didn't budge. Of course they would make these windows from glass-stone. *Imported* glass-stone no doubt, because there would be none of it in the ground here. The place to find glass-stone was Barresh.

"Why not use the stairs?"

"I want to get on that roof down there so I can pick off anyone who enters that courtyard."

She pushed her cloak back and took her gun from its bracket. Turned it on, and the safety off. Normal glass, you could melt, but glass-stone you couldn't.

With the gun on moderate setting, she fired at the frame where it was attached to the wall. The room filled with the acrid scent of smoke from burning paint. She yanked at the handle. Something popped. Another yank, and the whole frame came loose.

She peeked outside, but saw nothing except the courtyard paving lit by flapping oil lights. Where were Wairin and Dashu?

Izramith lifted one leg to the windowsill and heaved herself up. She half-slid down the roof that sloped away steeply from underneath the window.

The courtyard was empty. A light burned behind a window in the opposite wing. That definitely hadn't been on before. Where was everyone?

The door on the porch opened a fraction. Izramith used the infrared sensor on the gun to track movement. There were three people at the door, armed and crouching.

By their stance and shape, she judged that all three were men. None were Coldi. She would be happier knowing where Wairin and Dashu were, but—

The first man came onto the porch. Definitely Mirani.

She fired.

He went down without a sound. The door shut again.

Shit.

"Do you know how far away Rehan is?" she whispered to Daya, who had remained inside the window, but he didn't seem to hear her. He wouldn't know guards' hand signals; she wasn't even sure that he would be watching.

She could just see the tip of his crossbow protruding from the window frame. Why the fuck didn't he get the gun? Sheesh, she wished she had Braedon at her back. He wouldn't persist with stupid old-fashioned weapons for the sake of being interesting. Or something.

Something was now happening under the porch where she

had shot the man. A faint glow of light and dark figures moving. And more light behind the windows to the left of the door.

Ah, she spotted Wairin, on the far side of the courtyard. Dashu would be with him, and Braedon with the prisoners on the stairs.

And Rehan . . . She held her breath to listen, but heard nothing unusual. Then again, the Rhion was known as a silent craft, especially the smaller models such as this one.

Did Wairin and Dashu know that there were a bunch of soldiers behind that door? What were they even doing on that far end of the courtyard?

Izramith wriggled to slide further down the steep slope of the roof until her feet hit the gutter. She lay flat on her back, holding the gun in front.

The door on the porch opened again.

One man came out, and then another. Izramith watched them through the infrared screen on her gun. A third man came out, while the first one left the porch and inched along the building's wall.

She sensed movement in the courtyard and the next moment a flash erupted where the men stood. Her gun's visor tracked the shot back to the source. All right, that was Dashu's position. Good shot, that one.

More soldiers came out the door. She counted at least five.

From somewhere in the distance came the unmistakable roar of aircraft engines.

Damn, they were outnumbered and there would soon be a firefight in this courtyard. They couldn't have that when Rehan was supposed to land in here.

Options: ask him to land somewhere else, or make sure the firefight was over by the time he arrived. But there were by now at least ten soldiers in the courtyard and more still streaming in from that porch. Dashu made short work of a couple more soldiers, but that group inside the building was at least twenty strong. The windows of the building were glass-stone and charge gun proof.

She'd ask Wairin to blow it up, but if he caused an explosion and a fire, Rehan could definitely not land the shuttle here.

In rapid succession, she picked off all soldiers that showed up in her infrared sensor as being outside. But the sensor showed that others still sheltered in the building.

The roar of aircraft engines was getting louder. Those soldiers in that building probably knew of the approaching craft and had been ordered to hide.

The Rhion came into view.

The door opened on the porch. At least twenty soldiers streamed into the courtyard. Dashu was firing, Wairin was firing. Braedon was hopefully smart enough to keep low.

The men had left the door open. Izramith aimed and fired into the room. The flash lit up part of the building, showing the corridor and stacked old furniture in skeleton vision.

Something chinked into the roof tiles next to her. Damn, they had a sniper somewhere. She scanned the surrounding roofs with her infrared scanner. Didn't see anything.

But this person would possibly shoot at the craft.

Damn. She needed to stop this guy. Several times, she swept the gun from side to side. A small light spot showed up over the highest point of the roof opposite her, but it could be a chimney outlet. She wished for her guard-issue gun. The screen quality on this thing was utter rubbish.

The Rhion approached, bright lights shining down and messing with her infrared setting. Damn it. That guy up there was still shooting.

"Let me deal with this." Daya had come down out of his hiding place. He was going to shoot this guy with a fucking crossbow?

But the moment he pressed the release and the bolt shot free with a metallic *zhiiing*, the air turned cold. Charge gun discharges were invisible until they hit something. The bolt crackled with blue light as it streaked through the air and as it hit the roof opposite. It was a crap shot, hitting much lower than where the guy was sitting. Damn, if only Braedon—

Blue light crackled over the roof.

A flash.

An entire section of roof caved in, taking the slate tiles, the beams and the sniper down in a cloud of smoke.

Izramith turned to Daya. "What the hell is that thing?"

"Fighting with their own weapons, slightly modified." His face showed amusement. Did this have something to do with that thing called *avya* that he'd used in the valley behind the airport at Hedron?

The walls of the building were still crackling with blue light, which forced its way between bricks, pushing them apart. Men shouted and ran into the courtyard, into Braedon and Dashu's fire. The wall of the collapsing building crashed outwards, sending an avalanche of bricks into the courtyard.

Izramith shot at anyone she could see, but now that she had given away her position, she came under fire.

Wind from the landing craft tore at her hair. Its lights were so bright that she couldn't see anything else.

Time to get out of this spot. Izramith let go. She slid down the roof, over the gutter, into the air, shooting at the other side of the courtyard as she fell. Something whizzed past her and grazed her side.

She landed hard on the courtyard's pavement. Ouch, her side hurt.

A blinding glow from the shuttle's downlights turned everything in the courtyard white. She sensed Daya coming down next to her. There were at least ten people waiting in the alcove where she had entered the building. Her vision was too blurry to tell her who they were.

Clouds of dust blew into her face. The ramp was down.

Oh shit, that hurt. Clutching her side, she fell to her knees.

People were now running across the courtyard to the craft, which hovered over the ground.

"Izramith." A figure ran towards her.

Braedon.

She struggled to get to her feet. Pain shot through her side. "I think . . . I've been hit."

He looped an arm under her shoulders. They were barely at the bottom of the ramp when soldiers burst out of a couple of doors.

"Duck! Stand back!" Daya was already at the entrance of the craft with his crossbow. He coolly fired bolts into the buildings. Wherever he hit a wall, the spot glowed blue and then the building would collapse. No ordinary crossbow indeed.

Inside the craft, Braedon helped Izramith into a seat. There were people around her, but she didn't register faces. She ran her hand over her side. It came away wet with blood. Something had managed to get in between the two sections of her armour.

"Retract the ramp!" Braedon yelled.

"Hold on everyone." That was Rehan's voice.

The floor lurched. The pressure increased. Black spots encroached on Izramith's vision.

She must have fainted, because the next thing she knew, her armour was off and she lay uncomfortably stretched out over a couple of adjacent seats. Braedon sat next to her, sticking a bandage to her side.

"That was a nasty hit." He was packing away his supplies. "I fixed it up temporarily, but you'll have get it properly treated when we get home."

"Did . . . did everyone make it in?" She tried to lift her head. There were many people in the seats around her. "Are we still in Mirani airspace?"

"We are, but Rehan managed to apply for protected status while we were gone. There are a couple of Mirani craft escorting us, but they should leave us alone."

"Should is a word never to associate with war."

He smiled, and suddenly looked very tired. "At least you've lost none of your proverbs."

31

A GOOD NUMBER of guards were waiting for them when the craft arrived in Barresh. They escorted the group of rescued prisoners to the hospital, where the council had set up a light and airy room for them. Izramith went with them, still sore and dizzy. A lot of people were already there, including medical carers and officials to record their stories. Anmi was there, too, with all four of her boys.

A couple of nervous keihu and Pengali relatives waited and family reunions came with tears and shouts of joy from the relatives, and bewilderment from the captives.

A girl hugged her mother, but looked over her shoulder at another keihu girl, a friend amongst the captives, who held her hand out.

"They should not be separated," Braedon said to Daya.

"They won't be. They can all stay together in our accommodation. We'll sort out later where everyone should go."

Izramith sat quietly on a bench, watching the emotional reunions, happy to be out of the talk, wanting to be treated and go back to the guesthouse. Reyar came to sit next to her for a bit, but neither seemed to know what to say. Then a council worker asked her to come to a small room.

He explained. "We're having *gamra* inspectors arriving in the next few days. They will make detailed investigations and interview all the victims, but I understand you will be gone by that time, and we hope your statement will satisfy them so you won't need to be recalled. I understand you were the first person in that upstairs room?"

She recounted the events to the best of her memory, feeling slightly ill.

Time was passing too quickly. Already she had come almost to the end of her contract with still no clue on what she would do next.

When she was finished, she met Wairin in the corridor, and he went into the room to record his statement next.

In the big room, council workers had brought a meal and tea for all. A young man offered Izramith some, but just the look of food made her feel sick, so she leaned against the wall close to the room's entrance, watching the prisoners eat and drink. Reyar sat talking to a couple of other Hedron *zhadya*-born, all of them gaunt and unhealthy-looking. She would ask him if he could do anything for her nephew, but with the whole Aghyrian group here, that was no longer necessary. Someone would look after him, Anmi had said.

She felt reluctant to approach Reyar. Coming to him only when she needed something would probably justify his hostile position towards Hedron. Things were not all happy and carefree, especially with the Hedron group. But just seeing the keihu mothers reunited with their daughters made her certain that she had done the right thing.

Miran had apparently lodged an angry complaint against the violation of its borders, but the *gamra* outrage over the plight of the prisoners was greater.

What had the group been doing in Miran?

They'd been subject to experiments, the more vocal prisoners said. They showed scars from having devices inserted in their arms. To attempt to harvest or harness the energy their bodies built up. Except in most of them, the ability was nowhere near as strong as in Daya and experiments didn't seem to be leading anywhere, after which the Mirani started breeding experiments.

Izramith didn't know what made her angrier: the injuries or the idea that Miran had carried out experiments with these people.

"How are you holding up?" Braedon had come to stand next to her.

She shrugged. "All right, I guess. Some of these people look like walking skeletons."

"Don't forget to look after yourself."

"I'm all right."

"You will have that wound properly cleaned and glued."

She turned to him at the insistent tone of his voice.

"I did a temporary job. I'm not even properly qualified to do that work. It's a nasty cut."

"Sure."

"All right then. Am I going to have to drag you to this medico?" He glanced at the door where a Pengali woman stood. She wore a dark blue hospital gown that rippled at the back where her tail pushed up the fabric.

Izramith went with her to a small room further down the hallway. A bed stood in the middle of the room. Shelves packed with medical supplies crammed all the room's walls. Well, Braedon certainly had done his job for this hospital.

The place smelled like sickness and death. She was reminded of the hospital at Hedron and how she should go and get Shada to bring him here.

The woman told her to undress and lie down on the bed.

She proceeded to take off the bandage that Braedon had put on by yanking hard at the tape. Ouch. That was really quite uncomfortable.

"Hmmm. Quite nasty." The medico woman took a bottle with clear fluid from a shelf. She splashed some on a towel. "Have to clean this."

She dabbed at the edge of the wound. Pain shot through Izramith's side so stabbing that she almost cried out. She tried to lift her head. For fuck's sake, woman, what are you doing there? Sweat broke out on her face. Blackness encroached on the edges of her vision.

Damn.

Why had she gone so soft? She never used to be like this. She had even watched when the guards cut the crosshatched pattern into her upper arms; she had welcomed the pain. And now she was sweating, and feeling sick.

Fortunately, the gluing of the wound was relatively painless and quick. The medico stuck a large bandage over the top. "Must rest and keep clean."

Izramith nodded. Like that was ever going to happen. Then she thought of something else. "Please, can you give me something to balance my adaptation?"

The woman gave her a sideways look while washing her hands. "I thought you arrive many days ago."

"I did, but it's still upsetting me."

"Hmmm." The tail curled up. She dried her hands. "Need to have tests."

She disappeared, and a keihu nurse arrived to take samples of all kinds of fluids.

"I only wanted some extra medication," Izramith protested, but the man wouldn't comment. He probably didn't speak Coldi.

He left, and she waited while seated on the bed in the room, frustrated. She had a lot of work still to do, and these *gamra* officials to speak to and she only wanted some damn pills, not tests. There was nothing else wrong with her.

The Pengali medico returned. "Have your tests."

Izramith sprang to her feet. "Great. Can I have my medicine now? I'm very busy—"

"Sit."

Izramith sat. The serious tone to the woman's voice chilled her. "I am all right, aren't I? I mean—I've only been feeling bad with this adaptation since I came here. The first night was really bad, but it never went away—"

"There is no medicine you can take for symptoms."

Wait. "But everyone says—"

"Not adaptation is problem."

"Isn't it?" Something in the water or the food?

"You are pregnant."

What? "That's impossible." Fucking impossible. She spread her hands. "That's ridiculous. I never—"

The only man she'd been with was Braedon, and she'd flushed and not held back, because Mirani Endri didn't breed with any other races and neither did Coldi and if they bred with each other, certainly someone would have discovered that before now?

"Girls say ridiculous a lot of times, but if you sleep with man, you get pregnant. Simple. You not sleep with man, then, well, is a different matter. Because you need head looked at."

"No, no." Izramith held up her hands. "That's not necessary."

Izramith went back to the guesthouse in a daze.

Fucking pregnant.

Yet, she should have known. Hot flushes and sweats could be caused by anything, but the failure of her flush to fire when enough time had passed between the previous flush and when she wanted it to happen should have been a big flashing sign. Allowing a flush to happen was much easier than stopping it.

Even if she hadn't been with the guards and had slept with a man before leaving for Barresh, there was only one option: this child was Braedon's.

And that was impossible, right?

She sat on the bed and searched all the medical records. Soon enough, she came up with Anara Teren, Anmi's institute, where they did genetics research.

In the section about *Aghyrian markers and cross-species breeding,* she came across an article that stated, *While rumours of Coldi companion girls getting pregnant with Mirani Endri men are rife, there are only two documented and proven cases: Amandra Bisumar twice fell pregnant with Ydana's child, and twice miscarried, once early and once mid-term.*

There were pictures, too, of a tiny foetus in the palm of someone's hand, with all the little fingers and toes already formed.

Shit.

So, she'd likely be headed for a miscarriage, and would have to hide that from the guards. Or resign, admit that she was pregnant and then what? Lose the child anyway and be lonely?

Because if Braedon had been serious about her, she'd given him plenty of opportunity to tell her so.

32

A WARM BREEZE ruffled Izramith's hair. The light of both suns was low and she had to squint into it to see across Barresh's main square and down Market Street where thousands of people lined up, waiting for the parade.

There were locals in their family colours, guest workers in their native costume, or just any kind of costume. Long robes, colourful frills, gold and silver embroidery, brightly coloured veils, patterned skirts.

Izramith had not yet seen the wedding party, but they could not possibly outdo the spectator crowd in brilliance.

Already, the sound of the drums echoed over the markets. Behind her, the large guesthouse was a riot of colour, with people leaning out the windows cheering. Wairin was up there some-where, and Eris sat in a security station opposite her, facing a bank of screens. Their eyes met and he nodded.

Going well.

Yes, it was going well. Dotted throughout the crowd were Barresh council guards in black, looking alert, talking to each other on their comms, continuously scanning the spectators. They were no longer expecting much trouble, since the *gamra* team had descended on Barresh and was interviewing the freed prisoners and they provided a shield against hostile action. Barresh was, people joked, an expert at using such political shields. Miran could be heard gnashing its teeth across the border. Its council had given the matter the silent wall treatment. There had been no official statement, no comment, no acknowledgement of the incident.

Someone shouted at the first level window of the guesthouse. The Mirani Nikala workers up there cheered.

The party was coming across the markets.

First came the drummers, a combination of Mirani Nikala and local young people, the men with oiled upper bodies glistening in the light. Izramith spotted Jocassa amongst them, his face beaming.

Then the flower bearers, younger girls and boys dressed in white with baskets and headdresses made from flowers. They scattered small bunches of flowers into the crowd. A young woman next to Izramith caught one and she and her friend or sister went into squeals of excitement.

Then came the happy couple, in traditional Mirani wedding dress: matching long, dark red robes, embroidered with glittering beads in the same colour. Mikandra's hair was spiked up with a couple of longer strands of beads dangling down both sides of her ears. Her slender neck displayed the green tattoo of a string of flowers and leaves. Rehan's hair hung loose over his back, a curtain of silver.

Rehan held Mikandra's right hand with his right hand. The silver wedding armbands glittered on their wrists, with the chain linking them up still attached.

Whatever else Izramith thought about Rehan and his pompous assumption of power and privilege, they both looked amazing. And the expedition to Miran had initiated a shattering of many of her assumptions. It took a special kind of bravery to stand up to the people you had grown up with and fire a gun at them, because you believed deeply that they were doing bad things. It took bravery to extract your financial interests from the culture that supported you. She had seen Braedon suffer for that decision, but surely the entire business would have suffered.

So, Izramith was no longer sure what to think. Society *needed* champions, and the Andrahar family had become such champions.

People in the street clapped and cheered.

Rehan called out and the parade came to a halt. The drummers formed a wide circle on the corner where Market Street joined the square and the flower bearers lined up inside the circle.

Izramith eyed Eris across the street. It was not in the script that they would stop here. In fact, they weren't scheduled to stop anywhere until they arrived back at the markets, where cooks were setting up a big feast.

Eris shrugged, gesturing with his hands *I don't know*.

Izramith turned around to the guesthouse's façade. They'd finally been able to do the audit and all was deemed safe, but she didn't want to run unnecessary risks. She tried to find Dashu, who was meant to be walking with the group, but who had become lost in the bunch of the participants in the parade who followed the couple: the brightly-dressed children, the keihu men dressed as marsh eels—they made Izramith shudder—the flag-wavers, musicians, a couple of Pengali on stilts.

The couple entered the circle of drummers, and the entire Andrahar family followed. The brothers were in full ceremonial Trader uniforms, the women in puffed-up, tight-bodiced Mirani dresses, the children in white, including Vayra standing straight-backed next to his mother. Izramith wondered if his jerkin hid the silver chain with the Foundation stone, or if Mikandra still wore it. She understood that he derived no rights from it until he was legally an adult, and that wouldn't happen for a number of years yet.

Everyone stopped.

The drummers settled into a different rhythm.

Braedon stepped out of the family group.

He bowed before his mother and again before his brother and

bride. Then, under deafening drumbeats, he crossed the circle, squeezed between the flower bearers and their costumes and extended his hand . . . towards Izramith.

Their eyes met. He wore a ceremonial Trader uniform with gold embroidery, but his face looked gaunt as if he hadn't slept for days.

He mouthed, *come*, although the drumming made it impossible for her to hear him.

Everyone looked at her.

She shook her head. "I'm working."

"Come," he said again.

Two council guards in black came up behind her. One waved his hand for her to go. Damn, he had planned replacements. What the . . .

Watched by the entire crowd, Izramith took Braedon's outstretched hand.

"What?"

His expression was oddly intense. He led her back into the circle, between the drummers and the flower bearers, into the space left open in the middle. She felt horribly underdressed in her dark outfit, bristling with guns and knives. She was a killer; this family were sophisticated people.

Braedon faced her while the drums increased their intensity, if that was at all possible. He stepped back and bowed to her. In a sweeping gesture, he undid the clip of his cloak, took it off and swept it over her shoulders, where it hung rather ungracefully, because the sheer fabric clung to the rough material of the armour.

Izramith froze, while it dawned on her stunned brain that this was how Traders officially proposed for marriage.

All around, the crowd went mad with cheers.

"Braedon?"

"I believe the position of head of security in Barresh is open." He shrugged, his face tense, trying to look lighthearted and failing miserably. "Please. There is nothing in the universe I want more than to have you in my life."

Become part of that big, rambling family. Sit at the table in the house surrounded by laughing, talking, sometimes bickering people. Play games in the yard with the boys. Sleep every night next to someone loving and warm.

"I know about your news." He continued to meet her eyes.

"That's not a reason for you to do this. If you read the medical articles, it's unlikely that there will ever be a child anyway."

"That's no longer true. Things are different now."

"I still don't want you to think you have to do this for the sake of being proper."

He reached out and lifted her chin. "Izramith, look at me."

She regarded his pale face, his intense eyes.

"Do I look like a man who would ever ask for marriage for the sake of rumour or appearances?"

She shook her head. He didn't.

He looked like a man tormented, a man who had just as much trouble expressing his feelings in words as she had. A man who'd spent the entire night before his brother's wedding pacing the floor, because he was too nervous to ask that one question, the question she herself had been dodging for days, because she'd been afraid of the answer. *Would you be interested in sharing your life with me?*

"The moment I set eyes on you, I was sold. I asked Mother and she said I was crazy. I asked my sister-in-law and she never said that you'd never want me, but she sure as hell thought it. That night in the forest I had all I ever wanted, and then you had to propose this horrible . . . arrangement. I thought fine, love is a shock to you, but the more I tried to convince myself that it would never work and distance myself and go on with my life . . ." He looked down. "The more I couldn't."

He raised his head. His eyes glittered.

"So please . . . Will you be mine?"

Her vision blurred. She had been trying to catch his attention; she'd thought he wasn't interested in taking the relationship further; she'd wanted him to take notice of her, secretly longed for him.

"Yes," she whispered. "I will share your life."

Then his arms were around her shoulders and she was enveloped in the scent of perfumed soap.

The cheers of the citizens were deafening.

The wedding festivities officially ended Izramith's contract with the Barresh council, and Braedon sent someone from the house to pick up her belongings and take them to the Andrahar house.

Izramith started in her new position. It involved an office, a lot of electronics and many black-clad guards who jumped at her command. And endless amounts of politics. When Dashu went back to Asto, Izramith appointed a fellow Indrahui veteran, and also accepted into training a group of seven keihu youngsters, four of them girls, and five of them from the Semisu and Emiru families.

A few days after the wedding, a Pengali woman arrived at the house, sent by Daya, she said, to look after Izramith's health.

Thanks to adaptation medication to keep her temperature down, the pregnancy held and her breasts started growing. Each day she would stand in front of the mirror and stroke her expanding belly.

When the midwife judged it safe to do so, Izramith travelled to Hedron. She had not let Mother or Thimayu know that she was coming, and took great pleasure in seeing their faces when she walked in.

Thimayu started screaming, "You selfish bitch! You know he'll be *zhadya*-born, right?"

"She, actually." Scans had confirmed that and Daya was elated. "Yes, I know, and I know how they can be 'cured'. They're not sick anyway. I'll be taking Shada."

They looked strangely at her and she realised that they didn't even know the boy's name.

Their relationship was well beyond repair.

And so was her relationship with the place of her birth.

Where the rigid, monolithic structure of the Hedron Mines and the all-Coldi population had once given her comfort, they did no longer.

~

When Izramith flew back to Barresh, she had her discharge notice from the Hedron guards. It was not a good one— discharged for breaking the guards' celibacy rules. Commander Blue had been saddened to sign it.

"I thought you'd do well," she said. "But this . . ." and she gestured helplessly at Izramith's belly.

"I am doing well."

If the birth of a child was sad thing, then a lot was wrong with this culture.

But no one outside Hedron would care. Barresh valued her experience. She was now allowed to openly declare herself as ex-Hedron guard, and could get security jobs based on that.

Shada, now strong enough to sit—and bounce up and down, apparently—sat next to her, pointing out the window and babbling. People asked how old he was, and she gave up telling them the truth, because they didn't believe her, because a baby of his age wasn't meant to be doing all those things.

The child inside her kicked her in the ribs, as if wanting out to play with her brother.

Life with two *zhadya*-born children would not be easy, but there was help, and she'd take it over life with no family any time.

~

It was dark in Barresh when the shuttle landed. Looking out the window, and seeing the glow of lights display familiar streets, eating houses and shops still doing brisk trade, Izramith felt a type of inner calm she hadn't experienced for a long time. Not since the first season of having joined the guards.

Back then, she'd believed that signing up with the guards

meant she belonged somewhere. She wore the uniform happily when the scars on her upper arms were still raw and shiny, but over the years, and especially the past year, that feeling had been slowly stripped back until the certainty that she did not belong with the guards replaced it. Not belonging somewhere wasn't a life plan, because as much as she didn't belong with the guards, it left her searching for a place where she did belong.

Now she had found that place.

The doors opened, letting in the humid air.

Crew asked for parents to come forward first, so she lifted Shada to her arm and went forward. She was glad for the extra space, because she had been feeling tired and worn out, even more so than when she was still with the guards, and, having sat cooped up for the entire journey, Shada had plenty of energy.

Walking down the ramp, her mind flashed back to that time after he had just been born, when she'd seen the man coming down the ramp with his daughter and had thought she'd never have children herself.

Wrong.

She was now that mother and maybe someone else was watching her and hoping that he or she would have a family soon.

The walkways from the craft to the hall stood to the side, but the upstairs platform hadn't yet been finished. Evidence of building activity still lay scattered around: a ladder here, a couple of paint buckets there. The building would be completed soon, but she would not be flying anymore before the child was born.

Braedon waited at the door to the newly opened hall, his eyes bright with happiness.

She rushed into his open arms. His lips brushed hers.

"Welcome home," he said and then laughed. "Don't look at me like that, little fellow."

Shada had his head turned sideways and regarded Braedon with disturbing maturity.

He took the little boy from Izramith. Shada clamped his

chubby arms around Braedon's upper arm. A couple of fellow passengers glanced at the three of them. An older woman smiled.

"Let's go home," Braedon said. He put his arm around Izramith's waist and together they walked out of the building into the warm night air.

Thank you for reading Soldier's Duty. If you skip to the end of this book, you'll find an excerpt from Heir's Revenge, the fourth book in the Return of the Aghyrians series.

FROM HEIR'S REVENGE

RETURN OF THE AGHYRIANS BOOK 4

T HERE WAS a light in the yard next door.

Ellisandra stopped halfway through pulling the curtains shut and peered into the snowy dusk, where the grey buildings of the city faded into the murk of mist and falling snowflakes. The yard of her house was already covered in a good layer of snow, gilded by the glow from the windows downstairs. The wall that surrounded the yard had acquired a white cap, as yet undisturbed by the wind or the creatures of the night. On the other side of the wall, a snowy expanse stretched to the ruin of the house next door. In amongst the broken and fire-blackened walls stood a storm light, its flapping flame casting long shadows in the snow and on whatever remained of the walls.

That was odd. There hadn't been any activity at the Andrahar house for years. Why would someone come out to the ruin in the middle of this weather?

Behind Ellisandra's back, in the comfort of her upstairs room, the ladies of the theatre committee still chatted, accompanied by the chink of spoons on porcelain. The smell of sweet cakes hung in the air.

"Oh, no I don't think we should do that," Aleyo Hirumar was

saying. "I think everyone will be quite upset if we change the ending of the play. I know I would be."

"How would you stage it then?" asked Tolaki Telimar.

"As it is supposed to be. As it was written." The indignation dripped from Aleyo's voice.

Ellisandra should go back to the group and help Tolaki convince Aleyo to be a bit more adventurous, but now she spotted a man in the Andrahar yard, a tall figure shrouded in a thick longhair cloak. The light glinted in his curtain of hair. It was typical Endri hair, past the shoulder, silver-white, sleek, straight and loose. He wore knee-high boots with a strip of fur around the top, all very traditional, and very upper class.

According to the stories, the Andrahar family had been very traditional right until the moment that they decided to betray their home nation and leave. They had lived in Barresh since she was a little girl. Ellisandra was too young to have remembered the fire that destroyed the house or any of the riots and that treacherous trial that went before it, in which the family smeared Miran and tried to ruin the nation's reputation by trying to implicate it in criminal activities.

With his gangly appearance and fluid motions, this man next door was too young to be one of the four Andrahar brothers. Who in Miran still wanted to work for that family? No one she knew at any rate. No one local.

But the hair . . . she had heard jokes that the first thing Endri did when going to live in Barresh was cut their hair. Long hair was a pride thing, especially for the men. There was a saying that hair symbolised a person's ties with Miran. When a man moved away and kept his hair long, there was a chance that he might come back.

Behind her, the ladies of the theatre committee had gone quiet.

"Anything wrong, Ellisandra?" Tolaki asked.

"There's someone in the yard next door."

"Oh, let me have a look." Aleyo pushed herself up and

hurried to the window. She pushed her face to the glass, shielded from the reflection inside the room by her hands.

"There is, too." The window fogged up where her mouth was.

Now Tolaki also came to the window, and peered into the darkness over Aleyo's shoulder. "I see him. Probably just a groundsman."

"In this weather?" Ellisandra said.

"Doesn't look like a groundsman to me," Aleyo said. "Look at his hair. That's pure Endri. It's gorgeous, too. And who would employ a groundsman for a ruin like that anyway?"

Good points, both of them.

Even Sariandra had come to watch. But Tolaki and Aleyo were blocking the window, so she stood further back, looking forlorn and lonely in that dour dress of hers.

"Who do you think he is, then?" Tolaki asked, frowning at Ellisandra.

"No idea. Never seen him before."

"Do people still come to look at that ruin?"

"Very, very rarely. I don't think I've seen anyone there for years." The last time it had been a local surveyor. She tried to remember when that had been, but couldn't. Long ago. Possibly longer ago than she thought, because she remembered Father standing behind her looking out of the window and Father hadn't been able to do anything that remotely looked like "standing" unassisted for a long time.

Aleyo put on her conspiratorial voice. "What if we discovered something? I mean, no *normal* person would be out there in the dark in the middle of this weather. What if they're finally selling up but don't want anyone to know?"

That's what everyone had thought last time, too.

"No," Tolaki said. "Last I heard, Isandra Andrahar said that they'd sell the house and office 'over my dead body'."

"Maybe she died," Aleyo said. "She has to be pretty old—"

Ellisandra protested. "Not that old, I don't think."

"Well, if she died, then those sons of hers wouldn't care a bit about the house." Aleyo stuck her chin in the air. "I mean, it's not like any of us would want them back. I don't understand why they kept the house like this for all those years. The office, too, right in the prime locality downtown. Has to be worth a fortune."

Ellisandra thought she had an explanation. "Maybe they never sold because they didn't want any dirty Mirani credits for it." There was not much they could do with those outside Miran, not legally anyway. Not that it had ever before stopped any rich family from selling their house and leaving Miran for good.

Aleyo added, "Or maybe they were waiting for land prices to improve."

Tolaki laughed aloud. "Only to have seen the prices drop to a tenth of what they were when they left? Serves them right. We don't do selling for a lot of money here. We don't want foreigners to buy our houses."

Aleyo snorted. "Yeah, the Andrahars were arrogant, greedy pricks, even when they still lived in Miran."

This statement met with sage nods, even from Sariandra who had said barely a thing.

Oh well, no time to dwell on it. Surely the guards would keep an eye on this stranger. And no doubt he'd be gone soon and she'd never see him again.

～

You can get Heir's Revenge at all ebook retailers.

ABOUT THE AUTHOR

Patty Jansen lives in Sydney, Australia, where she spends most of her time writing Science Fiction and Fantasy.

Her career started in earnest when her story *This Peaceful State of War* placed first in the second quarter of the Writers of the Future contest and was published in their 27th anthology. She has also sold fiction to genre magazines such as Analog Science Fiction and Fact, Redstone SF and Aurealis, before making the move to independent publishing.

Patty has written over fifty novels in both Science Fiction and Fantasy, including the *Icefire Trilogy* and the *Ambassador* series.

pattyjansen.com

BOOKS BY PATTY JANSEN

More information:

pattyjansen.com

For a complete list of books, scan the image below with your phone.